Dear Becky Asselin

# VOYAGE OF THE SANDPIPER

## BOOK ONE: THE SEABIRDS TRILOGY

JESSICA GLASNER

I am so excited you won our first giveaway! I miss you and I truly hope we can see each other soon. Love you so much. ♥♥♥ XXXOOO Blessings! Jess G.

Edited by Hope Middlebrook



Printed in the United States of America

First Printing: **978-1-7337629-1-5**

Hope House Press

www.hopehousepress.co

www.glasnerhouse.co

*To Edith Piper*

*May the God of Hope be your foundation,*
*your peace and your comfort all the days of your life.*

# A HISTORICAL NOTE

I based this story on historical record, though I have taken creative license with a few dates. The characters are fictional, unless noted, but the political and military events occurred.

On the whole, the journey Agatha takes is very much like one any young American girl on the verge of womanhood might take at the exact moment the world ignited into the flames of battle.

It is worth remembering that history can repeat itself. If we do not learn from our mistakes, we are bound to repeat them.

Imagine Agatha's world. It is early summer 1939.

The globe teeters on the edge of falling into an abyss. We call that abyss World War II, the deadliest conflict in human history to date.

What pushed the world to the brink a *second* time?

The simple answer is the Great War, known today as World War I.

The massive loss of human life and property in the Great War was devastating. In the aftermath, Europe was financially, emotionally, and physically exhausted.

The situation took a turn for the worse after the 1929 crash of the US stock market and the collapse of the European economy. Many lost all they had—jobs, homes, and savings.

All over the Western world, trusted institutions like governments, monarchies, and banks fell apart. As a result, many come to believe that Western democracy and capitalism were flawed ideologies. Clearly, they argued, something isn't working. Perhaps, they wondered, there are other ways to organize nations and people.

In this space of unknowing, a few dynamic men promise stability and prosperity, in return for their followers unquestioned loyalty and submission. New political ideas—communism and fascism—argue that they will restore stability and national pride to countries brought low in the Great War.

Desperate for relief, a handful of European nations yield absolute power to these charismatic personalities and single political parties, leaving their former rulers and social structures behind.

In Russia, the Communist Party, led by Vladimir Lenin, overthrew the Romanov Dynasty in a violent revolution. The Party advocates the rule of the working class, public ownership of property and capital, and compensating workers by need rather than merit or ability. It sounds like a good plan, but the Soviet Government is a brutal dictatorship led by a ruthless and privileged elite. In 1929, Joseph Stalin took dictatorial control of the Communist Party. He managed to transform peasant Russia into an industrial and military giant—the USSR. In doing so, he systematically purged his political and religious opposition by murdering close to 20 million people. 20 *million*.

In Germany, Hitler rose to power, waving the banner of Nazism, fascism with an evil, racist twist. Fascists believe the will of the state trumps individual freedoms... Nazis believe that Aryan Caucasians are superior to all others. These include non-Aryan Caucasians, Asians, Africans, and, finally, Jews.

Hitler is a mad and evil genius. He argues (wrongly) that the

Jews betrayed Germany in the Great War and is obsessed with the lie that Jews corrupt others with ideas of individual equality and freedom, capitalism, and contradictorily, communism. These obsessions grow into a paranoia that Jews want to rule the world. Hitler uses fear tactics to manipulate his people with these twisted ideologies. He solidifies his power as an absolute dictator and begins his 'Final Solution'—the elimination of the Jewish people to create a Jew-free world.

Meanwhile, in Italy, Fascism ascends with military dictator Benito Mussolini at the helm.

Mussolini's foolish meddling in the Spanish Civil War drove a wedge between Italy and other European powers. As a result, he sides with Nazi Germany, convinced that such an alliance will restore Italy to its former glory.

In 1939, Stalin joins with Hitler to resist their common enemy, Western Europe, despite the fact that fascism and communism are ideologically at odds. In payment, Hitler allows the Soviets to occupy southeast Europe and the Baltic states—Estonia, Latvia, and Finland.

And meanwhile, in the Pacific, Japan seeks to extend her control and influence into China, Korea, and the greater Pacific Basin.

How does the West initially respond to these growing threats to freedom?

The British and French fear provoking Hitler's aggressive wrath. They choose a policy of appeasement, rather than confront the evil. And the United States, wanting nothing to do with another European bloodbath, tightens its borders and isolates itself from European politics.

So, as you can see, as Agatha sets foot on the *Grey Goose,* combustible fuel saturates the world stage that is moments from global conflagration. A match is striking the dark strip on the side of its matchbox. Within a matter of weeks, she, along with the rest of the world, will reach the point of no return.

And like Agatha, there will be no turning back. The only question that faces her is the same question that faces us: How will we move forward? And will we place our trust in God or in men?

*Only those who will risk going too far can possibly find out how far one can go.*

*T. S. Eliot*

# PART ONE

## A SANDPIPER ON SHORE

# CHAPTER 1

## THE START OF THE BEGINNING

"Don't look so embarrassed." My aunt adjusted my hair with a critical eye. "That's right. And relax your shoulders." Humming softly, she said, "I've read about painting live models. Thanks for volunteering."

"You volunteered me," I reminded her. I looked down at my hands. My fingernails were a little dirty, come to think of it. What was it that T.S. Elliot said, "On Margate Sands, I can connect nothing with nothing. The broken fingernails of dirty hands. My humble people who expect nothing. La la."[2]

Mother would have sent me straight upstairs to deal with them. At least, she would have if she were here. La la.

Coughing, Edie repeated, "Anyways, thanks. Now," she looked at the canvas, "lips a little closer together. Perfect! Do you draw, Piper?"

Taking out her pencil, she made small, short strokes on the canvas, her face hidden from view. "You look marvelous. One of the most lovely models I've ever had."

"I'm the only model you've ever had."

"Just so. The first is always the loveliest. Like your first love and first ice cream and the first scent of your favorite perfume. What's your favorite perfume?"

I didn't wear perfume, not yet anyways. "I have no idea," I answered.

"Mine's Tabac Blond." Her pencil moved quickly. "The woman at the perfume counter said brunettes and redheads always buy it because it has the word 'blond' in the name, but that's not why I buy it. I love my auburn hair. I'd never go blond. I like it because it makes me think of Europe. I imagine it smells just like Paris."

That was Edie. Always dramatic, always dreaming of faraway places and adventure. Yet she never left the safety of her fortress except to go into town on errands or her weekly poker game with the elderly Mr. Henderson. She was, simultaneously, perfectly content and terribly dissatisfied. Nearly impossible to read but wonderful to watch. Insecure yet comfortable in her own skin.

A part of me wondered if she knew that her purpose, the very reason my parents had sent me here, was to distract me. Edie, my aunt. She was a woman vaguely remembered from childhood. My parents kept in frequent contact with her, but I truly knew very little of my father's only sibling, who lived on the polar opposite side of my world. As far as I was concerned, Maine was as far from San Francisco as the moon. I had only been in Maine for two weeks, but my old life was already beginning to feel distant.

"Nearest neighbor's five miles up coast," my father had said when we'd first pulled up to Edie's place. He had been distracted as he gripped the steering wheel and rounded the bend, her lighthouse coming into full view.

It wasn't used as a lighthouse anymore and hadn't been in over three decades. Now it was just her home.

"Seems lonely."

"My sister likes it that way," he'd said. I wondered if that was true.

Strong wind hurled itself at the solitary structure, as lonely as she, threatening to push the building into the sea. But the wind never won, he had said. The house clung on, just like her.

She'd run out to the car, skin ruddy from years in the sun and with hair streaming behind her, wild and untamed. It was a dark auburn that paired well with her light brown eyes. Her freckled face further signified a life spent under sunshine. She'd been wearing a thick flannel shirt (colored like her hair), men's work boots, and trousers. Yet she was still quite feminine. Pearls graced her neck, and matching earrings were half hidden behind her long mane. She —my Aunt Edith, *the* Philipa Edith Gordan—seemed as sturdy and impenetrable as the house.

That night, after my father had departed, I explored the house a bit. It really was nothing more than a collection of rooms filled with artwork of birds that she had painted over the years. It was a smaller place than I'd assumed it would be. After completing my self-guided tour, I meandered into the kitchen where my new guardian was brewing tea. I innocently said, "This is an interesting house, Aunt Edith."

"Aunt Edith?" she'd said dramatically. "You make me sound as though I was your spinster aunt or something."

She was, and my expression must have said the same thing because she had regained her composure and said seriously, "Call me 'Edie,' like everyone else."

"Edie?"

"Yes." She licked her dry lips. "And you? We can't go around calling you 'Agatha.'"

"But that's my name. Everyone calls me that."

"But I'm not everyone." Contemplating me, she tilted her head slightly to the right. "How about 'Agi' or 'Atha?'"

I was just about to insist that she call me by my christened name, when something, a bird flying directly overhead and calling loudly, caught her attention. "No! I have it! We'll call you 'Sandpiper.' No, just 'Piper,' I should think. You both have long legs." She flashed a marvelous smile then turned away, as lithe and athletic as a young girl.

She was brilliant, creative, beautiful, and a bit strange from years of living all alone.

Papa, the grandfather I'd never known, had left her the lighthouse when he'd died and enough money for her to live in comfortable independence for the rest of her life.

Edie kept the windows wide open, and the curtains whipped violently, twisting this way and that in the salt-drenched air. The sound of the surf pounding in the distance gave off a distinct, strange loudness throughout the house. My aunt's bedroom was the only other upstairs room besides the guest room—my room now.

The room was simple enough. The mattress was a little old, but not totally uncomfortable. I'd brought only a few things with me from California, but I hoped that they would make me feel less homesick. There was an old photograph of my parents, which I set on the dresser, and my two most read books, a copy of T.S. Eliot's *The Waste Land* and an old pocket Bible. I placed them both on my nightstand. I had faithfully read that Bible each night since I had received it on my 12th birthday.

Well, I'd read it faithfully until just before I'd arrived. I hadn't cracked it open once since my mother and father had told me of their plans to leave me here while they went to Europe for a controversial new treatment. My mother had tuberculosis and was nothing short of being on death's door. This treatment was her last hope. I knew it was selfish to be pitying myself at a time like this, but I missed my parents fiercely and couldn't help but feel a bit abandoned. Why didn't they let me go to Europe with them?

I glanced down at *The Waste Land*. The pages were well worn; it had belonged to my mother before me. I'd always loved poetry. In fact, I'd won an award for my recitation of *Love Song of J. Alfred Prufrock* just the year before. "Would it have been worth while, to have bitten off the matter with a smile, to have squeezed the universe into a ball, to roll it towards some overwhelming question, to say: 'I am Lazarus, come from the dead, Come back to tell you all, I shall tell you all'"— I forgot for a brief second what came next.[3] Something about a pillow, I think.

Over the next few days, I learned all about my spinster aunt who lived in a lighthouse. Edie had written one novel, 20 years ago. The critics had called it genius, and she had newspaper clippings to prove it. Oh yes, Edie had been the up-and-coming star of the literary world. Her future had shone bright.

She hadn't finished one novel since.

Her writing desk was in the den, a big pine desk with papers, books, and magazines neatly piled all over it. A large, cozy fireplace faced by two oversize leather chairs on an old Indian woven rug rested dark and empty, seemingly not often used in summer, even in chilly Maine. A painting of a yacht, with the words "Grey Goose" scrawled elegantly on her prow, hung over the mantle. The room smelled distinctly of oranges and oil paint. It was a nice. I liked it. Bookshelves filled with glass canisters of seashells, bird feathers, sea glass, and books were pushed against the walls. An easel was propped up by one of the two windows.

Edie sat behind that desk every morning, sipping her coffee and clicking away madly on her typewriter with her perfectly manicured nails. Rumpled up papers filled the wastebasket with discarded words. This happened every day without fail.

Around lunch time, she would lean heavily over her desk and close her eyes, deep in thought. Sighing, she would say something to the effect of, "My character has no humanity. I hate him. I can't write about someone I hate." Then she would remove the paper, crumple it up, and throw it in the waste bin.

She was a creature of habit. Always tuna sandwiches for lunch. Always afternoons spent in the garden. Once a week, she had a poker game with Mr. Henderson, the single neighbor who lived five miles up the coast. She'd won a plethora of paraphernalia off of him over the years, including a couch, a 100-year-old bottle opener, and his deceased wife's false teeth. "Never lost a game," she'd told me proudly.

While she did all this, I banged around the house, reading here and there something from her library. I wandered around outside, watching the sea. At home, summer was always my favorite season. There were bonfires with the gang from school, hours to spend reading, and day trips with my mother to go shopping or to the art museum. We always had a lot of silly little adventures. I was an only child and Mother was more like a best friend than a mother.

I inhaled sharply, pushing back fear. A newly familiar numbness crept over me. It had been like that ever since I found out she was ill. Whenever I felt a cold shot of fear, I subconsciously reminded myself that strong people don't feel pain.

~

"PIPER!" Edie called again. "Today is the day! It's finally warm enough." She gave me a contented grin.

Outside, blinking in the sun, Edie stood decked out in an old-fashioned wool swimsuit that nearly covered her knees.

"Where's your suit?" she asked, looking down at my shoes.

"Can't swim."

"But you're from San Francisco!"

I shrugged, at a loss for words. My parents were not outdoorsy people, and we only lived there because that was where the medical practice my father had taken over was located.

Adjusting the picnic basket slung over her arm, she muttered, "Can't draw. Can't swim. Oh, Piper! We have much to accomplish this summer."

It was true. I couldn't draw, much to my aunt's chagrin. She had me sketching the last few mornings "because she 'couldn't have me being lazy all summer," and I needed 'something to occupy my mind.' Something other than my mother, I knew she meant, though she didn't come right out and say that.

"Here," I said, taking the basket, "lead the way."

I carried the basket and followed her down the rocky path to the beach. It was a bit warmer than it had been the past few days, but I still wore a sweater. We put the basket on a large flat rock, and I sat down, but Edie stayed standing. She threw her arms up and stretched back. "Swimming and sun are good for the soul! It clears the brain. And that's good for writers. You really ought to learn how to swim, you know."

Edie took off running towards the water, ignoring the fact that it was probably going to be freezing. She dove in and began to swim long, hard, strokes. She kept on going till she reached the buoy where she climbed on and waved to me, yelling, "You really ought to try this, Piper!"

And with that, she dove back in and began the long swim back.

Wet and dripping, cheeks flushed, she laughed, "Give me that basket! I'm starving. Nothing like a good swim to give you a healthy appetite. And a healthy appetite is a sign of greatness in an artist." I could never tell if she was serious or only poking fun at me. It made me feel vaguely uncomfortable. She laughed again and took a large bite of bread and a slow sip of coke while she threw off her cap and shook out her long hair. Looking out at the sea, I watched her face darken suddenly with some internal thought. As quickly as it appeared, it vanished, and I wondered if I imagined it.

I MUST HAVE FALLEN ASLEEP AGAIN. I was always falling asleep these days. Edie was gone, and I was all alone on the rock. The sun hung low in the sky. I stood up and gently shook the blanket out and made my way back to the lighthouse, shoes and blanket in hand.

Edie was sitting on the front steps, watching as I made my way up the path to her.

"I was about to come wake you up. You were asleep nearly three hours, and a lot's happened in those three hours."

"What happened?" I asked.

"King Edward just abdicated his throne to marry a certain Mrs. Simpson, a twice divorced hussy.[4] Quite scandalous gossip, don't you think?" Her eyes twinkled. "Want to help me with supper?"

"Sure," I followed her inside. I wasn't very hungry.

"What does your mother think about everything going on in Germany?" she asked quietly.

"Not much. She never really talks about politics."

"But your cousins still live there, right?"

I gave a nod.

We were in the kitchen now. She took out a cutting board and passed me two cans of soup to open.

"I'm planning a trip to Europe," she smiled as she began cutting a cucumber.

I was surprised. "When are you going?"

"When I finish my next book. No time right now, too much work. I'm in the middle of a big project, you know."

Every few days she would come up with a new idea and ditch the one she was working on, and her pile of unfinished manuscripts would grow. I realized that maybe my aunt was a creative genius after all. Only, she was a genius who seemed incapable of finishing any of her masterpieces.

"Where else do you want to go?"

"Argentina, where the penguins are." There was that dark, sad look again, the one that had crossed her face on the rock. "And I will see them and lots of other places, just as soon as I finish my next book."

"Are you happy here all by yourself, Edie?"

She didn't answer right away, and for a moment I thought she might not at all. Finally, she said, "I'm as happy as I've ever been, I suppose. I'm always happy by the sea. I can sing my opera here, and it gets drowned out by the noise." She gave a soft chuckle, and I grinned. The sea sure didn't drown out her Italian songs when she was in the shower.

I knew she was lying about being happy. She wasn't happy. I wasn't happy. We were both lonely. She feared her ship had sailed. Mine actually had, and it had carried both my parents away from me.

I heard my mother's voice in my head. "Agatha," she had said. "I want to rejoice in even this. I want character and hope. And so I'm clinging to the promise that hope does not disappoint. I want nothing more than for you to hold on to that promise as well," she had plead. "Will you?"

It was not a question of whether I *would*. It was a question of whether I *could*.

"Edie?" I put the can opener down. "Can I ask you a personal question?"

"I'm your aunt! Shoot." She kept chopping methodically.

"Why aren't you married?"

"Well, why aren't *you* married?" Her eyes narrowed.

"Because I'm 15!" I retorted.

"Yeah, and I'm 42. And a half." She looked at me with a feigned expression of horror, then said in all seriousness, "Piper! I am too young to marry. Don't marry until you have lived some life. I am still living my life. I have my writing career to think of!"

I thought about all of her unfinished manuscripts and stared at my aunt. I thought of all the places she hadn't gone, all the penguins she hadn't seen.

# CHAPTER 2

## THE FISHERMAN

"Well, when you *do* want to marry, what do you want him to be like?" I baited, playfully jabbing her in the ribs with a piece of driftwood. "And don't kid around."

We were back on the beach. Another picnic. Like I said, Edie was a creature of habit.

Tilting her head back, she thought for a moment and then said quite honestly, "Like a familiar sweet dream. The kind you dream every so often and can't remember when you wake up, but you long to dream all day long. Or like a favorite book you loved as a child and forgot about until you found it in an old box in the closet."

Cryptic. I was getting nowhere. I knew what I wanted in a relationship. I wanted what my mother and father had in each other. A rapport and easy harmony. There was that dull ache again. We still hadn't heard from them, though I supposed they were too busy to write. Still, it made me afraid, the unknowing. It was the vague dark storm on the horizon that was threatening all I knew and loved. Talking to Edie kept my mind off the black cloud of doom looming over my heart. I think she knew it too. There was something in the way she glanced at me when she thought I wasn't looking that said she understood.

"Come on!" She tapped me and jumped up. "Peter's coming by."

She wasn't going to get off topic that easily. "But do you even *want* to get married?"

She ignored me. "He'll need help, you know. It's a two-person job. Your mind might be more mechanical than mine, so if you don't mind helping out, I'm sure he'd appreciate it." She was making her way back to the lighthouse now, walking quickly.

"Well, do you?" I continued to press.

"Of course!" She ran ahead of me into the house, adding over her shoulder, "You wait out here for Peter, and do whatever he tells you. Tell him the bike's behind the shed. I'm going to change," she said decidedly as she ran inside and left me to wait for Peter, whoever he was.

"But who's Peter?" I yelled after her. "What's he going to tell me to do!" She couldn't hear me.

After a while, a man came into view, walking slowly up the lane. He was tall with blonde hair; it was so light that it was almost silvery, and his beard was just as blonde as his hair. He wore a black turtleneck with a sailor's jacket and carried a toolbox. It had to be him. He was the first stranger I had met since coming to the lighthouse.

He saw me and called out, "Are you Piper? Edie's niece?" He had a nice voice. Pleasant.

I nodded. "Actually, my name is Agatha, but Edie started calling me Piper."

He stretched out his hand, and I shook it. "Then I'll call you Piper too."

"And you're Peter?"

"My name's actually Sam, but your aunt started calling me Peter when I was a kid and it just kind of stuck." His eyes sparkled blue and were filled with laughter. He must have noticed my confusion and so tried to explain the choice of nickname. "Because I like to fish, um, like Peter in the Bible."

I raised my eyebrows. "So should I call you Sam or Peter?"

"Whatever you like. Most people call me Peter." He gave a wide smile, and I noticed his straight white teeth. He had the kind of smile that made you want to grin back. He reached out his hand and jovially shook mine. "So, your aunt has a bike that needs fixing?"

"Apparently. She said it's behind the shed."

"Lead the way!" he smiled.

Behind the shed, we found a dilapidated old tandem bike. A note attached to the handle read, "Your winnings from Thursday. I always pay my debts." I deduced that this was the result of last week's poker game.

"Do you think you can fix it?"

He believed so. "Most broken things can be mended."

I plopped down next to the box and watched. He appeared in his early thirties. Sam, or Peter or whatever this tall man's name was, was kind and easy to talk to. He didn't really need my help, but he was the first person other than Edie I'd seen in days. It was refreshing.

"She's always calling me to fix the stuff she wins from Old Man Henderson. Last time, it was that radio, the big one in her living room."

Edie, now dressed in her worn trousers and a wool shirt, brought us out some lemonade and gave Peter a bright welcome.

"Glad to see you, Peter. Haven't seen you since you got back." They exchanged a friendly hug. As Peter once again knelt by the bike, she asked a weighty, "How's your uncle?"

Peter gave my aunt a sideways stare and answered warily, "He's fine, as usual."

"He's like that. A more robust man I've never met. Good year I take it? Heard he's acquired three or four more boats for the fleet."

"Five actually."

She looked pleased. "He would. So ambitious. Always was. He always gets what he wants."

"Not always."

Edie blanched a little. "Well, I've got things to do inside. When you're done, come on in and I'll have supper ready for you both." With that she returned to the lighthouse.

Peter examined the bike carefully. "I've known Edie my whole life," Peter remarked after a while.

"I've only known her a few weeks," I stated simply.

"Well, she's about as strong-willed as they come. Doesn't know what's good for her. And that's the truth." He pursed his lips together. "Pass the Torx wrench, will you?"

I handed him the box because I didn't know what kind of tool he was talking about. "What do you mean, 'good for her?'" I asked.

"Oh, you know. She's always writing about fake things. Can't see the real life right in front of her. That's what my uncle says anyway. In my opinion, she's just been cooped up in that house for too long."

He tinkered with the chain. "I think that's as good as it's going to get. You and Edie should be able to make it into town without killing yourselves."

~

"THANK YOU FOR YOUR HELP, PETER," my aunt said as we sat eating dinner.

Peter stuffed another pile of beans in his mouth and replied, "Sure, I'm happy for the extra work."

"And I'm sure Piper was happy to be your sidekick." She threw in, "She's been moping about long enough."

I glanced sideways at Edie, "I *do* need a break from portrait sitting."

Peter chuckled. "Doing portraits now? Run out of birds to paint?"

Edie coughed slightly. "Eat your food."

"Thanks, Edie. Haven't had a home-cooked meal in a while." He cut into his ham.

Edie examined him shrewdly. "You look healthy, Peter."

"I try to stay outdoors as much as I can. Never liked libraries much." He liberally buttered his bread.

"Are you a librarian?" I asked, surprised.

Peter looked confused and asked, "What would make you say that?" I shrugged. Peter looked back at Edie.

"What are your plans for the next season? Are you going to stay in the East?" she asked.

"I suppose so," Peter answered with a mouthful of beans. "Unless there's a war. Everything's pointing to a big explosion over there in Europe. Could change things with the business."

"Oh, Peter," Edie set down her glass. "There may *not* be a war."

"There'll be a war."

He sounded so confident, so sure of the whole thing. Then it hit me; Mother and Dad were in Europe. Edie must have read my thoughts. She reached over and held my hand comfortingly. "Well, if there is going to be a war, I'm sure it won't be for a good and long while. Let's talk about something else, something more dinner appropriate." Looking at Peter, she said, "Right? Your uncle raised you better than that."

"Okay." Peter put down his fork and looked at my aunt squarely. "How about we talk about my uncle?"

A faint blush crept up my aunt's neck. "When's he coming back?"

"Next week."

Abruptly, Edie stood up and began clearing the table, despite the fact that neither Peter nor I had finished eating. "Remind him of our yearly, standing dinner date. I hate it when he's late."

"When *he's* late?" Peter looked incredulous.

She carried her dishes into the kitchen and called, "When he comes to pick me up, you come with him. I can't leave Piper here all by her lonesome. She needs other people around. I'm sure she's exhausted of spending all her time with me!"

"You would think people their age would just get over themselves and get married, instead of tripping all over each other and dragging me along into their melodrama. It's like a bad play." He said vehemently while grabbing a piece of ham left on a platter with his fingers.

"What are you talking about? Edie's never said anything about a fiancé." It dawned on me that there was much to my aunt that I did not know.

Chewing thoughtfully, "They aren't engaged yet." Peter saw my expectant stare and whispered conspiratorially, "I suppose it began twenty years ago. Every year he asks her to marry him, and every year she turns him down. He'll probably ask her again next week."

"Why only once a year?"

"His work. He is the founder and president of Scottish Lobster. And he does other stuff too, for the British Government. His job keeps him away. He returns to town only for a week each year and only for your aunt."

"And the rest of the year?"

Edie, from the kitchen, yelled, "What are you two talking about so secretly!"

"You and Horatio!" Peter yelled back.

"Don't go telling any tall tales to my niece!" Then we heard the sound of a glass shattering on the floor and an "Oh shoot!" by Edie.

He turned his attention back to me. "He's mainly on his yacht. But he has a big, old house in Scotland. Belonged to his grandparents. They left it to him years ago. That's where he's from, Scotland." An image of a weathered lobster baron formed in my mind. "He never did marry. Says he can't find any woman who compares to Edie, and he'd rather keep trying for her than settle for second best."

I leaned in and asked, "Does she love him?"

He smiled and raised his shoulders. "In her way, I guess. She hasn't married anyone else. But twenty years is a long time, and

Horatio has had just about enough of her games. But you didn't hear that from me."

Glancing at his watch, he said, "Oh, it's later than I thought. I've got to go. Tell your aunt thanks for me, will ya?"

I nodded yes and watched as Peter unfolded his lanky body from the chair and slipped his jacket on. "I'll be seeing you, Piper."

~

"EDIE," I began, while taking the wet plate she offered me to dry and place back on the shelf, "why do you want me to help Peter so much? Certainly he has enough to do instead of hanging out with a kid like me."

"I'm pretty confident he's got nothing better to do. He doesn't have a summer job. You have nothing to do either, and I've got a boatload of stuff that needs doing around here. Besides, he's got two things you need for your future."

"What?"

"Painting skills, I've got two pails of paint waiting for the shed, and friendship."

"I have friends!" I countered.

"And they are all thousands of miles away."

She had me there. "But Edie, he's quite a bit older than me."

"He's not that much older, is he?"

*Only fifteen or twenty years, give or take,* I thought to myself.

"Besides, you can have friends of all ages. Is he really that bad, Piper?"

I finally assented. He wasn't that bad. Actually, he was very nice.

Neither of us spoke for a moment.

"If there is a war..." I continued.

"Don't think about that, Piper. Thinking about things that may never happen never helped anyone." She scrubbed a pot vigorously.

"But my parents?"

"They'll be fine. She may be better before the summer is out.

We've got plenty of time," she said firmly, though her eyes showed that she didn't quite believe it herself.

Edie put the pot down and wrapped her arms around me. "Come now, that's no way to talk."

But I wasn't talking anymore, I was crying very hard on her shoulder. I didn't want to paint the shed with Peter. I wanted to go home. I wanted my mother.

My heart sunk. "People don't get better from tuberculosis, Edie. They die from it."

"Plenty of time," she murmured again. With my head buried in Edie's shoulder, I could almost hear my mother's voice on the waves below;

*"I know this is not what we planned, but I want you to know that I completely trust God in this matter, though my own heart is a bit shaken at the moment. I wish you could have come too, but this is simply not a place for children. You must know that things are not always as they seem. God's plan for our lives is not always what we want. Whatever happens, I want you to know that I love you, and God loves you too. Agatha darling, no matter what anyone may say, don't give up hope."*

I had memorized her last letter to me. It'd been weeks since she'd written, her handwriting spindly and weak. I'd read it a thousand times. A thousand times and a thousand more.

"I wish I could have gone with them."

"We all wish for things that can't or didn't happen." Her arms loosened a bit, and she dried my face with a napkin. The sun had just set, and an orange pink glow lit Edie's face, setting off her red hair in a blaze of color. "No one," she said sadly, "gets everything they want."

Those secret battles peeked out from Edie's stormy eyes, and I wondered what fears and questions she had faced all alone.

"Want to know something?" she asked. "You and I are going to be alright. Keep your hopes up."

"Hope." I tasted the word. It was deceptively sweet, and I spit it out amid distant rumbles of thunder. A storm was brewing.

Through the window, I could see dark purple clouds on the horizon. It was coming fast.

I looked at her and repeated what she had said. "Keep my hopes up. How do I do that?"

"Well, I will if you will."

It didn't quite answer my question, but it would have to do for now.

"Do you believe in miracles?" she asked me suddenly.

"Um, do you?"

She looked out the window at the storm clouds. "A long time ago, when I was just a little girl, before Papa bought this place and fixed it up, the lighthouse had been abandoned for nearly two decades. There was an awful storm one night. Came up real suddenly. Charlie, an old fisherman, was caught in it. He would have gotten caught on the reef, but, as the story goes, he saw a light coming from this tower. It was impossible. Everyone knew it... But Charlie saw the light, and he was able to navigate the reef. He lived. They called it the miracle light. Charlie's miracle light."

"Do you believe it?"

"Well, I saw Charlie with my own eyes, and he was still breathing."

"So, you really think my mother will live?"

"I think, no matter what happens to your mother, God doesn't want you to stop living, if you know what I mean."

"What about you?"

Her voice faltered. "I don't think he wants me to stop living either."

# CHAPTER 3

## EDIE'S YEARLY STANDING DINNER DATE

"Piper! I only have three hours to get everything ready!" She exclaimed as she hopped off the bike and ran with her groceries into the kitchen. "Peter's uncle is coming to take me to dinner, and Peter is going to stay with you here," she reminded me for the dozenth time.

I followed slowly with the packages and began to put the groceries away as she ran around picking up sweaters and papers off the floor and madly dusting the shelves in the den. "Piper dear! Go pick a bouquet from out back."

"It's just Peter and me. We don't need everything so clean."

Running her fingers across her sweaty forehead, she said as a matter-of-fact, "Peter's uncle will come back with me after dinner for coffee and brandy, and I want everything to look nice."

When I returned, Edie was still in the den straightening up.

I stood in the doorway and watched as she removed the painting of the *Grey Goose* above the fireplace and faced it against the wall. *That's curious*, I thought. Why did she remove it?

Edie ran up the stairs two at a time, and in an hour and a half, she was back downstairs.

I was sitting at the kitchen counter, paging through an old edition of *Ladies Home Journal,* when Edie sauntered into the kitchen wearing a gorgeous black evening gown. Her hair was twisted up in the most becoming way. She was absolutely breathtaking.

"Your hair is lovely like that," I said. "You look just like a model!"

Blushing, she replied, "Horatio always liked my hair like this. He's so elegant, you know. He likes things to be elegant."

I asked whether Horatio was a nickname or not, knowing her penchant for calling people by things other than their given monikers.

"Oh no. Horatio is his real name. Horatio could never have a nickname."

Then the doorbell rang. Edie gave a start and ran for the door. Flinging it open and striking a dramatic pose, she said, "Welcome! My dearest, oldest friend!" She reached out her hand, and a large one took it and shook it gently. The hand's owner stepped through the door, followed by Peter, who shot a knowing glance in my direction.

So this was the man who had the power to make my aunt do her hair.

He was about the same height as Edie, sophisticated, and proud in his bearing. Like his nephew, he sported a beard. Though his was as black as Peter's was blond. There were merry wrinkles around his eyes. He was instantly likeable.

"Edith," the man said, voice low and gravelly.

Scottish. He definitely had a Scottish brogue, the kind that rolls over R's and lilts and sings with the gust of a mighty emotional wind, even when asking for something as rote as a glass of water.

"Horatio," she paused and pulled me next to her. "This is my niece, Piper."

Horatio smiled and turned behind him. "Stay dog," he commanded a beautiful collie that immediately sat down on the porch.

"That's my life-companion, Miss Piper. That dog has been with me for years and loves the sea as much as I do."

He was holding a package and handed it to me. "Peter told me you were living with your aunt for the summer, so I got you a little gift." I paused and thanked him, holding it awkwardly.

"Well go on, open it up," he urged.

Carefully tearing open the brown paper, I held up a giant white sweater, the kind sailors wear. It must have been for a man twice my height and four times my width. I saw Peter stifle a smile.

"It's a sweater," I managed.

Horatio smiled proudly. "Fine Scottish sheep's wool. Well, put it on!" he urged. I slipped it on over my head.

"She'll grow into it, I'm sure," Edie said.

I looked at the sweater that hung just above my knees and a good four or five inches past my fingertips. Five of me could have fit on the inside. I certainly hoped I wouldn't grow into it.

I saw everyone staring and waiting for me to say something more. "It's... it's a beautiful weave."

The sea captain broke out into a huge grin, and as we made our way into the dining room, he told me in his loud baritone, "Yes, the patterns of the sweaters. Interesting story there. Each fishing family from long ago had their own weave in case there was ever a shipwreck and the bodies of the sailors were washed ashore, the families could identify their own." He was in front of me now, so he couldn't see the look of horror that spread across my face.

Edie took a step towards Horatio, her eyes never leaving his visage. "I'm so glad that Peter and Piper are here with us this summer, aren't you, Horatio?" Still looking at him, she said to Peter and I, "We're going to have a picnic on Stern's Rock. We should be back within a few hours. There's a set of cards in the drawer, but I don't recommend poker. I've been teaching her all my tricks."

Horatio chuckled, "I bet you have."

~

SOON AFTER THEY LEFT, Peter and I sat down to dinner. I hadn't noticed before, but Peter was quite handsome. If he hadn't been so much older than me, I would probably have had a crush on him. I resisted the urge to ask him why he wasn't married, but I was a bit curious how this man hadn't been swooped up by some girl.

While we ate the meal that Edie and I had cooked earlier that day, we talked about things to do in Maine and the new Jimmy Stewart film. Finally, after exhausting all chitchat, Peter looked at me seriously and asked, "Why didn't your parents bring you to Switzerland, Piper?"

"A sanitarium is no place for a healthy teenager."

A questioning look flickered across his face. "Sanitarium? I thought they were on some sort of vacation. You know, one of those grand tours of Europe."

"I wish they were."

He waited for more.

"It's tuberculosis."

"Oh." He looked down. "Is it bad?"

"It's a chronic cough where you cough up blood. You experience fevers, night sweats, weight loss... and there's no cure. But there is a specialist there with a new treatment my father read about. He's a doctor too, and maybe—" My voice broke, and I looked down at my plate. "Yes. It's bad."

"My mother died when I was about ten. At least your mother is still alive."

I bit my tongue and nodded. Yes, she was still alive, but for how long?

"Your mother passed away?"

"A boating accident. Horatio took me in and raised me after that. No siblings, like you. My dad passed away when I was just a baby. Horatio's a great man. Closer-than-a-brother sort of person."

"I like your uncle," adding, "even if his sense of size is a little off." I looked down at the sweater, grinning.

"Well, no one is perfect," he chuckled, and the mood lightened.

We'd finished eating and went to the den, waiting for my aunt and his uncle's return from Stern's Rock.

"Mind if I turn on the news?"

I shrugged. "Sure. It's dull as tombs around here." I hated listening to the radio without having my hands occupied, and I grabbed my journal, settling into the leather chair to try to sketch my namesake bird, the sandpiper. Unfortunately, my drawings were not improving.

Absentmindedly, I took in the news about Germany, Hitler, and the ever-present, increasingly notorious, Wallis Simpson. I was barely listening though. The news was never right anyway. At least, that's what Dad always said.

"Germany is in for a host of trouble, if you ask me. What a mess." Peter leaned back in his chair and sighed a contented sigh. "That dinner was good. Your aunt sure can cook."

"My mother came from Germany when she was a little girl," I mused distractedly. "I still have family there."

Peter sat up and stretched while I examined my bird. "Sure hope they aren't Jewish."

I blinked once or twice. "They are. My mother's Jewish. I mean, she's a Christian, but she was raised in a Jewish family."

"Well, at least she's in Switzerland." What was he thinking, why so serious all of a sudden? "It's funny your parents left for a sanitarium in Europe at a time like this."

"As if they wanted to make a trip overseas. They're trying to save Mom's life! And what do you mean 'at a time like this'?" I sat up, more than a little upset at this man. I knew what he was getting at. The war. A war that hadn't happened yet and might never happen for all he knew.

"Switzerland is neutral," I retorted. "Everybody knows that. Besides, it's where she could get the best medical care available." That ugly feeling of fear and anger simmered beneath the surface, uncomfortably threatening to explode all over Peter. "You should mind your own business."

"Sorry," Peter mumbled. He turned his attention back to the radio, or rather, pretended to. He knew he had hit a nerve. Standing up and moving towards the box, he said, "I'll change the station. Maybe 'I Love A Mystery' is on. Do you like that show?"

"Too scary. I want to sleep tonight."

"How about music then?" He fiddled with the dial.

The events leading up to my parents' hurried departure played through my mind. My mother had been coughing a little more than usual, but there was nothing to give us cause for major concern. My father had run some tests, and they had come back not looking good. We moved slowly. There didn't seem to be a rush. It was as though we were all three pretending nothing was the matter.

Then she had suffered a debilitating attack and struggled to breathe. We got through it, but barely. My father contacted one of the leading specialists on tuberculosis in Los Angeles.

Apparently, the best possible bet for her survival was a specialized clinic in Switzerland. It had the best climate, the most advanced treatments, and a new type of surgery.

The next attack was worse. Much worse. Now there was no choice but to go to Switzerland. War or no war. And I was left here, in this lighthouse, in Maine.

Soft strings played through the speaker. I felt Peter looking over my shoulder at the sketch.

"Nice bird."

"Well, at least you can tell it's a bird."

"They'll get better," he said. As kind as he meant to be, I only felt annoyance. It felt like he was patronizing me.

"No." I shook my head. "They won't get better. Nothing will turn out the way I want it to."

"What's the matter, Piper?"

That numbness I'd been feeling was gone. All feelings of apathy washed away. Anger, pain, and frustration were right there at the surface. Try as I might, I couldn't stop the words coming out of my mouth, "I am trapped in this empty house and there is nobody and I can't even draw! I hate it. I hate everything about this! I hate everyone here!" My heart was beating very loudly, and there was ringing in my ears. Was this a panic attack? Was that my voice shouting? A strange dizziness came over me.

"I don't think you mean that."

I didn't mean it, but I was so angry. I was so, so, so angry that she was sick and there was nothing I could do about it. And for some reason, God wasn't doing anything about it either.

"Piper, you need to calm down," Peter said quietly. He looked worried. "Do you need to breathe into a paper bag or something?"

Calm down. I needed to calm down. I sat down on the edge of the chair and tried to control my breathing. After a minute, I was able to say, "I'm all right." My heart slowed down. "I… I'm all right." I choked back a sob. "I didn't mean to say all of that."

The truth was, I hadn't known all those words were inside.

Peter ran to the kitchen and came back with a damp rag and put it on the back of my neck.

"You're sure?" he asked.

"Quite sure," I answered, though I felt nauseous.

After a moment, he asked, "Does this happen to you often?"

"Panic attacks?" I tried to laugh. "No. This was the first. First time for everything, I guess."

"You've had a lot simmering under the surface. Anger and disappointment. Guess it just decided to come out." Carefully, he continued, "Disappointment is a part of life, Piper. We all go through things we don't understand."

I was not ready for a deep conversation. My adrenaline was still pumping.

"It doesn't mean you should give up hope though."

Ugh. That word again. Hope? Hope for what?

"I see that cynical smirk. I'm not an idiot."

I looked up, my cheeks burning red with offense.

"You want to know what my uncle told me? He said that if I'm only happy when I get my way, I'm not worth my weight in salt."

"How can you say that!" I was shocked by his boldness. "My mother is dying! I don't have anything I want. Nothing!"

"For crying out loud. Your parents are alive. They love you. You are staying with a wonderful, quirky woman who loves you too. So what? Life didn't turn out how you thought it would? Life never does. It's the nature of things. You're a Christian, right?"

"Yes." Eyebrows arched, I felt like a cat, my claws barred.

"Then you know better than to go blaming God for your problems. He brought you here to learn to trust him more. For all you know, getting what you want could be the worst possible thing for you. God knows best. You don't know what's going to come of this. But he promised he'd work all things out for your good. You're old enough to know that. Stop acting so juvenile."

No one had ever spoken to me like that. "You don't need to throw my age in my face!"

"If you want to talk about age, I would say you were acting like a 3-year-old who didn't get her way."

"Are you accusing me of being selfish?" My voice rose, and a big fat tear slipped out and trailed down my cheek. I turned away so he couldn't see.

"If you ask me, that wasn't a panic attack. That was a temper tantrum. This is about trust, Piper. Whether or not you trust God."

More tears. I wiped them away. "You don't understand!" But he did understand, I thought. He understood more than I.

His face softened. "I didn't mean to make you upset. It's just that I know, in a way, what you are going through. Look, Piper, I'm sorry. I said too much. I was just trying to help, that's all."

Peter came over and put his hand on my back and awkwardly gave me his handkerchief. I hiccuped like a kid.

Peter looked awful. Like for most males, a crying female was "above their pay grade," to quote my father. "Look, I'll do anything to make it up to you," he patted my back, as the tears streamed down my face faster, pooling on my chin and sliding onto my shirt.

"I have a big mouth. I shoulda shut my mouth, even though I was right."

I looked at him sideways as the sound of raised voices filtered inside from the open window.

It was Edie and Horatio. They were shouting at each other. Our argument was immediately placed on the back burner as Peter trotted over to the window. Following him and drying my running nose on the giant sleeve of Horatio's sweater, I stood by his elbow. We could see Edie walking quickly up the path with Horatio at her heels. She was trying to look composed, but her hair had fallen down and she was carrying her pumps so she could walk faster. Horatio was holding the picnic basket, but after a few more steps, he slammed it down and shouted at Edie to stop. They were now just several feet from the front door, so Peter and I ducked beneath the window.

"You are an insufferable woman!" Horatio bellowed.

Edie was breathing heavily from emotion. "Horatio, I just… I can't!"

Peter raised his eyebrows, whispering, "What did I tell you? Every year."

"Just like you 'can't' finish a single novel. You know something?" His voice was angry. "You can't commit to me like you can't commit to one of your stories. And the only story you ever finished was when you were engaged to me. You wrote it, and it was good. Not great. But good. And you could have been great. If you had married me, you would have known the ending to all of your stories."

"I broke our engagement because I had important work." Her voice sounded like a woman trying to hold on to something that was slipping inescapably away from her.

"What could be more important than this, Edie?"

"Just give me more time, Horatio."

His voice bellowed back, "More time! Isn't twenty years enough! Edith Gordan, this is the last time I'm going to ask you. Will you marry me or not?"

"I don't know."

"You don't know? You don't know if you love me or not? Well then, make up your mind!" he demanded.

The front door slammed open, and suddenly Horatio was towering over where Peter and I cowered beneath the window. We sheepishly stood up. "Get your things, Peter. We are leaving this house for the last time!"

Edie ran inside and up the stairs to her room without looking at me or Peter, who silently grabbed his coat and followed Horatio out the door, shutting it quietly behind him with a final, "Every year. Every single year. I guess I'll see you around Piper."

The house was eerily quiet. I sniffled the leftover sobs of a wretched evening.

Later, I found Edie standing at the sink, washing a teacup very gently and slowly.

"Edie?"

She looked up at me and turned the faucet off, putting the cup on the rack.

"Are you all right?" I ventured.

She stared past me at the wall. "When I was a little girl, Piper, I wanted so much to be someone special. To do something memorable. I wanted it so much. I thought that if I just kept trying, I could grasp it, taste it, understand it. Do you know what I'm talking about?"

I didn't understand what she was saying, not exactly, but I let her keep on.

"Purpose. My life's purpose." The words tumbled out. "He would have held me back. I know it. I would have had to cancel all of my plans and live on a boat."

"Is living on a boat that bad?"

"I don't know now."

She turned back towards the sink. "You know what he said?" She paused. "He said I don't value people. He said I don't love anyone except myself and my work."

"I don't think that's true," I said quietly, trying to calm her down.

"Oh Piper, that's the thing. It is true. It is! I picked success over him. And now I don't have either. I've nothing at all. I'm a nobody with no one." Her shoulders sagged as the weight of the truth sank in. "I missed the boat. The ship waited for me a long time but couldn't wait any longer. I'm a poor little fool. A selfish, poor little fool."

Selfish. It was the same word Peter had used to describe my bad attitude.

## CHAPTER 4

## EDIE AND PIPER GROW UP

My ship, the one I was supposed to be on, was sailing away without me. My mother and father waved from the bow. There was utter silence. And then a massive black wave crashed over my head and forced me under. I couldn't breathe. Suddenly, a strong hand grabbed my arm and pulled me up. He was standing on the water. He looked remarkably like Peter, but different. Younger, but older. Stronger. He held me up and willed me to stand with him. An inner strength I didn't know existed welled up within me, and I stood on my own, locked in the strong man's gaze, out of which poured light. A miracle light? I was confusing things. Was I now that fisherman Charlie who had seen the lighthouse's beam? Tossed in a stormy sea, about to crash on the rocks?

The man was now a rock. No, he was a house built on a rock. A lighthouse. The light beckoned me to step out of the boat, to walk on water. I knew that the choice to stand was my very own, though it was the lighthouse-man's strength that held me up. *Help me, God. Help me,* I pleaded wordlessly.

"Wake up, Piper," Edie said gently.

The dream faded away as I gently opened one eye and then the other. It had been three days since that horrible night.

Peter and Horatio were glaringly absent.

We were glaringly alone.

Edie hadn't even tried to write. My portrait sessions had grown longer and longer as she avoided her typewriter. Both of us had been painfully quiet, and when Edie had spoken, it was to quote depressing Bible passages like, "Be careful, for the writing of books is endless, and much study wears you out." She had even returned from her weekly poker game without having won a single thing, muttering, "I'm losing my edge."

The dream was quite gone now. Only the silent prayer, *Help me*, remained. It was early morning, judging by the light.

She put a tray full of breakfast food on the bed, sat down and took a bite of toast. Light poured in. Mascara was streaked on her face from the day before, and her robe hung off her shoulder.

"You look like you were up all night," I began.

"I was."

"I dreamt all night."

"Bad dreams?"

"Yes. No. I don't know. Just dreams." I eased up carefully. "Breakfast in bed, huh? It's not my birthday."

"No."

"Is it your birthday?"

"Heavens no. But all last night I was thinking. There is something you and I have to do. And we have to do it today. I'm quite determined."

She took a sip of coffee and pushed a piece of buttered toast towards me. "It is the day you and I will both face our fears. You will learn to swim if it's the last thing I do. Maybe we can catch up to the boat if we swim fast enough."

The toast caught in my throat. What was she talking about?

"We will both be humbled. And in the process, we will be strengthened for the journeys to come."

The terror of the dream from only moments before rushed over me. I remembered it vividly now.

"Put this on and come downstairs. Ten minutes until we leave." She tossed me a swimsuit with the tag still on it. It was navy with white buttons up the front. "I picked it up for you last week," she called down the hall.

~

"WE'LL GO IN TOGETHER," she said firmly, stretching out her hand.

A mixture of anger and annoyance rose up in me towards my aunt. I pursed my lips and glared as the icy water nipped at my ankles, causing little goosebumps to run up and down my spine, but an unseen force pushed me onwards.

"Deeper, deeper!" Edie coaxed me on like I used to coax my dog Patty to come before she died.

I whined about the cold. And the wet.

"Your life will never be exciting if you're afraid to risk becoming cold and wet. For crying out loud, Piper, you are much too careful! You and I, we throw caution to the wind! We swim to great depths! We face the sea! Now take the plunge and give up control!" she decreed. "Besides," she added quietly, "your mother would want you to." And then she added to herself, "She would want me to."

Fear coursed through my body. Control was the last thing I wanted to let go of, imaginary or real. The spray of salt stung my eyes and I couldn't tell if what I tasted in my mouth was ocean or my tears. Edie's strong hands grabbed mine and pulled me under.

I felt my body suspend, perfectly supported by the water. Then came the shock of not being able to breathe. Panic set in, and I began to thrash about. *Help me, God!* I prayed fervently, terrified. *I'll let it go. I'll let it all go. I want to trust you! I'm sorry. I'm—* A hand pulled me up, and sweet sun and air struck my face. I heard Edie's voice telling me to stand. My toes found the solid ground, and suddenly I was standing, breathless and dripping.

"First lesson, lie on your back and float."

Nothing in me wanted to obey. Nothing. Yet I listened and relaxed as Edie instructed. We were quiet for a moment. "It's so important to let the ocean take you where it will. But it takes a certain amount of dying. Living always means dying. Real life, anyways," she murmured.

I wasn't sure she was talking to me. I pictured where the ocean had taken my mother. She had been forced to give up control, to trust God for the outcome, no matter what it would be. My mother's faith had always mystified me. So fearless and unafraid of the future. And my father? He believed as well, though on a more, say, academic level. He humored my mother.

Abruptly a wave made me lose my balance, and I came up sputtering and coughing, with the sun beating down and the water growing warmer. All the while, a sort of resolute expression grew more and more etched all over Edie's face.

Quite suddenly, I took my first stroke. And then another.

"We are going to die to ourselves, Piper! And in the process, we are going to live!" she shouted. "Keep going! Don't stop yet!"

Within an hour, I was swimming with relative ease.

Dripping and shivering with cold, we crawled back onto the beach. She held my shoulders and looked me square in the eye.

"I'll ask him. I will ask him."

I will never be exactly sure of how Edie managed to get Horatio to return to the lighthouse later that afternoon. Peter was by his side, looking suspicious of us and protective of his beloved uncle.

I answered the door, and Horatio responded curtly, "I won't step past the foyer. Call your aunt so she can say what she has to say, and I can get out of here. I'm shipping out early in the morning." He marched into the foyer and waited at the base of the stairs.

Yelling for Edie, I motioned for Peter to join me in the kitchen, all hostility between us dissolved the moment I saw his kind eyes. He turned to me and said, "Piper, about the other night, I shouldn't have been so hard on you, with all that you're going through."

Horatio's booming voice suddenly resounded through the house, rising above the waves like shattering glass.

"Where is that confounded woman!"

Peter and I rounded the corner and watched from the vantage of the kitchen.

"Philipa Edith Gordan, where are you!" he shouted up the stairs. "Edie!" His voice rang out, clanging like a ship's bell in a storm.

Edie appeared at the top of the stairs. She had changed into a floral summer dress and was barefoot. She didn't say anything, looking past Horatio and straight at Peter and I.

"Horatio. I..." She finally looked at him, but with an indiscernible expression. "I..." Her voice faltered.

"Stop, Edie," he commanded. "Don't come any further. I want to remember you the rest of my life just the way you are right now. Barefoot and flowers and not a day older than 42, for I won't be seeing you again. I'm leaving this forsaken town and you forever. I've waited and waited and waited."

Edie's eyes widened. "Horatio." I knew she wanted to say more, to stop him. But she said nothing. The habit of 20 years kept her rooted, alone, on the stairs. I saw her draw all her courage in with a deep breath. "Horatio, wait. I have something I must say to you before you leave." My own heart caught in my throat. "And no matter what your answer is, I want you to know the truth."

She paused for a long minute, not sure of how to continue. No one moved.

Horatio had had enough. Shoulders square, he turned on his heel, leaving a wake of resentment behind him. But in his hurry to leave, Horatio accidentally tripped over the rug and landed on his belly, arms stretched out in front of him.

Peter rushed from my side to help him up but in the process fell back a bit and knocked the painting of the *Grey Goose*, propped against the wall so Horatio wouldn't see it, flat. Instantly, Horatio's eyes fell on the painting.

He picked it up and looked at it while Peter and I looked at him.

"Edith!" Edie's face appeared around the corner.

"What is this?" he asked in a quiet voice.

"You know exactly what that is."

"And why do you have this?" His eyes softened.

"Do I have to tell you?"

Half to himself, he murmured, "Only those who will risk going too far can possibly find out how far they can go."[5] It was a familiar quote.

"Quoting Eliot?" Edith's eyebrows raised, her imminent victory tangible. I could imagine the voice inside her head: *Yes, Edith, you went as far as you could and found out where it got you. Nowhere. Alone. Thankfully, you had the brains to back up while you had a chance! Steady now, old girl. Don't lose the fish by yanking on the line too fast.*

Horatio slowly walked up to her and placed his hands on her shoulders. They were nearly eye-to-eye. "Edie, why do you have a painting of the *Grey Goose*?"

"Because... because I worry about you on the ocean every day and..." she trailed off.

"And?" he prompted.

"And when I see it, I'm reminded of you."

"You love me."

She tried to pull away and said something indiscernible to Peter and me, but she was caught by the firm gaze and grip of the lobster baron.

"Admit that you love me, Edie."

A strong wind came through and blew the front door shut. The noise scared Edie, and she jumped forward a bit.

"Tell me you love me, Edith!"

Peter and I were frozen like statues.

"I love you. And I want to marry you. I want you to marry me, if you'll have me."

"You love me?" he asked again. He seemed to not quite believe it. Slowly, she nodded her head up and down and let out a giant sob that half-scared me.

"I want to marry you. I've always wanted to marry you. I've been quite stupid and headstrong and selfish. And lonely. And afraid. And I'm sorry for all of it. Forgive me?"

He stood, a man stunned. Regaining his composure, he gestured around. "What about all of this?" I knew he meant the lighthouse, her life, Maine.

I could tell from the gleam in her eye that she didn't want it anymore. "The sailor's life is the life for me. I've been a landlubber long enough."

He looked down at her, utterly consumed.

"Room for another on that rust bucket of yours?"

"Maybe." His eyes were welling up with pools of tears.

She whispered, "Marry me, darling?"

He smiled vaguely.

"Do you still have it?" she questioned.

Laughing, he nodded yes and got down on his knee as he pulled out a ring. He put it on her finger, and she kissed him. Then she went upstairs without saying a word.

Horatio had caught his bird. The unmovable had moved. Peter's mouth gaped open.

Horatio turned and winked at me as he said triumphantly, "That's the way to get things done!" And with that, he walked outside and down the path, leaving Peter and I alone.

Peter broke out into laughter, hard and deep. "Never saw that coming! I was sure their story was bound to end tragically. Shows you never to count your chickens before they hatch." He gave me a grin, then followed his uncle down the winding path. My eyes followed his straight figure. His blond hair blew around wildly in the wind. The piercing blue heat of the day was a stark contrast to his wispy locks.

A sudden gust caused the front door to blow shut. How Mother would have laughed if she had been there. At that moment, all I wanted was her arms around me. I wanted to tell her everything, what Peter had said in the living room, how Edith was engaged, how I had learned to swim. I wanted to cry for hours and have her tell me everything would be all right and not to be afraid. And then she would flash her big, beautiful eyes and sing me something old and slow like when I was a child. And I would fall asleep in peace.

Quietly, I trudged upstairs and knocked on my aunt's bedroom door. There was no answer, so I gently pushed it open. She was sitting on the bed, facing the window.

"Are you all right?" I asked.

She nodded but continued to look out the window.

"I think so," she murmured. "I feel sort of funny."

"How so?"

"Like I finally grew up," she said, taking her hair down. "Don't know why I waited so long."

"Only fools rush in," I offered. "Look how wise you are! Twenty years? That's a long time to make sure you are making the right decision."

"Out of the mouths of babes." She slowly exhaled. "Thanks, I think."

"You really prayed for him whenever you looked at that painting?"

"Between me and you, I thought of him, prayed for him, and dreamt of him for nearly every waking hour of my life." She looked right at me.

I leaned against the doorframe. "Why did it take you so long to tell him?"

"Pride's an ugly thing, especially if you have a strong will. But our ship didn't sail, Piper! We still have a chance. Life is not going to pass us by, no sir! Not if I have anything to say about it! I've been painting birds too long! It's time to fly."

## CHAPTER 5

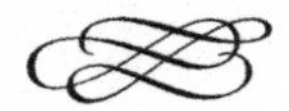

## TO CATCH A LOBSTER

I glanced at the clock. 3:00 in the morning. I had never dreamt so vividly before coming to Maine. It had to be something about the lighthouse. It was the same dream as before, just longer. I groggily tried to remember it.

The ship with my parents was sailing away. The same horrifying black wave forced me under and suffocated me. Once more the lighthouse-man pulled me up, willing me to stand on the water. *Let go, Piper. I made you to fly. But you must let me hold you up and put you down.* I soared higher and higher and higher.

I groaned. I'd never put much stock in dreams, but this one had to mean something.

My (much neglected of late) pocket Bible caught my eye, and I gingerly fingered it and opened up to Lamentations where I had left off weeks before. An old ribbon, frayed at the edges, marked the place.

"I remember my affliction and my wandering, the bitterness and the gall. I well remember them, and my soul is downcast within me. Yet this I call to mind and therefore I have hope."

Hope.

I read on, "Because of the Lord's great love, we are not consumed, for His compassions never fail. They are new every morning; great is your faithfulness."[6]

*God,* I prayed silently, *help me wait patiently for your compassions, new every morning. Help me understand your great love, even when everything seems and feels utterly wrong. Help me.*

The waves pounded on relentlessly, and I switched off my light and tried to get comfortable. I needed someone to talk to. I wanted my mother, but she was gone, obviously. Peter's face sprung to mind.

Peter?

Peter was the one person in the whole world I needed to talk to. He was the only person who knew what to say to me. He was so stable, so clear thinking. He would tell me the truth, even if it wounded me a bit.

I told him so, later that afternoon as we painted the shed.

Peter stopped painting for a moment, surprised. "I've always been sort of level headed. Just the way God made me, I guess. It takes a lot to get me upset. But when I get upset, watch out!"

"Takes you awhile to calm down?"

"Yeah."

"I know what you mean. Peter, everything you said the other night was true. It's become second nature for me to feel sad and angry. I feel like I've been grasping something very tight, something I need to let go of. But I don't know how to let it go. I don't know how anyone really lets things go."

"It's not so hard, Piper," he said kindly. "You just open up your hands and see what he gives you in return. I mean, look at your aunt!"

Just then, Edie rounded the corner. "Piper dear, drop that paintbrush. I need you to run into town. Can you manage the bike on your own?"

"Sure thing. What do you need me to do?"

"I've written a letter to your parents, telling them everything. I need you to post it."

I nodded. I had a letter to post to them as well. "Anything else?"

"Yes. Can you pick me up some orange slices at the grocery?"

"Orange slices. Sure." Ever since her engagement, Edith had gone on a sugar craze. Orange gummy slices were her current candy of choice.

"I'll take some Red Hots while you're at it." Peter's eyes twinkled.

A few minutes later, I was racing down the lane on the bike.

When I was young, my mother would race outside to meet the postman. He would give her letters from her family in Germany, and she would hold the letters to her face and smell them. Sometimes she had me smell them too. Happily, she would exclaim, "Don't you smell the cinnamon? My sister makes the most brilliant apple strudel with cinnamon and sugar and fresh butter. The butter there is different Agatha, really different."

Sometimes I almost imagined I could smell the cinnamon too. She would read the letters over and over and kept each of them in a beautiful, hand-painted wooden box. The scene on the box was of the Black Forest, lush and green. The stuff of fairy tales. She would hold the box and me in her lap and tell me stories of hikes through the woods, the medieval castles, and looking for mushrooms and wild herbs.

The post mistress took my letters and went into the back to check for Edith's mail. Meanwhile, I perused the corkboard on the wall that advertised local events like the upcoming clambake and the community theater's production of *Hamlet*. But another poster caught my attention. It was of a man holding a shield with the American flag and a snake. It said "Pro - American Rally" across the top, and then "Demonstration for True Americanism." It was signed, "The Friends of New Germany, the American Bund." Another poster below it was for a summer camp for kids, "The German American Bund Camp." The ad ran, "We extol German virtues to young, patriotic Americans of German stock.[7] It's the perfect place to spend the summer!"

Strange. I wondered what 'Bund' meant. It gave me a creepy feeling.

"Miss Agatha?" I spun around. The postmistress was back. She pushed two letters across the counter. I breathed a sigh of relief. Finally, my parents had written. All thoughts of the Bund were instantly forgotten.

Outside the post office, I held the envelopes next to my face and smelled them just the way she used to, hoping for some sort of familiar whiff of home. But none came. Just the smell of salt that stuck in my hair from that morning's swimming lesson.

Well, no matter. All I needed now was a bench in the sun to read them on. I'd seen one on the pier that would be perfect. I left the bike by the post office and nearly ran to the pier. Ripping open the envelope, I noticed that her words were still written in a shaky hand.

Dear Agatha,

I wish you could see this place. Beautiful. The Sanitarium is very modern, even though it is a sprawling old chateau (that is French for a large country house). There are about 70 other patients. They have us all lay out in the sun in the morning on the lawn, wrapped in big wool blankets. And there are a variety of strange treatments they've got me doing. They say the cold, clean mountain air is key.

The best surgeons are here, so here I am. They collapsed one of my lungs to let it rest. The procedure is called a plombage technique. I'm still recovering from it. The doctors are not sure if it did any good, but I am hopeful. Your father is wonderful, with me every minute. He won't leave my side except to go into the village for errands.

Your father said the bread is a revelation, but they won't

LET ME EAT IT. THEY HAVE ME ON A VERY STRICT VEGETABLE DIET. YOU KNOW HOW MUCH I LOVE A GOOD PIECE OF STEAK. WHEN I'M BETTER, WE'LL SHARE ONE TO CELEBRATE. WITH ROASTED POTATOES AND APPLE PIE FOR DESSERT. A LA MODE! (I LEARNED THAT MEANS WITH ICE CREAM ON TOP, IN FRENCH!)

GIVE YOUR AUNT A BIG HUG AND KISS FOR ME.

SENDING YOU BOTH ALL MY LOVE,

MOTHER

MY HEART SKIPPED A BEAT. They had collapsed her lung? What did that even mean? It sounded terribly dangerous.

At least it was a pretty place. Mother was always inspired by the great outdoors. It's where she met with God, she always said.

I knew that my father probably wrote more, explaining this lung business to me. After all, he was a doctor. Hands shaking, I tore into the corner of the envelope, unable to break the seal. I needed a letter opener. A bit crumpled, I scanned his familiar, nearly illegible scrawl, always an enigma to the nurses left to decipher his notes. His letter was even shorter than Mom's.

AGATHA,

I DON'T HAVE MUCH TIME TO WRITE. YOUR MOTHER IS HAVING A ROUGH WEEK. THE FEVER IS SPIKING. POSSIBLE INFECTION. THE PROCEDURE WAS NOT AS SUCCESSFUL AS WE WOULD HAVE WANTED. I WISH I COULD SOFTEN THE NEWS, BUT YOU ARE A DOCTOR'S DAUGHTER. YOU UNDERSTAND YOUR MOTHER'S CHANCES ARE SLIM. WE DISCUSSED IT ALL BEFORE I LEFT, SO THIS SHOULD NOT BE A SHOCK.

AS YOUR FATHER, ALL I CAN ASK IS FOR YOUR PRAYERS. SHE MISSES YOU GREATLY. AS DO I. I DON'T KNOW WHEN WE WILL RETURN. IF THE PROCEDURE HAD BEEN SUCCESSFUL.... WELL, AS IT STANDS, WE WILL BE HERE A WHILE LONGER.

YOUR AUNT WILL TAKE GOOD CARE OF YOU. KEEP YOUR CHIN UP.

DAD

THE WIND KICKED UP, blowing the sheet in my hands. I braced myself against his blunt truth. My father was never one to mince words.

"God, help me to hope," I whispered. "Help me let it go and trust you." I held my palms open and waited.

"Piper?" a Scottish brogue broke through my reverie.

Horatio and his dog made their way over to where I sat. The large man eased his way onto the bench. Glancing at my face, he took my hand and gave it a little squeeze. "Bad news, I take it." His hands were rough, the most weather-beaten hands I had ever seen. He grabbed my soft hand in his worn one and gave it a squeeze.

"You're practically my niece now, aren't you?"

"I guess I am."

"Then, as your near-uncle, can I tell you a bit of a tale?"

"You want to tell me a story?"

"Uncle's prerogative." He clarified, "You know, uncles have rights to tell their nieces stories. Especially when they've gotten bad news."

"Then I guess you have extra prerogative today. The news was pretty awful."

He leaned back a little on the bench, his face tilted up in the sunlight. "I grew up in a little village in Scotland. My mother was highborn, the only daughter of the local lord. But she fell in love with a common lobsterman. Her father disowned her, but she didn't care. She and my dad were so happy in their little cottage in the village. I started working with him when I was 10 years old. It was rough going there, learning the lobster business. I started with three cages and worked my way up. We woke early, 2 or 3 in the morning, stiff with cold beyond belief. In storms and gales and ice. Dangerous, backbreaking work. You have no idea what sort of work goes into lobstering."

He inhaled and then continued, "And then my dad died when I was 12, and there was my mother to care for. My grandfather would have nothing to do with us. Every storm threatened death, and my mother wore out her knees with praying. There was a little village church. It was beautiful and old and grand, like so many of the churches on the isle. Oh, how I miss Scotland."

Neither of us spoke. He was different than I had thought. Sort of like Peter in a way. He talked a lot more than Peter but had the same sensitivity. His rough hands and face belied the gentle soul beneath.

"Do you ever go back?"

"Rarely. My ma' passed on a few years back. So I've no one really there."

"What happened to your grandpa?"

"Funny thing. Never once saw the man, but he left me the old manor house when he died."

With that, he patted my back lovingly and pulled out a pack of peppermints. He popped one in his mouth and gave me one. "Things never turn out as you think, my dear. Never. It's not the way God works. Not to sound cliché, but the worst is never the worst. Besides, you're only fourteen."

"Fifteen," I corrected.

"Same thing."

"Hardly."

"Anyways, at your age, things always seem darker than they really are. Take it from me. I'm practically your uncle."

"Darker than they really are?" I looked at him doubtfully. "Things seem pretty bad."

He looked at me for a moment then shrugged. "You know what you need?"

I shook my head.

"You need to go fishing. Do you fish?"

Again, I shook my head, surprised at his suggestion. "I've never fished a day in my life."

"Nothing like fishing to shake a body out of the doldrums. Peter and I are going out tomorrow morning. You're coming with us. I'll pick you up quite early. Wear a sweater."

Not wanting to offend my new uncle, I agreed to go.

As Horatio stood to leave, I glanced down at his dog, patiently standing by its master's feet. Noticing the initials P.H.L. on the dog's collar, I asked, "What do the initials on your dog's collar stand for?"

Horatio mumbled, "They stand for nothing. You read it straight through."

I tested the sounds. "P.H.L. Phil?"

"Short for Philipa."

It hit me. Philipa Edith Gordan. "You named your dog after my aunt!

"Of course," Horatio grunted. With that, Horatio straightened his cap, whistled for his collie and briskly walked back to wherever he'd come from.

~

"ARE YOU OKAY, PIPER?" Peter asked.

"Seasick," I lied.

"Happens to the best of us," Horatio said sympathetically. "You'll be better next time."

I hoped beyond hope that there would be no next time. I was already longing for this awful morning to end. I couldn't look at Peter without blushing, which only made me more nauseous.

I replayed the last few minutes of conversation in the small little rowboat that bobbed up and down on the water.

Out of the water and into the bottom of the boat, the first catch of the day had thrashed.

"Salmon," Peter stated.

I smiled widely.

"Well, at least you learned something at that college last year," his uncle had said with a belly laugh.

I had glanced at Peter. College? "What do you mean, college? Are you a professor or something?"

"Professor!" Horatio had slapped his knee and laughed while Peter looked at me in a confused sort of way. "He's 18 years old, for crying out loud. I sent him to college to learn the business so he can take over the lobster company when I retire.

Squinting, I had examined Peter.

"And he came back with a full beard, of all ridiculous things!"

Peter touched his beard. "I thought it made me look older."

You got that right. I was shocked, and a bit horrified. Peter was only three years older than me.

A wave of nausea came upon me with a vengeance. I was completely speechless and horribly self-conscious. I had shared my guts with a mere *boy*? I had let him in on my deepest fears and confided in him my failures? I had let him, a *child*, council me! Preach to me! Like some "better than thou" self-righteous prig! (I chose at the moment to forget that he had been absolutely right.) The rest of the fishing venture passed in a strange and uncomfortable haze.

That afternoon, as Horatio and Edie happily cleaned and cooked the salmon, I avoided Peter like the plague and sought the solace of my room, complaining of a headache.

"Could it be sunstroke?" Edie asked, concerned, stopping me on the stairs.

"Nothing a little rest won't put right. She's seasick! Seen it a million times," Horatio answered.

"But now she's on land." Edie put her hand on my forehead, "No fever..."

I hated being 15. I hated that I could be so immature as to be so unhinged by some, some... boy! Or man. I wasn't sure which. It was embarrassing. I felt more pathetic than ever. Assuring Edie that I would feel better soon, I excused myself and ran upstairs.

She nodded, smiling, "Good! The Salmon Conqueror deserves to celebrate her catch. And quite a first catch!"

The idea of facing Peter again was horrible. What was I supposed to do? Pretend nothing had happened?

Nothing had happened, come to think of it. Nothing real, anyways. I talked myself back into some sort of composure. I was mature, a near adult. I could handle this with grace and poise.

There were much more important things to worry about. My parents, for one thing. Or the upcoming wedding. Or the state of Europe. Anything was more important than Peter and what I thought of him. Because I sure thought a lot of him. A whole lot. I thought of him so much that I might, just might, have had a crush on him.

# CHAPTER 6

## PIPER TRIES TO GET PETER TO NOTICE HER

It took me all night to finally calm down. I had returned downstairs for the salmon dinner but hadn't looked at Peter once, even when he asked me questions. I had picked at my meal for a total of 20 minutes before returning to my room. After lying in bed for hours awake, I felt intense hunger. Conflicting emotions of guilt (for being so rude to a boy who had done nothing to me and for thinking about Peter more than my parents or Edie) and the reality that I did indeed have a whopper of a crush on Peter made for a whopper of an appetite.

I snuck down to the kitchen for some leftover salmon and was not totally surprised to find that Edie had arrived there first.

She was in her robe, sipping tea at the table and carefully examining her ring.

"He had it engraved. It says *My Big Catch*. I can't decide if that's terribly romantic or terribly presumptuous," she said without looking up. "Pour yourself some tea. Water's still hot."

I retrieved a cup for tea, also making myself a plate of cold leftover salmon.

"You certainly were moody tonight."

So she had noticed.

"Worried about your parents?"

"Something like that. I don't really want to talk about it, actually."

"Mmhmmm." She was preoccupied. Of course, she had plenty to be preoccupied with. "Can't sleep. Can you believe it? Engaged one week and married the next. What's the world coming to?"

"If you ask me, I think Horatio was worried you might change your mind."

With a smile, she responded, "Once I make my mind up, it's made up." She stood up. "Want to see what's on the radio? I doubt either of us are going to sleep much more tonight."

I nodded and picked up my plate, following her into the den.

She turned on a small lamp and switched on the machine. Turning the dial, she found a station playing soft music (I was pretty sure it was Billie Holiday) and stretched out on the floor.

I sat carefully on one of the leather chairs. Salmon finished, the empty plate set on the floor, I grabbed my sketchbook and examined a few of my pencils of birds, lazily critiquing my pathetic attempts at art and pretending not to think about Peter.

Edie held the ring above her head and read the engraving over and over again. She almost looked like a teenager, lying there, arms in the air.

The song stopped, and a news bulletin started.

"Germany, led by Adolf Hitler, has officially annexed Austria with little to no response from other European powers…"[8]

This voice was replaced with a recording of Hitler's angry yelling in German.

"The Nazis are currently putting pressure on the Sudetenland, or certain areas of Czechoslovakia comprised of those with a primarily German ancestry. His calls for a racial purification and a pure Aryan super race… All Jewish professionals have been boycotted… The United States is determined to remain neutral in the case of war…" The voice continued to drone on and on.

All thoughts of Peter seemed so juvenile next to the urgent, real problems presented on the radio. It made me think of my parent's letters and my cousins in Germany; Lorelei, Grace, and Katrine. All three were just a few years older than I. They were my mother's older sister's children. I'd met them once when they'd visited the States years ago when I was little. They were pretty and sweet. I didn't remember anything else.

The reporter assured us that there would be no war and that life for the Jews in Germany, for the most part, would continue on as usual.

Switzerland is far from Germany, I assured myself. My cousins would be fine and so would Uncle Chaim and Aunt Judith. My parents would be fine. They would return. My mother would live. I was holding onto fine threads of hope, and I wouldn't let the radio rip them to shreds.

"Oh my." Edie put her hand to her mouth. "God help your parents." She caught herself and stopped mid-sentence, obviously not wanting me to catch wind of her worry.

She abruptly stood up and switched the station. A big band was playing a swinging number.

Pulling me to my feet, she began dancing around.

"Dance, Piper!" she commanded. "We'll shake the blues away."

She was so free, flailing about but absolutely on rhythm. "Nothing like a good dance to push away sadness." She squeezed my hand, and I smiled at her.

I couldn't help myself. I always loved dancing. We danced and twirled around the room, laughing almost to the point of tears, collapsing on the sofa when the song ended.

Another song came on, but Edie went to switch off the radio. She stood there a minute, thinking.

"Your parents will be alright. I feel it in my bones. And my bones are never wrong."

She winked at me, hinting that she knew something more about me than I knew about myself. "I met Horatio when I was your age."

Then she glided out of the room, leaving me to my journal of flightless birds. I felt like one of them just then, distorted, cramped, longing to soar high and away. Like in my dream, I needed to let it all go and trust. But once again, I wasn't sure how.

New every morning. It was a promise. I needed a new morning. I desperately needed a fresh start... again. Where was that elusive *hope* when you needed it? And what exactly was I supposed to hope for regarding this new complication in my life, a very kind, slightly older fisherman/boy sporting a golden beard and blue eyes that sparkled in the sun?

With all my strength, I willed myself to stop thinking about Peter as I crawled back into my bed. Finally, my thoughts stilled, and I fell asleep.

~

"THERE IS JUST SOMETHING SO 'UGH' about it," I later complained to Edie with a scowl. She responded with a stifled smile as she continued to paint a canvas.

"And what would make it un-'ugh'?" Edie sighed. "I'm telling you, it's a phantom flaw. Afflicts most women when they meet someone special. For me, it was my eyebrows."

Ignoring her, I replied, "A permanent wave." I knew exactly what I wanted and described my idea. I finished with, "It's so chic, and I want to look older."

"Chic and older?"

"Yes."

She inhaled before responding, "How you look doesn't matter. We've all already seen you, and we like you how you are. It's important for an aspiring writer to be comfortable in her own skin."

"I know that," I answered, but the pleading look was still firmly planted on my face. "But I'm not a writer. I'm not much of anything."

"And you think a new hairstyle will make you something?"

My face was pleading. She laughed that low laugh and thoughtfully tapped the brush on her forehead, narrowly avoiding painting herself. "Well, come to think of it, I really ought to get my hair done for the wedding. It's only four days away. Maybe we should head into town and get some new clothes and whatnot. There is a lot we will need."

"So I can get the perm?"

"If a perm is what you want, a perm is what you'll get. I just hope your mother won't kill me."

"She won't mind! I promise!"

"I'll call over to Belinda's Salon for an appointment. I wonder what one needs before one weds? I suppose I ought to buy Horatio some sort of wedding present. What do you think he would like?"

"A gilded lobster on a chain. Two of them, one for you and one for him," I joked.

"I like it. There is something there, Piper dear. Now, where can I get a pair of gilded lobsters?"

THE SALON SOUNDED like the inside of a chicken coup. Gossip and less-threatening chatter floated on the strong smell of acrylic nails and hair-dye. Ladies milled around with their hair bizarrely twisted this way and that with foil, or they sat underneath giant hair dryers that appeared to be imported from Mars. Pink of the Pepto-Bismol shade was the predominant color.

"So this is the first time you have ever gotten a permanent?"

"Yes," I replied.

The stylist leaned over me. She had big teeth and a slight lisp. Her lipstick was jarringly red, and her dress was so tight that I worried it would split down the middle if she bent over any further.

The next few hours were spent putting strong smelling chemicals in my hair, rinsing it out, curling it, rinsing it again, and applying more chemicals. Finally, the stylist announced, "Well, it's time!" She slowly unwound a lock of hair from the curler. To the horror of all, my golden hair fell out with the curler. The stylist stood there, stunned.

I screamed, "What happened! It's not supposed to do that! Is it?" I started hyperventilating. My vainglorious hopes of a perfectly curled and adult look were vanishing with painful rapidity.

Edie jumped up and stood next to the stylist. Her eyes were wide, and my face was beet red. Somebody gave me a paper bag to breathe into. A few more stylists gathered around my chair.

More hair fell out as they unrolled the curlers. I felt like I was going to pass out or throw up, but I did neither; I just stared at my ruined head in horror.

"How long did you leave that solution in?" someone whispered to the stylist.

"Too long, I guess. Her hair is really thin."

After what seemed like an eternity, every roller had been removed, and what was left of my hair stood out in strange waves and chunks.

"I'm ruined," I moaned.

The stylist looked worried. "Ummm. I'm sure we can do something—"

Edie interrupted with, "You better do something! My word, she didn't have much hair to begin with!" Her face looked grim.

"We'll try a strong conditioner." All of the other stylists nodded in unison that a strong conditioner was sure to fix everything. The conditioner was applied. They waited. They washed it out. They applied it again. They waited and washed it out again. Once more, the whole salon gathered around my chair to peer at my reflection in the mirror.

"I think we are going to have to cut it."

Edie nodded at the stylist. I just sat there as they turned my chair away from the mirror, submitting to the humiliation.

The stylist whipped out her scissors and started snipping away. Within a few minutes, I was pronounced 'finished.' A few of the women in the salon told me that they could hardly see the bald spots.

I was too terrified to look in the mirror, but I knew I had to. Slowly, they turned my chair around, and I stared at my hair. Everyone was silent. I looked a moment longer and came to the conclusion that I looked remarkably like a poodle. It was then that I decided that looking like a poodle was better than looking bald.

I looked at Edie. Her eyebrows went up, and I knew I had the decision to either laugh or sob. And wisely, I chose to laugh (though it took every ounce of willpower in me). "Well, hair grows."

"Yes, hair grows," Edie laughed. And the whole way home we laughed, though a few tears slid down my cheek.

Later that night, Edie carefully asked, "You are not too upset about your hair, are you?" She was looking over the purchases we had made before the awful salon visit. We had practically bought out Bowman's. Edie had acquired several new dresses and gorgeous lingerie sets that reminded me of the glamorous Jean Harlow or Dorothy Lamour movies. Silky, slinky robes and nighties. Everything was so elegant. She had bought me a lovely chiffon dress, in lavender, for a bridesmaid costume, with kid leather white gloves and white platform sandals. All quite stylish.

"Not much," I mumbled. We were in our pajamas and barefoot. "It was a juvenile decision I made without thinking."

Edie looked up and chuckled. "Oh, you were thinking all right. You were thinking about impressing a certain young man we both know."

I pursed my lips shut and stared at a photograph of my father as a child that hung on the wall. My eyes misted over. And my hand reached up to touch my shorn locks unconsciously.

My mother was dying. The boy I liked probably saw me as a whiny little girl. And to top it off, I had bald spots. It was all starting to get to me.

I looked angrily at my journal on the side table. I couldn't even draw a stupid bird.

Edie stood up and went to the window, struggling to shut it and keep the cold night air out. I went to help her.

Together, we were able to unstick the window, and it heavily slid down but not before a gust of wind blew in the rain, misting our faces and hair (or rather, what was left of my hair).

"Piper?"

Edie took my face in her hands and said lovingly, "All this will only deepen you as a person and give you plenty to write about as you age." She twirled her ring.

"I'm not a writer," I reminded her, once again.

Ignoring me, she looked back out the window. "I've been thinking. I don't want to go to Canada for my honeymoon."

"Why not?"

"I'd rather go to Switzerland, that's all."

"Really?" The weight and meaning of her words sunk in slowly.

"Yes, really. Horatio and I have already talked it over. And you and Peter are going to come. In fact, Horatio is already outfitting the *Grey Goose* for the trip."

Edie stood up and wrapped her arms around me. "No one should be away from their parents at a time like this."

As she spoke, I silently praised God and repented, feeling his mercy and love rush over me like a glorious sunbeam. Even in the wake of my hair's tragic end, he had looked down on me and smiled. The things that mattered to me, mattered to him.

Edie kissed my head and sauntered back upstairs. She stopped short, as though she had remembered something important. "And don't you worry about Peter. That boy has suffered too, more than anyone I know. He has gone through things not even I or his uncle know anything about. He may not see you as a grown woman, but it doesn't matter. He is true friend material. Don't you forget that and be a stupid woman like me. Hold out, he may come around yet."

Happiness surged through my body, and I ran and hugged Edie, long and hard. It was as though Charlie's miracle light had cut through my heart and planted, dare I say the word, *hope*. I felt like I was flying, soaring high. I had opened up my hands and received a very unexpected gift in return.

I could hope to see mother one last time.

I could hope that Peter would notice me in a few years.

And I did hope.

# CHAPTER 7

## EDIE AND PIPER ABOARD THE GREY GOOSE

I slept peacefully that night, dreaming dreams of my mother and Switzerland. I laid in bed for a long time, still feeling dreamlike after Edie's announcement that I would soon see my parents. That lovely feeling continued until I remembered the incident with my hair from the day before when I woke up with the dawn of the rising sun and rushed to the mirror. Yep, it looked just as bad, if not worse. My happy emotions began to drain, and I spent the next few hours shuffling around the house, trying to avoid seeing my reflection at all costs.

"My goodness, for someone about to set sail to see her parents, you're sure in a sore mood," my aunt said.

"Oh, Edie! I just can't bear the thought of everyone seeing my hair like this! I look like a porcupine." I didn't mind my aunt seeing me like this, but I simply could not face Peter. What would he say?

"I look diseased!" I continued to wallow in my anguish. Despite my inner joy at the thought of going to Europe to see my mother and father, youthful vanity and my crush on Peter made me painfully self-conscious.

"No, you don't." Her face appeared beside mine in the mirror. "I think the cut actually makes people focus on your eyes."

"Don't you have anything I could wear to cover it up?"

"Well, I guess I do have something," she mused. "Actually, two things. I have your grandfather's old fedora and a big straw hat I won in a poker game."

Wretched choices. "I was hoping for something closer to a wig, but I'll settle for the straw hat."

I followed her to her room. She awkwardly crawled under her bed, emerging triumphantly with a slightly worse-for-wear straw hat with a wide brim. It was plagued with holes. "I think a mouse got to it," I muttered as I gave it back to her.

"How about a scarf?"

I remembered seeing Greta Garbo[9] wear a scarf in a picture I had seen with my mother before she'd left. Greta had looked quite elegant in her scarf, neatly securing her curls as she drove around in a convertible. Maybe this was an even better idea than the permanent wave!

Edie rummaged around in a basket and chose a large silk scarf.

It was red, navy, and white, with a nautical pattern on it. She shoved me in front of her vanity and began tucking and folding and twisting. Within a few minutes, my tufts were well hidden.

"I think it looks sort of sophisticated," she said, obviously proud of her handiwork.

"Or sort of like a pirate," I responded.

"Better a pirate than a bird in molt."

She was right. I grimaced one last time at myself in the mirror and squared my shoulders. Unlike me, Edie looked luminous. She wore a beautiful sailor dress, part of her trousseau. It was silk. Her hair was in a loose low bun and hung wispy around her face. It was as though she had been born from the sea.

"What a strange ending to all of this." Her eyes scanned the room. "I thought I would never leave this house. How I wanted to at times."

"Are you ready to leave it?"

"What we call the beginning is often the end. And to make an end is to make a beginning. The end is where we start from."[10]

"What does that even mean?" I followed her out of her room and down the stairs.

"Who knows what T.S. Eliot means half the time. But it feels like this is an end and a beginning all at once, and it's made me so giddy I can barely hold still." Then she said with a gasp, "Oh, Piper! I feel everything is going to change. Adventure has blown right to my door, picked me up by my heels, and is carrying me away!"

THE *GREY GOOSE* was an imposing figure on the dock. It was 212-feet-long and gleamed in the sun with its bright white sides. There were 10 private guest rooms and 20 members on the crew. Edie had told me that it was one of the more extravagant yachts on the Atlantic. Horatio saw us coming and rushed down the dock to meet us, the collie following on his heels.

He swept Edie into his arms and kissed her so hard that she blushed. I blushed too. Then he took her hand in his right and mine in his left and led us up the gangplank and onto the main deck made of beautiful, perfectly oiled teak saying, "Welcome, my girls, to my home." PHL barked happily and licked my hand until Horatio bellowed for her to go below (an order instantly obeyed).

Crewmen hovered here and there. The sound of saws and hammering came from below. "I suppose I should have carried you over the threshold, my lovely young bride." He pulled Edie closer to him and dropped my hand, guiding us throughout the yacht.

As we toured, Horatio told us her history.

"She's going on eight years old. Built in the UK. Named her after Edie's first bird painting. Remember, the one you gave me?" Edie nodded and followed his finger to a painting of a goose hanging prominently on the wall of the narrow passageway.

"I bought her when I got out of the service."

"What service?" I asked.

"His Royal Majesty's Navy. I remained in the service after the Great War," he answered proudly. "I was in the Battle of Jutland."

I'd never heard of it, but I kept mum.

"What did you do?" I asked.

"No one knows," Peter interjected. "Top secret missions and stuff."

Horatio chuckled. "Oh, come now, that's all myth and legend. I was just a common sailor."

"Sure," Peter guffawed. "And I'm a monkey's uncle."

"Peter is right," Edie said gazing upon her fiancé. "Horatio is anything but a common sailor."

Puffed up with the admiration of his beloved, Horatio next led us to his private quarters. Workman were working feverishly to finish the changes that Horatio thought necessary to welcome Edie aboard his elegant and lavish floating palace. She oohed and awed over his color choices and the new fabric for the bedding that covered the cozy (and large) berth.

"Little Scottie dogs with red bow ties didn't seem appropriate for newlyweds," he said.

I had to agree with him there... though I personally thought that embroidered lobsters on silk was not that great of an improvement. But I conceded that he *was* a lobster baron, and he should have embroidered lobsters if he wanted them.

"It sort of matches your hat, lassie," Horatio commented.

"It's a scarf, actually," I answered.

"This is a yacht, in case you didn't know. Not a pirate ship." Peter's head peeked through the door. He playfully reached over and pulled it off, much to the horror of all, including the crewman who hung suspended on a ladder and dropped his toolkit onto the new lobster-themed bedding.

I am sure my bald spots flushed crimson.

Peter's mouth hung open slightly as he suddenly realized his grave mistake.

"The lass has been scalped!" Horatio said, disbelief written all over his face.

Edith rushed to my rescue. "You boys don't know anything about fashion. This style is all the rage in New York!"

"Well, I just came from New York and trust me, no one looked like that." Horatio was silenced after this with a swift jab to his ribs from my loyal aunt.

Peter just stood there. Stunned. I yanked the scarf from his hands. Shoving it back on my scalp, I glared at Peter and reminded myself over and over to be patient and composed and dignified. Drawing a breath, I said, "So, where will I be sleeping?"

Horatio cleared his throat awkwardly and led us down the hall to the last door on the right. The dark red, highly polished, wooden paneled walls reflected blurred versions of our figures. I would not think about Peter or my hair. I would not. I would hold it together. I would be adult. I would be poised.

Horatio pushed open the door, and all four of us entered the snug little cabin. The sleeping berth was wood paneled, along with the whole room. The bedding was chenille pink and had white satin lining and fringe. A matching bathrobe hung on a hook by the bed. A little writing desk made of the same wood was pushed up under the round window. A dusty rose plush rug and a cozy armchair with sage cushions finished out the furniture. Horatio showed how the panels opened up to reveal a little closet and drawers, and another one opened up into my own little washroom, complete with a shower. It was so feminine and lovely that I almost forgot the awfulness of the last few minutes.

"Why, Horatio! However did you finish this so quickly?" Edie gushed.

"I've got a good crew. They are all skilled carpenters, and I've hired a few mainlanders to help with the decorating and whatnot."

He turned to me. "So, Piper, what do you think?"

I gingerly sat on the bed. "I think it is the most beautiful room I've ever had. I don't think I will ever want to leave the ship."

"Good, because you'll be on it for a while."

~

EVERYONE FILED out while Horatio explained that Peter served as first mate and slept below with the crew.

"Can we see the crew's quarters?" Edie asked.

"Of course, my dear. But first, I want to show you the rest of the living quarters."

The living quarters included a dining room and a living area with leather couches, a pool table, a card table, a record player, and a small library. All throughout the tour I refused to look at Peter and kept self-consciously touching my scarf. We passed through the bridge, which was completely outfitted with radar and radios so Horatio could monitor his lobster fleet from the comfort of his own yacht.

Down below the deck, we met the crew who were on board. I had never met so many sailors before. Or, for that matter, seen so many striped shirts, tattoos, and piercings.

The ship's cook, Cookie, was a giant Jamaican. He had creamy dark skin and piercing blue eyes, the product of his mixed parentage. He was old, probably in his 70s, but powerfully strong. He shook my hand so hard that I thought it would fall off. "This one's a keeper, eh Captain? Look at her, ready to sail with a pirate's cap and sailor's colors! I like her. What do you like to eat, honey?" He turned to me. "Let me know all your favorites, and I will put in the orders ashore before we set sail. You just tell Cookie whatever you want, got it Princess?"

I desperately needed a new fashion solution for my, how to put it, *condition*. This one was drawing too much attention. Besides, it had utterly failed the "Peter test." Now that my secret was out, I might just have to bear it.

"Cookie's the best cook on the Atlantic. He's even better than the cook for the Prince of Greece's yacht, *The Trumpeldor*. Believe me, the last time we were together we had a little contest for roast beef, and Cookie's won," Horatio said.

"I didn't even know there *was* a Prince of Greece," I admitted.

"Everyone who is anyone buys lobster from Horatio. And if they are lucky, they get invited to dinner on the *Grey Goose*," said a tall, thin man wearing a butler's uniform. He gave me a stiff little bow and continued, "Ladies, if I may introduce myself, I am Agador Ferguson, the ship's steward. It will be my pleasure to serve you and make your stay aboard the *Grey Goose* as pleasant as possible." His eyes were deep set, brown and sparkly.

"Ferguson came highly recommended, all the way from London." Horatio winked at my aunt, who was looking more queenly by the minute. I guess this was what you could expect from a lobster baron.

"I didn't know you had a butler!" Edie was shocked and a bit delighted.

"Lots of things you don't know about me." Horatio's eyes twinkled.

Edie smirked. "Hmm. That'll change soon enough!"

The next few minutes were filled with so many names and introductions of the most diverse, nearly comical, cast of characters that I couldn't help but lump them into a blur. However, their faces and names would soon become almost as familiar as my own.

There was Frank, the third officer. He was in his late twenties and ruggedly weather-beaten, with skin so tan that it was almost red. There was a trained nurse, Nathaniel Amos Bounderby, who was virtually ageless, minus his shock of white hair. An accident from years before had left him mute. He spent his days mending the ship and the ship's men and his evenings playing the accordion in the open, salty air. Identical twin brothers Willie and Charlie Brophy had worked for Horatio for about a year as able-bodied sailors. What they lacked in brain, they made up for in brawn and general good-naturedness. There was Gorman, a man of medium build with intelligent, sad gray eyes and a large scar across his face.

Sebastian, the Puerto Rican Boatswain, kissed Edie's hand and garbled on and on about how beautiful she was. Sebastian kept kissing her hand to the point where Edie pulled it away, slightly disturbed but flattered nonetheless. She whispered in my ear, "We mustn't forget that sailors don't get out all that often."

"Well, that's almost everyone. But where is my second officer? Where is Frederick?"

Peter answered, "Freddy asked for an extra long shore leave."

Horatio's face darkened slightly. "To do what?"

"He was invited to speak at that Bund summer camp down south. You know, to tell all those German American kids what it's like in Germany and his experiences in the Hitler Youth and all that. I thought he would be back by now," Peter explained.

*Bund*. That word again.

"I am back now, Peter," a German accent answered, clambering down the stairs. His young, clean-cut face appeared at the end of the line of crewmen. He leaned forward to Horatio. "I apologize for being late, but it took longer to get back from the camp than expected."

He bowed slightly in my direction. I examined the face as it examined me. It was handsome, very handsome. Looked like it was chiseled out of marble. No lines, perfectly symmetrical. Hard. No, not hard exactly. Perhaps just serious. His eyes left mine to Edie's.

"So, this is the bride? It is my honor to meet you, madam." He bowed to Edie. And then, eyes back on me, he said, "And this must be Piper? Peter! You did not tell me your friend was such a beautiful creature! So has my bunkmate been a gentleman or just a big oaf? Americans have no idea how to treat women."

He was charming too. Now *this* was a gentleman. "You will, I'm sure, make this journey much more pleasant," I said. "You were speaking at a summer camp?"

He looked at me, pride shining behind his eyes. "Yes. My former commander in the Hitler Youth program moved here a few years ago. The Bund—"

"What is the Bund?" I asked.

"The full name is the 'Friends of New Germany.' They train young Americans in special military drills, and we instill the values of the Fatherland: good values; hard work, physical strength, beauty, German ideals. It creates strong and healthy young people and prepares them to serve their country."

"And which country is that?" Frank raised his eyebrows.

Ignoring the question, Frederick went on, "I was a very active member of the Hitler Youth, before I joined Horatio's crew. They are always excited to hear from a German brother who sets a good example." At that, Frank excused himself to get back to work, shooting Frederick a disdainful frown.

Peter laughed out loud. "Good example? You?"

Well, he certainly was more sensitive to a lady's emotions, I thought, glaring at Peter and putting on my most winning smile towards Frederick. *He* didn't say a word about my headgear.

Frederick spoke to me as if I were the only one in the room. "You would love it. Clean air. Mountains. Swimming. Hiking. Parades."

Peter looked uncomfortable and shuffled his feet awkwardly. Edie's eyes darted between me, Frederick, and Peter. She suddenly laughed, "Oh to be a bright young thing again! Horatio, lead us on. What else is there to show us on this boat of yours?"

"Our boat, darling. Ours."

So adventure had pulled me up by the heels. The end of the beginning was reached as the engine of mystery roared to life. I could almost see my parents waiting for me in Europe. I was close, so very close.

# CHAPTER 8

## A LOBSTER CAUGHT

The wedding day arrived. Through the wall, I heard Edie loudly singing a song from *Madame Butterfly*. She peeked into my room and whispered, "Piper! Are you awake?"

"I'm up." Flipping over in my bed, I groggily attempted to open my eyes. They widened instantly. Edie's face was plastered with a green face mask, her red hair in curlers. Her eyes shone out of her face, almost feverish with excitement.

She threw herself on the bed. "I'm getting married today," she sighed.

We laid there for a minute more, neither of us saying anything, soaking in the remaining few moments of life as we knew it.

Finally, Edie said, "Now, get up, Piper! The car will be here in two hours, and I need your help getting dressed!"

What a day. Edie was getting married, really getting married.

Two cups of stronger-than-usual coffee later, Edie and I were both a little jittery. We turned up the radio in her room and blared Lena Horne and Ella Fitzgerald, dancing like happy fools once more as Edie removed her mask and curlers. She pulled from her closet a stunning white suit, silk stockings, and beautiful cream pumps. A pearl necklace with little emeralds in between each pearl, a gift from Horatio, finished the outfit.

We styled her hair into a chic twist, and an antique comb from her mother was clipped in right above her left ear. Her makeup was simple but flawless.

I dressed in the bridesmaid dress we had bought in town and then sat down in front of the little vanity in Edie's room to figure out some sort of solution for my (remaining) hair. The pirate scarf just wouldn't do. Edie reached up into her closet and pulled down a box.

"I have a present for you," she said conspiratorially.

Lifting the lid to the box, I cried, "Oh my! Aunt Edie, it's perfect! Wherever did you find it?"

"I had it all along, but didn't think of it until last night."

Inside the box was a beautiful little cap, the kind that was all the rage when I was born. Worn close to the head, this one was decorated with art deco patterns in glass beads and sequins. It was the kind that flappers would wear. And it was the exact shade of lavender as my dress, almost as if they had come together as a set.

I put it on, and we both looked at my reflection in the mirror.

A wave of relief washed over me. "It looks like it was made just for me!" It really did. I actually looked pretty.

Now Peter would see what a fully grown, elegant woman I obviously was. I knew I had more important things to worry about, but right now I just wanted to impress Peter. Pulling my shoulders back, I pouted my lips like a movie star as Edie put just the littlest bit of rouge on my lips and cheeks.

We both stood up and gazed at our reflections approvingly. From this angle, I looked even better. "You know, I think this is going to work."

"I wish your father could be here, to walk me down the aisle," Edie said wistfully. "And your mother too. I would have had her be my maid of honor."

"That would have been nice," I agreed, feeling a familiar brush of sadness. "Guess you'll just have to settle for me," I smiled.

A horn honked above the noise of the radio and ever-present waves. Edie walked over to the window and waved to Ferguson, who was waiting with the car.

Stoically, like a soldier going into battle, she said, "The time arrives in every woman's life when she takes the plunge into the unknown. Into adventure, happiness, perhaps pain. Our time has arrived, Piper dear. We are taking the plunge. We, us brave women, you and I, are not normal. We are unusual. We are extraordinary. We were not meant to live ordinary lives. We are fearless. We fly above the realm of normality."

She paused and looked around her room. "This house has been good to me, but a new home awaits me. His name is Horatio, and he will be a stronger support than these old walls ever were." Placing her hands on the wall, she spoke seriously, "Dear house, Mr. Morrison will care for you from now on."

"Come, Piper," she said, extending her hand. "Our destiny awaits."

And so, hand in hand, we marched like soldiers to the car and Mr. Ferguson.

He bowed and opened the door to the back seat so Edie and I could slide in. "Beautiful day for a wedding, ma'am."

"Beautiful day indeed, Ferguson dear," Edie answered.

THE SUN WAS BRIGHT, clear, and perfect. Seemingly no time had passed before the car stopped in front of the white wooden chapel. It was a small building and quite old. It had that musty church smell. A bower of flowers hung over the open doors, and the organ was playing. Edie squeezed my hand and gently stepped out of the car assisted by Ferguson. I followed.

The chapel was filled with townspeople and the crew of the *Grey*

*Goose*. Windows were opened wide. The sea air and waves seemed to mingle with the chatter of the crowd and the organ. As soon as Edie stepped into the chapel, the room went silent and the organ began playing "The Wedding March." Waiting at the front of the chapel was Horatio, dressed in a suit with a little orchid in the buttonhole. Peter, his best man, was wearing a similar suit and orchid. He stood tall and proud next to his uncle.

It was time to begin the march towards adventure, the time had come to plunge in. I held a bouquet of small pink roses, a miniature version of my aunt's, in my hands as my feet steadily walked down the aisle. Right together. Left together. I kept my eyes glued on the priest who smiled confidently. He had done this a million times before, but I had never been a bridesmaid. Bowing my head like a princess to Horatio, I took my place, avoiding Peter's glance.

Then came Edie. She sort of disappeared into an ethereal glow, the music faded away, and I only heard the waves. The crowd faded too. I could only see her hands on the bouquet, moving through time and space towards Horatio. It was a moment forever etched in my memory.

She reached the front of the chapel, the music stopped, and the priest began. I only half-listened as the priest led them through their vows. I was too mesmerized by the look on Horatio's face to pay mind to anything else.

"Dearly beloved, we are gathered here today in the sight of God..."

"Do you Horatio Macleay"

"Do you Philipa Edith Gordan?"

"For richer or poorer..."

"To cherish..."

"Till death do you part?"

They exchanged rings, perfectly formed gold bands etched with lobsters.

Then, tears and kisses. And just like that, they were married. The chapel became a burst of cheers and applause as Horatio and Edie triumphantly exited as Mr. and Mrs.

Peter offered his elbow to me, and I took it. As we followed them back down the aisle, I felt his eyes rest on my lavender cap. Then he leaned over and whispered, "You really look nice, Piper." He gave my arm a little squeeze.

But he said it in the way a brother might to a little sister, which was *not* the way I wanted him to say it. There was a hint of an apology in the statement too, but I couldn't focus on it. There was too much activity.

We made it outside to the landing. A photographer was shooting photograph after photograph of the four of us, the wedding party. It was blazingly bright.

The crowd was throwing rice, and it hurt. Felt like tiny rocks being pummeled at my skin. No one had ever told me that the rice hurt. I couldn't understand why this was a tradition.

Horatio and Edie were pushed into the car, and Ferguson drove them away. Cans and old shoes rattled behind them, and a cheery "Just Married" was painted on the rear window. The crowd surged after them, carrying Peter and me along with them.

Peter yelled above the merrymakers, "Piper, why are you so mad at me?"

"I am not mad at you!" I couldn't very well tell him that I was angry because he was 18. And wonderful.

But I was mad.

"That's what women always say," he answered.

Surging ahead of him towards the reception site, I pretended I hadn't heard a word he'd said.

THE PAVILION for the reception was decked with white and pink bunting and had flowers hung over a long table. The crowd cheered as Horatio and Edie appeared, hands clasped and beaming.

Lobsters, hot buttered rolls, and corn were served on large silver trays. Under the pavilion, a long table held little cookies, deviled eggs, salads, and a giant punch bowl. The wedding cake, a gorgeous, white, fluffy thing topped with a tiny bride and groom, sat proudly in the middle, surrounded by trays of whoopee pies.

"A toast! A toast to the bride and groom!" someone shouted, clinking on his glass.

Everyone raised their glasses and laughed and toasted.

I snuck out of the party with my cake and went down to the water's edge, just out of sight. I slipped my shoes off and carefully removed my cap, letting the gentle breeze blow over my face and through my hair. My fingers ran through the thin strands. I grimaced and looked down at my cake. Vanilla, with raspberry filling. I picked at it and threw crumbs to the seagulls.

I had never been one for crowds, but the water soothed away the noise and activity of the day. I gingerly put my feet in the water and eased onto a large rock that was not too covered with barnacles and seaweed. The time passed by, minute by minute.

"Piper?"

I turned around and saw Peter coming up behind me. He was carrying his cake too.

"I thought I saw you head down this way."

I turned back towards the water.

"You know, your hair doesn't look that bad. Really, it doesn't."

"Thanks."

He paused before asking, "Won't you tell me why you're mad?"

"No."

"Well, if you are not going to tell me, how can I apologize?" he was beginning to sound irritated.

Sighing, I turned around. What was the use of telling him? He was oblivious so there would be no point. Besides, it would be too embarrassing. He was sorry after all. I could forgive him and move on like a normal person, couldn't I? I doubted it. But I could try.

I put on my best "it's water under the bridge" face.

"It was just me feeling upset about my hair, Peter." It wasn't totally honest, I know. But that's what came out.

"Your mother too?" he asked, genuinely concerned.

"I wish I could say it was that," I answered honestly. "And of course," I explained, "I am worried. I am so relieved to be on our way to her that I could cry. But it was just my vanity that was hurt. Imagine if your beard fell out?"

He laughed and said, "I don't think I'm as attached to the beard."

"Men have it a lot easier, mark my words."

"When it comes to beauty, I'll take your word for it."

Placing the cap firmly back on my head and strapping my shoes back on, Peter helped me up, relief written all over his face. "I'm glad we're still friends then."

I extended my hand and shook his firmly. "Friends."

"Forever?" he said with a wink.

My heart thumped a little faster.

"We're practically cousins now. I guess we're stuck together."

Frederick suddenly came running up and said breathlessly, "Piper, Edie's looking for you. She is going to throw the bouquet." He stopped dead in his tracks. "You look truly stunning today, if I may say so. An Aryan beauty. Are you German?"

"Aryan?"

"Pure German blood. The most beautiful women in the world look like you." He was so debonair. He was older, probably older than Peter, but not by much. And then I knew where I had heard that term. It was on the radio whenever news broadcasters spoke about the new German racial laws that were so controversial and put my non-Aryan, German cousins in a precarious position.[11]

"My mother is German, actually," I answered, but something inside warned me to stop. He had been a member of the Hitler youth. If the little I knew about Hitler was true, it was better to keep the details of my family under wraps.

"Then I am sure she must be as beautiful as you." He was polite, charming. "You must allow me to escort you back to the party." I hesitatingly took the offered elbow. He was so handsome, so polite. Certainly there was no real danger.

Frederick seemed like the type to have a lot of girls. I had never really met one of those sorts of boys, but I knew he was one of them. Somehow, you just know those things. I glanced back at Peter, following closely behind us, an unreadable expression on his face.

# PART TWO

## SANDPIPER SETS SAIL

## CHAPTER 9

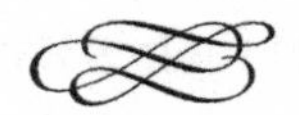

## SANDPIPER GETS HER SEA-LEGS

"Miss Piper?"

My eyes struggled open. A tall man wearing a monkey suit stood over me, and I heard water. Everything seemed to be moving. Where was I?

"Miss Piper, I've brought your breakfast."

The man opened the curtains, and light streamed in, bouncing off the shiny wood.

Oh yes, I remembered now; I was on the *Grey Goose*.

"Ferguson?"

"Yes, Miss Piper?"

I groggily sat up, and Ferguson placed a tray on my lap.

"Are you feeling better?"

I put my hand on my stomach. Still a twinge of nausea. "I think so. I don't really remember last night. What happened?"

"You went to bed feeling ill. I gave you a tincture enhanced with licorice and ginger. I believe the grogginess you are experiencing is a mixture of your new surroundings and yesterday's festivities. I ordered Cookie to make you a soft-boiled egg, dry toast, half a grapefruit, and some piping hot tea. It's a tried and tested combination for what ails you."

"What ails me?"

"Too-much-wedding. It's related to too-much-birthday if you've ever suffered from that particular strain of virus."

I gazed down at the breakfast and nibbled on the toast. "Do you always bring people breakfast?"

"Of course, Miss Piper. It's my job to serve Horatio and his family. I am your humble servant." He bowed a little bow.

"Well... would you sit with me while I eat, Ferguson?"

He coughed awkwardly and answered, "If you wish, Miss Piper." And with that, he sat stiffly in my little armchair.

"Ferguson, what happened after I went to bed?" I sipped the tea. I had a pounding headache.

He thought for a moment, then answered, "Mr. and Mrs. Macleay danced til midnight before retiring. Both are still in their cabin and do not wish to be disturbed. Peter and Frederick played cards before retiring to their cabin, and the rest of the crew went about their business. Is there anything else you would like to know, Miss Piper?"

I thought a moment. "No, I guess not."

"Then I will leave you to your breakfast." He stood up, bowed again, and firmly shut the door to my cabin.

The ship gently rolled as I carefully pushed the tray to the side and stood up. With just two steps, I reached the window and opened the glass porthole. Instantly, salt spray misted my face. There was not a cloud in the sky, and the sun shone bright. It was going to be a beautiful morning. In the bathroom, I splashed water on my face and brushed my teeth.

I selected some shorts, a blouse, and a pair of 'boat shoes,' a gift from Horatio. Then, I took a new white scarf and wrapped it a few times around my hair. Finally, I stared harshly at myself, muttering, "Yup, that's as good as it is going to get."

Emerging from my cabin and making my way towards the deck,

I passed Nathaniel on my way out. "Nice accordion playing last night." That was one thing I did remember.

The mute sailor smiled broadly and returned to winding up a large coil of rope.

The air was cool. No land was in sight. We were miles and miles from anywhere. I steadied myself after the ship dipped a bit and continued walking aimlessly on the quiet ship. Where was everyone?

I supposed that Peter was busy working, along with the rest of the crew. Who knew when Horatio and Edie would appear. I was on my own. Perhaps I could read something? Or maybe draw?

There were some cozy steamer chairs nestled against the cabins, and I settled in for a slow morning.

The sailors occasionally passed me and gave cheerful hellos, but there was no sign of Peter or Frederick. No one to talk to. Nothing to do. I was bored and anxious and excited all at the same time. I couldn't concentrate on anything and kept shifting in the steamer. Finally, Ferguson appeared.

"Miss Piper, would you like to order lunch?"

Was it already time for lunch? I'd lost track of the day. Gazing out over the ocean, I asked, "Fergie, how fast are we going?"

Ignoring my new nickname for him, Ferguson followed my gaze. "I assume we are traveling at about 30 knots." Then, after a quick calculation, he translated, "Roughly 35 miles per hour."

I groaned. At that pace, it would take us days and days to reach Europe. What if we didn't make it in time for me to see my mother again? I shook off the sense of dread that had been so familiar before the activity of the wedding and Peter had distracted me. "Can we go faster?"

"We are going as fast as the *Goose* can fly. And she is one of the fastest of her class." The butler must have read my troubled thoughts. "Patience, Miss Piper, is the key to enjoying this journey. We will arrive when we arrive, and that will be right on time. Not necessarily your time, mind you. But God's time."

"Yes. Yes, of course," I answered, doing my best to sound very mature and not like a child asking every twenty minutes if we're there yet. "I fear that time is not always on my side."

"You are far too young to say that!"

"My mother's not," I answered simply.

Ferguson patted my back and said, "Now, now. Don't give up hope yet. We are all praying for your dear mother." He coughed, once more in full on butler mode. "So, about that lunch?"

"Will I have to eat it alone?"

"Only if you wish. Where and with whom would you like to eat with?"

"I don't really care. Someone. I've been alone all morning."

"Young Frederick and Samuel, err, Peter are through with their morning duties. I will set an extra place for you with them in the officer's mess."

"Thanks, Fergie. That sounds perfect." Then, I said, "You don't mind if I call you Fergie, do you?"

He shook his head no, a smile flickering across his face, and then he disappeared down into the officer's quarters.

Having a butler was rather nice, I decided.

I SHYLY PEEKED around the corner and saw Peter and Frederick sitting at the table.

"Finally," Frederick sighed, catching my eye. "Now we will have some interesting conversation. Come on in and sit down." He pulled out a chair. "Welcome to the officer's club, with dear old Freddy and Peter, second and first officers, serving as your hosts. We dub you honorary chief officer of all that is beautiful and good." He took a butter knife and tapped both my shoulders as though I was being knighted, and I couldn't help but giggle.

Peter put his officer's hat on my head and said, "Now you've been officially initiated into the secret society of under-twenty-five-year-olds aboard the *Grey Goose*. Here, have a grilled cheese sandwich." He lifted up a tureen lid. "Apparently there is tomato soup too." He began to dish some out for himself.

"So, Piper," Frederick smiled mischievously. "Your lovely aunt and our fearless captain have disappeared. You must be terribly bored without anyone to entertain you. I will fill in, to the best of my ability, in their absence."

I giggled again, and Peter sort of grimaced, looking at Frederick out of the corner of his eye. But soon enough, the three of us were talking and laughing like the oldest of friends.

After a half an hour or so, Frank boisterously entered and began serving himself some soup. Frederick stood up haughtily. "Enjoy the company, Piper. I don't dine with his kind," he sneered.

Frank sneered right back, "Shut up, you German good-for-nothing kid."

"Alright men, settle down," Peter said. "We've a lady present." He looked in my direction, and Frank and Frederick visibly tried to control themselves. Frederick nodded gentlemanly in my direction and vanished as Frank sat down with a huff.

"You know why he was really late getting back from his leave?" He chomped down into his sandwich. Peter and I shrugged. "Well, I'll tell you. He was at that German American Bund Parade at Madison Square Garden."

"New York City?" Peter asked.

"Yeah. Marching along with all those German Nazi bums who call themselves Americans. They had the outfits and everything. Call themselves 'stormtroopers.' Marching around and 'heiling Hitler' and waving the American flag. Thousands of people turned up. Makes me sick." He was chewing with his mouth half-full. Swigging down a glass of milk, he continued, "He thinks he's so much better than everybody else just 'cause of some dumb Nazi pedigree. An old rum-runner like me is not fit to sit at the same table." His heavily muscled, tattooed arms flexed angrily, and he scowled at the door.

"Rum runner?" I asked, confused. There was so much I didn't know.

"Cute," Frank grinned. "She doesn't know what a rum runner is." He scratched his chin, "It's, uh, smuggling. I was in the smuggling racket before going straight."

"Oh." My mouth hung open. He was an ex-convict. Quite the crew Uncle Horatio had gathered.

"I don't think that's the reason he doesn't like you," Peter said.

"I know," Frank slurped his soup, contemplatively.

"What do you mean?" I questioned, feeling a little left out.

Frank looked at Peter and then back at me. I knew he wasn't going to tell me. "I mean..." he trailed off. "You want to know the story of how I got this tattoo?" He poked his bicep, bluntly changing the subject.

I looked at it. "The cross between an iceberg and a whale spouting water?"

"Nah, nah!" he said with a laugh. "It's a..." And he dove into a long explanation of why a mountain with a heart and a goat hiking up it symbolized his childhood in New Jersey and the love he left in Cuba. From there, he plunged into good old-fashioned pirate lore. I loved every minute of each hair-raising tale.

Hours later, I sat on the deck realizing that, for the first time in months, I did not feel very afraid of the future. It was as though the *Grey Goose* hung suspended in time, like a world unto itself.

For us, there was no approaching war, no death, no sadness. Just salt air and, dare I say it, *hope*.

A FIRM BELIEVER in dressing for dinner, Horatio insisted Edie and I have several evening gowns for the journey. Slipping into a creamy tangerine evening gown and a new pair of metallic gold heels, I felt every inch the princess of the ship. I swished and swirled into the dining room. I had covered my hair up with another matching scarf; it was becoming my trademark.

All the officers, Frank, Frederick, and Peter, were wearing tuxes. Ferguson stood to the side. Everyone was waiting for Edie and Horatio. Peter motioned for me to join the line of officers, and I waltzed over. Peter grinned. "Don't we look quite the set." And with that comment, I felt glowy all over.

It was time for their grand entrance. In came the happy couple. Edie looked radiant, decked out in a black satin gown. A large diamond necklace graced her throat. Horatio was the picture of a man who had bagged his first buck. We all applauded, and they bowed and curtsied, and Edie came and gave me a big kiss. Then we all sat down for our first meal as a family.

Everything was very proper. Mozart's "The Andante Piano Concerto No. 21" played on the record player. Ferguson served, and we chatted about the wedding and the glories of Europe. Glasses clinked, Edie and I whispered and laughed like confidantes, and the men discussed current affairs. I felt so very dignified. Horatio's eyes never left Edie's face though, not even for a moment. And Edie held his hand under the table.

After dinner, Horatio announced that Edie would give us a private concert.

"Darling, I don't know. I haven't sang publicly in years," she protested, feigning modesty.

"Now, now. We are all family here. Sing us just a little something. Perhaps our old song?"

"Well, if you insist," she said graciously, but quickly enough that everyone knew she was dying to perform. Edie stood up and motioned towards Ferguson. He left for a moment and came back with a violin which he passed to Horatio.

Horatio took the violin, and Edie took on the posture of a professionally trained opera singer. Horatio began to play the violin, a lilting Celtic melody. Then Edie joined in, singing a haunting song in Gaelic. I had never heard anything like it, but obviously Edie and Horatio had performed it together before. Horatio missed a few notes now and then, and Edie's soprano collided with the incongruent notes with such force that I struggled not to make a face. It didn't matter for Edie and Horatio though. The song ended, and they looked at each other, enraptured.

Finally, Frederick broke the moment. "That was nice."

"Thank you, Frederick." Edie bowed her head, then said, "How about some swinging music? Something we can dance to?" I loved how much she loved dancing.

We all got up from the table as Ferguson put a record on, a complex Latin rhythm with horns and strings. Horatio swept Edie into his arms and began to twirl.

Before I had a chance to think, Frederick had me by the waist, and we were whirling around the room. He was a good dancer. Very good.

Frederick pulled me in close, and I felt his breath on my ear. The music began to speed up, and we moved faster, matching its rhythm. "It's like a samba, but with a bit of a spring," Frederick said with a grin.

"Where did you learn to dance like this?" I asked breathlessly.

He bounced gracefully, leading me along. "All Germans are good dancers."

Frank cut in on our dance. "That's not true. Trust me." With no regard for the rhythm or the steps, Frank bounced and bobbed, dragging me with him around the room.

I glanced over at Edie and Horatio. They were keeping up amazingly well for their age. What rhythm! What poise!

Peter stood awkwardly alone with Frederick now, both leaning against the wall.

Horatio suddenly broke in, "I want to dance with my niece. Peter! Come dance with your aunt."

Horatio and I danced side by side with Peter and Edie, and then Horatio went back to Edie. By now, Frank had joined Frederick at the bar, and Peter stood in front of me.

"I can't really dance, Piper, not like Freddy."

"I can't really dance like Freddy either."

We looked at each other, and I knew we were both thinking that Frederick had acquired his skills by dancing with many women.

Peter wasn't that type. He wasn't charming in that sort of way. I looked up into his big, honest blue eyes that only spoke kindness and boyish playfulness. He was wonderful. He was who I wanted, I prayed silently. Or someone like him.

He held his hands out and smiled. "We can still give it a shot."

Frank turned the record over, and a slower song came on. Peter held me gently, and we attempted to dance. When he held my hand, my stomach filled with butterflies. I couldn't concentrate and forgot every step I had ever learned. I finally gave up and awkwardly excused myself to go join Frederick and Frank by the bar. Frank handed me a lemonade and winked. "Don't worry, there's nothing but lemon and sugar in there. It will cure you of what ails you."

“Frank, is there something wrong with me?”

“Now, why would you say that?”

“Everyone keeps giving me different cures for ‘whatever ails me.’”

Frank looked confused. I downed the drink in one long sip. Maybe it would make my crush on Peter go away.

Edie and Horatio started doing the tango. As they sauntered by, Edie grabbed a rose out of a vase and held it in her teeth as she did a backbend over Horatio's arm.

“It's Astaire and Rogers![1]” Frank laughed.

“Almost,” I grinned. “But not quite.”

Peter looked concerned. “They certainly are taking this honeymoon thing seriously.”

Frederick came and stood by my side. "Want to try?"

"No, I think I'm done dancing for tonight."

"How about cards?" Peter asked, now seated at the card table.

I shook my head no. But Frank and Frederick both accepted the offer and joined Peter at the card table. The tango ended, and

Horatio kissed Edie and joined the boys for a round of poker. "Will you join, love?"

"No, you can play for both of us tonight. I want to talk to my niece," Edie answered.

Ferguson brought over a glass of something red and said, "Snappy Tom, ma'am?"

"Snappy what?"

"A Snappy Tom. They are quite fashionable these days."

She peered into the glass and sniffed. "What's in it?"

"Tomato paste, water, chilis, and salt."

Edie's face contorted. "Chilis?"

"Yes, ma'am."

"Ferguson, bring me a lemonade." She waved the glass away. "Never let it be said that I let *fashion* take the place of good taste and common sense."

"Indeed, madam." Ferguson, straight-faced as ever, took the revolting drink away.

Edie settled onto the leather couch and patted the place beside her for me. "This is fun, isn't it! What new material we will have to write about!"

# CHAPTER 10

## PIPER'S VOYAGE

"It's like they've always been married," Peter said several days later as we played shuffleboard on deck.

Frederick shrugged, bored with the game. "So what?"

"So they seem like they've always been married, that's all."

It was true. I looked at Edie and Horatio, walking arm in arm, back and forth on the deck in a happy daze.

A shadow crossed my face. I looked up into the sky. A great dark cloud had blown over the sun, and a cold wind swept over the deck. The waves began to grow choppy, crested with white foam. Within minutes, the sky was black, and sheets of rain pelted the Grey Goose.

Edie yelled above the roar, "Horatio? Is this normal?"

"Just a summer storm, darling. Nothing to worry about! Go below!"

A giant swell lifted the boat, and it careened down the crest. Edie's eyes opened wide in surprise. "Are you quite sure?"

"Absolutely nothing to worry about. Now get below!"

As the *Grey Goose* began to pitch from side to side, and the wind rose to a howl, Edie and I clambered indoors and out of the rain.

For a few minutes, we sat in the uncomfortable silence of her cabin. We listened to the roar of the wind and shouts of the sailors, trying our best to stay upright with each pitch of the boat over the waves.

"I don't like this," Edie said abruptly. "I am not going to sit around on my thumbs. If we are going to be thrown about, we might as well make the best of it."

She threw open the door and stumbled to the sitting room, me at her heels. The enormous waves had sent the furniture sliding every which way. Edie sat on the sofa, only to have it immediately skid towards the wall. Back and forth we slid, trying to maintain composure.

"It's like sledding!" I shouted above the roar of the wind. That is, it was until you violently hit one of the wood-paneled walls.

"This is how we handle life and death situations!" she shouted back as the sofa thumped against the bookshelf (which was, thankfully, nailed to the wall). "We laugh at them! We ride the waves of life with anticipation!"

Ferguson fumbled into the room, struggling to stay upright. He looked green. Another wave dashed the boat. In a horrible miscalculation, Ferguson sought the stability of the dining room table which immediately began to slide, sending the poor butler on a crash collision course with the floor.

"Edie," I stared in horror, "he's not getting up!"

We slid down to where Ferguson was crumpled on the floor. He was unconscious.

"Oh my word!" I cried. "I'll run and get Nathaniel! He's the nurse, right?" Edie nodded, and off I went.

The ship was being tossed so violently now that I had to practically crawl towards the deck. When I opened the door, water splashed all over me. I was drenched. Rain was pouring so hard and fast that I couldn't see. The ocean seemed to have swallowed us.

"Piper!" Peter shouted. "Get below, right now!"

"Ferguson is unconscious! I need Nathaniel!"

"What!"

"Nathaniel! I need Nathaniel!" I screeched, trying to be heard above the din of the storm.

Willie and Charlie were securing the masts with ropes. Sebastian was huddled over a sail, fastened to the mast. The ship was almost sideways, and I feared he would be forced underwater. I screamed, and suddenly, the ship righted itself, only to be thrown the opposite way.

Gorman inched towards me. "Nathaniel, I need Nathaniel!" I yelled. He nodded and signaled for me to go below.

I retreated back to the sitting room and found Edie hovering over Ferguson, who was still out cold.

A moment later, Nathaniel, the mute accordion player and nurse, appeared and immediately began to take Ferguson's pulse. Then, he stood up, disappeared down the corridor, and returned with a bucket which he proceeded to dump on Ferguson's head. Ferguson stuttered awake, Edie slumped down in relief, and Nathaniel returned to the deck without any other acknowledgement.

Ferguson, Edie, and I were all very, very wet.

There was no formal dinner that night. Instead, we all ate downstairs in the galley where the pitch and roll were the least dramatic. No one was allowed on deck for fear of being swept away, but a terrible cracking noise forced Peter and the Brophy twins to go and investigate, worried the main mast had broken. I kept envisioning the three men being swept overboard, disappearing into the swirling black water.

Each second they were gone felt like a decade. Where were they? Why didn't they appear back in the hold? Why didn't Horatio do something!

"Don't ye be afraid now, lass," Horatio said to me. I realized my teeth were chattering uncontrollably.

Finally, they reappeared, totally drenched and exhausted.

"Like Peter walking to Jesus on the water," Frank muttered, the relief evident in his voice.

"They don't call me Peter for nothing." Peter squeezed out his jacket.

"What happened out there?" Gorman asked, his scar glowing oddly with the dim light swinging back and forth across his face.

"The mast is cracked but still standing. We were able to secure it temporarily, but another wave crashing from the same angle will be the end of it."

Edie looked pale but whispered, "God can still even the waves."

"But sometimes he asks us to walk upon them instead." Horatio rubbed his beard thoughtfully. "Haven't seen a storm this bad in years."

Frederick poured himself a cup of coffee, muttering that God couldn't care less about us at this moment.

"THAT ENORMOUS GALE pushed us terribly off course from the port in Spain where I planned to dock," Horatio explained the next day after supper. "What's more, the cracked mast demands attention. Casablanca is the closest port. We'll pull in for repairs."

"How much longer until then?" I asked.

"Two days at sea. Just in time for your birthday, your auntie tells me."

In all the frenzy, I had forgotten my birthday was coming up. It looked like my 16th year would show up just as we docked in Casablanca. I had hoped to be with my mother by then, and my heart sank a bit. I'd never celebrated a birthday without her. *Lord,* I prayed, *help her live until we arrive!*

It had been a quiet evening, and the boys had already settled in for a game of Hearts. Edie and I were on the couch where she was lazily lounging, her feet up on cushions, her head thrown back, looking at nothing in particular. She was describing to me a new idea for a novel, something that had been brewing in the recesses of her mind the past few days. "It's all about a butler who falls and goes unconscious. When he awakes, he thinks he is a maharaja."

Ferguson was looking at us, an unintelligible expression on his face.

"A maha-what?" I asked.

"A maharaja. That's an Indian—" Edie's explanation was shattered by Frank, who stood up violently from the table and hovered menacingly over Frederick.

"I don't know where you are getting your political ideas from, you dirty Hun, but if you're smart at all, you'll keep them to yourself!"

Frederick answered with total control, though his face was red with a sort of strange passion. He replied, "The Nazi Party is the only hope for ethnic Germans in light of the Communist threat. I can assure you that the only reason we took over the Czech Sudetenland is because of the ethnic Germans living there. It was for them. Germany doesn't want war with anyone."

"Anyone except the Jews. Have you heard about Nuremberg Laws? It put my uncle out of business." Frank was almost shouting.

So Frank was Jewish. And he had family in Germany as well.

"It was necessary to protect and save the German economy. Your uncle was no doubt a communist sympathizer, not unlike yourself. Besides, I don't see how they differ at all from your Jim Crow laws,[2]" Frederick answered, referencing the laws that oppressed so many African Americans in the South. The Jim Crow laws kept whites and blacks separated, giving the best housing and jobs to the whites and dishing out the leftovers to the blacks. Not to mention the disparity in education. It was the sort of thing that got my parents really riled.

My dad could rant for hours about the evils of the South and what was going on. My mother too. When she was in college, she'd written articles for the school paper on racism in the South, focusing on the Jim Crow laws. She painted a realistic, if negative, portrait of life for African Americans living in Birmingham, Alabama. She wrote about the separate water fountains, schools, and toilets they were forced to use, not to mention the pennies they were paid for what was essentially slave labor. She'd received four anonymous, threatening letters and two menacing phone calls warning her to quit while she was ahead. She didn't pay any heed though and went right on with the series of articles. And thankfully, nothing bad happened. Though it could have.

She repeated the story whenever she wanted me to remember not to give in to fear and to do the right thing.

A little chill crept up my spine as the reality sank in. What had poor Frederick gotten himself into? Did he really think that all that Nazi propaganda was true? In the shine of his charm and boyish smiles, I'd chosen to ignore his politics. Charm is charming, I suppose. But it was more than that. Beneath his thick veneer, I really felt he had a good, kind heart. Frederick was just misinformed, certainly! But then I remembered my first impression of him. Hard. Like his chiseled face.

"And what is so wrong with being a communist?" Frank glowered.

Horatio intervened. "Enough. No more talk about this. You know the rules. No politics on my ship. Frederick, you will keep your political views to yourself. If there is one more outburst like this from either one of you, I will let you go at the next port, do you hear me?"

The two men glared at one another.

"Now, shake hands and sit down."

Hands outstretched, they gave a quick, terse handshake. Frederick's handsome face had eerily morphed into something ugly with pride. Frank looked a bit shaken but began to deal the cards as though nothing had happened.

Peter looked at me and excused himself from the game. Edie, a little pale, clutched her drink. We didn't say anything.

I set my glass down and told Edie I would be in my room. Then I kissed Horatio on the cheek and said goodnight. As I exited the dining room, a hand reached out and startled me. It was Peter. He had been waiting. He put his finger to his lips and motioned for me to follow him to the bow.

"Piper, I don't want you to tell anyone about your mother on the ship, okay? About her being Jewish, I mean."

"But she's a Christian now."

"It doesn't matter to those guys... those Nazis. Frederick was a good guy, I've known him for a while. But he's changing. He's been reading stuff, listening to people. He came back from that camp with a file of papers from the American Bund addressed to some high-ranking Nazi officials. I saw him hiding it in his trunk when he thought I was asleep a couple of nights ago. I don't totally understand all of what he's been indoctrinated with, but it's dangerous. I've tried talking to him, setting him straight, but it's like he's been brainwashed. Always talking about how he wants to be a part of some glorious Germany of the past. I'm telling you, I don't think that *that* Germany ever even existed, and I don't think it will, either."

My thoughts turned immediately to my parents. "But Edie and Horatio both know about my mother's heritage. They know not to say anything, right?"

"I don't think they will say anything... not after that episode." He looked out over the bow, his hair blowing in the wind. "There is going to be a war. Soon."

"I know," I finally admitted out loud. The sound of the ocean rushed in my ears. What was left of my fairy tale world was beginning to cave in. The real world was back in full force. The coming war was on my doorstep, and my mother and father were stuck on a continent that was about to face a great battle. *Oh God, get this boat to Europe quickly,* I prayed silently.

"I'll see you in the morning." He placed his jacket around my shoulders and kissed the top of my head protectively, like a loving brother or even father. "I'm going to stay here a while."

As I returned to my room, I passed Frederick. He had lit a cigarette and was leaning against a wall.

"Piper," Frederick spied me. "Wearing Peter's jacket, I see." He said with a smirk.

I didn't answer.

"Well then... Gute nacht." He suavely nodded his head, and I wished him goodnight.

At that moment, he looked like a lost little boy. Lonely and afraid. He was so charming. Had so much potential. I hoped it was not potential for disaster.

# CHAPTER 11

## PIPER IN CASABLANCA

I awoke with a start and quickly dressed. I was in a hurry, though I didn't know what for exactly. It felt like there was so much to do! Turning 16 was proving very different from when I turned 15.

I had been just a simple kid when I turned 15. I was in California, worried about football players and math tests. Now? Well, I wasn't concerned about those things anymore. I was worried about life and death things, like wars and my mother. I had faced great storms on the ocean and in my heart. And I was in Africa. If you had asked me last spring if I thought I would be in Africa, and not in school, I would have laughed in your face. But I *was* in Africa. And I was officially 16 years old.

The docks in Casablanca were crowded and oppressively hot. Edie and I swatted flies away as we descended the gangplank to the shore. The African shore.

Ferguson had disembarked early to wire my parents about the change of route and to look for rooms in one of the city's many hotels.

Casablanca's heat and a cacophony of languages bore down on

us, along with swarms of flies. French, German, Italian, Arabic, and other foreign languages. Africa wasn't at all what I expected. There seemed to be just as many Europeans as Arabs and Africans. Out of nowhere, a loud, intense wail filled the air.

"What is that?" I shouted over the noise. The sound sent a shiver down my spine.

Peter stood by my side, taking in the scene. "It's the call to prayer, for the Muhammadans."

Ferguson pushed through the fray, looking stressed.

"Ma'am," he addressed Edie, "I've looked and looked for accommodations, but there is simply nothing up to par. We must stay aboard the *Grey Goose* for our duration in the port." Beads of sweat had formed on his brow. He wiped away the moisture with his handkerchief,

"The French, the Italians, even the Germans; all of them have taken the best rooms. I've never seen a city so bursting with refugees."

"But there isn't a war yet. Why are there refugees?" I asked.

Peter looked out on the wharf, concerned. "They know there will be one. A war, I mean."

"Funny," Edie answered. "They are all trying to get out, and we are trying to get in."

She took off her wide-brimmed straw hat and fanned herself, leaning against a post on the dock. Her white linen trousers glowed in the bright sunlight. Turning to Ferguson, she said, "Don't worry about the rooms. Horatio assures me that we will only be in the port for a day or two before pressing on to Marseille. The carpenters can steer clear of the living quarters anyway. And I'm sure that you and Cookie can find everything you need to outfit the yacht's pantry in the market. And get something extra special for the birthday girl. I have it on good authority she likes cake."

I grinned.

Ferguson looked doubtful, but Cookie assailed his fears. "Don't you go looking sour, Fergie. I can make a good mess out of anything. Maybe even a birthday cake."

"I never doubted you for a minute," Edie beamed. But Ferguson was still not convinced. "They had monkeys in the market, ma'am. Monkeys."

"Those are for pets. Not for eating," Cookie laughed.

Peter took off his coat. He too had broken out in a sweat. It really was dreadfully hot. "What are we supposed to do now?"

"I'd like to go see the monkeys," I offered. "As long as we have a day or two it could be fun to explore."

Horatio ambled down the gangplank, no longer in his captain's uniform but rather in a white linen suit complete with a white fedora. "So would I," he bellowed.

He gave me a little peck on the cheek and asked, "And how is the birthday girl this morning?" Then he whipped out a little box wrapped in red paper from his pocket and gave it to me. "Go ahead and open it." He and Edie smiled proudly.

I ripped open the paper and opened the velvet box. Inside was a gold pin impressed with a flying bird. I looked closer. It was a sandpiper.

"Look on the back," Edie said.

I turned it over. Scrawled in tiny letters was a message, "So you don't forget to fly."

Edie helped me pin it to my blouse and gave me a gentle hug. "I couldn't be prouder of you. You're so brave, just like your mother." She paused before continuing. "And your father. He's been very brave through all of this too."

He had been, it was true. Never panicking, never breaking down, he had been my mother's rock. He took things the way he always did, calmly, thoughtfully. Though admittedly, with a slight tremor in his hand and a tragic look in his eye. It was no secret he loved my mother, busy as he always was with his medical practice.

With that, Horatio took Edie's arm, and they led the charge, soaring ahead towards the large bazaar (an outdoor market,) with

Peter and I trailing behind. “Stick close to me, Piper,” Peter whispered. “Casablanca is known for pickpockets and thieves.”

I didn't tell Peter I wasn't carrying any money. It was nice to have him feel protective.

~

IT WAS the sort of world I had read about but didn't know really existed. Men wore tall round hats called “turbans” and long flowing robes. There were women covered from head to toe in large swathes of dark cloth, with only a small slit for their eyes. The buildings were ornately curved and carved, and the air smelled heavily of cardamom, cinnamon, and smoke. It was an earthy smell, warm and exotic.

“Come on,” Horatio yelled behind him. “The bazaar is this way!” He pushed through the growing crowd towards the stalls where men and women sold a myriad of goods. There were silk scarves, pieces of handmade lace, lamps, strange tobacco water pipes, and baskets filled with every imaginable bobble. There were spices, prime cuts of freshly butchered meat, and piles of sticky looking pastries. The noise and press of the crowd was overwhelming.

“The monkeys!” Peter called. “I found them.”

There were the monkeys, all five of them. “Oh! I must have one, Horatio,” Edie pleaded. “For Piper! It *is* her birthday!”

Not one to say no to his bride, Horatio gave the seller a few coins and passed the monkey to an ecstatic Edie. “Whatever will we name him the little thing?” she said, breathless with excitement.

Peter and I enthusiastically examined the tiny creature. He could dance and wore a funny little hat. He seemed to smile and laugh, just like a little person. He sat on Peter's shoulder, content to sit and watch like a parrot.

By the time we made it through the market, Edie had bought a beautiful tablecloth and Moroccan style dresses for herself and me.

Ferguson and Cookie waved to us from the food stalls. They had finished their purchases. Pushing our way towards each other, Horatio passed the parcels to Ferguson and gingerly took the monkey off of Peter's shoulder and placed it on Ferguson's. The monkey was, by all appearances, quite comfortable with the arrangement. Ferguson, on the other hand, looked a bit wary.

"Take all our loot back to boat, will you, Ferguson?" asked Uncle Horatio.

"Of course. And your plans, sir?" The monkey looked quizzically at us from Ferguson's shoulder.

"I suppose we will find something for lunch." Horatio looked around. "Are you kids hungry? Maybe after we can go for a camel ride?"

Peter nodded affirmatively, and I added that I could certainly eat something. The smell of spices was tantalizing.

"We really don't have time for the camel ride," Edie said, looking at her watch. "Not if we are going to get the paperwork taken care of in time."

"No, I suppose not. Well, there is a little place I went to long, long ago. We'll see if it is still open."

"THEY ALWAYS EAT LIKE THIS?" I asked, "At these low tables?" I felt awkward sitting on the cushions. The restaurant had turned out to still be open after all.

"Oh yes," Edie answered. "And notice there are no forks or knives. Only hands. And never the left hand. I've read all about this." With an air of authority, Edie ripped the bread apart and stuffed it in her mouth.

"Imagine," she said after swallowing. "Just a few weeks ago, it was tuna and oranges. I never thought anything would change. I would go on forever, like I always had. Swimming. Painting. Writing. Look at me now? Married. Having an adventure in Casablanca.

It's like I'm in one of my novels. Really, it is almost too much to fathom."

Horatio reached over and patted her hand.

It was true. It was almost too much to fathom.

The waiter appeared with little bowls of mashed beans and purees and salads, and piles of heavily spiced meat. I adjusted myself and re-crossed my legs as a platter of rice studded with nuts and raisins arrived, followed by a plate of dates and dried apricots.

Horatio looked perplexed. "This could prove rather difficult."

"I think it could prove rather fattening." Edie said, nevertheless, she plunged in with relish, ripping another piece of bread apart and stuffing it in her mouth. "This is delicious."

Ornate blue and white hand-painted tiles, covered in some sort of mysterious script, lined the walls and the ceiling. Tall ferns stood in the corner, and a record playing scratchy classical music droned from another room. I gingerly took a little rice in my fingers and took a nibble.

"Well?" Edie asked, all three watching me expectantly.

It was delicious, and I told them so. "Of course it is!" Edie was enthralled. "Everything is better abroad. This is so romantic, Horatio! A honeymoon in Casablanca!" She touched his face tenderly. Peter and I looked away from them and towards each other. We exchanged a grin. It was slightly embarrassing to see them so in love, but I think we were both just happy that they'd finally gotten married.

When the meal was over, the waiter brought us all tiny cups of coffee laced with cardamom. "We ought to buy some of that for the yacht, don't you think, Edie? Now that is coffee!" Horatio stood up to leave. "You kids head back to the ship. Edie and I are off to the consulate to obtain our exit visas."

"Sure thing," Peter answered.

Horatio helped Edie and I off the floor, and I tried to straighten out my dress. Edie winked, whispering in my ear, "What a completely inspiring day. I shall have to write about this in my book!"

Out of the courtyard, Edie and Horatio took off in the opposite direction of the harbor, while Peter and I returned through the bazaar.

"You seem different, Piper," Peter said. "Different than when I first met you."

"How so?" I asked, wondering if my rising blush showed. "Has there really been that big of a difference between 15 and 16?"

"You seem like you're doing better."

He was right. "I am doing better."

"What changed?"

I thought a minute. It was so simple to say but so difficult to do. "I'm trying to consciously make an effort to let go of my need to know the future and instead to trust God for the best."

He gave me a warm look, and we walked on in silence for a moment.

"So, you have a new pin and a monkey. Anything else you want for your birthday?" he asked with a grin.

"There is really only one thing I want. I just want to see my mother again." I didn't add that it might be nice, now that I was 16 and all, for Peter to ask me out on a date. It didn't seem really appropriate. Besides, he needed to come up with that idea on his own.

He grabbed my hand. "Let's pray then. I believe God works miracles."

"Me too."

"YOUNG LADY. PRETTY YOUNG LADY!" a fat short man called out from the inside of a store filled to the brim with dusty antiques and books. I turned around. "You come and see my store," he continued.

"Come and see what I have for you. Pretty things. One-of-a-kind things."

"No, thank you," I said, passing by. But the man reached out and took my arm, pulling me inside. "You must see my store, young girl."

"Let go of me!" I cried out, reaching for Peter with my other hand, the crowd pressing against us.

The man was remarkably strong for his small stature, and suddenly, Peter and I both found ourselves standing in the middle of his shop. It looked like it had gone untouched for a hundred years. Stunned, I scolded the man, "You really mustn't do that to people!"

"Piper," Peter said, engrossed in a display of curved swords, "take a look at these."

"Scimitars. An ancient weapon. Quite deadly," the man explained. A shiver ran down my spine. Had he taken us inside to kill us? Certainly not, I assured myself. He only wanted our money.

"How much for one of them?" Peter was like a little boy in a toy store.

"How much do you have?"

I whispered to Peter, "You're supposed to bargain, remember?"

"It doesn't matter. I don't have any money on me," he whispered back. We were two peas in a pod.

"How the guys at school would like one of these." He reached out and touched the blade. It was dull. The man smiled broadly. "You see, you like my store. I know these things. And for you." He pressed a delicate gold ring with a tiny ruby into my hands.

It was a stunning piece. Exactly the sort of thing I would choose for myself. A gasp escaped my lips. All fear of the man and shop evaporated in the simple beauty of the ring. I tried it on and looked at my hand. It fit perfectly.

"Your young man should buy it for you, I think." He looked expectantly at Peter, whose eyes opened wide.

"He's not my young man," I answered bluntly. "Come on, Peter. We have to go." I grabbed his arm and tugged him towards the door.

Peter looked at me, eyes still wide. And, for a second, he looked a bit disappointed. But all he said was, "Of course, yes, we really have to go."

It was then that something caught my eye; a tall blond man was furtively sneaking down the street just in front of the shop. Was it? Yes! It was! It was Frederick!

"Isn't Frederick supposed to be manning the *Goose*?" I asked.

Peter came to my side and saw Frederick's figure round the corner. Taking my hand and dragging me outside, he said, "You bet he is. That's definitely against regulation!"

Peter pulled me out of the shop and began to jog after Frederick.

"Where are we going?" I asked, breathlessly.

"We're following him! That's what!" he answered, searching the crowded street for a sign of the German.

The shopkeeper shouted after us, "But perhaps you will come back? Everyone comes back to Ali's." I looked behind me as Peter's grip tightened. "There he is!" he shouted.

I saw the shopkeeper, his smile still plastered on his face, amusedly watching us disappear into the fray, our feet pounding the uneven stones down the twisting passageways of the bazaar.

Twenty minutes later, we had ducked and weaved through countless stalls and streets, only barely keeping our wayward friend in our sights. Just as we were about to catch up to him, a vegetable cart manned by a figure in a dirty flowing robe, with an equally dirty donkey, cut us off at an intersection.

When the donkey finally made the decision to get moving again, we'd lost Freddy.

Lungs heaving, I sat down on a wooden crate pushed up against a wall. "What do you think that was all about?"

"No idea." Peter was also breathing heavily. "But I certainly don't like it. An officer never deserts his post. He's been acting so moody recently too. I'm worried about him."

At that exact moment, Frederick emerged on the street from a small alleyway a half a block from where we had stopped. He made a sharp turn and walked down towards the harbor. I squeezed Peter's arm and pointed. "Do you think we should keep following him? Or do you think he's going back to the boat?"

Peter checked his watch. "I vote he's going back to the boat. Probably thinks no one will notice he was missing, especially if he gets back before us."

Up on my feet again, I wiped the sweat from my brow. "How about we go see wherever he was."

With Peter on my heels, we plunged into the alley. Except, it wasn't an alley like I thought.

It was the courtyard of a palatial building. Moorish in style, big beautiful arches and cool trees shaded the interior. A guard stopped us at the ornate gate. "Kann ich Dir helfen?"

I looked at the uniform. Brown shirt, brown pants. Impossibly shiny black boots.

"Umm… I don't speak German. I'm, uh, we're lost," I stuttered. What in the world was Frederick doing here? And what was this 'here' anyways? I looked helplessly at the guard, who grinned good-naturedly.

"Das okay. I speak English. You need help? You are lost? You must be looking for the American Embassy? You are American? Or English maybe?"

Peter was at my shoulder, and both of us nodded yes. "American."

"Down another two blocks. It is confusing here. People are always getting the German and American embassies switched up."

"Thanks," Peter said, he put his arm around my shoulder and steered me away. "We appreciate it."

We pretended to move in the direction of the American

Embassy and then turned back towards the harbor. Both Peter and I were deep in thought.

"Maybe he needed to renew his passport or something? Or… or…" Or what? My brain was churning overtime to think of one good reason why Frederick would pop into the embassy for 5 minutes and then duck out, sneaking through the bazaar like a spy. Unless he was a spy? Was it possible? "Peter, you don't think Frederick is a…?"

"Spy?"

So he was thinking the same thing.

"What are we going to do?" I asked.

"Nothing drastic. I don't want to accuse Freddy of anything like that. He's our friend."

"But we have to do something! What if he's in some sort of trouble?"

We were in the dockyards now, nearing the *Grey Goose*'s gangplank. "I'll think of something. Might have to do a little undercover work myself."

## CHAPTER 12

## PIPER'S GIFT

"He brought back more papers. They're all over the desk in our room. All in German. Can't make it out though. I'm not familiar with a lot of the words," Peter said, trying to look inconspicuous later that evening. Everyone had gathered around the table to celebrate my birthday with the obligatory cake and candles.

There was no time to answer him. A giant pastry aglow with flickering blue and orange flames was headed my direction as the crew suddenly burst into "For She's a Jolly Good Fellow!"

Somehow, Cookie had managed to bake me an enormous, three layer, white chiffon cloud cake that was filled with a mixture of whipped cream, fresh fruit and nuts from the market. I'd never had anything like it. It was covered in more cream and topped with 16 candles.

It was hard to concentrate, given the news Peter had passed on. My stomach churned that we might have a spy in our midst. I wanted to pull Horatio and Edie aside that very minute and tell them. But Peter was adamant that we wait until we knew more.

To add to my concern, Frederick made a brief appearance at the party, took his cake, and then disappeared back into his room, complaining of a headache. If that wasn't suspicious… Well, it *was* suspicious. Period.

"We've got a little surprise for you, Piper," Frank said excitedly, pulling my attention back to the business at hand: my birthday.

"We all chipped in," Sebastian added. "Come on boys! Bring it on out! The señorita is ready for her present."

The Brophy Twins and Gorman stood to the side as Peter brought in a large box and set it awkwardly on the table. "Go ahead and open it," Sebastian pressed.

I lifted the lid of the box and looked inside. All I saw at first was a mass of tissue paper. Digging through the paper, I felt something hard and angular.

"Here," Frank came to my side, "let me help you." He lifted it out of the box.

"A camera?"

"We all thought you should commemorate the trip," Peter said. The crew stood there, shyly awaiting my response.

"Oh my." I bit my lip as a tear came to my eye. My heart had never felt so warm. "Thank you. Thank you all so much."

"It's a Leica. The newest model. 50mm lens and a coupled rangefinder," Frank explained. "There's film in there too."

"How do I use it?" I asked excitedly.

It took a few moments, but soon we had it figured out. "All right," I commanded. "Everyone together. That's right, against the wall. Now smile!"

Snap. I took the picture.

I liked the way the camera felt. It fit in my hands beautifully. Like it was made for me.

"Now, I'll be able to show my mother everything," I beamed. "This is the best present I've ever gotten. I love it."

"I thought you would," Peter said quietly, giving me a soft smile. And I knew it was all his idea from the start.

Then, he leaned in and whispered, "Follow me. We're going to confront Frederick! We need to give him a chance to let us know what all this sneaking around is really about. It's what a good friend would do."

Confront Frederick? "Do you really think that's a good idea?"

"I've thought about it all evening. It's the only way."

"Maybe you should let me do the talking," I ventured.

"Why?"

"Women are sometimes better at this sort of thing."

Peter led the way down the hold. "All right. If you really think so."

FREDERICK WAS SITTING at his small writing desk scribbling away on something that looked like a form. He looked up, surprised. "What's this? The social hour?" Looking back at the notebook, he said, "You kids go on and play with that new camera. I've important work to do."

"Work for the German Embassy?" Peter asked pointedly. So much for letting me do the talking. The atmosphere grew painfully tense, and I feared we had started out on a terrible foot.

Frederick put his pencil down, a hint of concern flickering across his eyes. "I am a German, remember?"

"Yeah! Well, you are a member of this ship's crew. And you deserted your post to make a clandestine visit to your countrymen in the bazaar. Now in my book that's enough to get court-marshalled. And I know this isn't the Navy, but on my uncle's ship it's enough to get fired." Peter was going about this all the wrong way. It was turning into a verbal fist fight, not the healthy intervention we'd planned.

He looked from me to Peter then back to me again. "Wait," he was putting two and two together. "You think I'm a spy, don't you?"

Peter and I glanced at one another. Guilty as charged.

"You do! Don't you?" He looked at us like we were idiots.

"Well," Peter answered, "you have to admit it looks bad. Transporting papers from those American Nazis. What mess have you gotten yourself into anyways?"

Frederick's eyes opened wide."You know about those papers? You went through my trunk?"

"You know me better than that! Of course I didn't go through your trunk. I saw you looking through them one night. I think you thought I was asleep."

"I'm going to tell Horatio you went through my trunk!" Frederick was indignant.

"Yeah, you tell him why too. Then see what happens." Peter's face was turning red. "See what he says when you admit you weren't manning your post!"

Now Frederick was annoyed. "I didn't leave my post. Frank gave me permission to run ashore for an errand. Do you really have nothing better to do than follow me around pretending to be detectives?"

"I'll verify that with Frank."

"Do!" Frederick's annoyance was quickly turning to anger to hurt. Not that I blamed him. Here we were, accusing him of being a spy and barging into his room. Well, at least it was Peter's room too.

No one spoke for a moment, and I put my hand on Frederick's arm and shot Peter a look that said, "Shut up. It's *my* turn."

"We do want to know what was in those papers, Freddy."

"I don't have to tell you what was in them, you know. I have every right to deliver anything anywhere. And Frank *did* give me permission to leave the ship," he emphasized. "But..." he stopped, "because you are my friend, and I would hate for you not to trust me, I will tell you."

His eyes stared into mine. "Those papers were nothing more than the American Bund's promise of loyalty to the Fatherland," Frederick explained, waving his hand as though that were nothing at all. "Are you satisfied?"

Satisfied was not the word I would use, concerned was more like it.

"Which makes them traitors to America," Peter interjected bitterly. "But that's beside the point. You probably think people can be pro-Hitler and pro-America at the same time."

His eyes haughtily challenged Peter. "I think the best Americans, and the smartest, are those who understand the good that Hitler is doing. Only a fool wouldn't!"

"Did you even read those documents?"

Frederick shook his head. "No, of course not. I am a gentleman. *I* don't look through other people's things." He scowled at Peter.

"So you don't really know what was in them, do you? It could have been codes, or money, or who knows what?" Peter pressed.

Frederick didn't answer.

I could tell that Peter was utterly disappointed in Frederick's lack of character. He rubbed his hands together and then stuffed them in his pockets. "I guess there's nothing we can do about the papers now. What's done is done. Who knows what harm your 'German ideals' have done to my country. Summer camps indoctrinating kids. Makes me sick. All that racist junk."

"Well, there you have it, don't you? It's your country. Not mine. And you have no idea what you're saying. Those communist Jews are taking over your government, and you don't even care. They are trying to take over the world! And my country is trying to stop them."

"Just quit with the Nazi diatribes, will you!" Peter was close to shouting.

"All right, calm down now," I put my hands up. "Frederick, if that was all that was in those papers, why didn't you just put them in the mail? Or why didn't they just mail them in the first place?"

For the first time, Frederick stopped and actually thought through what I had said.

"I don't know." The reality that he unknowingly might have been used as courier prompted a strange, almost proud look. "If they did use me to carry a secret message, then it was my honor to do so for the Fatherland. It shows they trust me."

Peter rubbed his temples. Consternation and alarming amazement gripped us both. What could we possibly say to convince him how wrong he was to trust people who touted such a twisted view of life.

I glanced at the paperwork on the desk. It *was* all in German, just as Peter had described. He was filling out some sort of form. Frederick saw me searching the sheet over his shoulder.

In answer to my questioning gaze, he said, "If you must know, it's my application for the Kriegsmarine."[3]

The weight of Frederick's words sunk in. "You are applying for the German Navy," Peter exhaled.

"The youth leader at the Bund Camp in America encouraged me to join. There is nothing I want more than to be back in Germany, fighting for my people, should the need arise. They need men like me back home."

"What about your contract with my uncle?" Peter asked.

Frederick shrugged as though he did not care. "I'll figure something out. Now you two get out of here. I want to finish this up before the morning."

"Are you going to enlist here, in Casablanca?" I asked, wondering if he had made arrangements with the embassy, perhaps to join a German ship that might be in the port.

"No. There are no training facilities for recruits here. I must go back to Germany to enlist. But I thought I might as well get the paperwork out of the way as long as we are docked."

I didn't know what to think or say. I just wanted to get out of the room, which seemed to be shrinking by the minute. My voice faltered a little. "I'm sorry, Frederick. We didn't mean to invade your privacy."

Frederick smiled at me. "Piper, you were only under the influence of Mr. Super Sleuth there. I would never hold a grudge against one as lovely as you. Besides, it is your birthday. It probably got to your head. All the excitement."

"Yes," I muttered, "too much birthday."

Peter stuck his hand out to his bunk mate. "Look, Freddy, I can't say I'm sorry for what I said. We are just going to have to agree to disagree on politics. But I wish you could try to see it from my side."

"You are blind, Peter. Just like the rest of the world. But you will soon see."

A creepy chill filled the little space, and I found myself walking as quickly as I could back to the deck. I needed some fresh air, immediately!

HORATIO SAT us down behind his desk in the ship's office. He'd locked the door and sat down heavily, listening to our tale.

"I can't fire him for his political views, now can I?" Horatio was troubled. "Though don't think I haven't thought of it. Truth is, I keep hoping he'll wake up to what a pain in the behind he's acting like. Not to mention how stupid he sounds. When I hired him, he was much more broad-minded and open."

"But the papers!" Peter interjected anxiously. "What if there was something in them that was traitorous?"

"A traitor to who? There is no war, at least not yet. Besides, America is neutral." He stroked his beard thoughtfully. "And it's not the papers I'm worried about. It's the boy's ideology. What's in his head. He's looked to the Nazi party as a surrogate father ever since his own dad died. It gives him meaning and purpose. And now, he hopes it will give him a future."

"So, what do we do?" Peter leaned back, defeated.

"There's nothing to do. Just go on like always. Nothing's really happened, has it? Frank did give him leave. He has every right to pick up enlistment papers and drop off a letter or two. I don't like it one bit, but that's the way it is. He's foolish, but he's his own man."

His bushy eyebrows frowned in unison with his mouth. "In my opinion, the lad is harmless."

"Not to Frank." Peter shook his head and murmured, "Or if he knew about Piper's mother…"

"Maybe he would change his mind. He likes me," I said.

Horatio sadly shook his head."I'm afraid that even knowing your sweet self is not enough to change years and years of the lies filling his head." He unconsciously paged through the ship's log.

"Okay," Peter said, unconvinced. "If you say so."

"But there *is* something we can do," I said quietly.

"And what's that?" Horatio looked at me, a little amused.

"We can pray for him."

He looked back at me in all seriousness. "That we can, lass. That we can."

We spent the next day up on deck as the sailors worked on the mast, only venturing back into the hubbub of the city to see if my father had tried to contact us and to pick up the letters of transit allowing us to leave the port.

The letters of transit were not ready, but my parents had sent a telegram, thankfully. Much to my dismay, it was not at all what I wanted to hear. "Message Received STOP Come as quickly as you can STOP Pray for a miracle."

Pray for a miracle? Pray for a miracle. Oh God, please help us make it in time. The claustrophobic heat bore down on me. After that telegram, I wanted nothing more than to be out of Africa and on our way. But all there was to do was wait. And wait. And wait. Until the mast was completed, and we had our transit papers, we were stuck. I tried to avoid Frederick at all costs. He went about his tasks on the ship like a cranky 8-year-old, making it abundantly clear he would rather be anywhere but on the *Goose*. He was counting down the days till his feet touched German soil. It was as though he was already turning into a soldier without a single day of training or a uniform.

Edie looked at me after reading the telegram out loud. "You know what you need?"

I shrugged. What did I need?

"You need something to do. Something to occupy your mind. If not, you'll just wander down paths inside your head that don't need wandering down."

I wondered if she was talking about me or herself.

We walked back up the gangplank, and I shielded my eyes from the glare of the sun. Everything seemed brighter here. More intense and sharp. Even the noises. I looked out towards the natural harbor, a great line of rocks. There was a bird, abnormally thin and long, black with a light orange beak and delicate white marks on its wings. I pointed it out to Edie, and she gleefully ran inside to grab the binoculars and a book on African birds from the library.

Peering through the lenses, I examined the creature while she paged through the book.

"It's a reed cormorant," she said after a minute. "Microcarbo Africanus."

"Pretty, isn't it?" I replied, passing her the binoculars.

"So pretty, I could paint a picture. Maybe I will."

An idea hit me. "I can do better than that." A moment later, I had my new camera in my hands. I focused the lens and aperture. Just then, a welcome breeze drifted across the water, and the cormorant extended its glittery wings and soared above us. *Click*.

"Magnificent," Edie breathed.

Watching the cormorant disappear into the blue sky, I saw Sebastian climbing up the mast. *Click*.

Later, the Brophy Twins posed by the mainsail. *Click*.

I made Frank and Peter sit in the steamer chairs and pretend they were reading the newspaper. *Click*. And another of Horatio and Edie dancing, she in her new Arab style dress.

All afternoon. *Click. Click. Click*.

Before I knew it, I had used an entire roll of film.

"I took a photography class last semester," Peter said shyly. "If you want, I can show you the basics to develop the pictures. Though I'll warn you, I'm no expert."

"I'd be grateful for the help," I answered, trying to keep my nervous excitement down.

"Horatio should have all chemicals on the *Grey Goose* we'll need to develop the film, and I had the boys pick up a safelight with the camera—that's a red colored light that won't expose the paper. But we'll need a dark room."

"How about the bathroom off the yellow guest room? No one uses it."

"Perfect." He was confident now, leading the way towards the storage room to grab the chemicals.

Peter and I quickly converted the small space into a dark room. Then Peter began teaching each step of the process with the precision of a scientist. Soaking the film in water to make the gelatin layer swell. Converting the images to macroscopic particles of metallic silver. Stopping the development with a quick bath in citric acid. Applying the fixer to make the image permanent and light resistant. Finally, now that we had produced a 'negative,' the last step entailed placing it in an enlarger and projecting it onto a piece of photographic paper.

Each step was part of a carefully orchestrated dance that could go terribly wrong, with one tiny mistake resulting in either over or underdeveloped photographs.

We worked in silence for the most part, carefully maneuvering around one another in the dark room. I held up a negative of Frank looking out at the horizon. The words Frederick said about Frank being a communist during their terrible argument and last night's outburst that Jewish communists were taking over the government came to mind. "Is Frank really a communist?" I ventured, swirling the film around in the acid bath. To be honest, I wasn't sure what all the differences were between fascists and communists. It was all rather confusing.

Peter was carefully hanging photographic paper up to dry. "No. He's not. His mother was though. Ever heard of the International Ladies' Garment Workers' Union?"[4]

I shook my head no.

"Well, it was a long time ago. When we were just kids. Anyways, garment factories used to be terrible places to work. The women were sometimes locked inside, forced to work long hours. There were a few tragedies. Fires and whatnot. A lot of women died."

"Frank's mother?"

"No. Frank's mother was one of the women who led the union. They fought with everything in them for better working conditions and pay. And they had some ties to the communist party. A lot of union rhetoric stems from socialism, and communism is just socialism taken to an extreme."

I nodded as though I understood. I really didn't though. I hadn't realized how smart Peter was. Of course, he *was* in college. He must know a lot of things I didn't know.

Peter went on, "Frank is always going off about workers' rights and the evils of fascism."

It hit me, "Oh, I see. And because Hitler is a fascist, and Frederick thinks Hitler is going to save Germany..."

"Exactly. They are like oil and water. Certainly doesn't help that Frank is Jewish, and Frederick is an Aryan snob."

"And maybe a spy," I added.

"Yeah. Do you buy it? All that stuff about not knowing what was in those papers?"

I thought back over the last week. Ever since the night of their argument, Frederick had turned increasingly hostile and superior to Frank, both in the way he looked at him and the tone of his voice. I thought of Frederick's mysterious adventure to the German Embassy in steamy, seedy Casablanca the day before.

I slowly answered, "To be honest, I do believe him. I really don't think he knew what he was doing or could be doing. We really don't know what was in those papers, they could have been harmless enough. But I do think that he hates whatever or whoever the Nazis tell him to hate."

Peter agreed. "The only reason something really bad didn't happen is because Frank is Freddy's superior officer."

We worked a little longer in silence, the sound of the water slapping on the side of the boat.

"In my opinion, Freddy is just biding his time. He'll leave the *Grey Goose* soon enough and be on his way back to the Fatherland. He's obsessed," he said after a while.

The boat gently rocked, and I lost my balance, falling into Peter. He caught me and helped me get stable. He was so close, and I felt my face blush a million shades of crimson. Thankfully, the room was dark, and the safelight made both our faces red anyways.

Peter glanced at the photograph in the enlarger. "Oh wow! Look at that!"

It was the photograph of the cormorant suspended in mid-air.

And it was magnificent.

# CHAPTER 13

## FROM ONE PORT TO ANOTHER

After dinner, Peter and I spread the photographs out on the dining room table, drinking lemonade and trying to ignore the heat.

"I can't believe you had all that equipment," I said to Horatio. "It was like you knew they were buying me a camera."

"I did know," Horatio answered. "I couldn't let them buy the camera without making sure there was a way to get the pictures out at sea. I'm not a patient man by nature."

"Could have fooled me," Edie chuckled. "Here, let me see that one, the one of me and Horatio dancing. We look elegant, don't you think? I think we ought to blow it up, like a movie poster. We could hang it right there," she pointed at one of the walls. "What do you say?"

Sebastian found the picture of himself and grinned.

"I am so handsome!" He puffed out his chest proudly. "Look at me, way up there on the mast. I am so brave too. Like the monkey!" He held the photograph up, examining the minute details. "Do you think that shirt makes me look fat?"

"No," said Frank, patting his shoulder, "it's just your muscular build."

The Brophy twins asked for a copy of their portrait to send to their mother. The only portrait she had of them together was when they were six. And they had changed a lot since then, they explained.

There was one of Nathaniel Bounderby. "Look at this one of Nathaniel," Edie said. "He may not be able to speak, but somehow, in the photograph, you captured him saying a thousand words. What depth his eyes hold. What stories in those weathered wrinkles."

But it was the cormorant that received the most attention. "Really, Piper, you have a gift. Your eye for placement, light, and timing… impeccable. I think you have found your medium. You were born to capture the poetry of the world on film," Edie proclaimed with passion.

The poetry of the world on film. I liked that.

I looked at the photograph. I could honestly say that it was good. Really good.

Edie tapped Horatio on the shoulder. "Don't you agree, Horatio?"

But Horatio was distracted by the monkey.

We had named the rascal, who turned out to be a female, Fanny. Whenever Ferguson entered the room, as he had just then, Fanny would swing off the furniture and lunge for his shoulder and there take up her perch. "I do declare, Ferguson, Fanny must think you are her mother or something," Edie said.

Horatio's collie barked menacingly at the monkey. "All right, all right." Horatio quieted the dog. "Take the zoo out please, Ferguson. We are trying to concentrate on art here." Ferguson acquiesced, pulling the monkey away from his head and holding her out in disgust.

"He'll warm up to her. I'm sure of it," Edie assured. She took a rather large gulp of lemonade. "I do think that Cookie's supper was abnormally salty. I could drink an oasis."

"It's the heat, dear," Horatio answered. Then, fanning himself with a magazine, he said, "Goodness, it is hot!"

The heat made it hard to sleep at night. I sprawled out on top of my coverlet in nothing but my slip, trying to ignore the sweat on my neck and the anxiety forming a pit in my stomach as our stay in Morocco stretched on.

TO MY GREAT DELIGHT, the next day we were finally back at sea.

Though it had taken my aunt and Horatio all morning to obtain the letters of transit, it often took people much longer. Sometimes even weeks or months.

Exhausted, hot, and irritable, Edie ranted, "That was the seediest office I've ever been in. Imagine, all that work just to leave the port." Closing her eyes and rubbing her temples, she described the large white shutters, the stuck-up French officials chain-smoking, the endless lines of refugees. "I'm sure they were taking bribes, darling. It felt so corrupt and shady."

"I know for a fact that they were taking bribes," Horatio stated simply.

"You mean you bribed them?" Edie was shocked.

"We don't have time to sit around here and wait and wait, just to have to bribe them after all that waiting."

"It's awful." Edie's voice broke into my thoughts. "Some of those refugees have been waiting on their exit visas for months.[5] The French have no idea what to do with them. And the Germans are hanging around like cats ready to pounce on a mouse. No offense to you, of course, Frederick."

The refugees. The poor. The wealthy. All were waiting. Biding their time. Meandering through the market. Sitting at the outdoor cafes, sipping strong coffee, and staring into space. What fear drove them to leave Europe for the Americas? What would make them so desperate to attempt the long circuitous route through Lisbon, the exit city in Portugal, to French Morocco? In Casablanca, they waited for passage on the one plane that flew in and out once a week, or by boat. Those with money had a much shorter wait than those without. Thankfully for us, Uncle Horatio could afford to go where he wanted, when he wanted.

Frederick, engrossed in the *Times* newspaper Horatio had picked up in Casablanca, looked up distractedly. He obviously hadn't heard what Edie had said. "You will excuse me, please," he said curtly and left the room.

"What's the matter with him?" Edie asked.

Horatio poured a cup of tea and joined Edie on the couch.

My eyes followed Frederick through the open porthole. He "accidentally" bumped into Frank as he passed him on the starboard. Frank lost his balance and toppled over while the mocking eyes of Frederick made his apology hollow and cheap. Frank popped up and appeared ready to sock the German right in the kisser, but he held back. Frank's temper was always on the verge of exploding, but he was no one's fool. It wouldn't do any good to start a fist fight.

"Just between us, darling, I don't trust him," Edie said softly to Horatio. They had also seen the little drama through the porthole.

Horatio didn't answer, still looking out the porthole. Edie went on, "I'm a writer, Husband. And I hate to say it, but villains exist in real life, and I think he might be one."

Horatio grimaced. "Real life is always more complicated."

"Good people sometimes go bad. Pain does that if you don't deal with it the right way."

Peter and I and Horatio looked at one another. Something had to be done about that boy. Horatio remained silent as the boat caught a huge swell, then settled once more. Finally, Horatio looked at his pocket watch. "We should pull into Marseille by midnight. I'll figure out what to do with Frederick there."

~

THE HEAT, even out at sea, was oppressive. It was difficult to be so still and so hot. There was barely a lick of wind. Everything was taking longer than I wanted it to. If only the ship would sail faster!

I ran downstairs and found Cookie feeding Fanny part of a banana. "What's for supper, Cookie?" I asked, peeking in a large pot.

"That couscous again." I knew he was talking about those little pasta bits that cooked up like rice that he had bought in Casablanca. "And chicken with spices." Edie had taken a great liking to Moroccan food and had requested it for the rest of the sea journey.

I went back up on the deck and worked my way to the bow of the ship. There was a large coil of rope, and I pushed it to the side so I could see over the edge, imagining in the sunset that I could make out the lights of Marseille. Of course, that was impossible. We wouldn't be dockside until midnight.

"I cannot wait to get back home." Frederick appeared close behind me. I looked over my shoulder. His handsome face so close, the cold eyes masking a world of hurt.

"You are going to enlist right away then?"

"I want Germany to become a great country again. After we were humiliated in the Great War…" he trailed off for a minute. "Hitler will bring us back the glory and honor we deserve."[6]

What had happened to him? What had made him so angry at the world, at the Jews? My mother would have playfully slapped him, told him he was smarter than that. My father would have explained that if he wanted to make Germany great again, he should work to oppose Hitler. But I didn't have their words. I didn't even know where to start.

"You would love Germany. The rivers and the forests, they are so beautiful," he continued.

"I've no doubt of that. My cousins told me the same." I looked out at the sea, willing Frederick to change. There was a part of him that longed for goodness, for beauty. I knew it.

"Your cousins live in Germany? What are their names? Perhaps we have met. Germany is a much smaller country than yours."

On no, I caught myself. Had I already said too much? Peter had told me to say nothing of my family to Frederick. "Their names?" I stammered. The ship's bell rang loudly, cutting off my voice.

"Change of the watch." Frederick looked up. "I'm on duty." He tipped his cap and retired to his post. Saved by the bell. I exhaled a sigh of relief and looked out once more at the vast sea.

A welcome breeze swept over the deck, spraying my hair with salty mist. The sails billowed and flapped. I could stand there with my face to the wind all night, waiting for the lights of Marseille.

It was still dark when I awoke, but I felt the night drawing to a close. Morning was almost upon us, and the port of Marseille was buzzing with activity. Bells clanged, and French voices shouted.

The docks never sleep, Horatio had said. I jumped out of bed, my bare feet on the wood-paneled floor. No need for Ferguson to wake me up today.

My small valise, packed the night before, was as ready as I was to disembark.

Splashing water on my face, I quickly dressed and tied my hair up in another scarf. It was getting easier now. I had it down to a science. I had a feeling in a week or two, my hair would be long enough to go without the scarf. Admittedly, that would mean sporting a Shirley Temple look, but she was cute, right? Not exactly the cute I was going for, but I would take what I could get. I took a quick glance in the mirror; my eyes looked irregularly alert, ready for action.

Then, reaching for my pocket Bible, I opened it to where I had left off the night before, in the book of Romans. "Now may the God of hope fill you with all joy and peace as you believe in Him, so that you may overflow with hope by the power of the Holy Spirit."

I wanted to be filled with hope and joy and peace. In that most desperate moment, our time possibly running out and a vast amount of ground still to cover, discouragement and fear were on my heels. But God promised that peace, and even joy, were mine if I only trusted him. The words washed over me, and my shoulders relaxed. We would make it in time. In time for what, I knew not, but we would make it.

Out on the deck, in the pale early morning light, Edie paced impatiently up and down. She was dressed in yet another of her new Arab dresses, the rich embroidery bringing out the deeper shades of the red in her hair.

"If only those men of ours would wake up, we could be off and on our way," she said, reaching out and giving me a slight squeeze.

"They *are* up," Horatio growled good-naturedly, taking both Edie and me by surprise. "And ready to go."

So we all must have felt the same need to get moving. But the train did not leave until noon, which meant we had hours to wait. The three of us stood against the rail, looking at the sea.

I could make out the vague outline of something a mile or so from the shore, a small island with a castle or fortress built nearly to the edge of the rock. "It is the Chateau d'If," Horatio answered my questioning gaze.[7]

From *The Count of Monte Cristo*? The infamous prison. I shuddered and snapped a photograph. Like Alcatraz, the prison off the coast of San Francisco, the dangerous currents made escape nearly impossible. "Over 3500 French Calvinists were imprisoned there long ago. For their faith," Horatio said.

"Frederick would probably love to visit it," Peter added, with more than a hint of cynicism in his voice.

"Now, now," Edie corrected. "Is that really necessary?" Then, thinking back to *The Count of Monte Cristo*, she said, "I never liked that book." Edie bit at a hangnail and changed the subject. "We've got time to kill. We really ought to do something. I don't think I have the stamina to just wait around here." She was as agitated as I.

"How about you and Piper go ashore?" Horatio suggested. "The Palais Longchamp is not far. Besides, you don't know the next time you'll be in France."

"What is the Palais Longchamp[8]?" I asked.

"It is a garden, a very famous garden with museums and fountains."

Edie didn't have to be told twice. She grabbed my hand, pecked Horatio on the cheek, and set off down the gangplank and through the meandering docks until we reached something called the Canebiere, a street that ran through the center of the city. We found a little pâtisserie and bought croissants and coffee. The buttery, flaky pastry melted on our tongues, and we bought a few extra for later.

The sun rose higher, and we pressed on towards the garden. It was not far, and soon we found ourselves staring up at the base of the most ornate, eccentric structure I had ever laid my eyes on. The glowing white facades, marble statues, and water features against the clear blue sky were striking.

"What's at the top?" I asked. Four sculpted bulls and three sculpted women posed at the summit of the fountain which flowed into a secondary pool and then a large pond. "There, behind the women?"

Edie squinted. "I think they are nymphs. And stalactites?"

Stalactites. Odd. "What are they for?"

"No idea."

We stared a little longer at the strange sculpture. "Turn around and face me," I directed, focusing the lens of my Leica. *Click.*

"I'm at a loss for words," Edie said, her mouth slightly open, turning back around to examine the sculpture. "It's not what I expected at all."

"What did you expect?"

She shrugged. "Not that. I've read about this place. I thought it would be prettier," she said with a chuckle. Then she grabbed my hand and pressed on. "Maybe it will be nicer past that monstrosity. I never did like big statues. Natural beauty is my personal bent. God's sculptures. Mountains, cliffs along the ocean, the frailty of a rose petal. Our own attempts look so pathetic compared to his handiwork."

Clambering up the hill and past the Palais Longchamps, we took in the admirable garden and lawn dotted with poppies. A few gardeners tended to the primly clipped bushes leading to the Museum d'Histoire. A few older couples taking their morning walks passed us and smiled kindly.

We wandered about the garden aimlessly. It was still too early to visit the Museum d'Histoire, which was only slightly disappointing. I had seen a stuffed camel back in the States. Come to think of it, I had seen a *live* camel just a few days before, in Casablanca.

Edie pulled out the last croissant and sat down on the lawn. The bright morning sun made her red hair shine and glitter, like the dew on the grass. I eased down next to her as she pulled the pastry apart and gave me half.

"Oh Piper, life never turns out how you think it will, does it?"

I munched thoughtfully. "You're happy now that you're married, aren't you?"

"I'm happy now because I obeyed God and stopped living for myself alone. In marriage you have to live for another person. You are not your own anymore. You're his and he's yours. It's not all about you." She stopped. "And I think that's why I'm happier now, because I'm not thinking about myself all the time." Laughing, she concluded, "God always knows what you need, more than you know yourself. For me, it was Horatio. I'm so grateful he didn't give up. Being with him brings me so much purpose."

She looked up at the sky. "And I know they all say that the honeymoon phase ends and all of that. And I suppose we will have a rocky moment every now and again. We're both strong-willed, he has a temper, and I can dramatize the mundane. But that won't steal our joy. We won't let it. We waited too long to waste time not being happy together."

"I think that is the most mature thing I've heard you say," I laughed. "You are starting to sound like a wise old woman of 42."

She patted my cheek. "I'm proud of you too. Proud of us both. We shall forever remember the summer of 1939 as the year Edie and her protégé grew up. It's amazing what wisdom comes with age." She looked up at the sky. The sun was now overhead, and it was growing hot. "Do you think we ought to head back to the yacht?"

"I suppose so."

Edie stood and helped me up, both of us dusting ourselves clean from the freshly trimmed grass.

As we began to walk down the hill, Edie turned to me. "Frederick stopped by our cabin late last night for a private word with Horatio."

"He did?" I asked, surprised. "Do you know what he wanted?"

"No idea. But this morning, Horatio promoted Sebastian to second officer."

"You mean Sebastian is now the second officer instead of Frederick? That's odd." I wondered what Horatio had shared with Edie about Frederick's extracurricular activities with the Bund in America and the German Embassy in Casablanca.

She sped up. "Who knew that life on board would be filled with such secrets and intrigue."

By 10:30 we were back on the dock by the *Grey Goose*. All of our luggage was neatly lined up and ready for transport to the train. Horatio gave his last instructions to Frank, who was to captain the yacht from Marseille back through the Strait of Gibraltar, around Spain and Lisbon, past France, and through the English Channel into the North Sea. From there, it was a clear shot to Brussels, where Edie and Horatio planned to meet the yacht, after spending a few weeks in Switzerland.

The *Grey Goose* was a beloved vessel, and it was the first time that Horatio had entrusted the ship to someone else. "I'll take good care of her, I promise you, sir." Frank lovingly touched the wood siding, spotless and gleaming in the sun. "You've nothing to worry about."

Horatio still looked like a concerned father. "No, no. Of course not. I trust you, Frank. But make sure you watch her keel—"

"I know, sir. I know. I've handled the *Goose* before."

Horatio laughed, and with a sigh, he seemed to relinquish his boat. "Yes. I suppose you have."

With that, the entire crew of the *Grey Goose,* except for Frederick, who was conspicuously missing, assembled for the last time. Tears sprung to my eyes as I realized that this was to be my goodbye to them. One by one, I went to each sailor and thanked him for such a wonderful time aboard the yacht and for my camera. I promised that I would never forget them, and we all agreed that we might meet once again.

Meanwhile, all of our luggage was carefully loaded into the cab designated to carry the luggage, while Peter, Edie, and I entered another, along with Ferguson, the collie's leash in his hand and the monkey on his shoulder.

A few minutes later, Horatio appeared, followed by Frederick carrying his own trunk. Frederick and one of the cabbies secured the trunk on the roof of the luggage cab, and then Frederick slipped into the front seat next to its driver.

Edie's eyes looked questioningly at Horatio as he slid in next to her. "Frederick was good enough to remind me that his contract runs out in a few weeks. No point in sending him on with the ship. He has asked if he might accompany us as far as Switzerland in return for ending his contract early."

So that's why Sebastian was promoted, I concluded. Peter whispered in my ear, "I guess it's always a good idea to keep an eye on the enemy.

I shhh'd him. Frederick was not *my* enemy (even if he did scare me just a bit). He was just terribly confused, I was sure of it. Well, I was almost sure of it.

Cranking open the window and slamming on the outside of the vehicle, Horatio exclaimed cheerily, "Let's be off then." The car's engine rumbled to life, and we began the final leg of our journey.

~

BY TRAIN, the journey from France through Italy to Switzerland was nearly 20 hours. That meant by evening on the morrow, we would be in Bellinzona, the small village where my mother's sanitarium was.

20 short hours! I could barely contain the jitters in my stomach.

Our first-class tickets bought private rooms for Peter, Frederick, Ferguson, and myself, and another for Edie and Horatio. P.H.L and Fanny were stowed away with the luggage, in special cages that we rented from the train.

This train was nothing like the train I had ridden from California to Maine. For one thing, we were traveling first class. Our car was plush and velvet and snobby. Everything was as lavish and luxurious as the people on the train. Women in furs, wealthy businessmen, a few families.

The other cars were filled with French soldiers. The constant babble of young male French voices, some tense, others overly boisterous, made me nervous.

Before the wheels had even begun to turn, Ferguson had taken two sleeping pills, falling immediately asleep. This left Peter, Frederick, and I to our own devices. None of us spoke for a long time. We just sat and listened to the chug, chug, chug of the engine winding up and the occasional sharp blows of steam. We were off, striking into the unknown. The train was going faster and faster. I pressed my face against the window, watching the city speed past. We were out of the city now, winding through vineyards and fields of lavender.

"I love lavender," I said mindlessly, nestling back into the cushions.

"Why?" Frederick asked.

I thought a second. "I guess because my mother does. She always filled up her drawers with little sachets of it."

"Reminds you of her?"

"Yes."

"I too am reminded of my parents with certain smells. My father smelled like wood shavings. He was a carpenter. A good one." He looked out the window and seemed lost in thought. Finally, he said, "He loved Germany. Like me."

Before he could go on, Ferguson began snoring loudly, and the moment was lost. Frederick stood abruptly. "I'll be in the smoking car." He looked disdainfully at the snoring butler. "I can't relax in here."

"Sure," Peter said and moved over so Frederick could get through. "Are you okay, Freddy?"

Frederick didn't answer, firmly shutting the door behind him.

Peter stared at the door. "I never know what is going to set him off."

"He's just really sensitive." It sounded lame, even to me.

"As sensitive as a time bomb."

With that, I looked back out the window. My thoughts turned back to my mother as the minutes ticked on. The lavender fields blurred into wheat fields, and then rows of vineyards. *Help her hold on God,* I prayed. *We are so close.*

# CHAPTER 14

## WHAT HAPPENED ON THE TRAIN

The afternoon wore on as the train wound its way through France.

I dozed off and dreamt I was flying, soaring over Europe. There were French soldiers like little ants beneath me. Some waved to me and pointed. I waved back but kept on flying. There was no time to stop. The clock was ticking in time with the chug, chug, chug of the train. *Don't give up Piper,* a voice said. *Don't lose your hope. You will get there in time.* My eyes fluttered open.

"You were out cold," Peter commented.

I sat up straight, stretching my tight muscles. We had been sitting for hours.

"I was dreaming," I laughed. "Oh Peter, ever since I first went to Maine, I've been having the craziest dreams. Do you think I'm sleeping deeper?"

"Maine does that to people. Gives them permission to dream again. Famous proverb." His blue eyes twinkled.

"You're joking. And besides," I countered, "we're not in Maine now."

"True. Maybe it's all the spices from Morocco?" he jibed.

"Very funny."

I inhaled deeply and looked back out the window. The sun was lower, casting long moving shadows of the train. The dream sat with me heavily, not giving up its grip. I was still half there, with the sound of the voice wrapping itself around my heart like a comforting blanket.

"Do you think God can speak to you in dreams?" I ventured.

He tugged at his beard and seemed to think before replying, "I think God can speak to us however he pleases."

I was not satisfied. "But has he ever spoken to *you* in a dream?"

"No. I don't think so." He extended his long legs as far as they would go in the cramped compartment. "But the Bible is full of stories of when God spoke to people through dreams or sent angels to visit people in their dreams and deliver a message." He looked at me and said seriously. "Do you think he was sending you a message?"

I felt uncomfortable. "I don't know. Maybe."

Before he could answer, the door to our cabin burst open and there stood Frederick, nose bleeding, a shiner of a black eye forming. I jumped up, gasping, "Whatever happened?"

I took out my handkerchief and pressed it to his nose. He brushed my hand away, rage burning in his eyes.

"Those pathetic French," was all he said. "He cut in front of me at the bar."

"A soldier?" I stepped back. "You hit him?"

"And he hit you back," Peter concluded with no sympathy.

Frederick was defiant.

"You could get us thrown off this train for your behavior. What were you thinking!" Peter was angry now.

"As if I care," he spat out.

"'*As if you care*?' Well you should care! We're your ticket out of France and back to your beloved Fatherland," he said in a low growl. "If you want to make it back, you'll shut up and behave yourself."

Ferguson once again snored an enormous snore, causing the three of us to stop and stare. He must have taken a lot of those pills. He had been like that for hours.

Relenting, Frederick bowed stiffly and sunk down into the seat. "You are right, of course." He dabbed at his nose. "It was careless of me." The words were all correct, but the eyes still gleamed rebelliously.

"Come on, Piper," Peter opened the door for me, and I followed him down the passageway. "We'll let him cool off."

I looked back at poor Frederick, sitting there, nose bleeding. He was so angry and so alone.

~

WE MADE our way through the smoking car. It was filled with soldiers drinking and singing "La Marseillaise," the French national anthem. Peter kept a firm grip on my arm, helping me around the press of soldiers. "You know what it means?" Peter asked. "The song, I mean."

I didn't.

"To arms, citizens, Form your battalions, Let's march, let's march! Let an impure blood. Soak our fields!"

I shook my head in amazement, happy to be out of the din and sliding into a booth in the dining car. We each ordered a Coke which promptly arrived. We sipped in silence, and a distracted Peter looked out at the countryside whizzing past.

"What do you think happened to Frederick to make him so angry?"

"His father died in France during the Great War, when Freddy was just a little kid. He often says he will never forgive the French. His mother had no money to speak of, and life was just very hard on him. I guess the hate grew to include anyone who was not German."

I considered Peter. His parents had died when he was young, but he was not eaten away by anger like Frederick. Somehow, he had let go and embraced what God had given him without resentment or fear.

Staring into my Coke, I was back in the water at the beach in Maine. I was letting go. It was the only way I could face the waves. We all had the choice to sink or swim, didn't we? We all had the choice to let go of fear and whatever else that threatened to drown us or to sink under life's unfair events.

"Newspaper! Newspaper!" A porter made his way down the narrow aisle, breaking my thoughts. Peter flagged him down and picked one of the two papers offered. It was in French.

"You speak French?"

"Not much. But I can usually make out the headlines and occasionally the main point." He looked at the front page. "This one is called *Le Point*."

"*The Point*?"

"Yeah. It's a right-wing news magazine, essentially. They didn't have a lot to choose from though. It was this or *Le Libertaire*, an anarcho-communist paper."

"I have no idea what that means."

"They probably don't either," he said with a small chuckle. He passed it over to me, and I carefully unfolded it. I could guess what it said without reading a word. Between the raucous soldiers on the train and the photographs of arms and parades on the front page, I knew; France was preparing for war.

"From what I can tell," Peter said, putting the paper down after a while, "The French think they will easily defend themselves against Germany, should there be an invasion."

An invasion? It seemed unlikely. Why would Germany invade France?

"The French Minister of War, Andre Maginot, has been building all of these obstacles and walls, fortifications really, to deter any German invasion along the borders of Italy, Switzerland, Germany, and Luxembourg. They call it the Maginot Line."[9]

I imagined the map of Europe I'd had in my room in California. Something was missing. Then it came to me. "What about all of the low-countries, like Belgium and the Netherlands?"

"I can't say for sure, but I think the French don't believe the Germans would attempt an invasion from below. They would have to cross the Ardennes forest. The terrain is too rough. Besides, the Germans have always gone for frontal assaults."

"I'm glad the U.S.A. isn't going to war."

"Every country will have to make a choice. And every person too. But I'm not afraid to do what has to be done."

"Aren't you afraid of anything?"

"Yeah."

"What?"

Peter didn't answer. A faint shade of pink crept into his cheeks. Was he too embarrassed to tell me?

"You can trust me," I urged. "What are you afraid of?"

"Asking girls out." He said it quite honestly. His face as straight as ever. I couldn't believe it. He was so wonderful, a dozen girls would have thrown themselves at his feet, at my high school anyways.

"Oh shut up!" I said playfully. "Certainly, you've asked a girl out before?"

"You up for cards?" Peter asked, abruptly changing the subject.

I shrugged, assenting, but I couldn't let him get off that easy. "Well, have you ever tried asking a girl out?"

The sun had begun to set, casting a warm pink-orange glow through the train car.

He pulled out the well-used deck we had played with for hours on the ship. Taking the cards, he dealt them out, one by one, not meeting my eyes.

"Not even for prom?"

He mumbled, "Didn't go."

"Wait. What?"

"I never went to prom," he stated again. I could tell that he was dying to change the subject, but I was so curious as to why.

"Tell you what, Piper. If I ever want to ask a girl out, you'll be the first one to know." His merry eyes were laughing. I wished I could tell when he was being serious! Why did he make things so difficult!

"Okay." I stared at my cards a few seconds.

"Let's play cards," Peter urged. "What's the matter? Did you get dealt a bad hand?"

"I'm not sure. You never can guess what sort of hand you are going to get, can you?" I said.

Behind him, coming down the car, floated Edie and Horatio. She waved in my direction, and both made their way to the table. She sat down and took a swig of my Coke.

"What I would do for a hamburger right now," she moaned, looking at the menu. "But I suppose I'll settle for the steak and pomme frites. I'm pretty sure those are French fries. Close enough, anyway. Have you kids eaten yet?" Peter shook his head as Horatio ordered a lemonade on the rocks. He looked like he had a headache.

"Are you all right, Uncle Horatio?" Peter asked.

"It's the trains. Never did trust them."

"He'll be alright. Horatio has never been comfortable on land. It's the stress." Edie gently rubbed her husband's back. "Where's Ferguson?"

"Sleeping."

"And Frederick?" Horatio took his drink from the waiter.

"I think we've lost him." Peter pursed his lips tightly together.

AS THE SUN SET, the train slowed and the soldiers departed to some section of the Maginot Line or so I assumed.

Meanwhile, a porter came through to check our passports. We were officially crossing over into Italy.

"You know, we have another five or six hours before we change trains," Edie said, yawning. "We might as well get some sleep. I'll call the porter to turn down our beds." She stood up to leave. "Are you coming, Horatio?"

"No. I could never sleep on a train."

I, however, longed to sleep. It had been a very long day.

Edie must have noticed. "Come on, darling. We girls need our beauty sleep." And she steered me to her room. We washed up in the tiny washroom and strapped ourselves into the clever bunks turned down by the night porter and ate the chocolate he had left on our pillows. I stretched out, my aching back relieved after a day of sitting. I felt Edie's foot bouncing my mattress.

"All this sitting is getting to my bones. I have barely exercised at all since we left, and I'm losing my figure. I need more blood flow to my brain!" She began to do sit-ups in bed. "What do you think those boys are talking about?"

"Are we turning this into a slumber party?" I asked sleepily. My eyes were shutting against my will.

"Well, I—" Before she could finish, the train lurched forward and began to screech to a halt. I heard muffled screams, and Edie tumbled off her bunk and landed in a heap on the floor. I heard myself scream and clamped one hand over my mouth and the other on the wall to brace myself. Slowly, the train came to a full stop.

"Edie! Are you okay?" I lunged from my bunk to the floor.

Edie, now standing, rubbed her behind gingerly. "Nothing that an ice bath won't cure."

"Do you think the war has started?" I asked, panicked.

Edie looked out the window. It was pitch black and silent. "I doubt it. But then again, I've never been in a war."

Suddenly there was a banging on our door. "Edie! Piper! Are you girls all right?" Horatio's voice was muffled through the door.

"What happened?" Edie asked, unlatching the door. Peter was by his uncle's side.

Horatio shrugged. "Something always seems to go wrong on these trains."

Everyone was out of their rooms by now, worriedly standing in the hall. Frederick, his face smeared with shaving cream, emerged from the washroom. Even Ferguson was wide awake now. For several minutes, no one knew what to do. The passengers spoke in hushed tones, wondering if it was safe to stay on the train. Finally, the conductor appeared.

"Everyone will please to remain calm," he said in a thick Italian accent. "We have a small problem with the track.

"What sort of problem?" Edie questioned.

"It was, uh, how to say," he searched for the words, "an accident! A very bad accident."

A few minutes later, we stood with everyone else on the edge of a precipice, looking at the trestle that had completely collapsed.

"You have got to be kidding me," Edie said, pulling her satin robe tighter around her as a cool breeze swept up the hill.

"How in the world am I supposed to get to Lake Como?" an elderly British woman moaned. "I paid to get to Lake Como. I'm meeting my daughter there in the morning."

"There will be a slight delay," Horatio muttered, "obviously."

The porter stood by Edie and Horatio and said quietly, "Perhaps it is sabotage."

"That or Italian engineering," a distinguished looking Russian threw in. "This is going to take weeks to repair." But we didn't have weeks. We had days. My heart quickened. Whatever was going to happen now?

*Don't give up, Piper,* the voice from my dream urged. *Don't lose your hope. Trust Me. You will get there in time.*

# CHAPTER 15

## LA CASA VERDI

Peter pulled out a map and studied it intensely in the moonlight. We had waited by the train several hours before Horatio couldn't take it any longer. Now we were marching down the country road, parade style. Horatio lead the charge and PHL, with Fanny perched proudly on her back, took up the rear.

"Are you quite sure we are close? We've been walking for miles and miles." Edie stopped, took off a shoe, and rubbed her foot. "You would think the railroad company would have sent a car or a wagon train or something by now."

Though my head throbbed with exhaustion, some adrenaline had kicked in, and so I lumbered forward.

Frederick was highly annoyed and growing anxious. "You've no idea where we are," he spat out. "You should have asked for directions."

"We are sailors." Horatio, unperturbed, glanced at the sky. "We don't need directions. We just need a clear night, which we have. We are almost to Milan."

I looked up to the heavens. Clouds blew in over the moon,

leaving us in darkness. There was a clap of thunder and then a flash of lightning.

"Oh great," Edie uttered, putting her shoe back on. "This is fabulous. Just fabulous." Big fat raindrops dripped down her nose.

Onward we trudged, the country lane growing muddier and muddier. I tried to keep pace with Peter but struggled with my suitcase. "Do you really think that was sabotage?" My hand was getting tired. I was tempted to pass it to Peter or Frederick, but they were each carrying two.

"Who knows? Anything is possible. Our train might have been carrying a secret shipment of arms. Or perhaps it was something else... someone somebody didn't want to arrive alive," Peter replied.

"Or it could have simply been an accident," Frederick sneered.

Peter shrugged. "I suppose we'll never know."

"Look!" Edie pointed. "I see something."

A faint glimmer of light shone in the darkness. Then two. Then four.

As we got closer, the warm glow of light streamed welcomingly from the windows of a large villa. "Do you hear that?" Edie said, excitedly. "It sounds like someone's home." The sound was of a piano and voices singing and laughing. It was some sort of party. "Do you think it is a hotel?"

"It certainly appears to be something of the sort." Horatio pushed the gate open and marched to the enormous wood front door, dark with age and warped from heavy use. He searched for the bell and rang it once, then twice. We huddled under the slight awning in silence for several minutes. Pushing wet strands of hair away from my eyes, I set my suitcase down and stretched my fingers, stomping my feet for warmth.

Then, the door creaked open, revealing a very, very old man. Craggy wrinkles stretched across his forehead. A coarse salt and pepper beard nearly hid his mouth. His eyes were pools of dark brown, nearly black.

He opened his mouth slightly at the sight of us, dripping wet, holding suitcases. There we were: a bedraggled Scott, his tall and red-headed wife, Peter, me, an angry German, a distraught British butler, a dog, and a monkey.

"Do you have any rooms available?" Horatio bellowed over the still overhead thunder.

"No Inglesi," he sputtered, growing concern evident in the tone. "Italiano. Me Italiano."

My legs were growing weary and exhaustion began to settle back in. I wanted a bed. And a bath. And some food.

Ferguson stepped up as I sunk down onto my suitcase. He tried his best to explain our predicament in his limited Italian, and a look of semi-understanding dawned on the old man.

He motioned for us to follow him inside.

As my eyes adjusted to the light, a soprano's voice wafted over our heads. More singing followed, then came the banging of a timpani. The hall, rich with dark oiled paneling and lit with soft yellow light from frilly lamps, felt as ancient as our guide. It all felt rather dreamlike. "They are in the middle of their nightly rehearsal," the old man explained through Ferguson.

Who were they? And why were they rehearsing at such an ungodly hour?

The unspoken questions lingered as we walked down the hall. Nearing the room from which the music emanated, the man put his finger to his lips as a signal for us to be quiet. Rounding the corner, an astonishing scene met us. An entire orchestra sat poised to play. The conductor raised his baton and then... the music.

"Rigoletto," my aunt murmured. "It is from Rigoletto." An Italian operatic piece. The old man understood and nodded affirmatively.

The shock, however, came not from the music, but from the musicians. The average age must have been 90 years old. They were bent over, frail, weathered, and gray. Some were in wheelchairs. Many of the singers supported themselves with canes.

The old man signaled to a woman near the door. She quietly made her way over to us and closed the door behind her, muffling the sounds of the opera. We all huddled beneath the stairs by a large statue of a man, darkened with time.

"Sì?" she said, looking at us, her eyes stopping on Fanny.

"Americanos," the old man grunted.

"Ah, I see." Her accent was very slight. Painted eyebrows arched slightly in understanding, lips betraying a small smile. "I speak English." She was very thin and carried herself with stately grace.

"Is this a hotel?" Horatio blurted out. "We need a place to stay for the night."

She laughed gaily. Little laugh lines spread around her bright hazel eyes. With a dramatic flair she said, "No! This is not a hotel, good sir." She opened her arms out in welcome. "This is La Casa Verdi!"[10]

Edie asked, "You mean the composer?"

It was then that I noticed the inscription below the statue. It read 'Verdi.'

We had, by some fortuitous turn of events, landed at the famed composer's final memorial to his music, conceived when he penned the notes of *Falstaff*.[11] And what was this memorial? As the elderly woman, Sofia, explained, it was a place for aging singers, dancers, and musicians to spend their last days on earth surrounded by music, without fear of where their next meal might come from.

"How romantic and beautiful," Edie sighed.

"He understood that great artists are often not great businessmen, nor do they always have families to take care of them in their old age. So, he decided he would take care of us, and he has," Sofia explained. "It runs completely off of royalties from his operas."

Sofia welcomed us to spend a night in La Casa Verdi and offered to make us a bit of food. Gratefully, we accepted and 10 minutes later were sitting around the large wooden table in the kitchen, wrapped in towels and blankets and holding steaming mugs of tea close. The walls were a creamy plaster, and everything was clean and simple. The wood-burning stove emitted a delightful dry warmth, and the whole room smelled of years of garlic, onions, and rosemary.

Apparently, concerts were held several times a week. Verdi's own piano held a place of honor in the small hall. At all hours, warbling voices and scales filled the dark paneled rooms. "We never really stopped living on artist's time," Sofia laughed. She was over at the counter, slicing thick crusty bread. "We are up at all hours of the night, and we sleep all day. But tonight's rehearsal is rather important. An esteemed guest is visiting for a private concert tomorrow." Her tone was flat, barely hiding a flicker of cynicism.

She brought over a platter of salami, cheese, and sun-dried tomatoes drenched in olive oil.

"I love Italy," Peter declared.

Sofia smiled. "The tomatoes come from our garden. We dry them ourselves."

Edie popped one in her mouth, and a look of total approval swept over her face. "You'll have to share the secret with me! Piper," she looked at me, "we could do this back in Maine with our tomatoes!"

"Ah, but they won't taste the same," Sofia said. "Our air here is very special, and the soil too."

A clap of thunder shook the old villa, and I choked on my tea. Horatio heavily slapped me on the back. The force of his hand shook my body intensely. I've always wondered why people think a slap on the back will help when you choke. As I caught my breath, the attention returned to Sofia.

"So, you were a singer?" Edie asked Sofia.

"Me? No, I was not a singer. I *am* a dancer." She held herself up proudly. "I will always be a dancer."

I saw Frederick look scornfully at the old woman. Impatiently, he put his mug down. "I would like to go to bed. It's been a long night." He stood up brusquely. His attitude had gone from bad to downright offensive. It was embarrassing.

"Of course." Sofia took no offense. "I am sure you all must be very tired. Follow me upstairs."

~

SOFIA LED us to three unused rooms on the third floor. There was one for the bachelors and the animals, one for Horatio and Edie, and one for myself.

Ten minutes and a wash later, I was cozied up in the big bed. It was irresistibly comfortable. Yet despite the night's events and my aching body, it took me a long time to fall asleep. The sounds of the rehearsal and our own journey gone so awry kept my mind spinning. Finally though, I must have fallen asleep, for when my eyes fluttered open it was nearly ten in the morning, according to the bedside clock. Bright sunlight streamed across the bed through the crack in the curtain. Barefooted, I ambled to the large window and threw the shade back.

Down below, I saw Sofia and Edie on a small patio eating breakfast. I quickly dressed and made my way down the silent halls towards the patio. Sofia hadn't lied, La Casa Verdi was quiet in the morning. Even at ten, almost no one was awake. There was no music, only the peaceful rest of the artists.

"Morning," I said as I sat down. The two women welcomed me, smiling.

"Horatio and Peter went into town to find some sort of new arrangement. He won't set foot on another train." Edie said, before taking a sip of coffee.

I would have a good attitude. I would. I would. I would.

"And my parents?"

"His first stop was to send your father a telegram with an update of our predicament." Seeing my worried face, she put her cup down. "Don't worry, Piper. Right now we have to trust that we are in the palm of God's hand, and he will get us where we need to go when we need to get there."

I grimaced. Some days were easier with the whole trust thing than others.

"You have a very nice husband, dear. You are newlyweds?" Sofia spoke to Edie while passing me a basket of small rolls. I took two and nibbled away.

"How can you tell?" Edie blushed.

"When you get to be 85, you can tell."

"You don't look a day over 80."

"Thank you, I think," she laughed.

Frederick, his dark mood growing darker, stormed onto the patio. He glanced at me and managed to eliminate his scowl for a brief moment, nodding curtly.

With a barely audible "good morning," he poured himself a cup of coffee and retreated back into the house. Sofia, Edie, and I watched him disappear.

"That young man is very unhappy. He doesn't think he belongs. As though his skin does not fit his heart," Sofia said. "Many artists have that problem. I understand it."

"You think Frederick is artistic?" That surprised me.

"Certainly. We are all created in the image of God, are we not?" Sofia said simply. "And God is the Master Artist. So we are all artists as well. Though some are more in tune than others."

"You know, I'm an artist too. A writer," Edie replied. "And I know what you mean. It can drive people to do awful things, that feeling of not fitting in. I once didn't leave my home for a year."

"A whole year?" I asked, shocked.

"Don't tell Horatio," Edie whispered.

"There are two directions you can take when you don't fit in," Sofia said thoughtfully. "You can let it take you deeper, making you more loving and understanding, allowing your art to reflect this. Or, you can become bitter and cynical. And slowly, you die. It is a lesson all of us have learned in this house, some the hard way."

Edie took a long, slow sip of coffee, silently agreeing with Sofia.

"I read Hitler was once in art school, before he took up politics in beer halls."[12]

"I read this too," Sofia said amiably, leaning back in her chair. "This is my point exactly!"

At that moment, Peter and Horatio ambled up the long drive and waved.

"No car?" Edie looked at Horatio. He stepped up to the table and took a sip of Edie's coffee.

"Nothing. Several horses and carts though, but everything was either too old or too small."

"You can thank our fascism for that. It is difficult to get what you need when you need it in Italy. It is not easy to find new cars, or old for that matter, in Italy these days."

At that moment, a young boy, around ten years old, appeared on the patio. He ran up to Sofia and passed her a note. "This is Pablo," she explained. "He lives in the village. His mother is my niece." She kissed him and opened the note. No one but me noticed her features pale slightly and her fingers tremble as she read it. She carefully put it in her sweater's pocket, shooing Pablo back home after filling his hands with a generous helping of bread and cheese.

"Is everything all right?" I asked.

Sofia narrowed her eyes. "You know, we have a truck you could borrow. It's old and needs work, but it would certainly get you to the border."

"We'll take it," Horatio said without blinking.

## CHAPTER 16

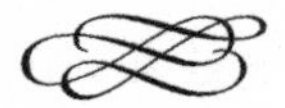

## THE GREY GOOSE, INC.

Ten minutes later, an old truck, slightly worse for wear, sputtered and coughed into the courtyard. A quiet "oh my" escaped from Edie's lips as she examined the ancient, lumbering vehicle.

Horatio and Peter emerged from the car, looking quite pleased with themselves. "It needs a little work, but we should have her up and running within a few hours."

Sofia proudly slammed her hand on the truck's dash. A cloud of dust rose. She rubbed her hand on her dress. "Well, I didn't say it was in good shape. Like the rest of us at Casa Verdi, some repairs are in order. But our hearts are strong, our bones, good. We have years of life left!"

Edie grimaced as the engine continued to choke. "It sounds like an asthmatic old woman." She looked at Sofia. "Uh, no offense."

Horatio shot Edie a look and growled, "I told you I could get her up and running."

"Have you ever even worked on a car before?" Hands on her hip, her voice dripped with doubt.

Horatio's temper flared. "Edith! I know cars."

"You know boats."

"Same thing."

"No," Edie shook her head, "they aren't."

Horatio popped the hood and looked into the filthy engine. "Just you wait and see." He turned to Sofia. "How much do you want for the truck? Does $150 sound all right? I've no idea what that would be in Lira, but in America, it would be a fair deal." He was still looking at the engine, poking around here and there.

"We will talk about such things later. It will be a fair price, I assure you."

Peter marched up to the table and took a couple of the rolls. "Don't worry, Edie. He may not know what he is doing, but I actually do know a little something about mechanics. Plus, I taught Piper here a thing or two about machines a while back." The bike we had fixed on Maine's shore seemed very far away at that moment. Almost a lifetime away.

He winked at me conspiratorially. Those beautiful blue eyes again. They still gave me butterflies. Why was he always winking at me? It was unnerving.

Edie pursed her lips and turned back towards Sofia. An idea seemed to have struck, and she held up her hand.

"Sofia, I have a request to make while we are here, which will probably be slightly longer than expected." Edie looked hopefully at the old woman. "Perhaps, it would be possible for me to have a small singing lesson with the maestro? I've always dreamt of singing at La Scala, and this is practically La Scala."[13]

"But of course. It would be our pleasure. We often give lessons to the local children…" Sofia answered but was only half present. She'd seemed awfully distracted ever since that little boy had passed her the note.

"Piper! Perhaps you would care to join me?"

"Nope," I said with a smile. "You are on your own for this one, Aunt Edie."

Sofia's eyes focused on Edie with a new intensity. "Actually, come to think of it, I think that a lesson is exactly what you need. In fact, we will begin immediately. Edie, come with me inside. Right now!" Sofia was distracted no more. She grabbed my aunt's arm and pulled her inside.

"If you insist." Edie looked back at me, slightly confused. "But there's no rush. It's going to take them a while to fix the engine."

"You have no idea how much of a rush there really is," Sofia answered, fully focused on the front door, marching steadily like a general off to war.

Peter looked at me. "That was odd."

"Very," I agreed, staring at the two women entering the villa. "Must be an artist thing."

"Yeah... or something else."

Horatio called Peter back to the truck. "Can you manage to crawl underneath and check out the exhaust pipe?"

"YOU WON'T BELIEVE IT!" Edie ran out towards the courtyard 15 minutes later. "You just won't even believe it!" Her voice was taut with nervous excitement. She grabbed my arms and pulled me off the low wall I had perched on in the sun. She looked at me, white as a sheet, and squeezed my arm till it nearly hurt. She was trying to tell me something. She spun me around and then practically threw herself into Horatio's arms, his wrench clanging to the ground.

"Confound it, woman! What's happened?"

Peter's head appeared from under the car. It was covered with grease. Oil spotted his shirt. "What's going on?"

"Galeazzo Ciano is coming here for tonight's concert, and I have been given the lead." Edie looked like she might faint.

Horatio blanched. "Whatever for?"

The name sounded familiar, but in the moment I couldn't quite remember who Galeazzo Ciano was.

Edie continued, "Remember how Sofia said last night that there was a special guest coming for a private concert?"

"That's absurd," Horatio managed.

Peter broke in, "Who's Galeazzo Ciano?"

Without any pause, Horatio said, "He's Italy's foreign minister. And Mussolini's son-in-law."

My heart dropped. Now I remembered why the name sounded familiar. Mussolini had been elected as Italy's Prime Minister in 1922, but within a year, all pretense of leading a democracy had been dropped, and he'd initiated a legal dictatorship that was drawing closer and closer to Germany by the day. It was the sort of information I never thought I'd need to know or even care about—until now. Mussolini's son-in-law, Ciano, was being groomed to one day be his successor and was already nearly as dangerous.

We were all silent for a long moment. Finally, Horatio looked at Edie and whispered, "Darling, what is going on?"

She leaned in close to Horatio and said, "Apparently word got out that a group of Americans had arrived at the Villa. They think we might be spies. Tensions have been flaring in this neck of the woods. You *must* get this truck up and running by tonight. We have to leave immediately after the performance unless we want to be detained in Milan for several days… or longer."

My stomach turned over. What had started as a journey to my parents was turning into something more than any of us had bargained for. Peter forgot he was under the car and sat up abruptly, only to hit his head violently on the bumper.

"Ouch!" he cried.

"Sofia had the rather brilliant idea that I pretend to be a famous opera singer from the States. Don't you see, dear?" Then, louder, she said, "In fact, they have parts for all of us."

"I don't understand, what are they afraid of?" I sputtered. "There is no war! Besides, America is neutral."

"But Horatio has a UK passport." Edie looked up at her husband.

It all became clear. A wealthy Scott, his crew, a British butler had all arrived at midnight and wandered around the town, sending telegrams, and supposedly looking for a car to go to Switzerland. It did look sketchy.

Edie straightened Horatio's tie. "You are now looking at the famous American opera company, The Grey Goose Inc."

"Ah," Peter said, getting the gist of the plan. "We've been scheduled to be here on tour for months. Nothing unusual or out of the ordinary, am I correct?"

"Exactly so." Flustered, Edie straightened her dress. "Now, I'm off to rehearsal. We expect you all inside in a few minutes."

I stopped her. "How do you know you can trust Sofia?"

Her eyes saddened. "She's Jewish, dear. In fact, many of the artists here are Jewish. There are rumors that..." Edie trailed off for a moment. "Well, she's asked if we could take her with us after the rehearsal. She has family up in the North, and it's safer out of the cities these days, even for a harmless, once-famous, old ballerina."

"That's the payment, isn't it," Horatio bent down to pick up the wrench, "for the truck?"

"Something like that, yes." Edie wrapped her arms around Horatio. "Life is not a dress rehearsal. But oh, how I wish we had some more time to practice this particular performance."

From inside the villa, Sofia yelled towards our small circle. "Do you think Frederick will be alright playing a Viking King?"

Frederick? Frederick, who had stayed inside all morning with a rotten attitude and a sour expression that displayed his obvious disgust at being cooped up with a bunch of old artists.

Peter answered loudly, "No problem there. He thinks he's one already."

The only reason he was with us, Frederick had made abundantly clear, was so he could get back to Germany. I was relieved he had stayed in his room.

"You should put something on that." I looked at Peter's forehead. "You're getting a black eye." Frederick's had already developed into a healthy shiner from the French soldier's offense on the train. Now our little opera troupe would tout not one but two young men who looked more like failed boxers than tenors.

"No time." He slipped back under the car. "Horatio, you and Edie go inside and figure this whole show thing out. Piper and I will finish the truck."

The hours passed by quickly. With the scanty tools in the barn, Peter was able to get the truck's starter to work. But all in all, the truck was on its last legs. "Keep your fingers crossed that it will take us over the border," Peter groaned as he slammed the hood down.

I handed him a rag, and he rubbed his grease-covered hands, then his sweaty forehead. Glancing at his watch, he said, "The concert's in two hours. That should give us enough time for makeup and rehearsal, right?"

Yeah. Sure. Why not? At this point, I was just trying to keep moving. Anything to not think of what might happen if we were detained any longer. As though not making it to my mother in time was enough of a strain, now it looked like we might get stuck in an Italian prison. If the devil was trying to steal my resolve to trust God, he was doing a pretty elaborate job.

I gritted my teeth and bore down with everything in me. I would not sink with fear. I would float. I would trust him. If it killed me, I would trust him. I would even pretend to be an opera singer for Mussolini's son-in-law. If that's what it was going to take to build character, so be it.

SOFIA, with an expert's eye, carefully applied the final touches of Horatio's makeup as we arrived in the large sitting room upstairs. He had a blue dress on, cinched in the middle. He looked like someone from *A Midsummer's Night Dream* or some other Shakespearean production. His muscular thighs bulked below the skirt, and the character boots barely fit over his calves. A long white cape, secured with a giant brooch, set off the entire ensemble into something quite royal. "They've got me playing Gaston, the Viscount of Bearn. And I'm a baritone!" He glowered at Peter and me.

"You'll hit the notes just fine, even if you're not a natural tenor, just like you did in practice. Besides, *Jerusalem* is the only Verdi opera you can passably sing with that heavy brogue," Sofia soothed. "We'll be in the wings. If you forget a line, one of our tenors will fill in. You just open your mouth. It is an old trick of the trade."

"And I am playing Helene," Edie waltzed in, "the Count's daughter." She wore a long, elegant gown of pink silk. A large cornet nestled into her unruly, red curls. "And you will be Isaure, my companion." She threw me a blue silk gown, not unlike hers. "Go put that on. And come back for your makeup."

"I can't sing!" I protested. Fear crept up my spine. "You know that!"

"You won't have to. Just twirl around the stage whenever I snap my fingers. We are skipping all of your solos."

This was bound to end in disaster. I had no doubt.

Behind me, I heard Peter ask, "And me? Who am I playing?"

"You are Raymond," Sofia answered.

"My squire," interrupted Horatio. "And we've got Freddy playing the soldier."

With that, Frederick stomped in. "This is humiliating," he said. Though surprisingly, I detected a glint of enjoyment behind his mask of surliness. It was the first glimmer of life I'd seen in weeks.

"I actually think you look quite handsome," Edie said, after taking him in a moment. The tunic was a little short. The boots a bit big. The sword too long. But overall, the look was convincing. He blushed slightly and sat down in a huff. "Why am I doing this again?"

"Because you don't want me to sue you for breach of contract," Horatio grunted. "Italy and Germany may be military allies young man, but that's not enough to keep the Italians from suspecting you. While Hitler and Mussolini may be cozy right now, with the same racist laws and their plots and schemes to take over the world—" He was on a role. Maybe it was the costume. It gave room for great, long political speeches.

That's when Ferguson marched in. He wore a bathrobe of sorts and a fake beard. An orange turban completed his look. "My goodness! If he isn't the most obvious choice for the Emir of Ramla I've ever seen!" Edie cried happily.

"Thank you, ma'am." Ferguson bowed. "My skill set does not include the theater, but I understand that under the circumstances it is necessary."

"We are grateful for your help, as always," Edie said. "I don't know what we would do without you."

Ferguson turned away, embarrassed by the praise. "It is my pleasure, ma'am."

Horatio clapped his hands. "Come sit down, every mother's son, and rehearse your parts!"[14]

Sofia looked pleased. "You know Shakespeare, Horatio?"

Edie answered for him, "Of course. *A Midsummer Night's Dream.* Act III. We used to read it to each other every summer. Midsummer, actually. Horatio thought it was romantic."[14]

"Didn't you?" Horatio asked, surprised.

"Sure. I love the great bard. Though this drama is a little more dramatic than I prefer," her voice quivered a bit.

"Be brave, my dear," Horatio said quietly.

Edie controlled her voice. "I'm trying."

"Remember Act V? 'Is there no play, to ease the anguish of a torturing hour?'"[15]

No one spoke.

Sofia signaled the pianist to strike a chord. "This is not a play. It's an opera. And we must get back to rehearsal and the escape plans. Horatio! Your solo. And Piper, go put on your costume!"

Right. My costume. I jogged to my room and slipped into my gown. Sofia had noticed my unusual haircut and so had offered me a tall conical hat made of the same blue silk as my dress. Without so much as a glance in the mirror, I hurried back to the sitting room.

Everyone gathered around Sofia now. Peter was dressed in his own tunic and pulling on character boots.

Sofia outlined the structure of the opera and finalized our plans for escape. Even Frederick listened attentively. His loyalty and politics might have put him closer to Mussolini than I cared to think about, but even he couldn't deny that his odds of not spending a week or two with Mussolini's secret police were lower if he threw in his lot with us.

~

"Now," Sofia waved her arm dramatically, "in the first act, we are in the palace of the Count of Toulouse. Gaston is about to leave for the Crusades, and Helene sings him a beautiful goodbye."

"I love that song," Edie interrupted.

Sofia silenced her with a wave of her palm. "Meanwhile, Roger proclaims his hatred of Gaston and plots to kill him with the help of the soldier." Peter and Frederick looked at one another.

"I thought that Gaston was framed by Roger for a murder."

"Yes, but not until later," Sofia explained.

"Oh, is that when I threaten to throw Helene's head to the dogs?" Ferguson pushed up the sleeves to his flowing garment.

Peter slid one finger across his throat. "And before my dramatic death scene, when I look at Jerusalem one last time before I croak."

"No! Yes... no! It is much more complicated than that. Don't worry about the story. Just follow our instructions. We've got people hidden in all the props who will be whispering where you should stand and when you should sing or not sing. And we've cut out the third and fourth acts for time's sake."

"Won't the audience be confused?" I threw in.

"No." She shrugged. "No one ever really pays any attention to the stories in opera. They tend to make very little sense. All the audience wants is grand music and majestic costumes. And that," she finished with a flourish, "is what we shall give them!"

"Sofia!" A tiny woman with a shrill voice interrupted us.

"What is it, Antonia?" Sofia snapped. In response, the little woman pointed to the window.

The crunch of tires and boots. It was Ciano.

"He is here," Sofia announced solemnly. "They say he and his father-in-law are quite insane."

Edie gathered her skirts around her and grabbed my hand, "Well, as theater people always say, the show must go on!"

## CHAPTER 17

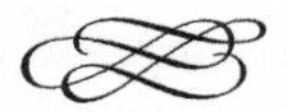

## FREDERICK FINDS HIS VOICE

Throughout the course of the opera, the residents of La Casa Verdi, hidden behind the various props and curtains, directed us on and off the stage. Their beautiful voices filled our mouths, and their chorus of knights, ladies, pages, soldiers, pilgrims, Arab sheiks, and the people of Ramla covered our clumsiness. Enrico, the stage director, kept the lighting very dim, so the audience could barely see our mouths move. And the elderly dancers kept moving in front of us whenever we had a solo.

"You know, I think we have them fooled." Horatio peeked behind the curtain, squinting to see the audience. The theater sat roughly 50 people, which was the entirety of Ciano's entourage. Frederick and I stepped up behind him, trying to catch sight of Mussolini's nephew, third-row center.

"You're stepping on my dress," I whispered fiercely to Frederick as we hid behind the curtain in the villa's small theater. He apologized and carefully stepped aside. "Truly, your aunt isn't entirely a bad singer."

I grimaced as she reached a high note. "Not entirely."

Peter stuck his head in between us. "Do we go on now?" The

music reached a crescendo, and the crowd politely applauded. A large fan was turned on for effect, the backdrop of Jerusalem swayed slightly. The fake palm trees threatened to blow over.

"Yes, now!" An unseen voice behind a bush whispered violently. Peter practically ran onto the stage, Frederick close on his heels.

Frederick unsheathed the sword as directed and took his place. Peter strode around the stage, his mouth open as directed. Somewhere, an alto filled the theater with music. He waved his arm in the air and tried his best to look very, very angry because someone had apparently been murdered. At least, I think someone had been.

The tympani pounded, preparing the way for Frederick's solo. He strode to the center of the stage, a new clarity in his eyes. Throwing his shoulders back, he held his arm out like a true star and opened his mouth to sing.

I don't know exactly what happened next. It took me by such surprise that I almost laughed out loud. From Frederick's own mouth flowed the most beautiful voice I had ever heard. And it was definitely Frederick singing. A clear, clean, penetrating note. It cut through the orchestra and hung over the audience like a miraculous dream. Frederick didn't know all the words, but he had learned enough in the hour of rehearsal to hit the melody spot on.

The combination of his profound "La La LAAAA" with the clanging of the tympani, horns, and chorus backing him up was astounding. He was completely in his element. Fully himself, fully alive.

"My goodness," Horatio breathed, "the boy's a prodigy. Why has he not considered pursuing the theater?"

The song ended, and the audience broke into a rapturous applause. Some even stood up.

~

OVER THE INTERMISSION, Frederick, a fresh glow to his face, collapsed beside Peter and me on the floor. "You know, this is rather fun. We have the Italians eating out of our hands."

"Frederick, you have a true gift. I didn't know you could sing!" I said.

Frederick looked down, suddenly embarrassed. "I haven't sung in a long time. Not since my father died."

"You *were* pretty good," Peter reluctantly agreed. "You surprised us all,"

"I used to love singing. I was in a choir as a child." His guard was down, more so than I'd ever seen. I wondered what it was that made him feel safe to do so now. He'd found his voice, years after losing it.

I put my hand on Frederick's shoulder and said, "I think he'd have been very proud of you tonight," I said softly. "You know, you don't have to go become a soldier and fight for the Germans. You could become a singer. You're the best singer I have ever heard."

He pushed my hand away gently. "Piper, you don't understand. I must do what I must do for my country. What is a song? Besides, what future could a German like me possibly have with a bunch of Jews? You know that the theater is filled with Jewish people. Hitler says that..."

It was the same old hard words, but this time Frederick was saying them as though trying to convince himself as much as me. I looked at him, hoping that sincerity showed in my eyes. "Stop while you're ahead, Frederick. These Jewish people are helping us. Like Sofia. And to be honest, I think you are just touting the party line because you have nothing else. But you could have something else if you wanted."

My boldness surprised even me. Frederick stood as though he had been slapped.

Edie pushed her way through the backstage props. "Frederick! You've been holding out on us. What a set of pipes!" She took his face in her hands and kissed both cheeks. "I'm prouder than a mother. The whole of Casa Verdi is agog. You could be the next great one. They all think so." He didn't meet her eyes and looked down at his feet.

Enrico hushed us with his finger. "He is coming!" His face was red with urgency.

"Who is coming?" Peter asked.

Before we had time to think, there he was. The polished black boots, the impeccable military uniform, the chest full of medals, the dark and gleaming eyes. We scrambled to our feet. Ciano himself was before us.

He broke out into an enormous sinister grin at the sight of Edie. "The grand dame of the American opera, here, in Milan!" he said in heavily accented English. He knelt to one knee and put a hand on his heart. "I am a true lover of opera, one of the last."

"That's nice," Edie choked. "I am a true lover of opera myself. That's why I am a part of an opera company." She was struggling to get into character, but Ciano did not appear to notice."

"Might I make a request, madame?"

"Request away." Her voice was strained, despite her attempt to sound light and gay.

Ciano stood back up. "My father-in-law is throwing a little dinner party tomorrow at his residence in Milan. You must come and sing. And the soldier, you know. He is very, very good." He bowed slightly in Frederick's direction. "The rest of your company is welcome as well."

"Such an honor. Perhaps we shall sing a collection of American ballads, 'My country tis of thee, sweet land of liberty'?" Edie asked archly.

This was met by the sharp laughter of Ciano. "Ha. Your humor is quite, shall we say, *brave*."

I almost blurted out that we could not possibly go perform tomorrow. We should have been in Switzerland by now, with my mother. Every minute here was a minute not spent with her. Every minute here was a minute wasted. Peter must have felt what I wanted to say, for I felt his hand on my shoulder, pulling me back, urging my silence.

"Your wish is our command," Horatio bowed, the feather in his cap wagging.

With that, Ciano, his eyes menacing, the air around him cold and tense, returned to his seat. In his wake, our little band huddled together. "Whatever are we going to do now?"

Frederick was sweating. He pulled at the collar of his tunic. "This thing is choking me."

"Here." Peter unbuttoned the back of the tunic. "How's that?"

Frederick rubbed the back of his neck. "Better."

I still felt shaky.

Enrico and Sofia pushed their way into the huddle. "We must get you out of here. You cannot go to Mussolini's residence."

"What would happen if we did?" My hat-cone thing fell to the side, and I pushed it back to the crown of my head.

Sofia spoke breathlessly. "They will question you and discover that you know nothing of opera. They will think you are impersonators, perhaps even spies. Then the prospect of your ever leaving Italy will become quite slim."

"We could come down with the flu? Horatio and Edie can hold their own with the music talk," Peter offered.

"They won't buy it," Enrico exhaled heavily. "No. You must leave, and you must leave now. We will call in the understudies."

"But they are, um, old," Edie replied. "The audience will notice."

"No, they won't. I will keep the lights so low that they will never see the different singers. And by the time they do, you will be over the border."

"How?" My mouth hung open.

He held his finger up and began whispering with such intensity that I thought he might pass out. "It is a long opera. And we will throw in a few scenes from *The Tempest* to add another few hours. We will keep them here all night!"

Horatio drummed his fingers together. "A play there is, my lord, some ten words long, Which is as brief as I have known a play; But by ten words, my lord, it is too long, Which makes it tedious."

Edie put her hand on his arm. "Enough with the Shakespeare, dear. However, I will admit it was apropos."

"And Antonia has tempted the guards into the kitchen for a dinner of pasta carbonara. They will be asleep by now and will never hear the truck depart." Sofia smiled.

"Her pasta will do that?"

"No, but the sleeping pills she dissolved in their wine will."

The next few minutes were hurriedly spent changing out of the costumes. We met outside the villa, in the woods where the truck was parked and packed. I climbed into the back of the truck, along with Peter, Frederick, Ferguson, PHL, and Fanny. Horatio was already behind the wheel next to Edie. Sofia squeezed in alongside them while Enrico quietly shut the door. Out the open window, Sofia planted a firm kiss on the old man's cheek and said, with a tear running down her cheek, "To have performed so many times with such a man as you is a blessing few artists can understand. Enrico, you have lit up my life with joy."

"And you, my lovely Sofia—" Enrico's voice broke, and he could not finish. He stepped back and raised his hand in a final wave before returning to the villa.

Horatio revved the engine and looked at the map spread over Edie's lap and the dashboard. In the moonlight, all of our faces, still decked out in rouge and lipstick, looked garish and rather frightening. "We head north, and if anyone asks, we are traveling mute gypsies! Got it!" Horatio leaned out the window, locking eyes with Peter.

"Right!" Peter answered.

"I said mute!"

Peter gave him a thumbs-up.

The last sounds I heard were those of the orchestra, the trumpets blaring the grand entrance to the gates of Jerusalem, drowning out the grind of our wheels churning through the gravel, carrying us to safety.

I pulled PHL close to me and leaned my face deep into her fur. The dog smell was comforting, as was her warmth in the cool night air. At least there was no rain. And we were finally on the road once more.

I COULDN'T GET my mind off the elderly residents of La Casa Verdi. We'd only been driving for an hour or so, but the night's chill had already crept into our bones. I was the first to speak, breaking the silence. "What do you think will happen to all of them when Ciano's men discover we aren't there? Will they punish them?"

Ferguson held Fanny, sleeping like a baby in his arms. "In my opinion, Miss Piper, that is a house of consummate actors. They will come up with something. I believe I overheard Enrico say that tomorrow they will regretfully inform Ciano that we disappeared in the night. And stole their truck."

"The guards will be questioned, but they will remember nothing, thanks to Antonia's sleeping potion," Frederick mused. "It really isn't that far-fetched of a story, when you think about it."

"Do you think they will shut the house down?" I wondered. "Many of them have nowhere else to go."

"They have risked losing everything. For us." Frederick paused. "Those stupid singers." Sadness etched his voice.

I hugged PHL closer, her rough tongue kissing my palm, and watched the blur of the trees, their silhouettes made menacing by the dark, whizz past.

IT WAS A STRANGE DREAM, filled with Vikings and Arab Sheiks and loud cymbals and trumpets. Just as the princess was about to fall into the arms of a horrible dark knight, I woke up. My head leaned heavily on Peter's shoulder, and his arm was wrapped around me, though he was still deeply asleep. The sun was nearly up. Only the last few stars were visible in the azul sky. We were still driving.

We hit a bump in the road, and Peter awoke with a start. Our faces were so close, and we stared at each other for a long moment. A jumble of thoughts and emotions struggled to the surface, and I pushed them down, carefully untangling myself and moving a few inches away. We sat in silence, looking straight ahead, both digesting the events of the previous night.

Frederick and Ferguson, both sound asleep, hadn't stirred a bit. The truck rounded a bend and shivered, as though it was cold too. The trees were capped with snow. We had spent the night steadily climbing through the Alps, which, even in late summer, held on to winter's chill.

I heard Sofia's voice in the cab telling Horatio to pull off on a small dirt road. We thumped along over potholes and around deep mud puddles. The sun rose higher in the sky, and all of us shook off sleep. There, in a clearing, was a little cabin and barn. Smoke rose from the chimney.

Horatio turned the engine off, and Sofia jumped out of the truck like a young girl.

"Paula! Paula!" she yelled.

Edie eased out of the truck, stretching her sore limbs. "I guess her sister is an early riser."

Peter helped me out of the truck, but avoided my eyes. I stamped my feet to get warm.

A woman, who I assumed must be Paula, emerged from the barn with a pail of frothy milk on her arm. She nearly dropped it with surprise.

The women ran towards each other, arms outstretched, and embraced, tears streaming down their cheeks. The two sisters favored each other greatly. So much was said, yet neither uttered a word. In one look, they seemed to reminisce of husbands passed on, speak of children living in the city, and discuss their uncertain future. Paula took her sister's hands and kissed them, waving us inside the cabin, speaking in Italian.

Paula's cabin was spotless and small. A little mezuzah hung outside the front door. In the corner, Shabbat candles and a tablecloth were carefully folded for the coming Sabbath. I stood by the fire, watching as she quickly arranged chairs and put a kettle on to boil.

The widow lived simply, carrying on every day as she had for years and years. Every movement was well rehearsed. A pitcher of buttermilk on the table. Freshly churned butter on the counter. You could hear the milk cows mooing and a rooster or two crowing from behind the cabin. It seemed that everyone was up and hungry for breakfast. We most certainly were. Paula poured us tall mugs of buttermilk and cut each of us a thick piece of bread as Sofia explained all that had happened.

If things had been different, I would have wanted to stay for hours, exploring the valley. But as things stood, we had to move quickly. After we'd eaten and stretched our legs, we rushed back outside to the truck. Sofia stood by as we loaded up.

"You will be safe here?" Horatio tenderly asked the old woman.

"Paula's husband left her the farm. It is far away from anywhere important. Besides, no one cares about two old ladies." Her voice sounded cheerful enough, but her eyes betrayed uncertainty.

"But who will take care of you? And what will you do if the Germans come?" Horatio pressed gently.

Frederick pretended not to hear.

"We will be fine. Paula's son is in Palestine. He can get us visas if it comes to that. But again, who wants to bother with two old women and their milk cows?" She stepped away from the truck.

"We really should be going," Frederick interrupted. His eyes were unreadable.

"Yes. Yes, you should." Sofia stopped and put her hand on Frederick's face. "Young man, know that I have seen you. Know that you have the capacity for greatness."

I was afraid for a moment. He knew she was Jewish. Would he pull away in contempt? Say something hurtful? But no, he did nothing like that. He just stood there awkwardly and then left to get into the truck. The rest of us followed him out.

"Paula says you are just a half of an hour from the border. You have enough petrol to get there. If the truck holds up, that is." She slapped the hood. "Godspeed."

The engine revved to life, and the two old women stood and waved until we disappeared down the road. I smiled as Sofia yelled, "Miss you already!"

A half-hour later, the sleepy border guards barely glanced at our passports before waving us on. They seemed hung-over from a long night of drinking and were more than happy to wave whoever through, no questions asked. All of us breathed a huge sigh of relief as we officially left Italy.

"You know, I think they really thought we were a troupe of traveling gypsies," Horatio laughed as the truck's engine sputtered back into gear.

"The monkey and dog cinched the deal, darling." Edie leaned over and kissed Horatio on the cheek.

I now sat up in the front with my aunt. My heart beat faster with every passing moment. Just a few more miles. The map spread out on our laps, we plotted a straight course for Bellinzona, the medieval village in Switzerland where my mother was. The truck's radio scratched in soft jazz.

We reached a turnout and Horatio let out a low whistle. "Everyone out! Piper, grab your camera!"

Down below, we could see the whole of the village, east of the Ticino river, nestled in the valley between the southern range of the Lepontine Alps and the Lugano Pre-alps. The red-tiled roofs of several hundred 18th century homes surrounded an enormous castle, the Castelgrande Bellinzona. "Certain views must be remembered," Horatio said. "We are all on my honeymoon, after all."

The castle was unlike anything I had ever seen. A group of interlaced fortifications built on a rocky peak overlooking the valley.

"It has belonged to everyone at some point. The Romans, the Pope, the French, the Italians, the Holy Roman Empire. The Swiss have had it for the last 150 years or so. They've been restoring the whole monstrosity. Apparently, there's a hotel in there now. Has a good bar. Says so, right here." He pointed at a guidebook he had picked up in Milan when he had bought the map.

"Well, I vote we stay there," Edie said. "I'm ready for a hot bath." Our rouge from the night before was still smudged on and mascara ran down all of our cheeks. We looked like exhausted, droopy clowns.

It was actually three castles; One built right on top of the other. We all stood near the edge, taking it in. "To think, we are so close," I breathed, looking down on the village. "Let's get going!" I pressed.

First, a photograph. Let's commemorate these past few days. We'll take it fast," Horatio begged.

Sighing, I arranged everyone in front of the lookout and focused the lens. *Click*.

The noise had a funny effect on me. For some reason, I felt that I just captured the last moment of my childhood, that everything from here on out was the real world. No going back. No more make-believe. Whatever I faced at the bottom of the valley would dictate the direction my life would take. Slowly lowering my camera down, I stared at the odd menagerie of people and animals. It was the same view as a moment ago, but my world had changed

"All right," Horatio bellowed. "Load up again. We've got to get to that sanitarium!"

I stood there, unmoving. Edie pulled me into the front seat. "Come on! We're almost there!"

~

WITH EVERY MOMENT that we drew nearer to the village, every breath came harder. I felt my throat constrict, whether from fear or my great anticipation to finally arrive, I didn't know. I gripped the door's handle till my knuckles turned white. What if she was gone by the time we arrived? What if the next few days would be the last I ever spent with her? What if this was the end? What if, what if, what if?

"Piper! Piper!" Edie shook me. I realized that I had been listing my fears out loud. I felt her pry my fingers loose from the door. "Stop! It's okay. It'll be okay."

Horatio handed his flask to Edie. "Give her a nip of that. Girl's gone white."

A bitter, burning liquid trickled down my throat. Coughing, I heard my voice saying, "Oh Edie, whatever will I do now that we are here? It's been so long since I've seen her. What will we do if she's gone? What will I do?" A tear slid down my face.

"Now is not the time to be asking 'what if?'" She looked out the window. "Trust me. It's in times like this that we forge ahead. Act now, ask later."

Horatio whipped the wheel around a hairpin turn, throwing us violently to the side. "It's a truck, darling, not a boat!" Edie yelled. "Slow down."

He pumped on the brakes, slowly easing the truck to a lower gear. "When I face a storm at sea, Piper, there is something I've learned to do. I trust God, and I do good."

"What?"

"I trust God, and I do good. That is what we are going to do when we arrive. We are going to trust God with your mother. And then, no matter what, we are going to do good."

I inhaled and exhaled. I could do that, couldn't I?

"Now where is that sanitarium?" He looked over Edie's arm at the map. Her long fingernails pointed at a spot.

"Got it. Nearly there."

# CHAPTER 18

## THE REUNION

"What do you mean! She isn't here?" I stood stunned at the reception desk.

Peter, Frederick, Ferguson, and the animals had taken the truck to the castle to deliver our bags and get cleaned up. I didn't care about how I looked. I knew my scarf was askew, my clothes were wrinkled, and makeup was sliding off my face from the performance. I had run up the long winding path leading towards the sanitarium, adrenaline coursing through my veins.

Attendants and nurses made way as I sidestepped the wealthy patients doing exercises on the lawn.

Now, the secretary looked at me blankly as I gasped for air.

No. She wasn't here.

"Is she alive?" I pressed. My stomach fluttered. Edie and Horatio were behind me now.

"I'm not authorized to give private information to unauthorized persons." Her nasally voice was irritating.

"I'm her daughter!" Inwardly, I coached myself to maintain calm.

"I'll need to see some ID." Could her voice be anymore grating?

"For crying out loud." I'd left my passport with Ferguson, who had all of our bags.

"Here." Edie reached around me and pushed her own passport into the receptionist's hand. "I'm Rose's sister-in-law."

Examining it over her glasses, she said in her vexing soprano, "Well, I guess that will do. Let me check the file." The woman disappeared behind a door and returned a few moments later.

"She was released. Two days ago."

"She's alive!" I exhaled, realizing I hadn't breathed in several moments.

"Where is she?" Horatio asked.

"I have no idea. Patients rarely let me in on their personal lives," she retorted.

"Not totally surprising," Edie muttered under her breath.

"She didn't leave any word at all?" I groaned.

The woman shrugged and went back to her typewriter. This was horrible.

"I did not plan for this." I shut my eyes. "Where could they possibly be?"

"It's the glory of God to conceal a matter, the glory of kings to search them out," Edie said. It was a proverb, badly timed, though true.

I didn't want to search anything out. I wanted my parents, and I wanted them now. I didn't think I was asking too much. I bit my tongue before throwing back something snappy.

The three of us walked dejectedly back down the path towards the castle. "We need a game plan," Horatio said. "Certainly they must have said something to someone! One of the nurses, her doctor?"

Excellent idea. We spun around and raced back to the garden as Horatio tossed out instructions. "I'll take the porch. You take the offices inside, Edie. Piper, you go to the garden around back." I nodded tersely and began stopping every nurse and every aide, anyone who looked remotely helpful.

Yes, some had known my mother and had seen her just a few days before. They had heard she had been released. But no, no one knew where they were. My heart sunk low, and a deep exhaustion set in. How on earth would we find each other? We didn't even know where to send a telegram. And they, not knowing where we were, could not send a telegram to us!

~

BACK AT THE CASTLE, I collapsed in a numb heap in the lobby, barely noticing the large ornate tapestries hung on the walls, the velvet couches and settees (upon which I sat), and the beautifully carved wooden tables. The lobby had been refinished to reflect the original room, which must have been the great hall long ago. I glanced up and disinterestedly watched Horatio and Edie at the front desk, signing the register.

And that's when I saw her: my mother.

On my feet, hands trembling. I tried to call out to her, but no sound came out of my mouth. A gesture, a tentative wave. And then, her eyes met mine.

She stopped dead in her tracks. I saw her form my name on her lips. She wasn't ill. She was shining. Brimming with health. I rubbed my eyes. Could it be?

She ran towards me. Arms wrapped around me. Both of us crying. Her hand on my cheeks, kissing me. "I was so scared! We had no idea where you were!"

"Mother?" I said. "Mother!"

"Your father and I were so afraid when your train never showed up. We heard about the bridge. We tried to reach you, but there was no return address. No telephone number. We were so worried."

I noticed my father now, his own eyes filled with tears. He must have been behind her the whole time. Mother and I, our hands intertwined, sunk into the deep cushions, afraid to let one another go. Dad stood behind the couch, then got down on his knees. We huddled our faces close together.

"When you weren't at the sanitarium—" I choked back a sob. "Oh Mother, I thought I might never see you again."

"I'm all right, Agatha." My name sounded foreign after not hearing it for so many weeks. "I'm all right."

"*How* are you all right?"

She adjusted the scarf questioningly and rubbed the rouge off my cheek with a loving gesture. "How about we get you cleaned up. Then we'll talk." Her eyes sparkled, sending shivers into my heart of joy and relief and mystery.

Edie and Horatio now saw us from across the hall.

"Rose! Nathan!" Edie cried out. Her hand rose unconsciously to cover her lips parted in surprise.

My father stood up and shook Horatio's hand vigorously. "So, you went and did it. You finally married the girl."

Edie laughed, "He took some convincing."

My mother hugged them both. "You're married! I can't believe it."

"Sometimes I can't believe it too! And you're alive," Edie said, holding my mother back and examining her closely. "We thought... Well, Rose, we hoped for the best but were prepared for the worst."

"I know. Us too," she answered softly, drawing me close.

"And somehow we all ended up at the same hotel," Horatio said.

"Providence!" Edie exclaimed.

"That," my father answered drolly, "and it's the only real hotel in Bellinzona."

We all sunk down onto the couches, staring at one another, no one knowing where to begin.

Finally, my father dove in. "We had no idea where you were or how to get in touch with you. When we heard about the train... I was about to hire a private detective, the Italian police are no help at all. Couldn't get through."

"I sent you a telegram from Milan," Horatio said.

"Never got it," he answered. "But then, the Italians are notoriously unreliable."

"I'm never letting you out of my sight again," Mother whispered in my ear.

"All of us, together again." Edie grinned from ear to ear. "Isn't this fun! Quite an appropriate end to our journey."

"Oh Edie," my mother said, "this is only the beginning. I can feel it in my bones."

~

AN HOUR LATER, I got out of the bath, scrubbed down and warm. With hot tea in my hands and my mother's bathrobe soft and familiar on my skin, I slowly relaxed as the reality that my mother was all right sunk in.

We sat on the small sofa in my parent's suite. My mother sat across from me, her knees tucked up under her dress.

I touched her face again and again. Cheeks, rosy red. Same laugh lines, deeper now than before. Real deep peace shining behind her eyes. "I'm just fine," she said, a grin spreading across her face.

Everything felt still, as though time had stopped. Of course, I was deeply happy. Relieved. Probably in a state of shock, truth be told. But it was as though there was something else, something I could not quite put my finger on. There was something more to all of this that I was not getting.

"I don't understand."

Mother began her story. "I was at the end. I had said my final prayers, begging God to let me see my little girl one more time. The priest had come. I don't think they understood that I'm not Catholic." Here she paused and laughed for a second before sobering again. "The doctors had done all they could."

"It's a miracle," my father interrupted from the bed, where he had propped himself up. "No one can explain what happened. Instead of breathing her last, she fell into a deep slumber. So deep, I was sure she would never wake up. But instead, she slept for nearly 3 days. When she awoke, she was well. Still weak, mind you, but all signs of tuberculosis were gone."

A chill swept up my spine. "Like Charlie's Miracle Light," I exhaled. "It's not your time to go until it's your time to go."

"Charlie's what?" he asked.

"It's a long story. I'll tell you later."

"God must have something left for me to do," my mother said.

Then she looked at me. "Agatha, it must have been very hard for you. Being so far away. Looking back, I should have kept you with me. I was afraid for you, afraid that you might see death. But, I shouldn't have left you."

All the memories of sleepless nights came flooding back. Being wracked with fear. Feelings of abandonment and pain. I held them in my hand momentarily, like stones, feeling guilty, then almost angry.

"It was hard," I answered, letting the stones go, one by one. "But I think God was in it. He teaches us what He wants, where He wants."

She looked at me. "You're different."

I looked at her.

"You've grown up."

"You're taller," my father added. "I'm proud of you, Agatha."

I laughed. "It's so odd hearing my name again. Edie started calling me Piper and now everyone does."

"How about those young men your aunt was telling me about. Do they call you Piper too?" my mother asked, her amusement evident.

Without warning, tears spilled down my face again. The months of tension and unknowing washed away.

"Everything is okay now, darling," she whispered in my ear. She held me close, and I breathed in her scent. Lavender, same as always. Familiar, safe.

When the tears stopped, my mother motioned towards my father. "Nathan, go get the present now." My father got up off the bed and walked to one of the suitcases. He opened it up and pulled out a small package wrapped in brown paper.

"You got me a birthday present? But how?"

"I may have been on my deathbed, but I wasn't about to forget my only child's 16th birthday." She kissed my cheek, and my father handed me the package.

"Go on and open it," he urged. "We had it made in town."

Ripping off the paper, I gently opened a small velvet box. Inside was a gold, heart-shaped locket with the word 'Hope' etched in a fine cursive script.

"It's on a chain, a necklace," my father said.

"But she hasn't opened it yet," my mother smiled.

I carefully snapped it opened. It wasn't a locket at all, it was a watch!

"The finest watchmakers are Swiss, you know." She beamed as Dad helped me with the clasp. "It's so you don't lose hope, because God's timing is always perfect. You may think you are too late when you are only too early. His ways are like that."

"If you stick with him, you will always be on time, and you won't lose hope," my father finished.

I gently caressed the golden heart. "You've changed too, Mom. And you Dad."

They looked at me questioningly. "How so?" my dad asked.

I examined them closely. My parents had always been high-strung, energetic people. They were high achievers with a strong work ethic. Now, the fight was taken out of them. They had nothing left to prove.

"When God does a miracle," my mother began softly, "you realize how little control you have. He's promised to take care of us, even if it looks different than we imagined. I am treasuring each second I have with you. I did before, but it's different now. I don't want to take our family for granted. What we realize in hindsight." My mother drew us both in close.

"Let's not lose another day. No more arguments or little

offenses. I don't want one minute lost in the silliness of those things," she whispered.

"We have much more important things to do," my father added.

"Like living." My mother straightened up and pushed away her tears. "You like your present?"

"I love it. I'll treasure it forever. But having you here, healthy, is the greatest thing I could ask for."

# CHAPTER 19

## HARRY

"Everyone!" I announced, barely able to believe it was all true. "Everyone, I want you to meet my parents."

We were all wearing the finest we'd packed, and Horatio was taking us to the hotel's restaurant as a five-star celebration, for we had much to celebrate. My mother was alive. Edie and Horatio were married. I had turned 16. We had escaped the Italians. My hair had grown out enough to go sans scarf, a la naturale! Life was good.

Peter looked at me and gave me a soft smile. His cheeks were a little pink, and his eyes were a bright blue. Yes, life was good and getting better, I thought with a smirk.

In a dreamlike daze, I took Peter's offered elbow and followed my parents into the dining room. The restaurant buzzed with energy. Wealthy guests, beautiful couples, everyone having a good time. It was the most elegant room I'd ever been inside in my whole my life.

So many different languages buzzed above the quartet playing in the corner. German, French, an indiscernible Slavic language. The mahogany table was decorated with candles on sparkling silver stands and a low floral arrangement of floating red chrysanthemums. Our table was right smack dab in the middle of all the activity.

My mother grabbed my hand under the table, and I never wanted to let it go. She kept looking at me as if to say, "Can you believe it? This is real!"

A part of me didn't recognize her. She was exactly the same, yet wholly different. Perhaps she felt the same, looking at me.

In the glow of the moment, I wondered if she would understand how much I had grown up. I glanced at Peter. How much I had faced without her. But that was a conversation for another time.

Tonight was a party. I ordered a Shirley Temple, in honor of my hair. It was sickeningly sweet. Pink. Lovely.

"Make that two," my mother threw in.

Then came the food. An endless stream of waiters in white jackets and bow ties brought large bowls of Zürcher Geschnetzeltes, proper Swiss fare, Horatio assured us. A braided bread and a variety of cheeses and fruit filled the middle of the table.

We raised a hundred toasts to my mother. To Edie and Horatio. To me. And even to Peter and Frederick for their masterful performances at La Casa Verdi. The whole restaurant seemed to partake in our joy, raising their glasses every time Edie stood up to announce yet another feat to applaud.

It must have been very late when the coffee was served, and we settled back into our chairs, worn out from all the stories we had told and retold.

Frederick," my father smiled, "will you give us a concert? I bet we could get the musicians to play you something you know. "

"Oh, Mr. Gordan," he floundered, "I don't know." His eyes darted to where a group of German officers on holiday were seated.

"Nathan, that is an absolutely brilliant idea." Edie stood up and began motioning for the violinist to come over to our table. She turned to my mother and continued, "You really will be impressed. He is so gifted!"

Frederick pulled her arm down, shaking his head. "I am much too tired to sing tonight."

The officers finished their meal, stood, and exited the restaurant brusquely.

Edie looked confused. "Are you sure, Freddy? We were having such a marvelous time."

"Perhaps another night. Actually, I think I must excuse myself. Goodnight, everyone."

Shaking my father's hand and bowing slightly to my mother, he said sincerely, "It was a pleasure to meet you. And I am so happy you are feeling better, Mrs. Gordan."

"Thank you, Frederick," she answered, giving him a kind smile.

Frederick pushed his chair in, gave me a final look, then turned on his heel and marched out of the dining room.

"That young man has a lot going on inside his head," my mother said after he was out of earshot.

"You've no idea," Edie agreed. "I do hope you get to hear him sing one day. I worry he will only open his mouth to sing to save his own hide. He doesn't know what it means to *give* of oneself. It is a character trait required of the best artists."

Ferguson stood up. "If you please, I must also excuse myself. PHL and Fanny have yet to dine, and I am responsible for providing supper for the zoo."

"Can the kitchen wrangle something up for the critters?" Horatio asked.

"I should think so. They have bananas, even in Switzerland, I assume," he said with a chuckle.

After he left, Edie looked at my father. "Having a butler is going to take me years to get used to. It's sort of like having a friend who spends his time cleaning up after you and making sure your life is comfortable."

"Could be worse," my father laughed.

Horatio smiled. "Ferguson is irreplaceable. Loyal to a fault. Kind to the end."

"He doesn't have a family?" my mother asked.

"Nope. Nobody." Horatio went on, "Probably the only reason he stays on. That and the adventure of having a boss like Edie."

No one spoke for a moment. I realized the restaurant was beginning to clear out. Only a few tables were full now, and the musicians were putting away their instruments.

I felt Peter staring at me intensely. "You look a lot like your parents, Piper."

"You really think so?"

Mom chimed in. "I think we have the same hands." She pulled mine next to hers and examined them. "What do you think?"

The three of us looked at our hands in the dim light.

"I think I see it," Peter said. "You both have nice hands."

"Thanks," we answered in unison.

Horatio leaned over his coffee, stirring methodically. "Well, now that you're alright, Rose, what are your plans? Nathan, are you going to hang around Europe? It's probably best to get back to the States as soon as possible. The news is that the tension is growing, and our window of opportunity to leave is closing. We all need to figure out a plan of action."

We all stared at Horatio. I heard Edie groan. "Do we really have to figure out a plan of action just now? It *is* our honeymoon, remember? Everything's all right now. Rose is better. Let's enjoy this one night. And in a few days, we'll all just... go home."

He sighed heavily. "But our honeymoon doesn't change the facts. I'm not sure we can just 'go home.' You heard the radio this afternoon. The danger is real. For crying out loud, we met Ciano. And it doesn't take a rocket scientist to know that that man is crackers. We have to talk about this, and we have to talk about it now."

My father nodded grimly. "I've been putting a lot of thought into it. We can get a flight back to Lisbon and from there hopefully get our letters of transit."

"But I really doubt we're gonna be able to get on a flight to

Lisbon," Peter threw in. "It could take weeks to get tickets for all of us. There's only one flight in and out every week."

"I've got some friends at the State Department. I can make a call," my father offered hopefully.

No one said anything. Edie crammed a little biscotti dipped in coffee into her mouth. "Well, if all else fails, we can travel under assumed identities. I *am* an opera star in Italy, remember?" Everyone smiled, but tension still filled the air.

Suddenly, I felt all the eyes turn from Edie to me. Did I have some chocolate on my face? I dabbed politely at my mouth until I realized they were not looking at me directly, but to something behind me. Or rather, someone behind me. I smelled him before I saw him. And I say "him" because it was a distinctly masculine scent. An expensive one too, not that I'm any judge of men's cologne. I shifted in my seat to face the looming figure.

"Certainly not! Can that be Rose? Rose Klein?" I craned my neck to see the voice's owner. The handsome man, for he was quite attractive, took a step closer. Like all the men in the restaurant, he was clad in an expensive tuxedo. His hair was swept back like a movie star, jet black and well-oiled. He sported a thin mustache.

My mother squinted, and then in beamed recognition. "Harry! Harry Stenetsky, what are you doing in Switzerland of all places? And it's Rose Gordan now." She jumped up and gave the man an enormous hug. "This is my husband, Nathan." She tapped Dad. "And my daughter, Agatha. Everyone, meet Harry, one of my old pals from high school."

"A wife and a mother all in one shot." His accent was deep Brooklyn, and he was focused on my mother and my mother alone.

"You look great, Rose. Real great." He held her out and examined her before shifting his view to the rest of us. "And who are all these other hotshots?"

Mother introduced Peter, Horatio, and Edie. "Nice to meet all of you. Any family of Rose is a friend of mine."

Horatio pulled out one of the chairs, and Harry sat down, energy pulsing through his body. He was full of nervous, taut intensity. His eyes were always moving, brain always thinking. He talked fast and moved faster.

"Harry, what are you doing here?" my mother asked again, searching. "We all lost track of you after graduation. You disappeared. And Gloria had been so in love with you," she scolded him. "She never forgave you."

I knew Gloria was one of my mother's best girlfriends growing up.

"Sweet little Gloria." Harry tapped his fingers on the table and chuckled. "I've been here and there. Busy. Real busy. Working with the National Jewish Fund. You heard of it? Been over in Palestine. Helping build a Jewish homeland. God knows we are going to need it."

"What do you mean?" I asked. "Going to need what?"

Harry looked at my parents. "You better educate your kid."

"I'm not a child," I countered, annoyed at this man.

Harry looked me over. "I guess not. Well toots, times are changing in Europe. Pretty soon, there won't be a safe place for a Jew to sleep. We need a country, and we need one fast. It's that or..."

The table fell silent. Edie cleared her throat.

Harry awkwardly stood back up. "Look, I would love to catch up more. Maybe tomorrow after you've had your family time and all." He came over to my mother and took her hands in his. "I really want to catch up, Rose, and get to know your husband. Tomorrow morning maybe? You are staying here?"

She nodded.

"Good. Breakfast then. In the garden." He pressed something into her hand, something only I could see from where I sat. "And bring your husband. Just your husband."

Then Harry went back to his table, filled with handsome men and beautiful women laughing uproariously. Like a tornado, he left us in a wake of confusion, wondering what on earth had just swept through our party.

"But Mom!" I protested, "We were going to have breakfast together, just the two of us. I have so much to tell you! We've been apart for months."

She looked at me and then at what he had pressed into her hand. A small piece of paper folded up tightly.

Peter leaned over and whispered in my ear as my mother read the paper. "Harry was watching for us. He was waiting in the lobby when you arrived. I've seen him staring at our party all night. He waited to come to our table until after Frederick left. That guy is up to something."

I looked back at Harry. Our eyes locked for a moment, and I quickly turned back to Peter. "He's watching us!"

"Hatikvah," Mom said, half to herself.

I looked down at her lap. The small paper had a word on it in a language I had never seen before. "It's Hebrew," she explained. "I learned it in school a long time ago."

"What does it mean?" Edie asked.

"It was the secret password for our old club. But in Hebrew, it means 'the hope.'"

Edie knitted her brows together. "What do you think he wants?"

"I guess we'll find out tomorrow. But my gut tells me it is Providence that we met."

Peter broke in, "I think it's more than Providence. That guy has been scoping you out. Best watch your back. I'm not sure I trust him."

"Peter," my mother answered, her eyes turning towards Harry's table, "if there is one person you can trust in this hotel, it's Harry."

## CHAPTER 20

## HARRY'S REQUEST

The next morning, my parents got up early to meet Harry for breakfast.

When I knocked on Horatio and Edie's door, I found Horatio wrapped up on the phone, attempting to arrange a new mode of transport so we could all get back to the States. Edie told me she had found an enormous pool in the garden and was working towards her goal of 1200 meters. "After all this travel, my muscles have turned into jello," she confessed. "Got to keep the old bones moving, Piper dear. Even on vacation!"

She pressed me to join her, but I really wasn't in the mood for a swim. I felt adventurous. I wanted to explore the old castle.

"You sure?" she asked once more.

"Quite sure."

"Well, take Peter with you. You never know what sorts of people hang around these establishments. Spies and everything. I wouldn't put it past that Harry fellow."

"You think he's a spy? Not like Frederick might be a spy, but a bonafide agent with contacts and codes?" My mind raced.

"Why not?" she shrugged. "I love some good espionage now and then. He certainly looks the part."

She had me there. "What do you think he wants with my parents?" This was certainly a turn of events, to say the least.

"Your guess is as good as mine. But my vote is that he definitely wants something."

~

"WHERE'S FREDERICK?" I asked Peter as he trimmed his beard. "Don't you think he might want to come exploring?"

"Sleeping it off. He met some Germans last night after he left the restaurant. In the bar. They were up late drinking and singing about the Fatherland." Peter sounded upset.

"And Ferguson?"

"I'm here, Miss Piper," the butler responded, emerging from the washroom. His face was wet and covered with foam. "Do you need something, Miss?" Then, remembering he was in the midst of grooming, he apologized. "Do forgive my appearance! Daily grooming is one of the few luxuries I allow myself."

"I'm glad to hear it," I smiled.

"So did you need me?"

"Not at all. I was just going to invite you to join Peter and I on our expedition to the roof."

Ferguson smiled, looking a little like Santa Claus. "I forget that you young Americans don't have castles. I've seen my fair share. No need to see more." He went back into the washroom. "And do have a good time!"

A good time is exactly what I planned to have. I couldn't remember the last time I'd felt so happy or curious or excited. Room service had sent up some sandwiches, and I stuffed them into a small knapsack. Then, with Peter trailing behind me, I set off for the ramparts, as directed by the front desk (who provided us with a small map).

We wound our way through endless rooms filled with coats of armor, enormous fireplaces, and handwoven rugs. We turned through little hallways and twists and turns, ever leading us up, up, up. Some doors were so low that Peter had to hunch over so he wouldn't hit his head. The castle was the town's main tourist attraction. As such, we passed little groups of people, all armed with their maps, traipsing through the great halls. But the higher up we climbed, the fewer tourists there were.

"The strain is probably too much for them. The strain is too much for me," Peter groaned. "Can't we stop for a minute? I've been counting. Over four hundred steps." He gasped for breath.

I was also breathing heavily. "Only another two hundred to go." I glanced at the map. "From there, we should reach the opening," I read from the description, "and a fantastic view of the village."

I leaned against the cool stone walls. "Can't you just imagine some knight climbing up all these stairs five hundred years ago."

"I feel sorry for the poor guys. Those suits weigh a lot. Up to 80 pounds."

"How do you know that?"

"Read it somewhere."

He took a drink from our canteen and started climbing once again. Breathless and with my side slightly tingly from a lack of oxygen, we finally emerged from the tower. And as the guidebook said, the view was spectacular.

"My goodness," I sighed. "It's absolutely gorgeous." The bright green hillside met with gardens and a vineyard or two. Cottages were scattered around the base of the castle. There wasn't one cloud in the sky, and a slight breeze cooled the sweat running down my forehead.

I slipped the camera out of my bag and snapped a shot of Peter against the rail, his face glowing with sunlight.

Then I adjusted the lens and zoomed in as far as I could. It was nearly as good as a pair of binoculars. I could see Edie down in the pool, swimming in long even strokes.

"Can I see?" Peter asked, and I passed him the camera.

"There's Edie in the pool. And look, I can see your parents talking to, uh, what's his name?"

"Harry," I answered, taking the camera back and looking for myself.

I saw the three of them sitting at a table.

Harry stood up and shook my father's hand. He quickly walked back inside the hotel, leaving my parents all alone.

Their faces close together, they were obviously deep in some kind of serious discussion. My father jumped up as though he was angry, but my mother pulled him back down, urging him to relax.

"Curious," I muttered. Putting the camera down, I turned back around and leaned against the rail.

"Are you upset with your parents for spending the morning with Harry instead of you?"

I kept my eyes glued to their table. "No, not really. They would never blow me off unless it was really important. I think their meeting had something to do with that note Harry gave my mother yesterday."

"Your parents don't strike me as the kind to be involved in any sort of intrigue."

"Me neither. What do you think of all this, Peter?"

"About all of what?"

"My mother getting better, just like that—" I snapped my fingers.

He looked up at the sky and said thoughtfully, "I believe God does mysterious things." Then he glanced at me. "Don't you?"

"Well yes, of course," I responded. "I just don't understand any of this. He could have healed her back in the States."

"I suppose so. But look what we might have missed out on." He took in the view. "Besides, you might never have come to Maine. We might never have met."

He had me there. It was getting warm, and I slipped off my sweater. "But we could have met some other time, under different circumstances. I could have stayed with my aunt for some other reason. It just seems like a lot of stress for nothing."

Peter looked back at me seriously. "It might not be for nothing."

"I guess only time will tell." I took one final glance at my parents below. "Let's keep going." I slipped my camera back into the knapsack. "I want to see the rest of the ramparts."

"Sure." He took the knapsack from me. "I'll carry that for you."

"My knight in shining armor," I smirked.

He bowed and took off an imaginary cap. "Just doing my duty, m'lady."

"My hero," I said playfully, grinning back at him.

"WHY IS it that men never stop for directions," I moaned, dragging my feet. "We've been wandering around for 45 minutes. And all of our sandwiches are gone."

"That's a cliché, and you know it," Peter retorted. "You could have asked for directions just as easily as me."

I stared at him blankly.

We had walked the majority of the wall and opted to take a different route to get back to the main part of the castle. Somehow, we took one too many turns and now were in the deepest recesses of the stone structure. "Probably the dungeon where they tortured people," I groaned. "I want to get out of here. It's creepy."

"I think it's kinda fun. Sort of romantic." He winked at me in that way that made me wonder if he liked me or if he was just kidding around. I wished for the umpteenth time he would be more straightforward.

The electric bulbs spaced down the dark stone hallway flickered.

Peter picked up the pace. "We're going east, right?"

I shrugged. "How should I know?"

"Well, the lobby is east. By the library." He pressed on. "Come on."

An hour later, we finally emerged into the large library off the main lobby. "Civilization!" I cried happily. "Well done, Peter. You haven't completely lost your navigator's skills."

"Ha ha. Hilarious."

"Now that we know where we are, let's go get a soda or something. How about you follow me this time?" I strode ahead and flung wide one of the solid oak doors and was immediately surprised to see a large conference room. Around the ornate table sat five men in uniform, all playing cards.

"Fraulein," one sneered, "please shut the door."

A chill swept over me, an evil frostiness I'd never felt before, not even when faced with Ciano.

"Sorry. Wrong door," I whispered quickly and shut it. As it closed, I realized that one of the five men was not in uniform. It was Frederick. In a split second, I saw embarrassment cross his features. He had pretended not to know me.

"Peter!" I shuttered, leaning against the closed door. "Frederick's in there. With a bunch of Germans."

Peter looked through the keyhole, then he stood up.

"Well, it's not against the law to play cards. And he is German."

"Just like it wasn't illegal for him to deliver those Bund papers!" I whispered. Peter stood up, and I looked in the keyhole after him. "We have to get him away from those people!"

He placed his hand on my shoulder and looked me straight in the eye. "Everyone makes their own choices. We have to let Frederick make his."

A few minutes later, Peter dropped me off at my room, and I opened the door to find my parents sitting close together on their bed. I had the distinct feeling I was interrupting something quite important. Their faces were furrowed with worry. Both looked up at me, surprised.

"Agatha," Mom said, trying to maintain calm. "I didn't hear you come in."

"What's going on?" I shut the door and locked it. I dropped my knapsack on the ground and sunk into the sofa, glancing at my watch. It was after 1:00 in the afternoon.

"Have you seen your aunt and uncle?" my dad asked.

"Not since this morning."

"Go find them." He looked dark. "We need to have a family meeting."

I hesitated, questions pooling in my eye.

"Go now, Agatha. It can't wait."

EDIE PACED UP and down relentlessly by the sofa where I sat, my knees drawn to my chest.

"A decision must be made by this evening," my mother finished.

Horatio and my father sat at the little table by the window. Peter had slumped down against the wall.

"We don't want to pull you into this. We know you're on your honeymoon." Dad exhaled heavily.

"It isn't like that," Edie sped her pacing up, "and you know it, Nathan. You're my brother, so I know you know that." She turned to her husband and said, "Horatio, I don't see how we can refuse. Not after all we have heard. And if what they say about Harry is true."

My mother wedged herself next to me, pulling me in close. "Oh, it's true. Harry is one of the best men on the planet. And the truth is, something is going on over there. I haven't been able to get through to Judith—my sister in Germany. It's peculiar, and I'm frightened."

My aunt in Germany was much older than my mother. Judith was married when my mother was a very little girl and chose to stay in Germany with her new husband when the rest of the family immigrated to the States. That's why my mother's German accent was so faint that you could only pick up on it when she was very, very tired.

"The Nuremberg Race Laws have been in effect for over three

years," my father said. "The Jews have been excluded from organizations, professions. Why, the mayor of Munich even forbade Jewish doctors from treating non-Jewish patients. More and more Jews are denied entrance to university, or they are not allowed to sit for exams. Jewish actors aren't allowed to perform on the screen or the stage. It's nearly impossible to get a job. By now, according to Harry, most Jewish-owned businesses have been transferred into 'Aryan' hands. The list keeps growing. Harry said there are now over 400 restrictions in Germany that are only for Jews. And the Germans decreed in January that Jewish men and women not bearing 'Jewish-sounding names' must add the name 'Israel' or 'Sara' to their given names and carry identity cards indicating their Jewish heritage. And in Germany that has nothing to do with faith and everything to do with lineage."

"As in?" I questioned.

"One grandparent is enough. They are closing in like a hangman's noose. They've even decreed that Jews must surrender all of their precious metals and stones to the state. Without compensation."

My mother began to cry. "Oh Nathan, what about Judith and the girls? And Chaim?"

We've tried to convince them to leave, but Chaim refused to leave his job at the University."

"Nathan," Horatio interrupted, "if what you said is true, Chaim no longer has a job."

"Do you think they've gone underground?" Edie asked.

"Do you think they would need to?" my mother asked, horrified.

"Harry has it from a very good source that soon, in fact, it might already be happening, something much, much more sinister may be in store for German Jews." My father stood up and went to the pitcher of water on the nightstand. He poured a glass and downed it. "And that is where we come in."

## CHAPTER 21

## HARRY'S PLAN

Room service brought trays of steaming soup and bread. Harry stuffed the bread into his mouth and pushed up the sleeves to his sweater. Tonight, though more relaxed, he still exuded intense energy. But his eyes betrayed the underlying exhaustion of a man who had been facing an impossible task for a long time. His hair was not oiled either. All natural, thick curls as wide as my thumb playfully brushed the top of his eyebrows.

Peter opened the door, stepped inside, and closed it. "I'm not too late, am I?" Peter said.

"Lock it, kid," Harry commanded.

Obeying, Peter reported, "Frederick is back in the bar with his new buddies. Singing like fools. The whole hotel is annoyed, but everyone is too scared to tell them to stop." He poured a bowl of soup from the tureen and settled beside me on the couch, sipping noisily.

"I'm not too scared of you to tell you to stop slurping!" Edie playfully smacked him on the head.

"I was just getting started," Harry continued sternly. "You've heard of the kindertransport?[16]"

I shook my head. None of us had heard of it.

"It hasn't gotten the press it should," Harry spoke quickly. "The United Kingdom passed a bill waiving certain immigration requirements so German Jewish refugee children can come into the country unaccompanied. We are allowed to transport 10,000 children. So far, we've helped nearly half that number get out."

"Who would let their children travel all alone to complete strangers homes?" Edie asked, her eyes narrowing.

"You'd be surprised," Harry grimaced. "Besides, at this point, most German Jewish parents just want their kids to survive whatever's coming. Once they start invading the surrounding countries, there will be more. Lots more."

He took a deep breath. "We've got everything prepared in Britain. A lot of good Christian families have opened up their homes. And we are working on figuring out a way to get more into Palestine, but it's complicated. The Arabs are afraid we might get enough in to actually get our country after all."

"But they are just children," my mother said.

"Children grow up," he said somberly.

"I thought the homes were temporary," my mother questioned. "They will go back to Germany after everything becomes normal again."

"Sure, Rosie. You go on believing that if you want to." He stood up and went to the window.

He brushed back a few curls that had fallen in front of his eyes. "We have it from a good source that war will be declared soon. Very soon. We have only a few weeks to get out the last train of children. The borders are already closing up. I can't get in or out of Germany anymore and sending messages to my associates has become nearly impossible."

"How can we help?" Horatio pressed.

"It's simple really. Continue your holiday. You're just a nice American family celebrating a marriage with a European tour. Go to Germany. Go see Berlin. But don't let the police know about your family there." He paused, making sure that we understood that last part very clearly. "And on the way, you could deliver some top-secret, you understand, highly sensitive material to Geertruida Wijsmuller-Meijer.[17]"

"Who?" my mother asked.

"She's the Dutch organizer of the children's trains. The Germans won't let us use the German ports, so we put the children on a train to the Netherlands. And from there to a boat that sails straight to the good ol' shores of England."

"Or Scotland," Horatio added.

Harry shrugged. "Sure. You get the idea."

For a brief second, a smile crossed his face. "Gertie, that's what I call her, is a real trooper. You'll love her." He came back to the table and sat down. Stress lines creased his forehead.

"I've only one question, Harry," my mother asked. "What made you come to us?"

"I am in Bellinzona pretty often. It's a midway point for several of us." I assumed he meant other members of the underground; perhaps the other handsome men and women in the restaurant last night.

"When I saw you in the lobby… Well, let me put it this way, I'm not sure I believe in God, but if I did, I would say he put you right in front of me and said, 'Harry, Rose and her family are the answer to your problem.'"

"And I speak German."

"Certainly doesn't hurt." He grabbed another piece of bread and began to butter it, then stopped. "I do have one concern though."

"What's that?" I asked.

"Your German friend."

"I assure you, he won't be any trouble," Horatio said. "As soon as we reach the border he'll be on his way. We have a deal. I don't think he would do anything foolish between now and then."

"You mean like what he's doing now?" Peter looked skeptical.

"We'll cross that bridge when we come to it." Edie put her hands together and sighed. "He's too wrapped up in himself to worry about us. Besides, he might be a good cover. We have a real son of the Fatherland as part of the wedding party."

That was true, I assented.

"He's a liability. I don't like liabilities." Harry strummed his fingers through his dark hair.

"Frederick's bark is worse than his bite. And like Horatio said, he's practically gone as it is," I threw in.

Horatio looked like he was trying to make a decision. I watched as his face went from pensive to resolute. He looked at Harry and said, "We can do more."

"What do you mean?" Harry asked.

"I've got a very nice boat. We could easily fit a few little ones on it."

"It's a yacht," Edie added bluntly.

"Yes, a yacht. How about I send word to my men on board to meet us in the Netherlands? Let us help with the children. I assume you need more hands on deck, so to speak."

Harry looked perplexed. "Well of course. But you are all..."

"No, we are not Jewish. Well, Rosie here is Jewish."

"I thought you were a Christian now," Harry looked confused.

"Does the fact I believe that Jesus is our promised Messiah change the fact that I am a Jew?" she questioned quietly.

Harry seemed at a loss. "I don't know. If you choose to do this, you must know that it is extremely dangerous. You yourself have a kid to think of." He looked at me.

"As if traveling through Germany with a secret message from an American working for the British underground and the Jewish National Fund wasn't dangerous enough," my father retorted. "Besides, we are talking about saving children here. Thousands of them."

"And, as I said before, I'm not a child." I put my bowl of soup down.

"Touché." Harry had been out-argued. The Gray Goose Inc. was about to embark on a journey into totally uncharted waters.

No one spoke.

"Shall I send down for dessert now?" Ferguson asked. "The chef said they have a very good Sachertorte."

"Definitely send for it," Harry said. "In fact, make it two. And some coffee. It's going to be a long night. Calls for sugar and caffeine."

~

THE WATER RUSHED over my body. It was quite cold but still warmer than the Atlantic ocean. This morning, the pool beckoned me.

"Curve your palm," Edie said from the side. "Like this." She showed me. "And don't strain your neck like that. You'll get a crick."

I tried to relax my shoulders and get into the rhythm. One, two. One, two. One, two. I still felt clumsy in the water, but Edie cheered me on. "You're doing splendidly. Just splendidly. I ought to paint you swimming." She yawned loudly. "Once I get my paints back anyways."

Reaching the end of the pool, I propped my arms up on the side. The steamer chairs were filled with sunbathers in big hats and sunglasses. Edie had dark rims under her eyes.

"Maybe you ought to get in," I suggested. "Might help you wake up."

She held a cup of coffee close, still in her bathrobe. "No. Nothing will help me wake up today. We were up all night," she whispered, "discussing secret plans with you-know-who."

"He's sort of charming," I said, referencing Harry. "In an abrasive way."

"It will take an interesting sort of girl to nab that guy."

I nodded in agreement.

Edie sat down heavily and threw her bare feet into the pool. "Your parents still asleep?"

"They were out cold when I left. That was about an hour ago."

I pulled myself out and sat next to Edie, looking at our feet side by side in the water. I leaned back and laid out flat on the pavement. Edie leaned back with me. Both of us stared up at the blue sky. No clouds again.

"Boy, Maine sure seems far away," I said.

"What I would give for a lobster roll."

"What would you give?" I asked.

She didn't answer.

A few minutes later she said, "Well, you better go rouse the sleepers. We've got to look good for our performance."

Before I could sit up, Peter's face suddenly hovered over both of us. His hair was unkempt, and his clothes were thrown on haphazardly. "I found you. Why didn't you tell anyone where you were going this morning?"

I sat up and shook the water out of my hair. "What's the matter?"

"I… I've got news."

Edie sat up and held her hands out for Peter to help her stand. He did, and once they were nearly eye to eye he said, "Frederick's gone. He just up and left. I found this note this morning. Must have left when I was asleep."

My aunt took the note and read it quickly, her eyes scanning the page. "So those Nazis got to him after all." After she finished reading it, I noticed tears had come to her eyes. "And I had so wanted him to join the theater. His gift was meant for the world to hear."

The sad but simple truth was that the small troop of German soldiers had swept him away with tales of glory and the Fatherland. By now, he might already be in uniform and on German soil. For crying out loud, his enlistment papers were already filled out. By now they were probably processed and stamped and approved, given Germany's penchant for efficiency.

In the note, he thanked us for getting him this far and wished us the best. There was not much else.

"So that's the end of Frederick." My towel felt rough against my skin, and a shiver ran up my spine with the breeze.

"I suppose so." Peter took the note back. "He didn't even have the decency to say goodbye."

"Perhaps he was afraid he might lose his gumption if he saw us again." Edie put her arm heavily on my shoulder and steered us inside.

Then a horrible thought crossed my mind. "You don't think that he would betray us!"

Peter shrugged. "Nothing we can do about it now. Besides, what does he have on us? Nothing at all. He doesn't know about Harry. He probably doesn't even know we are going to Germany."

Nevertheless, a knot had settled in my stomach, and I feared it would be there for quite some time.

HARRY MET us beside two cars that Horatio had secured. One was a Rolls-Royce Phantom III with 'Sedance de Ville Coachwork' and the other was a Rover 10. Both were under a year old and gleaming. I could tell Horatio was quite proud of the finds. "Almost a shame we will have to sell them in Germany."

"Indeed, sir," Ferguson agreed. "I'm looking forward to driving the Rolls. Marvelous looking machine!"

"You have the package?" Harry looked intensely at my mother.

She clutched her purse and nodded a terse yes.

"Good. Now, Gertie will meet you at the rendezvous in Berlin. What you give her will allow her to load over 400 children onto the next train to the Netherlands."

"I'm not getting on another train," Horatio grimaced.

"I know. I know," Harry muttered. "That's why we have you driving across the border. Hopefully, there won't be any issues. But if there are, you are going in with your eyes wide open. We won't be able to help you. Do you understand?"

We all nodded yes. I caught my mother's eye, and she gave me a tiny thumbs up.

"What's the point of life unless you live it." She looked at Edie. "Isn't that right, Edie?"

"You said it, Rosie girl. Now let's get this honeymoon on the road!"

# PART THREE

## THE GREAT NORTHERN MIGRATION

## CHAPTER 22

## ENTERING THE FATHERLAND

The distance between Bellinzona and Berlin was 930 kilometers; roughly a hard day's drive. However, we chose to break up the drive into three days in order to make it really look like we were pleasure-seeking tourists. The first day, after crossing the border, we would stop in Stuttgart. The next day, we would press through to Leipzig. Finally, on the third day, we would arrive in Berlin, where Gertie would meet us at the designated rendezvous.

Any number of things could go wrong. We could be stopped at the border getting into Germany and forced to turn back, or we could be stopped at the border leaving and detained.

If we were found to have any connection whatsoever to Harry and his people, we might be arrested. And if war was declared, well... while we might be neutral Americans, Horatio and Ferguson were both British.

Up until this moment, climbing into the Rover, my wings had only carried me so far on the winds of faith. Now, the invitation to soar to heights unknown beckoned from the whispers of heaven.

Perhaps, I wondered, this was why God had brought all of us to Europe.

The excitement and intrigue of the whole thing thrilled me and terrified me. My whole life in California felt like a dream, and now I was awake, wide awake. Quite wide awake. Grades, school papers, football games, and homecoming dances, things I once thought very important and all-consuming, felt small and insignificant now.

Peter could sense that I needed time alone with my parents, and he opted to sit with Horatio and Edie in the Rolls. Ferguson, back in his preferred vocation as butler and driver, opened the door with a flourish, and Edie gracefully entered, wearing a freshly pressed traveling suit of light gray, with a matching hat.

My mother was dressed in a similar suit, but brown. All the men wore wide trousers and preppy sweaters. And today, I looked more like them in my stylish men's style pants and coordinating jacket. All in all, we looked like happy vacationers. Eccentric, yes. Not many would travel to Germany with a monkey and a dog via car. But that was us. We were a special sort of family. Fanny had a new cage secured in the back seat of the Rover, and PHL lounged lazily in the backseat, a traveling pro.

Ferguson gave me a bunch of bananas for the monkey with strict instructions to not let her eat more than half of one at a time. "She doesn't know her limits. Trust me, I've had more than one negative experience." I slid the bananas into a basket with other commodities, like our water flasks, a hot thermos of coffee, and some sweet rolls studded with currents that Ferguson had procured at a small market near the castle. No one would go hungry on this drive; he was adamant we be prepared.

I slid next to my father in the large bucket seat, and Mother slid in next to me and shut the door firmly. Holding my hands lightly, she shut her eyes and her lips moved.

"What are you saying, Mother?"

"I'm praying for our journey, dear."

My father started the engine. "Amen to whatever you prayed."

I looked in the rearview and saw Harry standing there, watching us leave. He waved once and then turned back to the castle.

"He's a strange one, Rosie," my father said. "But a good man. Surprised you didn't marry him."

Playfully, she responded, "I always knew I could only marry a man with dimples just like yours. Harry doesn't have dimples." Then she said more seriously, "Besides, Harry was never settled. Always upset about this or that. Always moving from place to place. Never at rest."

"You were too smart for that."

"Yep."

"I've never been so happy." My father looked at us. "I've got both my girls." His voice caught in his throat.

He rounded a bend lined with enormous pines. "We aren't going to live the way we used to."

"What do you mean?" I questioned.

"I know what he means," Mother answered.

"What?" I pressed.

He thought a moment. "We were always okay. Your mom and I went to the right schools. We got married at the right age. We ate dinner together every night."

My mother kept going with, "We had a beautiful daughter who made us laugh and was thoughtful and smart. We lived in the right neighborhood in the right house. We went to the right church. Every Sunday."

"Almost," Dad interrupted.

"We were doing the best we knew to do. Better than most. And we had a lot of pride in that."

"So what exactly do you want to do differently?" I questioned.

"You and I never used to talk. I feel like we don't really know each other." He looked straight ahead.

"Dad," I squeezed his arm. "Don't be so hard on yourself. You know me. You know me better than most of my friend's fathers know them."

"But I can do better. I *want* to do better. You grew up, and I didn't even know it. But it's more than that," he continued. "We never asked what God wanted from us. We just did what we wanted and hoped he would bless it. With your mother almost dying, the months spent away from you, all the things I thought were important just aren't so important anymore. That's what I am trying to say."

I let his words sink in, fingering my new locket. "From here on out, Piper," Dad said, "this family is going to ask what God wants first. And then, we are going to do whatever it is he says."

"Like rescuing Jewish children," I said.

"Like rescuing Jewish children," he affirmed. "And whatever else he might have in store for us."

~

WE DROVE on until the sun had set, and each picturesque village flashed past in a blur. We stopped in Zurich for a quick bite at a small restaurant attached to a gas station. It had a long communal table, and the waitress brought us sausages and bread and something that looked like butter seasoned with herbs.

"I don't think it's butter," Edie said, smearing it generously on her bread and taking a bite. My mother flagged down the waitress and asked what the white stuff was.

"Head cheese," she explained after the waitress left. "I'd forgotten all about it."

"It doesn't taste like cheese," Edie replied.

"It's not cheese," my mother went on. "It's the head of a pig set in aspic."

"Aspic?" I questioned tentatively.

Horatio smiled broadly and took a generous portion. "In Scotland, we call it 'potted-heid.' A real delicacy. It's pig brains set in gelatin and vinegar."

Edie put her bread down. "I think I'll take my bread plain today. Pass me a new slice, please."

"Welcome to the foods of my childhood."

"Oh, come now," my father said, "you were raised kosher."

"True, but my mother used to make head cheese out of the head of a sheep or a cow. You know, so it was kosher. I never liked it much."

"What did you eat growing up?" I asked. "I mean, when you were still in Germany."

She thought back a moment. "Well, I remember lots of cabbage, sausage, and pickles. And my mother's cookies. She always had good shortbread cookies."

"My favorite," Dad smiled.

"Quite different from what mama made for you and me, Nathan." Edie pushed her bread away. "Lots of white bread and bacon and eggs. And cake. Mamma made a cake every week."

"Chocolate," Dad finished.

Horatio smeared another thick piece of bread with the head cheese. "My mother raised me on potatoes and oats. And Cockaleekie. That's a chicken soup made with leeks and chicken. Just the sort of thing to warm you up after a cold day of fishing."

"Sounds nice," I said. "I could go for a bowl of chicken soup about now."

"What? You don't like head cheese either?" Peter poked me in the ribs.

I giggled. "There is only so much pork and beef a girl can eat at a time. All we've eaten in days is salami and bread."

"I'm not complaining." Peter smiled and then pointed to my plate. "You going to eat that?"

I shook my head no as he swapped his empty plate for mine.

Ferguson excused himself to speak with the cook and see if he could find something suitable for PHL. Unlike monkeys, dogs cannot exist on bananas alone. "Perhaps a bone or two are left from some sort of roast. Might keep her quiet in the car. She's a good traveler, but I like to be prepared," he said, pushing himself up from the bench. I could see PHL's head lounging out the open window of the car. She looked calm and peaceful, enjoying the air.

"You know, when I was your age, Piper," my mother said after a while, "I always dreamt of doing the sort of thing we are doing now. Adventuring across Europe on a top-secret mission. I think when I went to college to study journalism, I thought this would be the sort of thing I would end up doing. But I met your Father, and the rest is history. Sometimes our dreams come true when we least expect it. I feel like I'm finally doing what I was created to do."

I listened to her words, leaning my head on her shoulder. I had no idea what I was created to do. How did one know what God had created them to do?

"While I was lying in that bed, with hours left to live, I did a lot of thinking." Now she was speaking just to me. "I longed to write you a letter, to tell you everything I hadn't told you yet. I realized there was too much. I could never write it down anyway. I was too weak."

"What were you going to say?" I asked, oblivious to the rest of the table watching us.

"It all boils down to how much I love you."

"I never doubted you loved me for a moment."

"I worried that you would think God didn't love you if I died. But you didn't give up hope, did you?" she said.

What could I say? What inner battles I had fought over that very thing. But some battles must be fought alone. The weight of the locket was heavy upon my heart.

The rest of the meal continued in silence; the seriousness of the task at hand settling on us like the fog that rolled in as we approached the border between Switzerland and Germany an hour later.

~

We edged up to the crossing. A guard in a crisp gray uniform, impeccably groomed, in his early 20s, tapped for my father to roll down the window. "Passports," he said curtly. We handed them over.

"Everything looks in order." He passed them back to my father. "So, you are in Germany for a holiday, yes?"

We nodded. My mother smiled broadly and said pleasantly, "I've always wanted to show my daughter the beauty of Bavaria. We hear that late summer is the best time of year for traveling along the Rhine."

"And you are with the car in front?"

"Yes, my sister- and brother-in-law," my father explained. "It's a family trip."

Satisfied, the guard gave the gatekeeper a signal, and suddenly we were driving across the border.

"Well, that was easy enough," Dad exhaled slowly.

"Hopefully it will be just as easy getting out," my mother whispered.

I turned and looked once more towards Switzerland and freedom.

# CHAPTER 23

## A GERMAN HOLIDAY

Stuttgart was nestled in a fertile valley, with hills covered in vineyards and the Neckar river weaving through the valley's numerous parks. It was remarkably well ordered and lovely, or so my mother told me. It was too dark to really see anything.

It was not a small city. Many of the German car companies, like Mercedes and Volkswagen, had major factories in the industrial district.

And of course, there were horses. "Stuttgart actually comes from the words 'stud' and 'farm' because the city was founded by a duke specifically to breed warhorses," Mom explained. "But that was over 1,000 years ago. The inn we're staying at is attached to a farm, a stud farm. Guests can go riding if they want. It's on the outskirts of the city."

"1,000 years?" I exhaled. "So long ago."

"Germany has a very long history, much longer than America's."

The road leading up to the old place was scantily lit. But after edging along for several minutes down the gravel road, we pulled up to an enormous farmhouse and stable, both of which looked over two hundred years old.

My legs creaked uncomfortably as they slowly stood up. I hated sitting for long periods of time. I stretched carefully from side to side as my father began to remove our bags from the trunk. There was the sound of horses, roused by our arrival, inside the stable. The air smelled heavily of hay and that earthy livestock smell.

A young man about my age exited the stable and walked towards our cars. He waved, smiling. "Honeymoon party? I speak just little English..." His accent so thick it was nearly impossible to understand.

He took a few suitcases under his arm, motioning for us to leave the rest. "Suitcases my job." He smiled in relief when my mother asked in German if there was any tea available this late.

Leading the way to the main house's newer addition for guests, he pointed us towards a private sitting area where a giant fire roared. "You sit. I send my sister, Greta, with tea."

Greta, a heavily pregnant, pretty young woman, arrived five minutes later carrying steaming cups of tea and slices of brown bread with homemade cheese.

"You are Greta?" my father asked.

"Yah, I am." She set the tray down. "I run the inn with my husband. Well, my husband is away now. And my parents run the stud farm."

"It's a big place," my mom said.

We have over 500 horses. It's been in the family a long time. Nearly four hundred years."

"Your English is very good," Edie said.

"Thanks. I once wanted to be a teacher... before I met my husband," she chuckled.

"Is it your first?" Mom looked at her belly.

"Yah," Greta smiled, "our first."

She bustled around the room, making sure everyone had a beverage of some kind, and then said, "You must make yourselves at home, please. If you need anything, just yell. I'm always nearby. You are the only guests at the inn right now, so really, make yourselves comfortable. Breakfast will be out at 7:30. I'll have my brother take your bags to the rooms upstairs."

Sensing our need for privacy, she shut the door and left us in the well-worn, cozy armchairs and couches.

"It's rather chilly, isn't it?" Edie asked, drawing closer to the fire.

"I've always remembered Germany as being a cold place," Mother said. "I was always cold as a child."

Horatio downed his tea and took Edie's hand. "It's because you're tired, dear. Let's go to sleep. Long day ahead of us."

"Hmm," she nestled further into the couch, not quite wanting to get up from the fire's warmth. "The fire is so lovely." But the lure of the soft bed was too much, and she and Horatio quietly left for their room. My parents were not far behind, leaving Peter and me by the fire's glow, Ferguson snoring loudly in his chair.

"If I had my way, I'd sleep down here too," Peter said.

"Nothing's stopping you," I smiled, setting my cup down gently. "How was the ride in your car?"

"You know Edie and Horatio," he laughed. "They sang the whole way, everything they could remember from *Jerusalem*."

"Sounds boisterous."

Ferguson let out a snore so loud that he shook himself awake. "Oh my," he looked surprised. "Everyone's gone to bed, have they?"

We nodded.

"I guess I'll head up myself. Right tired, the stress of facing the border patrol." He stood up.

"Were they that hard on your car? We thought the questions were rather easy."

"Oh, it was nothing out of the ordinary, I suppose. I just don't trust myself under pressure. I'm a butler and driver, not a spy, Miss Piper."

"Be quiet, Ferguson," Peter scolded. "Someone might hear you. We are in enemy territory."

"Indeed. See what I mean? All right, you two. Off to bed." Like a mother hen, Ferguson herded us off to sleep.

~

My room was on the third story with a connecting door to my parents' room. It was tiny, with a sloping, wooden roof.

I crawled into bed, my mind weary from the day's events.

The light and the sound of birds woke me up first. I felt just like Sleeping Beauty under piles of down and the crispest sheets I'd ever slept in. Out my window, several horses in a pasture grazed lazily, the bright sunlight reflecting off the dew with such intensity that I had to turn away, my eyes still heavy from sleep.

I wound my way towards the smell of food. Black coffee, hard rolls, and very thin slices of meat were served in the same little sitting room we'd spent the evening in. Every meal seemed to include lunch meat. Back home, salami was for sandwiches, not breakfast, lunch, and dinner. Thankfully, I found a hot dish of scrambled eggs and scooped a heap onto my plate.

Horatio and my father were each on their second cups of coffee and hunched over newspapers, but Edie, Peter, and my mother were nowhere to be seen.

"Where is everyone?" I asked, cramming eggs into my mouth.

Without looking up, my father answered, "Your mother and Edie are taking a tour of the stable with Greta. You can probably catch up with them if you hurry."

I stuffed the rest of my eggs into a hollowed out roll and walked quickly towards the stable, finishing my breakfast as I went across the lawn and towards the ancient structure.

I pulled open the heavy wooden door, amazed at the immensity of the building. There were at least 70 stalls and a large open space for training in the center. That's where I found Greta's brother working with a magnificent white horse. It was as though the animal could read its rider's mind. It hopped from side to side, then reared up on one foot.

"Piper," Edie waved at me from across the arena. "Come over

here." My mother and Greta stood next to her, leaning against the rails. I joined them, marveling at the horse's ability to dance.

"I'd no idea horses could move like that," I said.

Greta beamed and said, "They are not just any horse. They are the Lipizzaner. From the Spanish Riding School in Vienna. They are very rare and cost a fortune."

"The Spanish Riding School in Vienna, Austria. Europe is a funny place." Edie shook her head and asked, "Are they warhorses?

"No, no. Once, maybe a hundred years ago, but now just for show. Of course, we also have warhorses. Thousands of them and highly trained men to ride them. We provide many of the horse cavalry with stud horses. We are proud of our cavalry."

"Is your husband a horseman?" my mother asked.

"No, he is a member of the Panzers." Greta looked proud. "*Tanks*."

"How industrious," Edie said, looking away.

"Thank you," she said with a big smile.

"So you would like to ride one of them?" she asked. "We offer rides through the woods. It is very pleasant."

Edie and my mother looked at each other and shrugged. "What do you think, Agatha?" my mother asked.

"Why not?" I admired the lovely white animal. "We don't have to leave for a few more hours, right?"

Greta looked at my mother and Edie. "Our horses are incredibly gentle. You really must take a ride. You are all on holiday after all. And in Stuttgart, you must ride at least one horse!"

"ARE YOU QUITE SURE ABOUT THIS?" Edie asked hesitantly as she tried for the third time to swing her leg up over the horse's back. "I think I'm too tall for this horse."

One of the grooms, a grandfatherly man with sparkling eyes, held the horse steady. Another came and hoisted my aunt up onto the horse's back. The rest of us were already on our mounts. We'd all been assured by Greta that the trail horses were quite old and could be trusted with the clumsiest of riders.

"Are you quite sure you don't want to come, Ferguson?" I called to our butler, who was walking PHL and Fanny around the courtyard.

"Quite sure, Miss Piper. The menagerie needs their morning exercise and so does their handler!"

Horatio adjusted his seat on the saddle. "I've got a bad feeling about this, Thor." He slapped his horse's flank. "You better not buck me off." Thor answered by flicking his ears back and showing his teeth ever so slightly.

My horse's name was Odin. All the horses were named after one Norse god or another.

Our guide, the elderly groom who'd held Edie's horse's bridal, mounted his own horse and led us out of the stables and into the pasture. The day had turned gray and cold from a thick mist. It was the kind of weather suited to sitting by a fireplace with a good book. But Greta had insisted we take the ride, and we knew we must, if only for appearance's sake.

Our guide, who didn't speak a word of English, guided our little caravan of horses into the woods. Horatio and my father looked terribly uncomfortable. My mother was a natural because she had ridden at summer camp growing up, as had I.

The horses walked the well-worn path slowly as they seemed to have done thousands of times before. No amount of kicking or 'giddy-upping' would change their steady pace.

I dug my fingers into Odin's silky-smooth chestnut coat and bent over to his neck. I had always had a soft spot for horses.

Peter sat very upright on his horse and gripped the reins tightly. "You need to relax," I told him. "Don't be so stiff. Put more tension in your legs and sort of stand up in the stirrups. But relax your shoulders. You look like you're strapped to a board."

His shoulders slowly relaxed. "Look at you! Much better!" I said.

Turning back around, I noticed that we were falling behind. I gently kicked Odin to get going.

"Put gentle pressure on your horse's belly," I instructed. I heard Peter's horse trot for a moment, followed by Peter saying, in a tense voice, 'Whoa, Whoa there, Freya. Good girl."

Freya, a cranky gray mare, fell back in line.

"See Peter. It's just like riding a bike"

I looked back, and Peter grinned at me. "Couldn't do it without you."

"Sure you could have."

"I'm not so sure about that."

Something about his tone and the way he said it that made me stop and turn back around. How could it be that Peter could always leave me so confused and my insides so torn up?

"Piper, there's something I've been meaning to talk to you about."

"Come on, you two!" Edie called back. "You're missing out on Rosie's history lesson of Stuttgart. Get those animals' rears in gear and come and listen. It's fascinating. She's telling us all about the Duke who started the first stud farm. They were black stallions. Like my beauty!" She lovingly patted her horse's side. "That's why the city's coat of arms is a black stallion. Some of the vineyards are nearly 1,000 years old!"[1]

I could barely hear my mother at the front of the line, lecturing about the vineyards to my father and Horatio. Honestly, I couldn't care less about the history lesson. I wanted to know what Peter was going to say.

"What were you going to say, Peter?" I asked quietly, attempting to look as beautiful as possible.

Looking ahead, he thought better of himself. "I'll tell you later."

My hopes fell a bit, and I turned back around, listening to the hum of my mother's lecture, and the thump, thump, thump of the horse's hooves on the hard earth.

The trail ended in a pretty glen, bright green with the late summer rains and colored with the last of summer's wildflowers. A shimmering, crystal clear stream bubbled through its middle. I half expected Snow White to come singing out of the woods and the seven dwarves to emerge from behind the stream.

The groom helped us dismount. From his saddlebags, he procured little glasses and a bottle of a strong liquor, to "give us strength for the ride back." Specially made from a local vineyard, he explained and proudly clinked the glasses together. My mother translated, and we raised a toast to 'long life and success in all we set out to do.'

I held back after the toast, making my way towards the stream. I felt, more than saw, Peter by my side. He didn't say a word, just walked close by. Unable to take it one more second, "Peter, what were you going to tell me?"

"Only that, I, um... well, I think you're --"

"Peter! Piper!" my mother called. "Get on back here. Time to mount up!"

Peter groaned, and we turned back towards the horses.

## CHAPTER 24

## WHAT PETER AND PIPER SAW

We must have been a half mile from the house when it happened. Once again, Peter and I brought up the rear and fell behind. I won't say I didn't have a hand in urging Odin to go slower.

Who knows what set Odin off. Perhaps it was a twig snapping or some small woodland creature in the underbrush. Whatever it was, my horse became wildly spooked and rose up on its haunches. I screamed and leaned forward because I vaguely remembered one of the wranglers at camp telling me to do that in order to stay in the saddle. It worked. And for a moment, Odin stilled.

He stomped the ground, once, then twice. And then, without any more warning, he broke into a breakneck speed off the beaten path and into the dense brush of the dark woods.

My first thought was how surprised I was that such an old horse could move so fast. My second thought was how I could possibly stay on his back. I gripped the reins for dear life as Odin galloped over rocks and fallen logs, hardly knowing where he was going himself. A dozen tree branches threatened to catch me and pull me off Odin's back. I dodged and ducked and clung on as best as I could.

Vaguely, I heard Peter behind me, yelling my name.

Odin ran deeper and deeper into the woods. The fir trees were so thick overhead that the sun rays didn't reach the earth. And then, Odin stopped so suddenly that I was thrown off his back and onto the ground.

I landed on soft mulch, breathing heavily, afraid to move. Odin snorted, steam coming out of his nostrils, while I lay there looking up at him, hoping I wasn't paralyzed.

Moments later, I heard Peter's voice once more, calling my name.

"I'm over here!" I yelled. The stamp of his horse's hooves were nearing. "Piper! Oh my… Are you hurt real bad?" He quickly dismounted his mare, tied her to a branch, and ran over to me. Odin, still a little jumpy, moved away. Peter knelt down beside me, fear all over his face.

"Are you okay? Anything broken?"

I got up carefully, with his help. "Just my pride, I think," I laughed tensely. "I don't know what happened."

I was on my feet now, carefully testing my various limbs. "Where is everyone else?" I asked.

Peter helped me brush off the moss and leaves clinging to my hair and clothes. "You took off so fast, I was the only one who saw which direction you went. I assume they are all still on the trail. Probably preparing to send out a search party for us."

I looked at our surroundings. "You have any idea how to get back?" A thick mist began to fill the woods, giving it an eerie, creepy quality. I didn't like it one bit.

"Sure," he said, though he himself didn't sound convinced. "We just go back the way we came."

My legs were shaking. "I don't think I can get back on that horse."

"It's okay. We're both better off walking anyway." With Odin and

Freya trailing behind us, we plunged into the woods in search of the trail.

"Do you want to tell me what you were going to tell me earlier?" I ventured.

Peter looked at me. Was he turning pink? Yes! Peter was blushing. "Just that I think you're pretty swell, Piper. I hope we stay friends forever. Maybe even more than..." He stopped and looked to the right. "Did you hear that?"

"Hear what?" My heart thumped loudly in my chest.

"That mechanical thumping noise."

I breathed a sigh of relief. I had been worried that he could actually hear my heart.

Listening carefully, I could barely make out the sound. "Probably one of the factories. Maybe we're near the industrial district."

"Which means we must be near the main road! I don't remember hearing anything like this on the trail earlier."

We immediately changed direction and headed directly towards the sound, which steadily grew louder. Finally, we saw a large clearing and an enormous fence topped with barbed wire. A little closer and we could make out guard towers with armed guards.

Peter tied the horses up. "Let's get closer but keep down."

We half crawled to the edge of the clearing and then got down in the tall grass. "You don't happen to have that camera with you?" Peter asked.

I crawled back to Odin and removed my knapsack from the saddle bag. "You're in luck." I handed it over.

"This is bizarre," Peter adjusted the lens. "Take a look and tell me what you think."

There were rows of men all wearing striped uniforms of some kind. They were very thin and, from what I could tell, doing some sort of menial labor. Something about it felt very dark. I took as many shots of them as I could. "Is it a prison?"

"No. I don't think so. Forced labor is illegal for prisoners. I wonder if... Piper, it might be a concentration camp."

I looked back into the camera. An awful wave of dread swept over me. "A what?" I snapped another picture.

"A place for political prisoners. Jews and Gypsies and disabled people and who knows who else. Anyone who the Nazis consider inferior. That's what the papers say. I thought they were just rumors." He heaved out a sigh. "Communists. Socialists. Doesn't matter who. If they want to get rid of you, they have ways." Peter was whispering now. "We better get out of here. And fast."[2]

I slipped the camera back into my bag and followed Peter through the brush back towards the safety of the woods. Wordlessly, we untied Odin and Freya and practically ran in the opposite direction from which we had come. About ten minutes later, we were once more on the trail.

We arrived back at the stud farm to find the adults huddled around with Greta. They were discussing sending out a search party when my mother spotted our approach.

"What happened!" my mother cried. "We looked behind us, and you both had vanished!"

Greta looked relieved and emitted a stream of German. My mother smiled. "She said, the young man probably wanted to romance you in the woods." But though her voice sounded happy, her eyes betrayed the fear she must have felt at our disappearance.

"Something must have spooked Odin. He took off running into the woods and threw me."

My father came closer and took my hands in his, checking me for injuries. "I'm fine, don't worry," I told him. "Peter found me, and we made our way back."

"How long were we gone?" Peter asked. "We lost all sense of time."

"Just under an hour," Horatio said, stretching his legs out one at a time. I was surprised. It had felt much longer than an hour. "I'm going to feel this ride tomorrow, aren't I?"

"You have no idea." Edie tenderly rubbed her backside.

My own soreness from the fall was already setting in. "Maybe I could trouble you for an ice-pack, Greta?"

She nodded understandingly. "We've no ice," she apologized. "Perhaps a hot bath with special salt though?" My mother answered that, while I would no doubt love a bath with special salt, we had to get back on the road to reach Leipzig before dark.

"All right," Horatio bellowed, back in captain mode. "Let's get packed up and meet back here in 20 minutes. Ferguson!"

Ferguson emerged with the monkey in his arms. "Yes, sir?"

"Why are you always holding that confounded monkey?"

"Sir, the poor thing misses her mother." Ferguson sounded hurt.

"Well get rid of it and get the cars ready."

"Here," Edie outstretched her arms. "Give the little wombat to me. We need some quality time together."

Peter held me back before I could follow everyone inside. "Don't say anything about what we saw until we are in the car. I don't trust Greta or her brother."

Nodding gravely, I agreed. "Oh Peter, what have we gotten ourselves into?"

Peter caught sight of Greta staring at us through the kitchen window, her lips pursed together. He spoke louder and gave a wide grin. "Just between us, there is no one I would rather get lost in the woods with than you."

"You really mean that?" I asked, playing along.

His eyes went all serious, and he leaned in close. "With all my heart."

"Piper! Peter! Get in here and get yourselves packed and ready to go. Your uncle is in a mood," my mother shouted down to us from her room's window.

~

My parents' faces registered their horror. The rumors were true after all; concentration camps were real. I had seen one with my own eyes.

"Nathan," my mother said, her voice laced with fear, "you don't think that that is why we have heard nothing from Judith and Chaim? It isn't possible?" Her question hung in the air, for by this point, none of us really knew what was possible and what was not.

"I don't know, Rosie." He gripped the steering wheel. "I don't know." A sign whizzed past, announcing our arrival in Leipzig. The large city was supposed to be quite cultured, a center for learning and music. It had been for hundreds of years.

My father checked the map and continued following the Rolls. "We should be nearing the hotel now," he said. Not a moment later, he stopped in front a large palatial building: The Grand Leipziger.

Uniformed bellboys rushed out, opened our doors, and whisked us inside, along with all of our bags. It was one of the nicer hotels in the city. High-ranking German soldiers meandered through the lobby, elegant women on their arms. Laughter and classical music filtered through from the dining room.

"I suppose we must change for dinner," my mother sighed. "And I was hoping for a simple bowl of soup. I don't know if I can stand being around these people. I feel like I can't breathe."

"I'm sure we can get room service if you aren't feeling up to a show."

Edie stepped in. "You have to be up for a show. We're supposed to be vacationing. Horatio is working with the concierge for some entertainment this evening. After all, we are in one of the great music centers of the world."

"As long as I can sit down," I begged. My whole body was starting to ache from the fall. I longed for that bath. "My derriere is in rebellion, if you know what I mean."

"I'll send out for aspirin," my father said. "We could all use one, I think."

Another bellhop motioned for us to follow him to our rooms.

All were on the third floor and had a magnificent view of the city square. Each was small but elegant. The walls were painted eggshell blue with gold accents. Little chocolates were placed on the pillows, and fluffy bath towels and pink bars of soap were laid out by the sink.

As the bellhop arranged my bags, I went to the window and noticed a huge ruin. It looked as though a department store had burned to the ground. It was an awful view and a stark contrast to the pretty guest room. It stole my attention, demanding I look at it in all its horrific gaping emptiness. The remains of stain glass still stood upright, as well as large grand pillars. It was something out of a nightmare.

"Do you speak English?" I asked, reaching into my purse to pull out a tip.

"Yes, madam. A bit."

"Was there a fire?" I pointed to the gaping hole and broken walls.

He looked where I pointed. "Oh no. That was the old Leipzig Synagogue. The Nazis tore it down on Kristallnacht last April. It was the most stunning building in the city. Once." He sadly shut the curtain and took the change from my outstretched hand.[3]

"You are not a Nazi then, I take it."

"I don't like losing beautiful things to silly political drama. But don't tell my boss I said anything." He winked conspiratorially.

"No, of course not."

"I didn't think you would. You are American, yes?"

I nodded.

"One day, I hope to travel to America."

"I hope you can too," I sighed.

"Enjoy your stay, madam." He bowed and shut the door.

I turned on the tub. As the room filled with steam, I threw open my luggage and rummaged through for my loveliest gown, the one I'd worn to Edie's wedding. There, near the bottom of the suitcase, I found my old copy of Elliot buried in the folds of the dress. I'd forgotten all about it. My high school poetry class seemed as irrelevant and far away as it possibly could.

As I shook out the dress, the old lines from Prufrock's love song haunted me. I spoke the lines out loud. "Of restless nights in one-night, cheap hotels, and sawdust restaurants with oyster-shells. Streets that follow like a tedious argument of insidious intent. To lead you to an overwhelming question... Oh, do not ask, 'What is it?' Let us go and make our visit.[4]"

I wondered what drew me to the poem just then. Was it Prufrock's fragility? Why did his voice always echo in my mind? He displayed "pathetic passive humanness in the face of intense desire." Was that what my English teacher had said? I had no idea what *that* meant.

I hung the dress up in the steam-filled bathroom to let the wrinkles out and then lowered my aching body into the hot water. I splashed water on my face a thousand times, trying to wash away the vision of the tortured men at the camp and the shell of a synagogue outside my window. All the while, Elliot droned, "Of insidious intent. To lead you to an overwhelming question... Oh, do not ask, 'What is it?' Let us go and make our visit."

I didn't want to visit that place. And yet, here I was.

## CHAPTER 25

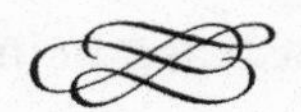

## THE HOTEL ADLON

That evening we listened to a concert of classical German pieces. As we walked back to the hotel, I noticed that my aunt and mother both seemed stressed.

"Wagner and Liszt. Wagner and Liszt," Edie fumed. "What about Mendelsohn and Meyerbeer. We are in Leipzig after all. I know Hitler loves Wagner but honestly.[5] There is only so much drama a woman can take."

I glanced sideways at my aunt.

"They don't play the Jewish composers anymore," Peter answered quietly.

"Wagner hated Mendelsohn," Horatio said thoughtfully. "Blamed Mendelsohn's success for his own failure.[6] I hope Ferguson speeds it up with the car. It's getting cold out here."

"Mendelsohn's statue is gone." Mother stopped, glancing behind us. "We should have passed it on the steps. We didn't."

"Perhaps you don't remember," my father suggested. "You were only a little girl when you left."

My mother was perturbed, "I may have been young. But believe me, I remember. My father took me on a special trip, just the two of us, to listen to a Mendelsohn concert. Afterward, we got coffee and cake and walked to the statue. I remember. It should have been right by the fountain. But it wasn't."

It was true, there was no statue near the fountain by the concert hall. There was nothing at all.

Later, back at the hotel, the front desk clerk clarified that "There once was a statue of Mendelsohn, indeed. But now, all such reminders of Germany's past are being destroyed to cleanse the nation."[7]

"Ah," my mother looked blank, "I see. To cleanse the nation."

"Indeed madam. I hope you enjoyed the concert," the clerk chirped.

"It was a very fitting end to the evening," she answered.

As soon as we were on the lift, my mother fumed, "Imagine. And Mendelsohn founded the Leipzig Conservatoire."

THE DINING ROOM was quite empty at breakfast the next morning. Without all the German officers, I was able to take in the beauty of the room, for it truly was quite exquisite. I wished things were different so that we could freely enjoy it. The whole room was a pale green. Enormous windows opened onto the square and the fountain. There were live ferns, lovely linen tablecloths and napkins, and porcelain silverware.

I saw Peter and Ferguson at a large table towards the windows. "Good morning, Miss Piper," Ferguson welcomed me, pulling out a chair between him and Peter. "I heard the concert was quite a flop."

I nodded, easing into the chair. "I much prefer crooners to classical anyways."

I looked over the table as Ferguson waved down a uniformed waiter and ordered tea and breakfast for our whole party. Each table was graced with a perfect bouquet of light pink miniature roses. Quite feminine, all things considered.

"Where is everybody?" I asked. Ferguson answered by nodding in the direction of the entrance. A moment later, in waltzed the rest of the family, everyone looking tired and more than a little tense.

"I had no idea music could take it out of a group so collectively," Ferguson said, rather surprised. "But then, I've always been a morning person. I do hope the coffee is extra strong. By the looks of it, you all need it."

Peter scrutinized the decor. "It certainly doesn't seem like a Nazi hangout. More like a place for a tea party."

My mother sat down, dark circles under her eyes. "You haven't seen anything yet. In Berlin, we will be staying at the Hotel Adlon. It is the finest hotel in Germany. Some say it is the finest in the world."

"Propaganda," Horatio huffed. "Where's breakfast, dang blast it!"

He was certainly in a mood.

"Hardly," my father responded. "I've read about this place. It's right up there with The Ritz."

A waiter appeared with silver urns of coffee, tea, and hot chocolate. Moments later came the usual bread with butter and jams, along with soft-boiled eggs and something our waiter described as "muesli."

"More like raw oatmeal with milk." Horatio let it glop into his bowl. "I'm a Scot. I eat my oats cooked, thank you very much."

Edie passed him the plate of sausages. "Eat these and stop complaining."

"You look tired, Agatha. Did you sleep all right?" My father glanced at my plate of uneaten food.

I shrugged. It was more that I hadn't slept at all. I kept seeing lines of emaciated men in striped prisoner's clothing marching to a terrifying symphony that sounded a lot like Wagner. Around 4:00 in the morning, I finally dozed off. But my wake up call came at seven, and I was not used to functioning on three hours of sleep.

"Well," my mother said, pouring herself a second cup of coffee from the silver pot, "you can sleep all the way to Berlin."

All the way to Berlin, I repeated to myself.

I held my own cup of coffee close and took a long sip. My mother looked surprised. "You drink coffee now, dear?"

Edie looked sheepish. "It's my fault, Rose. I'm afraid I got her hooked on it back in Maine."

"It's all right, isn't it?" I asked.

My mother thoughtfully looked at my father. "If it's all right with your father."

"Look at her, Rose. She's more mature at her age than I was at 25."

My mother laughed. "I suppose you're right."

"And you really like it black like that?" my father asked.

I shrugged. "Doesn't bother me."

He shuttered. "Her tastes are more mature than her old man's. If she can drink her coffee black, she can drink all the coffee she wants."

~

It didn't matter how much coffee I drank that morning; nothing could keep me from falling asleep for the 3 hours to Berlin, nestled up with PHL in the backseat. It was around noon when I felt mother's hand gently pressing me to wake up. "We are here, Piper."

My eyes fluttered open. I liked her calling me by my new name. "Where?"

"The Hotel Adlon."[8] Of course, the famous Hotel Adlon. Or perhaps infamous. Time would tell.

The enormous Brandenburg Gate was right outside my window. If I hadn't felt like I was in Germany before, I certainly did now. Directly opposite of the gate, through my other window, PHL and I gazed up at the hotel.

It was the picture of a luxury hotel. The first of its kind built in Germany, it was modeled after the Waldorf Astoria in New York and The Ritz in London. And it certainly was a contender for grandness, taking up the whole block in one big, imposing, ornate cube of windows and balconies. The scent of power and money wafted in the air. You could smell the hotel from across the city, I was sure of it.

In the lobby, enormous marble columns held up an intricate paneled ceiling. There were multiple ballrooms, several restaurants, a palm court, a lounge for the ladies, and a smoking room for the men.

Another floor held a music room, library, cigar shop, and barber's shop (which the men made a beeline for). And as with most glamorous hotels, they were quite accommodating to our pets. In fact, they had a private kennel on site. A guest had come through recently with a pair of tigers. What was a little monkey and a collie to that?

The porter did, however, hold Fanny as far from his body as possible as he took PHL's leash and disappeared into the recesses of the enormous building.

With our circus safely stowed away, Edie, my mother, and I were left alone.

"Well," Edie began after a moment of taking in the opulence, "I want to go see the interior garden. It's supposed to have a Japanese-themed elephant fountain."

"Lead the way," my mother said.

After stopping at the front desk for directions, we passed through the Neo-Baroque and Louis XVI styled halls and sitting areas, through the palm court, and into the interior garden. Everywhere buzzed with activity. Never before had I seen so much wealth and power in one place. And it wasn't just German people staying there; I heard French, British, and American accents as well. I saw Diplomats and reporters, a few European film stars and artists, and wealthy heiresses vacationing in the city. It seemed as if the whole world was gathered in the Hotel Adlon. It was thrilling and frightening. The air was charged with activity and mystery.

"And I thought the hotel in Leipzig was fancy," I sighed, sitting down on one of the gilded settees across from the fountain where water playfully streamed from the elephant's trunk. Unlike the rest of the hotel, only a few people were scattered through the garden. "I think the last hotel would fit in one of the ballrooms of the Adlon. Have you ever been anywhere so glitzy?"

"Yes," Edie said, "in a dream once."

"Berlin is the center of Germany. Everything important happens here." My mother's words were said in a playful tone, but her lips were tight.

"Oh come on, Rosie. You have to be enjoying this hotel just an ounce." Edie leaned back against the bench, stretching her legs out straight in front of her. "Anyone else feeling hungry? It's been nearly 5 hours since breakfast."

"Ladies," a gentle voice with a soft German accent spoke behind us, "perhaps I can offer you some coffee or tea? We serve tea by the fountain." One of the hotel's housekeepers, in her early 60s by the look of it, waited for our answer.

"I think that would be lovely. Bring everything you have. We haven't had lunch. And charge it, please. We are in room," Edie checked the key, "211."

Almost instantly, the woman reappeared, pushing a rolling cart that expanded to become a small table. On it was a steaming teapot, several small sandwiches, and something that looked like a donut. "They are berliners," she explained. "We always welcome our guests with them. This is your first time at the Hotel Adlon, no?" she asked.

We nodded, and I took a bite of the berliner. It was donut-like but slightly less sweet than I was used to. The center was filled with marmalade, and the whole thing was covered in powdered sugar.

"My goodness, this is absolutely delicious," my aunt complimented the woman. "I bet your guests leave the hotel 10 pounds heavier than when they arrive. My girlish figure is going out the window on this trip. But I guess you only have a honeymoon once. Ideally, anyways."

The housekeeper laughed. "Oh yes. We are known for two things. First, our food. And second, our illustrious guests."

"Have you worked here long?" my mother asked.

"Nearly my whole life." She poured the tea into our cups. "I started working here when I was just fifteen. The hotel was brand new then. Such a different time. Some wealthy people would just 'move in' for months. I remember a countess who lived in one of the suites for years. Actually, until she died."

"Well, I can imagine it was a lovely place to live," Edie said.

"And die," I bluntly added. My mother shot me a look to remind me of my manners.

Setting the pot down, the woman continued, "They had us learn English and French so we can serve our international patrons better. No one wants to feel they cannot communicate with the hotel staff when they are tired from traveling and whatnot. We at the Hotel Adlon strive to make sure every need is met before you know you need it. It is why we are one of the most famous hotels in Europe. Do you know who has stayed here?" She smiled proudly.

We shrugged. I examined the older woman. She was plump but strong. Bright eyes, still filled with wonder and excitement, like a little girl in her make-believe castle. This was her castle. She adored the hotel, it was her home. The staff, her family. The Adlon was a world in and of itself, set apart from the rest of Germany, which she watched through its gilded windows, happy to be safe inside. And now, with relish, she pulled back the curtain on who she had entertained as guests within its walls.

"Thomas Edison. I saw him on my first day of work. And Henry Ford and John D. Rockefeller and Charlie Chaplin. And that was in the old days. More recently we've had Marlene Dietrich and lots of politicians. American ones like your President Roosevelt. And also the Maharaja Bhupinder Singh of Patiala."

"A full-blown Maharaja?" Edie stopped. "I never. Was he the one with the tigers?"

She nodded her head yes. "Even Tsar Nicholas II, may he rest in peace. But that was a long time ago."

"It certainly seems like a political center," my mother commented.

"Well, that is really because we are so close to all of the embassies. International politicians prefer the Adlon to the Hotel Kaiserhof."

"The Hotel Kaiserhof?" Edie raised her eyebrows.

"It's a few blocks to the south. It is across from Hitler's Chancellery on the Wilhelmplatz and the Ministry of Propaganda."

"More popular with the Nazis then, I take it," mother said. "You must have seen a lot during your service here."

"Yes. More than can be imagined. Which is one of the reasons I stay on. Nothing here ever changes. That's why the people come back. They want something to depend on. And our berliners are dependable. Always the exact same. Always perfect." She surveyed the table, pleasantly concluding the interview. "Is there anything else I can help you with?"

"Thank you, no," my mother said. "You've been quite hospitable."

"Well, I'll leave you then. But if you need anything, don't hesitate to call for me. My station is behind those doors." She pointed to a nearly invisible door behind two enormous ferns.

As she left, Edie took another berliner and held it philosophically. "Do you remember that movie *Grand Hotel* with Greta Garbo?"

"I hated that movie," my mother said. "We'd better be quiet around here. The walls have ears." She eyed the hidden door.

"That's beside the point." She took a bite of the pastry. "I bet that movie is inspired by this place."

I remembered a line from the film about a fictional hotel in Berlin. "People come, people go. Nothing ever happens."[9] Of course, as the film would have it, everything happened at the hotel. Love, death, even a jewel robbery. I assumed the same was true of this place. The line echoed Prufrock's love song, "In the room, women come and go, talking of Michelangelo."[10] The poem was always cropping up in the strangest places.

I stared at the elephant fountain. It was as if the whole world was coming and going, talking about things that don't matter, ignoring the elephant in the room: the Nazis. The tea sandwich took all the moisture out of my mouth, and I coughed, trying to swallow. Mother wordlessly passed me her cooled tea to push the sandy crumbs down my throat.

Edie stopped and looked at her watch. "It's nearly 2:00. How long have we got till the rendezvous?"

"Another 2 hours. She's going to meet us at 4:00 sharp. Harry said Gertie would meet us in the lobby."

"How will we know who she is?" Edie asked, finishing off her berliner.

Mother sipped her tea. "Apparently, she will be the tallest woman in the room."

# CHAPTER 26

## GERTIE

At 3:45 sharp, our men, smelling like cologne, met us in the lobby. Peter's bare cheeks gleamed white, practically glowing. "Your beard!" I exclaimed. "It's gone!"

His hand rose to his chin, rubbing the spot that used to have hair. Peter's face was, as Horatio smirked, soft as a baby's bottom. He also looked about 10 years younger. "What? You don't like it?"

"No, no," I faltered. "I just wasn't expecting it."

I examined his face, his jaw. It was stronger than I had imagined it to be under that beard. He was, honestly, strikingly handsome. I turned away, embarrassed for my frank staring.

"I think you all look fabulous," Edie said.

"He was a real barber, Rose," my father said. "Straight-edge razor and everything. Haven't had a good old-fashioned shave like that in years. It was great. I feel wonderful."

Horatio stood by Edie. "The old man did give great neck rubs." He checked his watch. "Alright then, enough of this golly-wagging. We've got five minutes till the rendezvous. Places everyone!"

"Right. Piper, you're with me." Peter took my hand, and we strode towards an enormous couch facing the east door. Horatio and my father sat at a small table facing the west. My mother and Edie found a lovely archway by the north entrance and stood there, pretending to chat. And Ferguson planted himself under a fern by the south entrance. Gertie could not possibly get by without one of us spotting her.

Peter shook the newspaper he was trying to read. "Not that I really speak German or anything, but I bet this paper is chock-full of propaganda."

"Just like you don't really speak French." I kept staring at his bare cheek. He rubbed his chin again uncomfortably.

"You know what happened when I was at the barber's?"

"What?"

"I asked the barber what he knew about concentration camps."

"You didn't!"

"Oh yes, I did. And you know what he told me?"

"What?"

"That they don't exist. That it was all a lie from the Americans. And when I asked him about Jews disappearing, he told me he didn't know any Jews who had disappeared."

*All the women come and go/ Talking of Michelangelo...* [11] Ignoring the elephant in the room. My skin crawled.

"Where'd you go, Piper?"

I looked up at Peter.

"I lost you for a second."

Focusing again, I responded, "Maybe he didn't know any Jews to begin with?"

"My thoughts exactly. He's bought right into the Nazi propaganda machine though. Most of the people don't know those camps exist, and if they do know, they don't believe it's as bad as the rumors."

"Do you think they *are* as bad as the rumors?" I asked as I continued to study the definition of his jawline.

"Is my face really so shocking?" Peter looked back at the paper. "You keep staring."

"It's just so different. It keeps distracting me. But seriously, do you think the camps are as bad as the rumors?"

"You saw as much as I saw." He looked over my shoulder. "Hey, look. I bet that's her."

Turning around, I saw one of the tallest women I had ever seen — probably 6'3 with her heels on. Her face was bright and cheerful, and she had big blue eyes and golden blond hair. In her early 70s, she was absolutely stunningly beautiful. Like an angel. She stood quite upright and carried herself like an ancient queen.

The woman searched the crowded lobby, looking for someone or something. All eyes turned towards her, everyone parted in her path, giving the woman the obvious respect she deserved. She had the ability, I thought, to make even Hitler sit down and listen. As Edie would say, her's was a commanding presence. "That has to be her," I breathed.

Standing up and walking towards the woman, I gently lifted my hand and caught her eye.

"Excuse me, ma'am."

She looked down at me curiously.

"Are you looking for a parcel for your children? One that was delayed in the mail?" I dropped the code as discreetly as possible. Craning my neck to see her face.

"A package?" she said, quite surprised. Then a glimmer of worry set into her blue eyes. "Harry? Is he all right?"

Knowing not to say anything until the correct password had been given, I waited awkwardly. She got the hint and said quickly, "Oh yes. The package for my grandchildren. You have found it, yes. And my daughter will be so relieved you got it through."

It was Gertie all right.

"Harry is just fine," Peter said quietly. He was behind me now.

"But where is he?" Her voice broke a little.

"Couldn't risk crossing the river," he said, carefully choosing his words in case of intrusive ears. "The water was getting a little too deep."

For such an enormous woman, her voice was much more feminine than I expected. "Oh, I see." Such disappointment. "But he found someone he trusted enough to send." She gave each of us a kind smile.

I liked this woman. Her Dutch accent. Her fur stole. Even her high-heeled shoes that made her taller than she already was.

"So where is this parcel?" She took my hand in hers as I led her through the lobby.

~

AFTER MY FATHER carefully locked the door of our suite, my mother dug through her purse and passed the old woman the package Harry had given her in Bellinzona.

Gertie took the small box, roughly the size of my fist, and quickly untied the ribbon. Inside was a tiny music box. She wound the handle, and it began to play "Fur Elise" by Beethoven.

"Harry always liked Beethoven," she said softly, carefully listening for a specific note. Then, when the note was reached, the little handle stuck and came out. The whole box opened to reveal twenty diamonds hidden within the mechanism.

"My word," Horatio exhaled.

"Each one is between 5 and 7 carats, of the highest quality," Gertie said, counting them and placing them in a special velvet-lined box. "These will pay for the transit of another train full of children."

"Wherever did Harry get those?" My mother looked over Gertie's shoulder. "I can't believe I was carrying those around in my purse."

"You know Harry," Gertie laughed. "He has a way of convincing people to give to the cause. I believe these came from the Rothschilds in Britain."

"Why not cash?" my father asked. "Or a money transfer?"

"To say as Harry would, 'Thou shalt not carry cash into

Germany these days.' It would raise too many eyebrows. It's taxable. And would probably be confiscated or held up in the bank before I could get to it. Diamonds are much more portable. And they can be sold on the black market. They'll be used to bribe railroad workers and any troublesome German officials we may meet on the way."

She continued, "The Great Depression in Germany severely damaged Berlin's economy. It's one of the reasons Hitler was elected. There was utter chaos. The Communist and the Nazi parties were literally fighting in the streets. When Hitler seized control, he took over every civic organization, excluding the church. Meanwhile, thousands of his opponents fled."

"Or were imprisoned," I threw in.

"Exactly." She went on, "And that was only 6 years ago. What you see in this hotel is not what the rest of the city experiences. There are still shortages. Still money troubles. It's one of the reasons we can get so much for the diamonds." Her tone darkened. "It is also why so many have turned on the Jews. Hitler's rhetoric blames them for the country's economic troubles."

"That is ridiculous," my mother said.

"Certainly. It is the Great War that is to blame for that, but everyone wants a scapegoat. And then there are the scapegoat's' children."

Folding the box up and securing it in her stole, Gertie leaned forward. "So, are you quite sure you want to help with the transport? This is not child's play. The risk is real. If you want to back out now," she was darkly serious, "I will bear you no ill will."

Edie answered for all of us. "We are all in, you can count on us."

"All right. Here is the plan. It will take me a day or two to sell these. Another two days to arrange the children. You are motoring to the Netherlands, no? Your part from here on out is quite simple. Just be at the harbor in The Hague a week from today. We'll put a load of children onto your boat and whisk them off to safety."

"Is there anything else we can do?" Horatio offered. "Certainly, there is something."

"You are so kind. You have already done more than you can imagine." The tall woman stood to leave. "I will be seeing you very soon."

Before she reached the door, she paused and looked back. "And stay clear of the Gestapo. They are quite dangerous, even to foreign nationals like us. They can detain whoever they want."

"We'll be cautious," my father assured her.

"One thing, before you go." My mother pulled her aside.

"Yes?"

"My sister- and brother-in-law live in Berlin. Harry said to say nothing about our connection. They are Jewish, you see. I must have sent 10 telegrams in Switzerland and received not one response. I've tried calling their home 5 times since arriving, all from public phones, mind you. Not from anything traceable."

Gertie looked down at my mother, troubled. "I wish I had more comforting words for you. Many people have disappeared from Berlin of late."

"Then we must look for them!" my mother exclaimed. "Nathan, we must!"

My father looked at Gertie. "How long will it take to get to The Hague?"

Gertie shrugged and answered, "It's not more than a day's drive, if that. You have several days to search if you must."

My father looked at Gertie resolutely. "We must. It's family."

Gertie's eyes filled with pity. "Family. Of course. I understand. Well, may God grant you success." She walked towards the door. "And God willing, we will meet in the Netherlands before the week is out."

WE STOOD on the steps of a large townhouse a block from the University. My aunt and uncle had lived in this home since Uncle Chaim took the job as Professor of Applied Mathematics nearly 20

years before. It was four stories high, and some of the rooms on the top floor were rented out to students. The white stone facade framed large windows that opened out onto the street. Aunt Judith was a wonderful host and loved the students. The home was always open, always filled with young people. My cousins were practically raised in a student's dormitory, my mother used to laugh.

She'd described the home as clean and simple and warm. Filled with books and a huge dining room table, the one my mother always spoke of so fondly from her childhood that had been left with her sister. Judith loved to bake and always had plates of rugelach for the students.

We knocked and rang the bell again.

No answer.

We had discussed splitting up, some of us waiting at the hotel and another group going on the hunt for Judith, Chaim, and the girls, but no one wanted to miss out. To quote Edie, it was an "all for one, one for all" sort of adventure. And so, all of us had loaded up in the cars and meandered through the streets of Berlin in search of the house.

Turning towards my mother, Dad asked, "Rose, are you certain this is the right address?"

"Quite sure." She looked down at her pocket address book and put it back in her purse. "Besides, she sent me a photograph of the house years ago. You know, the one from when the girls were little, all seated right here on these steps. This is the place."

"Well, it may be the right place, but I don't think anyone is home." Edie stood on her tiptoes and tried to see in. "All the lights are off. Wait—someone is coming. A maid by the looks of it."

"Chaim could never afford a maid." My father looked confused. "Not on a teacher's salary."

"Professor," my mother corrected.

"Big difference," he retorted.

The heavy door creaked open, and a stern looking maid looked at us blankly.

"Yah?"

My mother shuffled uneasily and explained that she was looking for Chaim and Judith Adelman.

The maid tersely answered that the Adelmans had moved several months ago and that she had no idea where they were. "But why did they move?" my mother gasped.

"I don't ask why Jews do what they do," she spat in German.

With that, she shut the door with resounding firmness. My mother's shoulders sagged, and my father protectively put his arm around her shoulders. "Oh Nathan, whatever do we do now?" she said, a single tear falling down her cheek.

Gertie's voice echoed ominously, "*Many people have disappeared from Berlin of late.*" Peter and I glanced at one another, both paling.

"Perhaps we should try the University?" Edie wondered out loud. "Maybe someone there will know where they are."

"Edie's right." My father agreed. "I'm surprised we hadn't thought of that. Okay, everyone back in the cars. Ferguson, lead the way!"

# CHAPTER 27

## THE JAZZ CLUB

The University of Berlin was enormous. Like any university, there were students scattered about the campus studying. Professors, distinguished by their flowing dark robes, walked quickly to and from class. An enormous flag with a swastika hung bleakly from the top of the University tower.[12]

Ferguson waited with the cars while the rest of us walked as calmly as possible into the university's quadrangle. Mom pointed out that the lush garden that had once filled the center had been replaced by cold pavement. It was a bleak place, as gray and cold as the sky.

"There must be a directory somewhere around here," Peter said, "You know, of where the different departments are and where everyone's office is."

A young woman, her blond hair in a soft bob and wearing glasses, noticed our confusion. Her sensible block heels clumped along the hard brick pavers to where we stood. "You are Americans?" she asked in English. "You need some help, yah?"

"Yes," my mother said. "We are looking for Professor Chaim Adelman?"

"Adelman?" The girl tilted her head. "What department?"

"Maths and Sciences."

"Oh yes, you'll want the building over there." She pointed to a large brick hall. "There is a receptionist on the first floor who can help you." She looked at Peter and I. "You are prospective students?"

We shook our heads no, just looking for an old friend.

Her eyes narrowed. His was clearly a Jewish name. "A professor named Chaim Adelman?" she repeated.

I felt my father's hands on my shoulders, steering me towards the building she had pointed out. Turning back towards the young woman, I said cheerfully, "Thanks so much for your help."

She watched us cross the courtyard, and we all exhaled in relief once safe in the Maths and Sciences building.

The feeling was short-lived. Just 10 minutes later we were back in the quad, quite confused and with worry growing.

"Professor Adelman has taken another job," the receptionist had explained. "And no, I have no idea where or why." With that, she had dismissed us with a flick of her hand.

We stood shivering in the damp with nowhere to go, no leads at all. It was awful. Peter and I sank to a bench. My father held my mother tightly. Horatio and Edie stood close to one another. "Perhaps we ought to go to the authorities?" my mother asked weakly.

"I think that would just make things worse," Edie replied. She looked at the sky. "Oh God, have mercy." Her breath made a thin vapor in the cold air. "Show us what to do."

Peter stood up abruptly. "This place is giving me the creeps."

Horatio shuffled his feet. "Look, evening's setting in. How about we go find a coffee shop and regroup, come up with a new plan? There has to be something we can do. It just hasn't come to us yet."

A loud gong rang over the campus, adding an eerie quality to the horrible moment.

A young man, about Peter's age and pushing a bicycle, stopped. He leaned the bike against the back of our bench and came around to the other side.

"You are looking for Professor Adelman, no? I overheard you asking around." His eyes searched furtively to the left and to the right. No one was within earshot. I realized he must have been waiting for the crowd in the courtyard to thin before approaching us.

He was a handsome sort. Big green eyes, fair skin, light brown hair. He was small, not more than 5'6, and quite thin. He had an appealing, honest quality.

"Yes!" My mother stepped towards him. "You know what has happened?"

"Keep your voice down, madam," the young man said quietly. "Why are you looking for the Professor?"

My father looked at my mother, wordlessly warning her not to share too much.

"His wife, Judith, was an old friend. I've been trying to get in touch with her, but they moved out of their home, and it appears that Chaim no longer works at the university."

"All of the Jewish professors were let go a few months ago," he said, extending his hand. "I'm Rolf. I was good friends with the Adelman's. Actually, I rented a room from them until the Nazis took the house."

"The Nazis took the house?" My father looked appalled.

Rolf shook his head sadly. "It's been nearly two months since they were evicted."

"Do you know where they are? Chaim and Judith and the girls?"

"I know where the girls are," he said simply.

"But what about Judith and Chaim?"

Rolf looked around tentatively. "Look, we can't talk here. Where are you staying?"

"The Hotel Adlon," Horatio stepped closer.

Rolf's face darkened. "That won't do either. Look, there's a place we go, all the students. It's a jazz club. Do you like jazz?"

"I thought Hitler outlawed jazz.[13] Called it degenerate," my father pressed.

"It's underground, if you know what I mean."

My parents looked at each other. "You mean, it's illegal. Like a speakeasy?" my mother whispered.

"Look, do you want to know about the girls or not?"

Shaking her head emphatically yes, she looked at my father, then back to the young man.

"All right then." He scribbled the street and house number on a scrap of paper and passed it to my aunt. "Here's the address. It's not too far from campus. Come tonight at nine. I'll meet you there."

THE CLUB WAS LITERALLY UNDERGROUND, in the basement of an apartment building in a not-so-fabulous part of town. Horatio kept Edie close to his side and begged her not to wander off alone. There was no sign of the club from the street, only the dim glow of lights and a faint hum of jazz music.

"What does degenerate mean?" I asked.

Edie looked back towards me. "Debased, degraded, corrupt. Hitler thinks jazz is the evidence of mental and moral decline."

The rowdy music grew louder. Edie went on, "Stupid reasoning really. Jazz is alive. It's progressive. New, moving, *real*. Music that you can feel. I'd much rather listen to jazz than Wagner."

She paused before saying, "Wagner, now that is degenerate."

Descending the smoky, badly lit stairs, with highly disreputable characters lounging about, I began to have serious doubts that we should have trusted Rolf. "Peter, this was a terrible idea. A completely terrible idea. We are going to be murdered," I whispered.

But Peter actually looked quite relaxed. "Don't worry. I'll protect you," he chuckled. "Besides, haven't you always wanted to visit an underground speakeasy?"

No, I had absolutely never wanted to visit a place like this. I could smell stale smoke and sweat from the stairwell.

"And who is going to protect us when the Gestapo storm the place?" I muttered.

My parents, like two fish out of water, pushed the door open, and a wave of smoke and a blast of a trumpet exploded over us. I almost expected to be blown backward by its power.

The badly lit room was packed full of people, old and young. They sat around tables smoking, drinking, and eating bowls of what looked to be cabbage soup. A small platform crammed with musicians was the center of activity. A large black woman crooned a song in French, her voice husky and rich. Some students were arguing over a book loudly in one corner and nearly coming to blows by the look of it. I hung back, but Peter pulled me forward.

Edie beamed, "How lovely." She swayed slightly to the music. "Maybe we should dance, Horatio. This place it pretty romantic."

Horatio took in the room. "Where? In the 2 foot by 2 foot corner near the bathrooms?"

Rolf saw us from his table on the far side of the club and waved us over. He kicked a few students out of their chairs and offered them to us. When we finally were seated, Rolf ordered us bowls of soup.

"You like the singer?"

She was wonderful, yes. But then again, we hadn't come to hear the music. Why had Rolf brought us here?

"It's one of the only clubs she can perform in. And Jews performing jazz? Doubly dangerous."[14] He looked at the performers. "The violinist? He's world famous, used to be in the Vienna Philharmonic. Now he plays here and makes pennies. Happy to get a bowl of soup for a song."

"Jewish?" I asked grimly.

Rolf nodded and slurped his soup noisily. He looked at my mother and father squarely.

"Why are you really looking for the Professor?" Rolf said bluntly. "These are dangerous times. How do I know I can trust you?"

"How do we know we can trust you?" Peter retorted.

Rolf rolled his eyes. "I lived with them for two years. Lorelei and I were... We are... Look, all you need to know is that I think of the Professor like family."

"Prove it," Peter said again.

Rolf pulled out a photograph from his wallet. It was him and my cousin Lorelei. She was standing there, her hand in his. They were by a river. And they looked very happy.

My mother took the photograph in her hands. She looked up at Rolf, eyes brimming with tears. "I'm Judith's sister."

"Oh," he said, taking the picture back. "I see." Understanding washed over Rolf's face. He looked utterly relieved and completely pained at the same time.

Folding the photograph carefully and putting it back in his wallet, he said, "Your sister and her husband were like my parents. I even called them Mom and Dad, if you can believe it. We were very close." He paused, his face awash with grief.

"So you have information of where they are?" my father asked.

"See for yourself," Rolf answered, his eyes turning towards the stage. The singer finished her song and stepped off the platform to raucous applause. The musicians stepped back and formed a little circle. The trumpeter replaced his horn with a ukulele.

Three beautiful young women, all in their twenties, stepped gracefully onto the stage. They wore matching, simple black suits, but each woman was quite different from the other. Something about them was familiar, and as I looked closer, I realized who they were.

"Mother," I gasped. "It's Lorelei, Katrine, and Grace!"

My mother, mouth open in shock, stood up, but my father pulled her back down, whispering to wait.

The sisters stood close together. The ukulele struck a chord, and then they were off and running. For girls who looked so different, their voices melded in perfect unity. I couldn't pick out who was who, their harmonies were so tight. The song was a silly American one that the Andrews Sisters sang called "Hold Tight, Hold Tight, Want Some Seafood Mama."[15]

The audience loved it. They laughed and sang along, clapping and joining in on the chorus.

The next ballad was a slow one in German. Katrine took off on a solo, with Lorelei and Grace singing a lilting hum in the background. Of course, I had no idea what she was saying, but I knew the song was sad. It almost looked as though she was about to cry.

Just as the song ended, Katrine scanned casually over the crowd. A double take, then a gasp. She turned to the violinist and whispered something in his ear. He nodded in understanding and began to play a gentle melody. Then she jumped off the stage and ran towards my mother.

"Aunt Rose?" she called. "It can't be!" Her sisters were close behind her.

## CHAPTER 28

## THE COUSINS

We sat huddled together, the table filled with empty bowls of soup. The musicians were putting away their instruments. It must have been close to midnight. All the patrons were gone. All except us.

Katrine's face was drawn and haggard on closer inspection. Dark circles were under her eyes. She was small, with long, dark hair. Lorelei sat very close to Rolf, his arm around her shoulders. Her green eyes were still wide with astonishment at the night's turn of events. Grace was wedged between my mother and I, clinging tightly to Mom's arm. Her blue eyes revealed a woman who had experienced too much tragedy for one so young.

"The Gestapo took them away. I don't know where." Katrine's voice was exhausted and tense.

"What do you mean, you don't know where?" Horatio questioned.

"It's not like I can go to Nazi headquarters and ask where they are. I could get arrested myself."

"On what charge?"

"On the charge of being born a Jew," she spat out.

Rolf stepped in. "I've put out some feelers. I have some connections. They are most likely in one of the new concentration camps."

"But whatever for? Chaim was a math professor," my mother stuttered.

"He was also vocal to his students about his feelings towards the Nazi party," Rolf answered.

The story came out in bits and pieces. The Nazis had confiscated the house not long after Chaim and Judith's arrest. The girls had nowhere to go, but Rolf was able to secure them a small apartment near his own. Katrine was forbidden by the Nazis to take her final exams for her Masters in History from the university. Lorelei had been let go from her position as the chief clerk at a successful law firm. And Grace was flatly denied entry to the university at all.

All of their parent's money had been confiscated, along with the house. The only way they were able to buy enough bread each week was by performing at the underground jazz club.

"It's a miracle really," Grace said, "that mother taught us how to sing. And you can live off of soup and bread for a long time."

"As long as there is coffee." Lorelei gave a thin smile.

"But why didn't you write us? Why didn't you let us know what had happened?" I asked my cousins.

"It's not that simple," Lorelei looked down. "We are in hiding. We can't send messages or letters. They would throw them away if we said anything against the Reich. Or they would track us down and send us wherever they are sending everyone else."

She broke down suddenly. "So many people are gone." Edie drew her in and held her, allowing her to cry. Rolf rubbed her back comfortingly.

"We've got to get the girls out of here, Nathan," my mother said firmly.

Katrine sat upright. "No! I'm not leaving without my parents," she said staunchly.

Lorelei echoed the sentiment. "And I'm not leaving without Rolf."

Grace looked from one sister to the other. "Well, we have to do something. If you ask me—"

"No one asked you," Katrine silenced her little sister. "Lorelei and I are the eldest, and we are not leaving."

Rolf looked crestfallen. He crumbled up a crust of bread, sadly shaking his head. "But you must. All of you must."

Lorelei turned on him. "How can you say that?" she cried. "How can I live without you, now that my parents are gone?"

"How can you live if you don't go? You know what they are saying, Lorelei. It is only going to get worse. Much worse!"

"And what of you? They'll make you join the army!"

"If they do, I'll keep doing what I'm doing now. No doubt the underground needs those on the inside."

"You'll be shot, Rolf!"

"I could be shot now. Everyone in this club could be shot. You're going, all of you are going." He looked seriously at the girls. "Your parents asked me to take care of you, and I'm telling you what they would want. They would tell you to get out now, while you still can."

Katrine started to protest, but was silenced by a look from Rolf.

"I'm doing everything I can to find your parents. What good would it be to them if you are arrested? The political climate is only becoming more dangerous. Escape before it's too late."

Katrine hung her head and breathed a sigh of defeat. "All right. You are right. I don't want to leave, but I suppose we must."

The question was, how?

Their papers identified them as Jews, and as such, all travel was restricted.

Getting my reluctant cousins out of the country was going to take a lot of creativity. And at the moment, no one was feeling very creative. Rather, we were all depressed and anxious.

Grace stood up. "I'll go make us something warm." She disappeared into the club's kitchen and came back with a pot of exceptionally strong coffee.

"Good thinking." Horatio poured a mugful of the thick brew. "Reminds me of Cookie's coffee. My goodness, I am looking forward to being back on the *Goose*. And I thought I knew how to navigate storms. No storm I've faced at sea comes close to what we are dealing with now."

Edie slapped his arm. "Be quiet. I'm thinking."

Edie was in one of her moods. She was now pacing back and forth, a great idea brewing just beneath the surface, ready to explode like a geyser. "I've got it!" she finally said, clasping her hands together.

"Horatio!" She spun on her heel and faced the table. "You are about to become a father!"

Horatio blushed crimson. "What!"

Edie laughed. "No! Not that!" She kissed his cheek, looking at my cousins. "We are going to adopt three German girls."

We all turned and looked at Lorelei, Grace, and Katrine. "Umm... Edith," Katrine said confusedly. "We are all in our twenties. Besides, the adoption process is quite long. It can take months."

"You don't understand," Edie exclaimed, her eyes bright with excitement. "We'll get forged documents. We'll change your names, stretch your ages a bit. Without makeup and with more simple hairstyles, I think we can pull it off."

"Forged documents?" My father's brows furrowed.

"Matching sweaters and bows. Flat plain shoes." My mother tilted her head to the side. "It just might work. We've only got to make them look like teenagers."

"The papers will take the best forger," Rolf said, absorbing the idea. "And we will need the documents quickly."

"We have 4 more days before we need to be in the Netherlands," Peter offered.

"How are we going to find a forger this late in the game?" my mother asked. She looked down. "I never thought I would hear those words come out of my mouth. But then again, I never thought I would be in an illegal jazz club either."

Edie looked mischievously at my mother. “It’s never too late to start acting a bit rebellious, Rose. We’ve been good girls our whole lives. I wouldn’t want to die without pressing the limits a little.”

Horatio looked sideways at Edie. ‘Reign it in, dear. We wouldn’t want your wild side to draw too much attention.”

“What, like smuggling three adult women out of Germany might raise an eyebrow or two back home? No one will believe me when we get back to Maine. No one!” She sat back proudly. “It will make great fodder for my next book.” Then, her courage waned. “That is, if we can pull it off.”

My father drew our attention back to the task at hand. “So we have to find a forger?”

Rolf sighed. “It’s not really a matter of finding him. It’s a matter of getting to him.”

His name was Jean-Baptiste Renauld. He was French. Conniving. Dashing. And he was the forger. The best in Berlin, explained Rolf.

When Rolf said it was a matter of getting to him, he meant just that. And the only people who got to Jean-Baptiste Renauld were those who got a seat at his poker table in the Smoking Room at the Hotel Adlon.

“Well, at least we are all staying at the same place.” Peter stared at the dregs of coffee in his cup. By this point, Grace and I had stretched out on the floor, nearly asleep.

“Jean-Baptiste is more than just an expert forger. In fact, forgery for him is sort of a hobby. His actual profession is gambling,” Rolf said. He was quite alert and awake, and I wondered whether he ever slept.

“How do you know all this?” my father asked Rolf.

Rolf gave my father a look that said, “Don’t ask me questions that I can’t answer.”

According to Rolf, the gambling forger, or forging gambler, was protected by members of the mafia. Just which mafia, Rolf declined to expound upon. The infamous character had ties to every underworld thug you could imagine. He took no messages and allowed no one near him unless they were willing to put down big money in a game. The stakes were always high, and Jean-Baptiste always came out on top.

He allowed top Nazi officials to win just enough to keep himself from getting arrested. Even Nazis liked to gamble, so they ignored his other hobbies. But he cleaned everyone else's clock to support his decadent lifestyle, which, luckily for us, was based at the Hotel Adlon. His poker games in the Smoking Room were legendary, and entry to the table was both difficult and dangerous. And when he felt like it, he put his artistic skills to use. That is, for those willing to pay.

"We just need to get into that Smoking Room," Peter said.

"You know," I said after a minute, "Edie is a rather good poker player."

I remembered the drawer in Edie's kitchen in the lighthouse, the one with her neighbor's wife's false teeth. What was it Edie had said, that she had never lost one game? "You won that bike, remember? And the couch."

Edie nodded, but said, "I never play for money though!"

"Couldn't you play for money," I pushed, "if you had to?"

She bit on her coffee spoon and said in an apprehensive tone, "I suppose I could. But how would I get a place at the table?"

Horatio looked worried. "I'm not sure I like this. For one thing, we could lose a lot of money."

"Darling," she said reassuringly, "we have a lot of money to lose. You are a very wealthy man."

Horatio went on, "And we could end up wasting precious time if he refuses to help us."

"He won't be able to refuse," Edie said firmly.

"Why?" I asked.

"I'm going to take him for all he's worth and then some." She still sounded a little nervous, but her confidence seemed to be growing by the minute. "And you are all going to be praying in the upper room! We have goodness on our side!"

Rolf looked at the clock. "It just might work. If she's as good as she says."

"She is," I assured him.

~

WE FURTIVELY STOLE through the streets of Berlin back to the hotel. My heart was thumping loudly in my ears, and I jumped at every shadow. When we finally arrived back in the lobby, I nearly collapsed. My parents had barely spoken a word, except to mention how thin the girls looked. And pale. Probably from spending all their time indoors, we agreed.

My mother clung to me long and hard outside our room as dad shuffled the key in the lock.

"What is it, Mom?" I asked. Though I knew what was wrong. She was afraid, terrified for her sister and brother-in-law. For her nieces. It was all so unexpected. So horrible.

I slipped off my necklace and clasped it around her neck.

"What are you doing, Agatha?"

"I think you need this more than me right now."

She looked at me questioningly. "What do you mean?"

"You told me once to not give up hope, no matter what."

She fingered the heart. "The Hope. Ha Tikvah." Her Hebrew roots were a stark reminder of what we faced ahead.

"Hope does not disappoint," I said, willing myself to believe once again. "No matter what, God will see us through to the end."

"No matter what," she answered, "even if we face the worst."

I squeezed her hands. "In the end, the battle is already won. No matter what happens down there."

"You've been reading your Bible," she smiled softly.

"I take after my mother." It was true, I had been faithfully reading everyday, whenever I could spare a minute or two. Scripture always seemed to still my racing mind and quiet my troubled heart.

"Thank you, Agatha." She fingered the necklace. "I'll give it back. I promise."

"I'm sure I'll need it soon. You can be brave the next time. We'll take turns."

She shakily took off her coat as she walked into the suite. "You have yourself a deal."

## CHAPTER 29

## THE POKER GAME

Edie smoothed the satin black dress and adjusted her pearls. Mom and I had fixed her hair in a fashionable pile of curls on top of her head. We'd also done a fabulous job on her makeup. Not one freckle showed. Approvingly, we stepped back and stared at her in the full-length mirror in our suite.

"I guess that's as good as it's going to get," Edie sighed.

"It's more than good," Mom said. "I would say you look like a very, very wealthy woman who has some money to spend and some secrets to keep."

"You don't look half-bad yourself," Edie replied to her. My mother glanced at herself behind Edie. She too wore an evening gown, but it was simpler than Edie's, not intended to stand out. Only Horatio and Edie were actually going to be in the Smoking Room. My parents would be at the bar, keeping watch for any funny business.

Meanwhile, Peter and I were relegated to room service in my parent's suite.

There was a polite knock on the door before Horatio, Peter, and Dad entered the room.

My father gave a low whistle. "You ladies look gorgeous. Ready for a night out on the town?"

"Something like that," my mother groaned. She gathered her purse and said, "You think the girls are alright?"

"I'm sure they are just fine," he assured her.

"Besides, it would have raised too many eyebrows to bring them to the hotel," I added. We had all agreed it was much safer if they continue their routine, and we go on with our "vacation."

"They are adult women. And smart as whips, all three of them. They've been doing a good job taking care of themselves so far. They'll be fine for another day or two," Edie said, checking her own bag, "30,000 marks? You think that is enough?" She fingered the wad of cash.

"It should be. But if it's not, write an IOU," Horatio said. "You have the girls' papers?"

She patted the bag. "Passports and extra photographs, just like Rolf said."

Edie turned her head and looked at the back of the dress in the mirror. "You don't think the scoop back is a little too revealing?" she asked.

"Nah," I said. "Besides, you've got swimmer's muscles to show off."

"If you say so, Piper." She held herself erect. "Well Horatio, my dear, lead me to the Smoking Room!"

Horatio held the door open and called over his shoulder, "As they say in showbiz, I hope we all break some legs tonight."

"Sort of like the old days," Peter said, gnawing on a chicken leg from the dinner the kitchen had sent up. "Me. You. All the adults in our lives doing something exciting, and us doing nothing."

"We're adults too, Peter."

"Sure. Whatever you say." He threw the bone back on the plate. "What do you think's happening now? It's been what, three hours?"

I glanced at the clock. "Yup. Three hours." I picked at my plate. "What'd you do this morning?"

"Nothing much. Ferguson and I took the animals for a walk, and I wandered the hotel a bit."

Hmm. While Edie and my mother had shopped for the appropriate evening wear, and Horatio and my father wired in for the appropriate cash for the game, I had opted to stay in the suite and catch up on my beauty sleep. Now I was fidgety from lack of activity and nervous to boot.

The way Peter kept tapping his fork on his glass of milk confirmed he felt the same way.

"That's it." Peter stood up after a minute. "I can't take it anymore. I'm going down there."

"You can't go down there," I protested. "What are you going to do, sidle up to the table and put down the five-dollar bill in your pocket? 'Deal me in guys!' Seriously! Those men play for real money. Besides," I pushed my plate of uneaten food back, "we are under strict instructions to stay out of sight."

"Which is exactly what I plan to do," Peter said, throwing on his colorful sweater.

I had to make a quick decision.

Done.

If Peter was going, I was going.

I popped up and threw on my shoes. "Give me a second." I ran into the bathroom and dragged a brush through my hair. It was, thank goodness, actually growing into something quite stylish and sophisticated. The effects of the perm-gone-south were almost gone.

"How exactly are we going to work this operation?" I yelled out to Peter. "Famous opera stars again?"

"Without Freddy we wouldn't make it past the bar. I was thinking of something more undercover."

"What? Are we going to hide in the potted plants?" I asked cynically. "In that sweater, you'd stand out a mile."

"Not quite. Like I said, I did a little snooping earlier today."

"You've been planning this?" I asked, shocked.

"Not exactly. Well, yes. Sort of."

Satisfied with my hair, I grabbed my camera and followed Peter out of the room. We went down the hall to the enormous grand staircase, where we walked four flights down to the ground floor. When we reached the entrance to the Smoking Room, instead of going inside, Peter turned into a little alcove on the left that led into one of the grand ballrooms.

"No one is using the west ballroom tonight," he said. "I checked."

"So what?"

"The west ballroom has a large balcony that runs along the outer edge. I climbed the stairs to the second level, and that's when I realized the balcony opened out on the other side, allowing us to look down at the bar and the Smoking Room, completely unnoticed. I'm brilliant." He leaned against the wall, smirking at his own ingenuity.

"This is perfect," I whispered, eyes wide.

"What'd I tell you. I'm brilliant."

I PEEKED down over the edge and strained to find my parents at the bar through the lens of my camera. Their glasses remained untouched, their faces glued to the large wall lined with ferns opposite of the bar. The wall's opening was guarded by a tough-looking goon in a pinstripe suit.

"The Smoking Room?" I asked.

Peter nodded. In the Smoking Room, various groups of German officers played cards and smoked cigars. The smoke hung in a dreadful haze, nearly blurring the view. Off to the side was a pool table.

"They don't call it the Smoking Room for nothing. It stinks, even up here!" Peter said.

"What's the point of this balcony anyways?"

"It's a service hall. So the staff can quickly move between the ballroom and the bar."

"I guess that makes sense." I scanned the Smoking Room, zooming in with my lens. I spotted Edie seated at a table with a small group of men, all dressed to the nines. I pointed, and Peter followed my gaze.

"Just a gentleman's game of cards," he said under his breath.

Edie was playing her part quite well. Horatio stood behind her, attempting to look as relaxed as he could under the circumstances.

"Which one is Jean-Baptiste?" I asked.

"Probably the one with the red carnation in his tuxedo pocket."

I looked closer. Yes, he had to be the one.

The dealer shuffled the cards, and Edie cut the deck. Then the betting began.

Peter and I settled in, sitting cross-legged on the thick carpet and peering through the ornate wooden lattice work, completely invisible to the gamblers below. Peter pulled two boxes from his pocket. "Red Hots or Tootsie Roll Pops?"

"Where'd you get those?"

"Been saving 'em for a special occasion."

He held up the two boxes tantalizingly and whispered in my ear, "I would have brought popcorn..."

"Give me the Red Hots. Tootsie Roll Pops stick in my teeth."

He tossed me the box. "Suit yourself."

We ate the candy, piece by piece, watching restlessly and trying to hold still.

Peering through the lattice, Peter popped the last Tootsie Roll into his mouth. "They must be on their sixth or seventh game."

"How's she doing?"

"By the looks of the chips on the table, Edie is doing well. Very well."

"I told you she was good," I smiled.

Peter looked back at me and broke into a grin. "Your teeth are stained red."

Self-consciously, I shut my mouth.

"You know, if we go to the north end of the balcony, we'll be able to hear everything," Peter whispered. "They are probably about to finish up."

We crouched and crawled along the balcony until we were huddled just above the table. It was true, we could actually hear what was going on, but we couldn't see as well. The smoke from the table wafted up in thick plumes. I let out a bit of a cough. It was difficult to breathe.

Peter motioned for me to be quiet. "Listen! And stay down so they can't see you!"

A distinctly French accent rose loudly. "I think you, madam, are bluffing!"

Edie laughed gaily, "Oh, Jean-Baptiste! I never bluff. Never, never, never!"

"You are a liar!" he shouted.

Not being able to see anything, I imagined Edie was laying her cards on the table.

"What'd I tell you," she laughed again.

"A full house!" He was raging now. "Impossible!"

"I would say you owe me roughly 60,000 marks. How much is that in American money, dear?" she asked Horatio.

Horatio guffawed, "Enough to buy another yacht."

"How did she do that!" Jean-Baptiste demanded.

Horatio shrugged. "Beginner's luck."

"Everyone leave! Except you and your husband!" the French voice commanded. I heard the sound of chairs scraping against the wood floor and men's voices heading towards the bar.

Jean-Baptiste was peeved. "I don't have that sort of money here. I'll have to go to the bank in the morning. In the meantime, will a bank draft do? Or perhaps you want to play another round?"

"Oh no, Jean-Baptiste." Edie spoke to him as though he were an old friend. "Then you would pull out all of your tricks and win it all back. Oh no. That wouldn't do at all."

She coughed a feminine cough. "But, just between us, a bank note *won't* do."

"Whatever do you mean, madame?"

"I have another form of payment in mind." Edie tapped her fingers on the table. "Perhaps we can talk in the privacy of our suite?"

PETER and I raced as quickly as we could back to our room. Just thirty minutes after our arrival, my parents and Edie and Horatio arrived. All four were wide-eyed with excitement.

"It worked. I can't believe it worked!" Edie threw herself on the bed.

"What happened?" Peter and I asked simultaneously.

It was all quite simple, my father explained. Instead of paying Edie her winnings in cash, she made a trade for use of his special services. My father slumped in one of the armchairs.

Edie took her jewelry off and shook out her hands. "My wrists sometimes seize up. All my years of typing."

"Stress," my mother said. She sat on the chair's arm, flinging her arm over my father's shoulder.

"I told him I wouldn't hold him to the money if he did a little favor for some friends of mine," Edie said proudly.

"A favor he's been asked by many others, I take it." Horatio sat on the bed's edge.

"I'm telling you, he cheats," Edie said, popping her head up.

"A forger and a cheat! I despise those sorts of people!" Horatio stood up again. It had been a stressful evening for him too, and the creases on his forehead looked more furrowed than ever.

"Don't be too hard on him," my mother argued. "He is doing us a favor."

"A favor? I'm doing him the favor. My wife won 60,000 marks! He's getting off easy if you ask me."

"If he's a forger and cheat, how did you win?" Peter asked.

"I know all their wily ways. My old neighbor, Mr. Henderson, was a terrible cheater. He taught me everything."

"No wonder he was so angry," my mother looked at Edie. "He must have thought you were a member of the Gestapo out to expose him![16] No doubt there are more than one or two high-ranking German officials who would happily confiscate his bank account and take back the money they lost at his table."

In all reality, that was possible. But on the other hand, Jean-Baptiste let enough of them win to keep them coming back, and the numbers were high enough to protect his little business. And even German officials could have use of a forger at times, I reasoned. That said, he must have had many enemies.

"I won't say I didn't let something like that slip out. It was simple. He does the papers, no questions asked, and I don't have him arrested," Edie said with a grin.

"You are very clever, my dear. I had no idea how you excelled in the fine art of blackmail." Horatio helped her off the bed.

"I surprise even myself sometimes," Edie chuckled.

"And if I ever decide to quit the lobster business, we can go into the poker business."

"But I told you, I never gamble for money."

He grimaced. "No. You've graduated to gambling for lives."

Edie yawned loudly. "I'm completely exhausted. But that was a good day's work. Much more satisfying than sitting in front of my typewriter with writer's block. I'm ready for bed."

"When will the papers be finished?" Peter asked, gathering his things to go back to his own room.

"Two days," Horatio said.

"What do we do in the meantime?" I asked.

"We wait," my mother said, "and we pray."

# CHAPTER 30

## FREDERICK'S FINEST HOUR

A sharp ring on the telephone jolted me awake. It came from my parents' adjoining room in the suite. The clock read 3:00 in the morning. I could hear my mother's muffled, "Hello? Edie! What happened?" as I slipped on my robe and quietly padded into their room, sitting on the edge of their bed.

We'd spent the last 2 days anxiously awaiting the forged documents. And just when we thought that Jean-Baptiste was not only a cheat and forger but also a dishonorable fop who refused to pay his debts, he had, apparently, knocked on Horatio and Edie's door in the middle of the night.

My mother whispered to us, as Edie's voice talked non-stop through the speaker, "He apologized for the late hour. He said he spends his 'nights awake and days asleep and was never quite sure when other people were awake anyways,' or something like that."

She paused and listened to Edie before continuing, "The adoption has gone through."

Edie's voice had risen in excitement, and I could hear her plainly for a moment. "Horatio and I are now the proud parents of three

German teenagers, who also happen to be underground singing sensations."

"So he did it? He fixed the passports?" I asked. Mom put her finger on her lips, motioning for me to be quiet.

Finally, Mom exclaimed, "Oh! What good news, Edie! Thank you, dear! And give that husband of yours a kiss for me. See you in the morning. Goodnight!" She gently hung up the phone and ran her fingers along the starched sheet.

"So?" my father pressed.

"We have the papers. We have the papers!"

The next morning, Edie and Horatio came to our suite to give us the whole story. My mother's hair was still in curlers, my father's hair wet from the shower. Edie and Horatio looked like they hadn't slept all night.

She wearily sat down and watched as my mother took the curlers out of hair. "So," my mother said, "tell us everything!"

"It was all very clandestine." She yawned. "Who shows up at three in the morning?"

"Jean-Baptiste, that's who," Horatio interjected. "He was quite complimentary. He told Edie she was remarkably good at poker."

"He said that?" I looked at Edie. She gave me a wide grin and answered, "Yes. He actually said I was better than he was. All credit to dear Mr. Henderson, of course."

Horatio jumped back in and said, "He was very angry after she won. And then, after contemplating how brave Edie was to risk so much for a few girls, he concluded that the girls must be very special."

Edie said, "'I told him, 'Jean-Baptiste, every human life is special. And right now, there are many more who need your talents to help them escape what is coming.'"

"What did he say?" my father asked.

Imitating the Frenchman, Edie said in a deep voice, "True, madame. But even one such as I must make a living, no?" My uncle smirked and replied, "A living is not exactly how I would describe his lifestyle. I don't think he cares about people one bit."

"Don't be so hard on him, dear. He did help us." Edie patted his arm.

"Here are the papers." Edie pulled them out of her handbag for us to examine. With her keen artist's eye, she declared them masterpieces. "He really is as good as Rolf said. They are perfect."

Horatio groaned, "I'm thankful this whole sordid business is over. What an unlikeable fellow. No morals at all. You know, he had bodyguards waiting outside the whole time? Worried someone is going to murder him, no doubt!"

"He liked me well enough," Edie laughed "He said he would be proud to work for me anytime. And if I ever want to get in on an underground poker ring back in the States, he has connections. But I told him that I *never* play for money."

"I hope we never see him again." Horatio stood up and moved towards the door.

"Don't burn the bridge, dear," Edie said, putting the passports back in her purse. "You never know when we might need an expert forger again."

"I never expected that I would need one to begin with."

WITH NO MAKEUP, their hair in braids wrapped around their heads like schoolgirls, flat lace-up saddle shoes, and plain dresses, Katrine, Lorelei, and Grace easily passed for three girls in their teens.

As the forged papers showed, their parents had died in a tragic automobile accident, leaving the girls under the protection of Horatio and Edie. The accident had occurred only the month before, and Edie and Horatio, along with the rest of us, had collected them and were now off to Scotland. It was all perfectly legal and would be quite simple... if the border police bought the story.

Our departure immanent, the girls' downcast, tear-stained faces only added to the story of three sisters who had lost their parents in a tragedy. And after considering it for a moment, I realized that they had. The Adlon had seen such sadness before, and the staff looked on our little group in the lobby pityingly. "Yes," they whispered and gossiped, "they are sisters. And the parents are dead. Now they have to go with that couple all the way to Scotland!" "Yes, the one who won all that money a few nights ago from the Frenchman." "Tragic, isn't it? Look how sad they are! And so pretty." "I would be sad too if I had to go to Scotland. Good German stock like that."

As we walked to the restaurant, Lorelei clung to Rolf, at times begging him not to forget her and to write her, and other times pleading with him to come with us. But he could not. He would not. He was needed in Germany. Many more would need his help in the weeks and months to come.

"I know that. I know." Lorelei tried to stifle her tears. "And it breaks my heart." Her big green eyes were rimmed with red. "A khave iz nit dafke der vos visht dir op di trern nor der vos brengt dikh bekhlal nit tsi trern."

"Don't speak Yiddish here, Lorelei!" Rolf whispered fiercely. "Besides the fact that I don't speak it, other people could hear you!"

Reprovingly, she translated, "A friend is someone who wipes your tears, he's someone who doesn't make you cry."

"You know it's more complicated than that." Then he rubbed her shoulder and said, "Come now, I don't want to remember you like this." But his eyes were also red, and he turned his face away to hide his own tears. "It's our last supper together. Let's try to enjoy it, for old times' sake."

"This is nothing like old times," Lorelei fumed. Seeing his pleading eyes, she softened. She took his hand and followed Katrine, who stoically led the way to the restaurant where we all sat for what we hoped would be our last meal in Germany.

"I don't think I will ever come back here," Grace said, looking angrily at her plate of food. "No. I will never ever come back to Germany. And I refuse to speak any more German. Starting now, I will speak only English."

No one said anything.

"That could prove rather difficult, dear," Edie said softly.

"I don't care." Grace looked ready to throw her plate across the dining room. "You hear me!" She was almost shouting, and the tables nearest us turned and gawked. "Never again!"

~

WHILE WE WAITED for our cars outside the hotel's lobby, Rolf and my cousins clung together in one final embrace.

"I will always treasure my memories of your family. And I pray to God that we might be together again. That we might once more sit around your mother's table, singing and saying the Shabbat prayers," Rolf softly said.

"It really meant so much to you, even though you are not a Jew, Rolf?" Katrine asked searchingly.

"It meant the world that you shared your family and your traditions when I had none."

Then the girls tore themselves away from the last vestige of their old life, disappearing into the back of the Rolls.

Peter and I got into the back seat of the Rover. PHL hopped onto Peter's lap, and Fanny settled in my arms. The engines roared to life, and I watched as Rolf waved goodbye, tears streaming unashamedly down his face. Then he disappeared from view, and we pressed forward to the Netherlands and freedom.

The quickest route to the border was to head west to the coast and from there, south to the Netherlands. The crossing, in between the Dutch city of Groningen and the German city of Leer, was located on an inlet of the North Sea and was operated by the German Navy, not the usual border police. This wasn't totally surprising, given the fact that the region was not particularly populated, and the road was primarily used for transporting goods to the German port.

"Now, act calm," Mother directed, her voice tinged with fear as we approached the line of trucks awaiting inspection.

Nothing could possibly go wrong, I assured myself. Jean-Baptiste was an expert. No one would ever know that the papers were falsified. No one!

I held Fanny close, feeding her a bit of banana.

"You really think you should be doing that right now?" Peter asked.

He was right. I put the banana down, and the monkey squealed in protest.

I watched tensely as one of the guards approached a large truck. The burly guard took the driver's papers, examined them, and roughly motioned for the driver to open the back.

The driver, a sullen-looking peasant, grumpily complied and opened the back of the truck. Poking around with his rifle, the guard must have felt something was off. He signaled for back up, and a small group of soldiers began emptying the cargo.

"This could take a while," my father sighed, turning the engine off. He sniffed apprehensively.

"What do you think they are looking for?" I searched through the window.

Panicked, my mother leaned forward. "Oh my, what is the driver doing?"

The man was in the process of slowly backing away from the truck. Gathering momentum, he made a mad dash for the woods.

One of the guards saw him slither off and yelled the alert. All the soldiers checking the line of cars and trucks dropped what they were doing and ran after the escaped driver. That left the rest of us under the surveillance of one officer and one guard.

No one moved. I don't think anyone even had the courage to breathe.

"All right!" one of the soldiers finally shouted in German. "Everyone out of your cars. Now! Hurry!"

"Oh Lord, help us," my mother prayed as we all filed out of the car. I clinged to the monkey, and Peter held PHL's leash. We joined Horatio, Edie, and my cousins by the side of the Rolls. The eight of us huddled together, waiting for whatever was going to come next.

The same guard who had shouted the alert strode haughtily between the cars, demanding that we all open our trunks and suitcases for inspection. He began to rifle through our things.

Then, out of nowhere, we heard the sound of a gunshot followed by an explosion. The guard ran into the woods, leaving us alone with the officer in charge.

I turned to see the young man who was about to take our passports and gasped. Frederick was striding towards us. In a full German navy uniform, no less.

"Imagine meeting you here of all places." He looked very stern, and the smile was forced and thin.

"You are already an officer?" Horatio was surprised.

"My time aboard your ship worked out to my advantage. They need experienced seamen. So while I'm still technically in basic training, I already have the status of captain," he explained.

Peter and I looked at one another. Already an officer? That meant Germany was preparing for war.

"Good for you, Frederick," Edie said, forcing a smile.

He was all business. "Alright then, papers."

As he read over the documents, his face registered complete surprise. He looked at the girls, then back at Horatio and Edie. "You are now parents?"

"It's a long story, Freddy dear," Edie laughed, drawing my cousins close to her. "We adopted them. It's all there," she said. "They are good children."

My cousins stood gawky and awkward. Katrine was glaring at Frederick. Lorelei was looking down at her shoes, and Grace was growing paler by the second.

"You adopted three adult women? I knew you were strange but..." His confusion was met with dread. The truth had hit him; I saw it all on his face. Somehow, Frederick just knew. He knew the papers were forged. He knew exactly what we were doing.

He said quietly, "They are Jews, aren't they?"

"Please, Frederick. Please," I begged, my voice barely above a whisper. I remembered Sofia telling Frederick that he had greatness in him, and I willed him to tap into that greatness now.

"Look at that one!" He pointed at Katrine. It was true, her dark hair and petite frame gave away who she was. Even her defiant stare. Everything about her screamed "Jewish."

I could hear the soldiers returning from the woods, dragging the screaming driver back. There was a sharp noise followed by a terrifying silence. I started to tremble uncontrollably, and, for a split-second, even Frederick looked afraid.

At that moment, our lives hung in the balance. His eyes darted to the woods and then back to our cars.

*Oh God, work on our behalf.* I prayed over and over again.

Frederick's face contorted in confusion. He was completely distraught. My heart broke for him. "Come with us. Get in the car, and we'll make a run for it!" I whispered tensely. "Don't stay with these people."

Caught between the truth and what he wished was true but knew was not, he choked, "I can't, Piper. This is all I have."

The soldiers returned. The driver of the truck was nowhere to be seen.

The captain in charge shouted at Frederick.

Frederick shouted something back, giving a salute. Without meeting any of our eyes, he waved us on.

"Get in and drive," he said firmly to Horatio and my father. "Don't *ever* come back to Germany."

When he turned back to his superior officer, he was all military bearing, uncompromising and in control.

Of course, what he'd said wasn't true. The German Navy wasn't all that Frederick had. I sunk into the backseat, my head pounding. I didn't understand. I had watched a friend die, right before my eyes. He had us. He could've had a family. And now?

"He's lost. Forever." A sob rose before I could stop it. A deep, pain-filled sob. Tears poured down my face, and my hands shook with leftover adrenaline.

"But he didn't betray us, Piper," Peter comforted me. "He helped us in the end."

"God will protect his people, Israel." My mother thoughtfully looked back at me.

It was Frederick's greatest performance.

Indeed. Frederick had helped us in the end. Deep down, he had pulled out what little goodness was left. But it wasn't the ending I had wanted. Not at all. But then, many things in life don't have the ending we want, do they?

# PART FOUR

## A WING AND A PRAYER

# CHAPTER 31

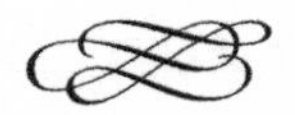

## THE BIJENKORF AND WHAT HAPPENED NEXT

The North Sea was different from any ocean I'd ever seen. Unlike the coast of California, which was a fiercely deep blue with long stretches of warm sand, or the coast in Maine, which was rocky and jagged, the North Sea was one long strip of gray stormy water and harsh wind. The farther we traveled on this journey, the harsher the landscape became. It made me feel lonely and more than a little afraid.

We stopped for a late lunch at a little seafood shack on the beach, shivering as we ate fried fish and chips.

When Horatio finally spoke up, relief was evident in his voice. "What a joy to be by the sea again. Home at last."

We were a quiet group, eating on the nearly deserted beach, freezing wind whipping around us.

"How far to The Hague?" my father asked.

"Not far," Horatio answered. "Half an hour's drive at most."

"I want to get out of these clothes," Katrine said after a moment. "Do you think there is a place we can shop?"

"I could use a jacket," I shivered. "I didn't come prepared for this cold of weather."

None of us had, and with a sea voyage on the North Sea staring us in the face, we all needed some more weather-appropriate gear.

"I know exactly where to go, ma'am," Ferguson said. "The Bijenkorf. It's a department store. The best in the Netherlands."

"How do you know all that sort of stuff?" Peter questioned.

"That's what I pay him for," Horatio answered.

"It's my honor to be of service, sir." Ferguson bowed slightly.

"Will they have everything we need? The girls don't have a single item fit for anything other than a boarding school." Edie looked at their saddle shoes.

"Oh yes, I guarantee they have everything you could possibly need."

With that, we all loaded back into the cars after wiping our greasy fingers in the sand, brushing them off the best we could. Out of the biting wind, I started to warm up with the help of the collie on my lap, a living fur coat. My stomach hurt, whether from the stress of the morning or the fried fish, I couldn't tell. I didn't want to go shopping. All I wanted was to nestle next to the collie and sleep for a very long time.

WHERE GERMANY WAS all rolling hills, little villages nestled in valleys, and well-ordered cities, the Netherlands was remarkably flat and watery. It was an intriguing flatness and watery-ness that wasn't a marsh exactly, though it was damp.

It was unlike anywhere I'd ever been. We drove past fields of flowers and saw cattle roaming around large farmhouses. Waterways and dikes crisscrossed the road and railway track. Farmers in thick wooden shoes and wide hats stared silently at our cars as we drove towards The Hague, or Den Hague as they said in Dutch.

Den Hague was a large city full of diplomats living in mansions lined up neatly on the edge of the river near the Court of International Justice, opened by the League of Nations at the close of the Great War. It didn't bustle like New York or San Francisco. It moved along steady and slow, like the little houseboats floating on the dikes. No one hurried. Nothing was out of order.

19th-century townhomes, with their cookie-cutter lattice work and window boxes overflowing with tulips and roses, lined the wide streets surrounding the ancient Old City Hall, a grisly building of red-brick, hundreds of angles, and hidden tunnels and passageways from the looks of it.

It was near the Old City Hall that the Bijenkorf stood. It was the mother of all department stores, a shrine to shopping, a material watering hole for both the bargain hunter and the luxury lover. Women in thick furs and men in heavy wool coats smiled gaily, entering in and out of the five stories high building, arms laden with pretty packages, cheeks rosy, and eyes happy.

We'd gone from escaping the Nazis in the morning, to contemplating which cashmere sweater to buy in the afternoon. Nothing could shock me now.

Delicate classical music, played by a little woman on the white ivories of a Steinway, floated over our heads as we plunged through the revolving glass doors into the department store. I inhaled the thick, sweet perfumes wafting our direction from the perfume counter near the entrance.

The first floor housed a tea room and chocolate shop, selling delightful pastries, warm drinks, and little sandwiches to hungry shoppers. There were many other wonderful things on that floor. Scarves and hats of the finest silk and wool. Men's and women's shoes for every possible occasion or need. Cosmetics and imported specialty foods like caviar and champagne.

Our harried border crossing seemed to disappear like early morning mist that burns up as the sun rises as we stood in the atrium.

The second story was filled with suits and men's hats and ties. The third story held women's evening wear and lingerie. The fourth story was women's day clothes. And on the fifth story was housewares, furniture, and a grand restaurant boasting the best Dutch apple pie in the country.

It was all enormously grand and delightful, a far cry from its origins as a yarn and ribbon shop owned by a humble Jewish family, the Goudsmits.

We stood there a moment longer, slightly stunned. It was as if we'd been transported into an alternate reality. A man wearing a chef's hat and an apron walked over and offered us chocolate made in the Bijenkorf kitchens.

"I think the Germans must have shot us at the border. I've died and gone to heaven," Edie sighed, taking a piece of chocolate covered in bits of toffee and cranberries. "It's delicious. You all ought to try some."

Peter took a large handful from the grinning chef.

Katrine took my mother aside. "Can you come with my sisters and I and help us find what we need? I'm so tired, and my mind is so full. I can't think clearly. And we have nothing really. Not even an extra set of socks." She touched my mother's face. "You look so much like my mother. Younger, but so similar."

Tears welled up in Katrine's eyes, and my mother pushed her own tears away. Straightening her shoulders decisively, she said, "No, Katrine. We'll not cry now. Now is not the time for that. We've too much to do." She sniffed and thought out loud. "Let's see, you'll need undergarments and night things. Stockings. Two pairs of sturdy shoes. Two skirts, three blouses, and a sweater. A good wool jacket. And a dress for nicer occasions. We have a lot of work to do." Rubbing her hands together, she herded her nieces upstairs. "All right, off we go girls."

Thankfully for all of us, at the Bijenkorf we really did not have a lot of work to do; there were people for that. A swarm of pretty, young saleswomen swooped in like a flock of doves, hovering over the girls.

Within an hour, each was outfitted in a perfectly fitting, lovely new wardrobe. The hairdresser gave them each brand new styles.

There were so many boxes of merchandise that Ferguson had to tie them to the roof of the Rolls. Horatio thundered that he was buying out the store, to which Edie responded with, "But you're a father now, dear!"

Lorelei fingered her new silk blouse gently. "I've never had clothes this fine. Professors don't make much, and typing clerks make even less," she laughed. "I never was cut out to be a secretary anyway. I hated working in that firm."

"What would you like to do?" I asked, sitting next to her on the velvet couch, trying on a pair of outlandish heels.

"Oh," she sighed, "I don't know. I always wondered if I should go back to school."

"And study what?"

She shrugged again. "I don't know. Who knows if I will ever get to go back to school now. Nothing is turning out the way I thought it would."

"You're telling me," I agreed, taking the shoe off and handing it back to the clerk.

Peter waltzed up wearing a smart new blazer. "What do you think, ladies?" He spun around.

"Very handsome," Lorelei laughed. "Rolf would look good in that too."

"You care a lot about him, don't you?" I asked quietly.

"He is my dearest friend." She looked away, not allowing me in any further.

Ferguson was not far behind. In his hands was a brand new bowler hat and a rather spiffy cane. He looked pleased with himself. "It's got an ivory handle. On sale!"

"Quite the fashion accessory." I looked at it questioningly. "But do you really need a cane?"

Just as he opened his mouth to answer, a small commotion drew our attention away. The pianist stopped playing, and a group of the store's staff gathered in the corner of the café across from the shoe department. There were several shop-girls, the manager, and a couple of chefs. The café's patrons put down their sandwiches and cookies and stood in twos and threes, looking out the window and whispering tensely. Someone turned the radio in the corner up, and the tense voice of the Dutch newscaster rang out. They buzzed like bees, and concern and fear filled the formerly carefree air.

"I'm going to go figure out what's going on." Peter left us on the couch and approached the gathering.

He came back a few minutes later, his face white. "Where is everybody?"

Horatio and Edie were in the fur department. My mother was with Grace and Katrine, working their way through hat after hat in millinery. And my father was picking up a few pies from the restaurant upstairs for us to have for supper back at the cottage we'd rented for the night.

"Hitler's invaded Poland. France and Britain have declared war on Germany in return. They are allies with Poland. It's starting. The war is starting."

Lorelei grasped my hand, her face blanching. "So it has started, has it? How strange, how very strange," she said. "Not what we planned at all." Repeating to herself now, she whispered, "Not at all what we planned."

~

THE SEASIDE COTTAGE was more of a house than an actual cottage. It was three stories high with big windows opening out to the sea. About a quarter mile of seagrass and reeds formed a visual barrier from the grey waves.

As soon as we'd arrived, Mom, Dad, Horatio, and Edie had holed up in one of the bedrooms on the ground floor, speaking in hushed tones.

Ferguson busied himself in the kitchen with what he had found in the market. The table was filled with over 200 pounds of chocolate that my aunt had insisted we purchase before leaving because,

"With the war on and everything, there will be shortages. Mark my words."

Wrapped up in big blankets on the deck chairs looking over the ocean, my cousins and I were quiet. Fanny nestled on my shoulder, sleeping peacefully. Peter was out near the waves, playing with PHL, throwing some drift wood for the collie to fetch. Grace, just barely older than Peter, stared at me knowingly. "You like him, don't you?"

What was the point of denying it? "Who wouldn't?" I responded. "He's a very likable guy."

"Good-looking too," Grace chuckled. "Hand me your camera." I passed it to her, and she shot a picture.

"Do you think I'm dumb to be interested in an older man?" I ventured.

"Older man my foot!" Grace put the camera down in her lap. "Katrine was interested in a man 15 years older. *That's* older."

"What happened?" I asked, for 15 years older did seem quite a bit older.

Katrine cut in with, "Are you seriously bringing Mathew up?" Her face was a mixture of pain and embarrassment.

Ignoring her, Grace continued, "He liked playing the field. She was just another trophy."

"That's not it at all. And it wasn't his age either. He was just wrong altogether." Katrine pushed her hair out of her face.

"I can't believe you are talking about boys when the whole world is falling apart," Lorelei said.

Katrine argued back, "It fell apart when Hitler became Chancellor."

"Girls," my mother poked her head outside, "it's time to come in for supper." She had dark circles under her eyes.

There was not enough room around the table for everyone to sit, so we all took our bread and cheese and ate with our plates on our laps, huddled around the warmth of the small fireplace, the radio droning on in the background. We could just barely get a clear signal from the BBC. The other stations were all in Dutch. The static finally won, and we gave up on knowing what was going on for the evening.

War was no longer just around the corner. It was on our doorstep.

"It's funny how cold it is, and it's only the first of September." Ferguson shivered, adding another log to the fire.

My mother looked at my plate. "Just pie, Agatha?"

"If it's the end of the world, I might as well go down eating Dutch apple pie." I stuffed the layers of apple and cinnamon into my mouth.

"Odds are you'll go down eating chocolate," Peter answered. "All the same, my sentiments exactly. Just pie for me, Fergie."

"You'll thank me later, trust me," Edie said seriously. "I'll also take a piece of that pie, Ferguson."

"Of course, ma'am." He stood and ceremonially cut another slice.

Horatio checked his watch. "The *Goose* should arrive in the port by midnight. We'll go out and meet her first thing in the morning."

"And then?" my father asked.

Horatio continued thoughtfully, "Our goal is to load the children onto the boat and be off with the next tide. Then Scotland and home."

Scotland and home. That sounded perfectly beautiful to me. I couldn't wait.

EARLY THE NEXT MORNING, we drove down to the harbor. There was the *Goose*, right on schedule, sailing straight through the harbor and carefully docking.

Frank's beaming smile was the first one I recognized.

"Piper! Piper!" Frank waved wildly from the side of the *Goose*, shrouded in the morning mist. He ran down off the pier, picked me up, and spun me around. "What a sight you are for sore eyes!"

I laughed. "It's so good to see a familiar face."

"Your hair is growing in real nice. Look at you! You're right gorgeous!"

I blushed.

"And who are these lovely ladies?" He whistled as my cousins got out of the Rolls.

"My cousins." I poked him in the ribs. "And they are real ladies, so you better treat them well."

"What are they doing here?" he asked.

"It's a long story, but we helped them escape the Nazis. They are Jewish, remember?"

He nodded, eyes widening. "That's right. I forgot that our families had that in common. Not a good time to be a Jew in Germany." He looked around a moment. "Frederick is long gone I take it?"

"Yes," I said simply. What was the point of trying to explain?

"Good riddance."

By then, Horatio had made his way up the pier and clasped Frank by the hand. "So, Frankie my boy, how's the old girl doing?" He lovingly looked at his boat.

"Never better, sir. And ready to sail as soon as you are." Then a bit more quietly, Frank said, "I did as you asked, sir. I brought the pistols you ordered. What are we smuggling boss? I know when something's up. I've got experience. Where are we taking the cargo?"

"It's not cargo. More like a nursery."

"You're smuggling a nursery?" He looked confused.

The sound of honking drew our attention to five buses pulling into the harbor.

"They're here," I said.

"Right on time."

Gertie, like a mother hen, got out of the first bus and waved energetically at Edie and Mom. "You made it!" she yelled happily.

The children began to get off the bus slowly. They looked wide-eyed, in shock. Some cried softly. "It will be alright, children. You are all so brave!" She comforted them with hugs and pats.

"Look who I've brought!" Gertie said proudly, pointing to the second bus.

There on the steps was Harry. He looked like he had been up all night. He marched towards us. "So you made it through the land of sourkrauts in one piece. I owe you all big time." It took me a moment to get the joke.

"How did you get here?" my father asked, obviously glad to see him.

"I took the French-Belgium route. Long and anything but direct. But I made it." His suit was crumpled and his hair was messed up. He rubbed his jawline. "I need a bath, and I need a shave. A drink wouldn't be too bad either."

"Harry, it's six thirty in the morning," Gertie laughed.

"Could be midnight for all I know." He looked at the children disembarking from the buses.

There must have been nearly 400.

"They won't all fit on the *Grey Goose*," I observed.

"Don't worry, kid. We've got five more boats in the harbor. We'll get them all aboard, no problem. They'll be taken all over the UK."

Frank stood there, mouth open slightly. By now, he had been joined by Nathaniel, the Brophy twins, Sebastian, and Gorman. Even Cookie had come topside. Seeing the whole crew together again was a stark reminder of simpler days.

Horatio took his men aside and explained the situation. He told them he understood that because there was now a war with Germany, many difficult decisions had to be made on the parts of all. But for now, he requested that all concentration be focused on the task at hand.

The children were all under 12 years old. Some had a small suitcase, others had nothing at all. Each was marked with a tag telling their name, age, and parents' names. They were allowed to take no more than 10 German marks out of the country.

"Ladies, come help me," Gertie called to us.

My cousins, Mom, Edie, and I immediately went to her side and began to lead the children down the gangplank and into Peter and Frank's arms. Many of them were just babies and had to be carried. A tiny girl clung to my hand as though she would never let go, her eyes wide with fear as I handed her over to Peter. I wished I could speak to them in German, but I couldn't. Instead, I spoke as calmly as I could in English, believing they could understand my tone.

The rest of the crew worked tirelessly to safely stow the children below and organize their suitcases. Cookie got right to work preparing snacks. We worked as a unit, one child after another, one traumatized tiny face after the next. Nearly an hour passed before our forty children were settled.

In the meantime, sailors and volunteers from the other boats loaded their assigned precious cargo.

On board, Grace, Katrine, and Lorelei sprang into action, holding the babies and singing songs with the toddlers. Grace had promised that she'd never speak German again, but she broke her vow, telling an animated story, replete with hand motions and different voices, to a group of children gathered around her.

Frank looked on approvingly. "I like these cousins of yours. They are real ladies, just like you said."

I was proud of them, all of them. My cousins, these children, they had all been ripped away from everything they had ever known and everyone they had ever loved.

"I'll run back up and see if there are any stragglers." I jogged back to the deck, finding my parents and Edie and Horatio huddled around Gertie at the bottom of the gangplank.

I joined them just as Gertie looked at her notebook and said with satisfaction, "Not one left behind. We've got them all on board."

"That just leaves us," Edie said. "We ought to board too, shouldn't we?"

Harry ran up the pier. "You got room for me on that junkbucket of yours? I've got some business in Scotland."

"Sure thing, Harry," Horatio said. "Got any bags?"

"Just one. It's already on board, actually." He smiled smugly. "I knew you wouldn't say no."

"Gertie, which boat are you taking?" my mother asked.

The old woman looked back at the busses. "I'm staying here."

"Gertie! Seriously? You think that's a good idea?" Harry was no longer smiling.

"Oh Harry, don't worry. The Dutch have declared neutrality. And my husband is here. I can't ask him to leave his job. He's been at the firm too long to just up and leave. And we are old. Our lives are here."

"You think the Nazis are really going to leave the Netherlands alone?" Harry sounded angry. "They won't. And they will do what they are doing in Germany. And people like you will be their first target."

"No," Gertie reprimanded him, her voice strong and commanding. "Their first targets are the innocent and defenseless. People like those children."

She paused before saying, "I will stay right here and work until I die to make sure they are given a chance to live. Now get on that boat, all of you, we don't want to lose the tide."

As the boat set sail, I watched Gertie from the stern. She stood on the pier until all the boats were out to sea. Little did any of us know that these were the last boats of the kindertransport to set sail. Gertie had saved all the children she possibly could.

From here on out, getting anyone out of Germany would be very, very difficult. If not impossible.

## CHAPTER 32

## ON THE NORTH SEA

It was not a full-on storm, but the weather was rough enough to separate the seafarers from the landlubbers. The North Sea is not known for calm waters.

Dark gray water pitched the boat from side to side from the moment we set out, and within twenty minutes, half the children were seasick, along with Grace, Lorelei, and my father. I was spared this time around, thankfully.

The very nauseous children were kept in the hold, where the rocking was least intense. In order to fit all of them, it was two children to a bunk in the crew's quarters. They were kept under the watchful eyes of the Brophy twins and Sebastian, who sang to them in Gaelic and Spanish and tried to make them laugh with funny antics, while keeping them hydrated with spoonfuls of Cookie's rich chicken broth. My father lay flat on his back in my old bedroom, eyes fixed on the ceiling, face green.

The rest of the children were corralled in the library, which had been turned into a large play area. Our primary goal was to distract the little ones from the reality that they were being taken from their families, possibly forever. A difficult task but not impossible.

For one thing, we had the monkey keeping the older ones entertained with her shenanigans. And PHL was adored and petted by a swarm of loving hands. Swing music blared from the record player. The children ran raucous about the room, screaming with delight on our main attraction — the old 'sliding the wave ride.' (We pushed the furniture to the edges of the room and slid and tried to keep our balance with the rise and fall of the waves). Katrine, my mother, and I led the charge, sliding back and forth on the couch cushions. Even Ferguson got in on the action, upon the special request of the children, all of whom had taken a particular liking to our butler. If you hadn't had known, you would have thought it was a pleasure cruise for children.

Finally, when we'd exhausted every nursery game we could think of, Cookie brought in a tray stacked with rolls with butter and jelly. Harry was just behind him with several pots of hot chocolate for the children and strong coffee for us.

The children fell upon the bread ravenously, and it was then that I realized how thin some of them were. Pale too, as though they had not been outside in a long time. I wondered how many had been hidden away in basements and attics.[1] However had Gertie found them?

A tiny little girl with golden curls, probably about four years old, sat in Edie's arms, eating her bread with gusto. With jammy cheeks and sticky fingers, she nestled into my aunt's arms and yawned loudly. Seconds later, the little angel fell asleep, at peace for the first time in many days.

Mom had her arms around two identical twin boys with dark hair and giant brown eyes. I assumed they were around seven years old. Both were silent. Fearful. Perhaps my mom reminded them of their own mother.

I switched records to something a little more peaceful. I found some soft Bing Crosby ballads. Seemed like good naptime music to me. Glancing at Ferguson on the couch, I noticed that he looked dog-tired. "Are you all right, Ferguson?"

"Oh, you know me. A life of intrigue and adventure is one thing, a life of intrigue, adventure, and becoming a nanny all in one week is something else. I just need some time to - you know - *adjust.*"

"Can I fetch you a cup of coffee for a change?"

"That would be greatly appreciated, ma'am." He sighed and leaned his head back on the cushions. "And an aspirin."

"You got it." I stood up and went to the table where Harry was pouring a mug of coffee for Katrine.

She took the cup with two hands and thanked him softly. "You are the one responsible for all of this?" She took the scene in. The children were scattered throughout the room, some nestled up on cushions, some eating their bread, some falling asleep.

"Nah," Harry brushed her comment off. "There were a whole lot of people involved. People like your aunt and uncle and your new parents." Chuckling, he said, "That was a good one."

"Yes." She took a sip. She looked very beautiful just then. I poured the coffee for Ferguson, but noticed he had fallen into a deep sleep, with three children slung over him asleep too, like little monkeys. I took a big gulp of the coffee.

"What are you going to do when we get to Scotland?"

Katrine looked at him blankly. "I never saw myself leaving Germany. It was home." She stared into the distance. "Edie and Horatio are wonderful, of course. They've offered to let us stay with them until, well, until we figure out what to do. Until my parents can be reached."

Harry's face clouded darkly. "Right. That's, uh, a good plan. They are great. Edie and Horatio."

Sipping Ferguson's coffee, I realized I was completely invisible to Harry and Katrine, though I stood less than two feet from where they spoke.

"And what about you? What are you going to do?"

"Me?" Harry took a gulp of coffee. "I've got to get all these kids settled. After that, I've got some people to meet. Things are going to be much more difficult now. I worry we've missed the window of opportunity."

"The window of opportunity to what?"

"To get as many of us out of Germany before—" He didn't say it, was stopped by the look on Katrine's face.

"I understand," she said quietly. "What is it that you do, exactly?"

"I'm a Zionist," he said proudly. "You know what that is?"[2]

"Harry, if I may call you Harry," she said hotly, "I've got a Master's degree in history from the University of Berlin. My father is a top professor, and I am a Jew. Just because I am *not* a Zionist doesn't mean I don't know what Zionism is."

"So why aren't you one?" Harry retorted accusingly. "Don't you think the Jews deserve a homeland of their own? In Palestine? Don't you think that it is the only way we will survive?"

"Oh, come now," she protested. "My family has lived in Germany for decades. We are Germans. I've always resonated more with being German than a Jew. We aren't really religious. My mother always made a chicken dinner on Shabbat, and we sang Kiddush, but we don't keep kosher. We even celebrate Christmas with our Christian friends and have Christian family members. It's just the stupid Nazis."

"You *are* a Jew. You're different. And when times get tough, there will always be someone to remind you just how different you are."

"That's not true." Katrine was angry now. "And you are very rude!"

Undeterred, Harry kept going, saying, "There will always be someone out to destroy us, and the only way we are going to survive is if we have a country of our own. A way to defend ourselves! And we need people like you, Katrine. Like you and your sisters. People who are strong, smart, brave. We can't do it alone."

"You really need historians? You just need bodies who can dig in your precious swamps in Palestine. I've read about what it is really like over there. The dust. The desert. The Arab Riots. They don't want you there! They won't let you stay either. Once all this craziness ends—"

"Don't be a fool, Katrine. Look at the Russians. Systematically working their way to wipe us off the face of the map. One pogrom after another. And if it isn't them, it's someone else. Angry Polish noblemen. Crazy communists. Now the Nazis. It doesn't matter. You can believe that if Hitler is defeated, everything will go back to normal if you want to, but it won't change the truth. Things will never, ever be the same again." Harry set his cup down and went to the deck.

Katrine's lower lip parted just barely, but no reply would come out. It was a verbal battle, and Harry had just won round one. "I need some air."

"My goodness, that man has a lot of opinions," she finally huffed under her breath. She was normally the smartest person in the room and was not used to being trumped by anyone. And she didn't like it one bit.

"He's sort of charming though, don't you think?" I said, staring after him.

Realizing for the first time that I was there, Katrine looked at me, then at Harry through the porthole. He was leaning against the ship's railing, his dark curly hair whipping about in the wind. "That's not the word I would use. Not the word I would use at all!"

ROUND TWO OF Katrine and Harry's brawl took place at dinner. *Our* dinner, that is. We'd fed the children and bedded them down early under the watchful eye of Ferguson, giving the Brophy twins and Sebastian a break. Gorman and Nathaniel were doing the work of five men running the ship. Gone were the days of dressing for dinner and dancing to Ethel Merman. Yet, despite the communal exhaustion, spirits were high. Well, not exactly high. But they were not as low as they could have been.

My mother took the bowl of chicken soup Cookie had made to my father. He was still in bed, and she was hoping to get at least a few drops of liquid into his system. Dehydration only made sea sickness worse.

With Frank at the wheel, Horatio collapsed next to Edie on the couch, both of them so tired they could barely speak.

"I've always heard that parenting is harder than it looks. I've judged so many parents." She leaned her head on Horatio's shoulder. "I couldn't get that one little girl to let go of me, the one with the curls. I held her till she fell asleep and had to pry her little fingers off of my jacket. Poor thing. And then I accidentally woke her up, and she wouldn't stop crying. I didn't know what to do."

"Don't worry," Horatio gave her a little hug. "It's just our first day. We'll get better with practice."

"You really want children?" she asked, wide-eyed.

"No. Well, I never really considered it. How about we talk about it once we get back to civilization?"

Edie nodded and gratefully took her bowl of soup from Cookie.

With a gust of wind, Peter blew into the dining room and shivered. "My word, it's getting cold. Cookie! Please pour me a bowl of that." Looking around the room, he asked, "Grace and Lorelei still feeling under the weather?"

I nodded. "My dad too."

Harry took his soup and boldly sat across from Katrine. She stared straight at him. Like a cat ready to strike, I thought.

"You know what I think about people like you?" Harry stuck his spoon in his bowl.

Raising her eyebrows, she asked in an even tone, "What? What do you think about people like me?"

"You're like sheep. Led to the slaughter. You don't want to know, so you pretend not to know."

"What's that supposed to mean?" Her voice rose.

"Az a nar gait in mark, fraien zikh di kremer," he said, nonpulsed, the Yiddish words rolling easily off his tongue.

"What did I miss?" Peter looked at me, but I motioned for him to be quiet.

My mother translated, "When a fool goes shopping, the storekeepers rejoice."

Harry was on a roll and spouted, "You liked your nice, comfortable life, everything just so. You knew people suffered. You are smart, so of course you knew. But you didn't really care. You still don't"

"I do care! How dare you say that!" Katrine struggled to control herself.

"If you go on pretending that everything will one day be normal and the way it was, that Hitler will just go away and your parents will come back—"

Interrupting, she yelled, "But they might! You don't know what's going to happen."

"Shut up, Katrine and listen to reason."

Without missing a beat, she responded coldly, "And you think that moving to the middle of the desert and setting up a tent with some Bedouins is going to fix everything? Going to be a real life?"

"It's better than that pretend life you're living, kid. At least in my world, we are going to actually be alive. In yours, we all end up dead."

"And in yours, we won't? As if the Arabs would let us stay? They've been there a long time. They are not about to just give up their land!"

"We've got a better chance with them than the Germans. And it's not just a desert. We've got mountains and the ocean and yes, we have some swamps too."

"Sounds lovely. Like a real paradise," Katrine sneered.

*"A klugar farstait fun ain vort tsvai."* He frowned.

My mother once again translated for him. "A wise man conceals his intelligence. The fool displays his foolishness."

*"A klugar vasit vos er zogt; a nar zogt vos er vaist!"* Katrine's spat without missing a beat.

"A wise man knows what he says. A fool says what he knows." With a small smile, my mother added, "At least, I think that's what she said. My Yiddish is a bit rusty."

Katrine was on a roll. *"A behaimeh hot a langen tsung un ken nisht reden; der mentsh hot a kurtseh un tor nisht reden."*

"Animals have long tongues but can't speak. Men have short tongues and shouldn't speak." My mother was getting faster. It was coming back.

"Whoa, whoa, there." Peter put his hands up. "Timeout. Ding, ding, ding," he laughed awkwardly.

Katrine stood up, her shoulders erect. "I'm going to go check on my sisters. Excuse me." Without so much as a glance at Harry, she left the table.

As the door slammed behind her, Harry looked at me. "Your cousin is one strong-willed dame. For someone so smart, I marvel at her stupidity."

"I'll pass on your sentiments." I took a sip of soup.

"You do that." He was red-faced. "I can't believe my own people sometimes. Blinder than bats."

Horatio appeared behind Harry. "Don't be so hard on her. She's lost everything she thought her life would be in the blink of an eye. If she wants to be blind for a while, let her. She'll open her eyes in good time."

"Some of them don't open their eyes," Harry answered sadly. "I've tried so hard, Horatio, to tell them. But no, they stayed. And now, they are in those camps. And who knows what else Hitler has up his sleeve." With that, Harry strode out of the room.

"What a pair those two make," Edie said. "A more volatile match I've never seen."

My mother grinned and shrugged. *"Fun krume shidukhim kumen arois glaikheh kinder."*

"You forget we don't speak Yiddish," Horatio chuckled.

"From bad matches also come good children."

# CHAPTER 33

## SCOTLAND

"They really are precious children," Edie said. She was holding the little girl with golden curls again. "So sweet and well behaved. For everything they've gone through..." Edie didn't say anything more, but kissed the top of her head. The girl, Anna, and my aunt had become inseparable.

"I wish I could speak German," Edie went on. "I'm really going to miss them, their precious little selves."

Our journey was practically over. In another hour, the *Goose* would pull into the harbor at Edinburgh. All the children had been bathed, had their hair brushed and their bellies filled with more of Cookie's treats. He had gone overboard with the sugar, and he knew it. He couldn't resist the joy his sugar cookies evoked on their faces. It might not have been the best way to ease their tears and homesickness, but it certainly seemed to help. We'd probably gone through 30 dozen in the last two days.

Katrine and Harry maintained an open hostility, butting heads over everything from the right way to hold babies, which was funny as both were single and had little to no experience caring for children to whether or not cream went in the cup before or after the tea. If there was a point to be argued, they did. And when there was no point to be argued, they maintained a stony silence.

Now, as we waited for land, they sat on opposite sides of the dining room table listening to the wireless. The refined BBC voice blared out loud and clear for the first time in days.

"This morning, the first air-raid sirens sounded over London. However, thankfully, they were a false alarm. Chamberlain has reformed the government, creating a War Cabinet. Winston Churchill was named as First Lord of the Admiralty. Also, the National Service Act was officially passed this morning. All men between 18 and 41 are liable for conscription. And now, for the music program, we proudly present the London Philharmonic's live performance of Beethoven's 5th."

With that, the first movement began, and I turned the radio down a notch. It was much too intense a piece for the moment, in my opinion.

Peter poked his head inside. "Piper, come here. Come see!"

"What is it?"

"The coast of Scotland!"

Slipping my sweater over my shoulders, I followed him out to the bow. Pressed up on the deck close enough to feel his warmth, I took in the coastline. It was marvelous, daunting, rugged. It evoked freedom, safety and home all at once, though I'd never set foot on its shore.

"That's Edinburgh's Leith Harbor," Peter said, looking at the docks and the city's outline beyond it.

There were low clouds hanging like a thick mist above the ancient city which rose like a medieval fortress above the sea. It was a welcome sight that seemed to urge us onward, promising rest and reprieve. A strong wind blew up behind us, increasing our speed. I studied the white crests on the dark blue waves, the sea-foam of the ship's wake thick behind us. With each rise and fall of the sea, my breath came easier.

Grace and Lorelei joined us and we gazed onward, our hair

blowing wild from the wind, enjoying the ship's motion and the feel of the salt-spray on our exposed skin.

"Does Horatio live in the city?" I asked finally, as the sounds of the harbor reached our ears. Sailors were shouting and ship's bells were ringing. We heard the steady drone of machinery and smelled the scent of fish. I grinned a little at that thought. Always the same smell of fish in these harbors, no matter the country.

"No," Peter answered. "He lives further north in a village outside of St. Andrews called Kingsbarns. It's just a short sail up the coast. We should be there by this evening."

It was then I noticed I had been looking at Peter, not the view. And I had been for a long time. He looked down into my eyes, smiling shyly before turning away.

"After we drop the children off at Leith Harbor," he finished.

"Kingsbarns." I tasted the name. "It sounds lovely."

WE PULLED into Leith Harbor before noon, met on the dock by a small crowd of families awaiting their wards. One by one, the children's guardians packed them off into cars or cabs and took them to their new homes.

Some were older couples, in their 60s or 70s. They were still strong and healthy and had empty bedrooms to spare. Others were young couples who could not have children of their own. Still more were those who had so many children that one more mouth to feed wouldn't make much of a difference. "Why not?" I could imagine them convincing one another. "Take some little refugees in? It's the right thing to do, of course. The British thing. The Christian thing."

The process of distributing the children took time. There was much paperwork to fill out, and of course, the children needed looking after. In the midst of all the activity, it was nevertheless impossible to ignore the obvious; the port was readying itself for war.

We'd passed two warships coming into the harbor, enormous gray monsters so large that the sailors on board looked like grasshoppers. The children stared wide-eyed at the ships. A little one asked if they were Noah's Arks.

The pier itself was swarming with activity and men in uniform. A few stopped for a little too long and were a little too friendly to our little enterprise. Specifically, a little too friendly to my cousins and me. Frank flexed his tattooed muscles and pushed them back with all the grace of a bulldog.

"You've got to watch out for sailors. I don't trust 'em around women one bit." He winked at Lorelei. She rewarded him by blatantly ignoring him, turning on her heel, and heading back into the confines of the *Grey Goose*.

"What's the matter with that cousin of yours? Does she not like sailors or something?"

"All three of them are a little moody," I said, trying to soothe Frank's hurt pride.

"Yeah." He gave a shrug. "I figured that out on my own. Still, most girls I know are not able to resist the charms of good ol' Frank. I was just trying to get her to smile."

Horatio bellowed from the starboard for Frank to help him prepare the yacht for departure. He wanted to be out with the next tide. "Aye aye, sir!" Frank jogged back on board, and I heard him mutter, "I need a break from all these women anyways."

Sebastian watched from the bow. He whistled low and slow. "Those senioritas getting to you, Frank?"

Frank pretended he didn't hear the jibe, busying himself with a pile of rope.

Harry looked at his list. "Oh no," he groaned.

"What is it?" Edie asked, holding little Anna in her arms.

"We've got three kids left over." He looked at Anna and then at the 7-year-old twins, Willem and Raffi.

"What do you mean?"

"I mean we have three extra kids. No more foster families. Dang blast it!" He rubbed his hand through his hair. "Now I'm going to have to get them to Exmouth in England. This is going to put me behind schedule."

"What's there?" Edie shifted Anna to her other hip. At four years old, she was a little too big to be held, but neither she nor my aunt seemed to notice.

"There's a hostel there for the extras. Got it set up in an old summer camp. The National Jewish Fund's running it.[3]"

"You mean, you are going to take these babies and put them in a summer camp? The cold weather is about to set in!"

"You don't have to make it sound so bad. We've got good people taking care of them."

"They don't need people," she sounded panicked. "They need parents! Besides, you don't have time to take them to what's it called..." She shook her hand in the distance.

"Exmouth," he finished.

"Right. Exmouth. You have important espionage things to do, right?" Her voice continued to rise.

"Well, yes. I do," he conceded. "But could you please keep it down a little, Edie?"

She stood protectively in front of Willem and Raffi. "Boys, go downstairs in the *Goose*. Get out of this cold."

"They don't know what you're saying," I reminded her.

"Well somebody translate for crying out loud!" She pointed at Harry. "You are not taking these babies anywhere. You hear me?"

My mother stepped in, suddenly understanding what Edie meant. "Edie, are you sure? You don't know the first thing about raising children."

"Oh, come on, you sent me your kid. She lived through the experience, didn't she?" Everyone looked at me.

"A 16-year-old is a little bit of a different ballgame," my father joined in, looking down at the twin boys.

"Don't try to argue me out of it, Nathan. My mind is made up!"

She turned to Harry and said, "No point in wasting the train trip. Trains aren't safe anyway."

"Okay, okay. You want the little rascals, you got em." He was smiling and holding his hands up in mock surrender. "I guess my job here is done."

He looked over at Katrine. "Maybe not 100% successful." Katrine refused to give him eye contact and crossed her arms hotly.

"If you ever need a place to stay in Scotland, you are always welcome at our home," Edie said with a flourish. Harry hugged Edie quickly and pecked her cheek. Giving her a small smile, he responded, "You're a peach. You know that, right?"

Edie patted his cheek. "Now be a good boy, and go do whatever it is you have to do. But don't do anything stupid. Try to stay safe."

My mother reached out for Harry, and he hugged her too. "You heard what Edie said. You've got important work to do. You should get moving."

"I've got one more thing to do here," Harry said.

He walked up to Katrine and stuck a piece of paper in her hand. "Look, Katrine," he said firmly and quietly, "I know you don't want to listen to me."

"So stop talking." She pushed his hand away, but he would not be so quickly deterred.

"British Policy is facilitating 3,400 of the older kids to stay here only temporarily."

"What are you saying?" Her hostility on hold, she listened carefully.

"I'm saying that I'm working on getting them to Palestine. It's a program called Youth Aliyah. We've got a boat headed out from Chelsea in a month. The details are on that paper. We could use help."

"What does this have to do with me?"

"I'll spell it out for you. If you happen to wake up one morning and discover how right I am and how wrong you are, be at the port in Chelsea. We need girls like you. Smart, strong, spunky. It will take all of us working together to survive this."

"Unlike you, I think it is only a matter of time before the German people come to their senses." Her jaw was set, her fist clenched.

"Come on, Katrine!" he plead, begging her to understand. He repeated, "We need you."

"I'm sure you'll find all the help you need somewhere else." Katrine spun on her heel and walked quickly back up the gangplank and into the Goose.

"Yeah. I guess so," he said quietly to himself. Harry stepped back and saw me watching him. He had a sad half-smile on his face, and his shoulders drooped. "Well, you can't say I didn't try. Bye, kid." He thumped my back like he would an eight-year-old boy, pushing me off my balance momentarily. "Guess I'll be seeing you."

"Keep yourself safe, Harry."

"Sure, kid, sure." He slung his duffel on his back and disappeared down the pier into the crowd, his hand waving one final time, his face staring straight ahead. And then he walked into whatever battle it was that he was determined to win.

IT WAS late afternoon when we were all back at sea for our short journey up the coast to Kingsbarns, the home of Horatio's family castle. It had belonged to his clan for years and years, with mountains of lore and mystery surrounding the old place.

Edie slid the last couch back into place. We had officially dismantled the nursery, and the library was, once again, just a library. Edie looked over at Horatio. "The children are going to need warmer clothes. They've nothing appropriate for a damp castle."

"What?" he replied, thinking he'd misheard her.

"Warmer clothes. For the children."

"Whatever do you mean, woman?" He poured himself a cup of strong coffee from the urn. "I just spent half a fortune on those girls' new wardrobes. Everything from evening dresses to riding clothes. And I don't even have horses."

"Not those children," she said. "Your *other* children."

He stopped, coffee midair. "What other children?"

It was at that moment that Ferguson appeared with Anna clinging to his back, the monkey on his shoulder, and Willem and Raffi clinging to each hand.

"So, now you're telling me I'm actually a father."

"Something like that."

He let out something between a laugh and growl. "Well, I guess it was about time we got started on a family."

"It might be only temporary, you know," my father said, straightening the paper on his knees. "They have parents of their own and will need to go back to them at some point."

"God willing," my mother added.

Ferguson eased Anna off his back and set her down at the table with the boys. "Now, be good children and stay right there. Good." He wiped sweat off his brow. They looked at him quizzically.

"Doing all right, Ferguson?" Edie asked.

"Never better, ma'am. I think they are starting to understand English."

"Geniuses. All three of them," Horatio said with a grin.

The three children looked up at Edie, eyes wide and questioning. Edie swept them up into her arms and hugged them tightly. Little Anna giggled, and the boys wrapped their arms around her neck. They may not have understood what she said, but they certainly understood that they had found a friend.

## CHAPTER 34

## HOME AT LAST

The castle clung to the crags of an enormous cliff jutting out over the sea. Half of it was crumbling, and it looked quite mysterious shrouded in the evening's mist.

It was a strange sort of house. The medieval walls were crumbling, along with a tower and what was left of the ramparts that lined the outer boundary along the cliff. The great hall and living quarters had fallen into terrible disrepair in the late 19th century. And instead of restoring the old place, Horatio's grandfather built a new mansion, of the Gothic Revival style, backed right up against the ruins of the castle. The whole thing blended together into a mess of brick turrets, angles, and sharp jagged edges. Not unlike the cliffs, I thought.

"It almost feels like home. Right out on the edge of the sea and everything. If I close my eyes, I could almost be in Maine," Edie said with what can only be described as a contented sigh.

The roar of the ocean's surf pounding against the rocks below did make one feel at home. Except it was much colder than Maine, even in the summer. And the damp was intense, the kind that bites into your bones and won't let go.

"All right, all right!" Horatio pushed through our little crowd. "Let me carry my bride over the threshold."

He pulled out a skeleton key and unlocked the door. As it creaked open, he swooped Edie up into his arms and led the parade inside the dark hall.

"Watch your back!" Edie cried as Horatio set her down carefully and flipped on the lights. "I've gained weight on this trip. I'm not the skinny slip of a girl you married." She needn't have worried. Horatio was as strong as a bear. And she had never exactly been a "skinny slip" of anything. A more apt word to describe Edie was "sturdy."

"I had it wired for electricity a few years back, just in case I decided to move in permanently," Horatio said proudly. "Never really expected to need the old place though. I usually sleep on the *Goose*."

The lights revealed a foyer and a grand staircase leading up to the second and third stories. Everything was done in dark wood. Dozens of ancient swords, muskets, and coats of arms hung on the paneling.

And it was freezing.

Edie took a long sweeping look. "It's very masculine," she said simply.

"But you love it?" he prodded, smiling hopefully.

Throwing her arms around him, she said, "I'll adore it. Once I find my bearings." She rubbed her hands together and shivered.

"What about heat?" my mother asked. "It's not healthy for the children, the cold and the damp."

Katrine shrugged. "They're German. They're used to cold and damp."

My mother seemed unconvinced.

"Right," Horatio said, "heat. We've got radiators in most of the bedrooms, don't we, Ferguson? And we can get the fires roaring in no time at all."

"Of course, sir," he nodded. "I'll see if I can get a fire or two going in the main living areas. It shouldn't take more than a few hours to warm this place up." Ferguson set off down one of the halls and disappeared.

"A few hours?" my mother shivered.

"It takes a long time to heat these buildings. It's the insulation." Horatio answered.

"Or the lack thereof," my father added.

We all stood there, wondering what in the world we were supposed to do next. It had been weeks since we'd had a moment of peace. How does one wind down when one has been wound up for so long?

"Well, considering you're all our guests," Edie said, suddenly slipping into hostess mode, "I think a tour is in order."

"Well said, well said," Horatio nodded, proud that his wife had taken ownership of the house so quickly. "A grand tour of the old family seat."

Frank walked beside Peter and I. "I wonder why some castles are called family seats. Do you think it actually has something to do with some sort of chair?"

"Perhaps a throne," I concluded. It was a very royal place. There was a massive ballroom, an immense library, and countless drawing rooms and sitting rooms. I counted 21 giant bedrooms that each had a four poster bed hung with heavy curtains. A few had more than one bed.

Edie chose the bedroom next to her and Horatio's to convert into a nursery, leaving another 19 bedrooms for the rest of us to choose from.

Grace and I both didn't really want to sleep alone in a giant empty room, so we opted to share one of the rooms with two beds that looked out over the garden. Lorelei and Katrine took the connecting room next to it. We dubbed it 'the women's dormitory.' The men's dormitory for Frank and Peter was on the floor above.

The rest of the crew stayed on the *Goose*, preparing for her annual overhaul. Once the ship's hull was scrubbed, and she shone as clean and bright as new, the men would enjoy a few weeks of a much deserved vacation.

Ferguson, Frank, and Peter lugged our trunks into our room. "The fire is lit, and the sitting room is cozy and warm, Miss Piper and Miss Grace. If I might be so bold, you two go downstairs and rest up a bit. Let me undo your trunks, and I'll light the fire in here while I'm at it."

"Is he always so helpful?" Grace asked.

"It's nice, isn't it?" I smiled at Ferguson. "I don't know what we'd do without dear Fergie."

"It is my pleasure to be of service, ma'am." He bowed slightly and made way for us to pass.

Lorelei and Katrine poked their heads through the connecting door. "Those two are ours," Lorelei said, pointing to two of the trunks. Frank hefted one of the trunks onto his back and carried it into their room. "See, I can be helpful too." He flirtatiously winked at Lorelei, determined to win her over.

She rolled her eyes.

Frank dropped the trunk with a thud. "What? Not even a thank you?"

Poor Frank. He wasn't making much headway. "Would you light the fires in our room too, Ferguson?" Katrine asked.

The butler nodded, and with that, we wound our way to the hearth of the roaring fire in Horatio's favorite sitting room. The room was neither too big nor too small and had a thick rug and comfortable worn-in couches. It was the most homey of the rooms, and it was also the room with the radio.

Horatio and my father huddled in front of it, listening intently to news about the war, barely moving. Edie and Anna sat on the floor, along with the boys. She'd found some paper and colored pencils in Horatio's desk and was attempting to give her a rudimentary lesson in primary colors and shading. This was quite difficult to do, given that they didn't speak the same language. (Also difficult to do if you are four years old and are not quite sure of all your colors yet in any language.)

"Where's Mom?" I asked my dad. He glanced up from the radio. "Down in the kitchen. She offered to figure out some sort of supper."

The kitchen. Where was that again? Katrine looked at me and grinned. "She'll probably need help, seeing as there are so many of us. I'll go with you."

We took one or two wrong turns before we finally found the kitchen and my mother raiding the pantry.

"It is too late to go into the village for supplies." She moaned at our arrival. "All we've got is baked beans and tinned tuna. We'll have to wake up early to get bread for the children in the morning."

"And us," Katrine laughed. "We've been rather spoiled, haven't we? Between all the hotels and Cookie?"

"Do you think you remember how to cook?" I asked. Mom had never exactly been a gourmet cook. She shot me a look and replied, "I can handle canned beans. Trust me."

I surveyed the kitchen. "Not very modern, is it?" Katrine said, putting the cans down on the long farm table. The stove was a huge wood-burning one. "Looks like nothing's been updated for a hundred years. That is, except for the electric lights."

My mother, hands on her hips, said in an exasperated tone, "I can light a stove, I should think. I saw my mother do it dozens of times. Are there any matches around here?"

I found a pack in a drawer and tossed it to my mother. Hardly paying attention, she caught it. She'd always had good hand-eye coordination.

It took several tries to get the stove lit. But in the end, we succeeded, and Mother was soon shouting through the old halls to, "Come and get it while it's hot!"

Gathered around the farm table in the kitchen, supping on beans, it was not the most elegant meal of the journey, but it was my favorite.

And for the first time in many weeks, I exhaled.

~

THE BROPHY BROTHERS and Sebastian rented a truck and delivered all the cargo from the *Goose* early the next morning. I'd forgotten all about the souvenirs that Horatio and Edie had bought in Casablanca. There were boxes overflowing with spices, strings of glass beads, and little carved camels (which Anna promptly adopted as her own). The men also brought in all the chocolate from the Netherlands and my cousins' clothing. We had enough stuff to fill the back of the truck twice.

Edie and I oversaw operations from the base of the truck. "That box goes there, Sebastian!" I called. "Bring the inlaid boxes to the sitting room. We'll put them on the bookshelf," Edie directed. On and on it went.

Edie gasped as Horatio walked into the courtyard from the house. "Oh my! Horatio, whatever are you wearing?"

I turned to face my uncle. He was wearing a skirt! We both gaped, wide-eyed. Horatio looked down self-consciously. "What is it?"

Confused. He was honestly confused.

"Oh Edie," Sebastian laughed. "It's a kilt. A kilt!"

"Of course. How silly of me. I did marry a Scotsman, didn't I? It's your traditional dress, isn't it?"

"I always wear my kilt when I'm back home," he said. "You wouldn't believe how much more comfortable it is than trousers."

Regaining composure, Edie replied, "Of course, I'm sure. And very becoming too."

Sebastian laughed, "I was confused too, the first time he wore one, señora. In my country, we would call that kilt a skirt!"

Horatio bristled. "Real men wear kilts. Get back to work, Sebastian!"

Sebastian tossed him a suitcase. "Here, boss! Whatever you say!"

With that, Horatio marched back into the castle.

"Piper!" Sebastian called. "Where do you want this stuff?" He pointed to three large boxes, the last on the truck bed.

"What is it?" I asked.

"The equipment for a dark room."

Peter joined us at the truck's edge. "Anything else for me?"

I shook my head no and turned my attention back to Sebastian. "Maybe there is a basement or something?"

"For what?" Peter asked.

"A darkroom."

Peter looked thoughtful. "There's a gardener's shed out back. It'd be a perfect dark room. Follow me." He instructed Sebastian, "We can set it up now."

Following a pace behind, I called, "But are we needed inside?"

"Nope." Peter glanced behind in my direction. "Your parents and cousins ran into town to pick up some groceries and cleaning supplies. We've got the whole morning to do whatever we want."

And he wanted to set up a dark room with me? My heart skipped a beat.

An hour later, once again, Peter and I were hunched over chemicals in the crimson glow of the red light. Old pros by now, we worked as a team, watching the film develop before our eyes.

The first picture was a doozy. It was the men in striped uniforms at the concentration camp.

"It's a good thing the Germans didn't confiscate your camera at the border. If they'd found that picture…" he trailed off.

I hung it carefully to dry and didn't answer. There was no need.

Next was a shot of Edie and the gamblers that I'd taken from the balcony. Then there was one of Harry and Katrine standing with their backs to one another, both of them angry and proud. It was a split second moment, but I'd caught it.

"What a picture," Peter said, still looking at the camp.

I sat down on the small stool and turned to face Peter. "What do you think is going to happen now? Do you think we'll get to go home soon?"

"I don't know. I guess we'll just have to wait and see. We can't make any real decisions until we know more."

~

WHEN WE GOT BACK to the house, Edie, my mother, and my cousins were hastily unloading crates of jars and bags of sugar onto the kitchen table.

A loud knocking at the back door was followed by a stream of middle-aged village women plunging into the kitchen, chattering loudly like a flock of chickens.

"Whatever is going on?" I asked, pushing through the crowd to my mother and Edie. "Who are all these women?"

"The war has started, dear. We are doing our part," Edie said, slightly distracted.

"Our part for what?"

"To feed the troops, of course," Edie replied as if the answer was obvious.

"They're members of the W.I.," my mother said, gesturing towards the gray-haired matrons in floral dresses and knotty wool sweaters, "the Women's Institute."[4]

"What's that?" Peter was right behind me.

"It's a club your aunt and I joined this morning in town. They've asked to use the castle's kitchen because it is the only one big enough."

"Big enough for what?" He made room for one of the matrons carrying a stack of pots.

My mother put down a heavy sack of sugar. "Due to the draft, a great number of farm laborers have been called up. Now there is an enormous amount of fruit that might rot if not preserved right away." She looked at the door. "Strawberries, actually."

With that, a troop of adolescents carrying baskets and buckets of strawberries marched in, leaning the containers of fruit up against the far wall of the kitchen.

Edie sat down heavily on a chair near my mother. "The government gave the W.I. over one thousand pounds for the sugar. A representative from the Ministry of Health should be by soon to give us some instructions. Apparently, it is very regulated. I've never made jam, so this ought to be interesting."

The whole crew of the *Goose* was in the kitchen now, unloading the heavy canning equipment and firing up the stove. Cookie looked ready to charge. "We'll do anything we can to help with the war, ma'am. We'll make jam all night if we need to."

A portly woman grabbed one of the stools and leaned heavily on Peter's arm to help her up on top. Rapping a big wooden spoon against an empty pail, she silenced the crowd of women.

"Thank you all for coming!" she said, smiling broadly. "And thank you, Edith, our newest member of the community, for volunteering your kitchen."

"My kitchen is the Women's Institute's kitchen," Edie said magnanimously, nodding her head like a queen. "Anything for the war effort!"

"Right," Mrs. Sybil Butterfield (for that was her name) continued, "the war effort. That is why we are all here. With our men being sent off to fight, we have our own battles to wage right here! We can beat Hitler right out of his senses, and we'll do it by keeping our boys fed and happy. The Ministry of Health has said we must start by not letting our food go to waste. If it grows, we can it. And we'll send it to our men going to the front." Her voice had risen to a shout. "Who's with me?"

A bevy of feminine cheers rang out, punctuated by the deep bellows of the seamen.

"Then let the jam-making begin!"

And so it began. We boiled and stirred, cranked and boiled. Sealed and tasted. Sealed again. I had sugar crusted in my fingernails, and the whole kitchen was steamy hot and smelled of cooking fruit.

The farm women chatted and gossiped, Edie right at the center of it all. Finally, at one in the morning, the last pail of berries was preserved. Mrs. Sybil Butterfield warmly shook Edie's hand. "Now that ought to show those Huns a thing or two," she growled good-naturedly. "So, we'll see you at the meeting next Tuesday? We meet every week in the chapel."

"Of course," Edie said tiredly, pushing a loose red curl away from her face. Her cheeks were flushed from exertion.

"Next month we do the elderberries and pears."

Edie nodded. "Sounds like a plan. Would you like to just leave the equipment then? I'll have one of the crew stow it below until the harvest comes in. Horatio mentioned that the cellar has plenty of room."

"Capital, capital." Mrs. Butterfield said. She fully relished her role as Commander-in-Chief of Operation Preservation.

"We'll be heading back to the *Goose* now, if you don't mind, Edie," Cookie said, taking his hat off the peg on the wall and following Mrs. Butterfield out the door with the rest of the crew.

"Of course, Cookie. Thanks for your help, all of you," she looked exhausted. To no one in particular, she murmured, "Wars are rather tiresome. Don't you think?"

Cookie gave a short laugh and agreed.

"I've got a great idea," my mother said after the door slammed shut.

We all looked at her expectantly. My father was scrubbing pots over at the sink. My cousins were slouching on the floor. Anna and the twins were asleep at the table, jam all around their mouths. Horatio, wearing an apron over his kilt, was stacking jam in a crate.

"Let's do nothing at all except sleep."

"That is an excellent idea," I agreed.

"Capital, capital." Peter did a stunningly good imitation of Mrs. Butterfield.

## CHAPTER 35

## WORTH A MILLION WORDS

"Up here in the north, it rains 265 days a year," Horatio said stoking the fire after our late breakfast. A thick sheet of rain held us indoors the following day. A rain which I would soon grow used to.

Peter, after a mad dash through the garden to our darkroom/shed, returned with my photographs safely stowed under the protection of his mackintosh.

I looked through them briefly, then passed them to my mother. She wordlessly stared at the one of the concentration-camp motioning for my father. After a moment, he passed it to my cousins, who handed it back and forth amongst themselves, their faces going white.

When the photograph finely made it to Edie, she looked at my mother. "It's completely frightful. Terrifying. Don't let the children see it. Ferguson, move them to the corner." She directed, "It might give them nightmares." She shooed the twins back to their colored blocks on the floor. "It might give *me* nightmares."

"Well someone has to see it," Grace said. "We've got to show somebody!"

My mother, puzzled, took the photograph back and stared at it hard. Looking over her shoulder, Frank frowned. "You two really saw that? Wow. So the rumors are true."

Horatio in his leather chair pulled up near the fire said, "I've got a friend in Edinburgh. He's the editor-in-chief of the Scotsman. Went to school together back in the day. I want to drive there this afternoon. Ferguson just finished getting the Bentley working again after it sat in the garage all year."

"The Scotsman. You mean the newspaper?" Edie asked.

Horatio nodded yes.

"You mean, you think Piper should publish it?" my father asked.

"She must publish it. The world has to know what's really going on." Katrine looked up. "We have no choice. My parents could be there or one like it."

~

JUST HOURS LATER, I was wedged between my parents and Edie and Horatio behind the editor-in-chief of the Scotsman's desk. He scrutinized the photograph closely with the keen eye of a professional. He also wore a kilt, as the editor-in-chief of the Scotsman must.

"Did you take this photograph, lass?" he asked finally, looking up at me. "It's obviously not a fake." His light eyes were penetrating, and his unbrushed hair was askew. The office was in such a state that I assumed he lived there half the time. Life of a newspaperman, I supposed.

"I took it," I said quietly. "I wish it was fake."

The stress wrinkles around his eyes and mouth deepened as he probed, "What were you doing in Germany? Right dangerous for a young thing like you to be gollywagging round the Hun's countryside."

"It's a long story," I said flatly.

"Well, I'm going to need it if you want the photograph to be published."

"Then you want to publish it?" my father asked.

"We are one of the oldest publications in Scotland, but we don't print photographs without stories." He put the photograph down carefully. "And this photograph has a story that must be told."

"Must be told?" Edie repeated to herself. Her eyes were fixated on some unknown point on the wall. She stood up slowly and said once more, "Must be told."

"You bring me the true story, say by tomorrow, and I'll print it. Front page. The Sunday paper. All of Scotland will read it. Any later and the photograph will be too old for a front pager. I want to paint this as a current event."

"All of Scotland?" Edie had moved toward the window and was looking down at the street below.

"Indeed," the editor said.

My heart sunk. By tomorrow? "I'm not a writer. I don't think I could..." I stammered, not knowing what to do. There was no way in a million years that I could write down what had happened in a way that would do the story justice, much less by tomorrow.

"Piper," Edie asked slowly, "would you mind if I have a go at it?"

"I would be relieved," I answered honestly.

Turning back, with a quick step towards the desk, Edie reached over and clasped the editor's hand. "You have a deal. A story by tomorrow."

"But will you have time?" my mother asked.

"I always have time!"

Back in the Bentley, Edie hummed to herself, "Time for you, and time for me, and time yet for a hundred indecisions, and for a hundred visions and revisions, before the taking of a toast and tea."[5]

"Before the taking of toast and tea?" I knew those words. Elliot. Of course.

"Edie, you know *The Love Song of J. Alfred Prufrock*?"

"Who?" Horatio asked.

Edie nodded distractedly. "If only I really did have the time. I'm afraid I don't even have time for one revision." Edie tapped her fingers together impatiently. "Drive quickly, Horatio. We've work to do!"

~

A LOUD SCRAPING OVERHEAD DREW Grace's and my attention to the floor above. Peter and Frank had found an old roll top desk in one of the unused bedrooms and were shoving it down the stairs to Edie's personal sitting room.

"I can't work without an office," she said, hands on her hips, those long nails practically twitching with excitement at getting to click away once more. "Everyone knows I must have my own workspace." Edie's years-long streak of writer's block was finally broken. Her days of painting seabirds and portraits were over, at least for now.

She glanced at Grace. "Go get your sisters. I need to interview all of you. And tell Ferguson to keep the children as quiet as possible. I must have absolute silence to fully concentrate. It's imperative that writers have quiet!"

Edie was more focused than I'd ever seen her.

"I haven't seen that look in her eye in decades," Horatio smiled proudly. "I've missed this side of Edie."

"What look?" I turned towards him.

"It's the look she gets when something genius is forming. You just wait and see what happens next. When that gleam is in her eye and her fingers hit the typewriter, the words that come out demand attention. They are the sort of words that can change the world."

~

MY COUSINS WERE in that room for hours. They emerged pale and tired. Lorelei's eyes were red rimmed from crying. Frank passed her in the hall and shot her a sympathetic glance. She walked by as though he was invisible. Mother made tea and sat with them in the kitchen, all three completely out of words.

Edie had given strict instructions that she was not to be disturbed. No tea. No dinner. It was definitely one of her mad rushes of creative energy, Horatio confirmed.

"She'll be up all night. Nothing we can do to stop her," Horatio said as he dropped a tray of supper off outside her door. "Her fingers won't stop typing till she runs out of things to say."

"Then what will happen?" Peter asked, setting his fork of potatoes down.

"She'll sleep for 18 hours."

She was indeed up all night, but she finished the article. Proudly descending the stairs, still in her dress from the day before, hair all over the place, she held a handful of papers aloft, pearl bracelet gleaming triumphantly.

"Ferguson," she called, "get the Bentley ready! Piper, grab your coat. Time is of the essence!"

Back in the editor's office, Edie and I hunched forward on our seats as he read Edie's piece. He looked up approvingly, even admiringly.

"You wrote this?" he asked.

"I'm a novelist by trade," Edie answered.

A slight trace of concern etched on his forehead. "But this is not fiction?"

"Oh no. It is the testimony of my three adopted daughters. All true. Every breath of it."

He shook his head sadly. "Terrible times we are living in. God help us." He faced the window, looking out over Edinburgh. "Tomorrow morning, front page. And thanks for bringing it to me."

As he shook my hand, he stopped and looked at me. "Hold on to that camera of yours. You have a gift. Ever thought of being a reporter?"

I honestly hadn't.

"Come to me in a couple of years if you're interested in a job. I like brave girls who can get shots like that. No shots have come across my desk that are as important as that one. And by a 16 year old girl, no less."

I felt my face blushing.

"I wasn't alone. I have a partner, my friend, Peter."

"My nephew," Edie added.

"But it was your niece who took the picture." He came around the desk and opened the door, ushering in the sound of an army of reporters and secretaries typing in the newsroom, the thud of the press upstairs clanging away. Pressing his card into my hand, he gave me a smile. "Don't lose that. I meant what I said."

I fingered his card in my pocket the whole drive back to the castle, putting it inside the soft leather case of my Bible when we got home. Perhaps he was right. Perhaps I would make a good news photographer. It was certainly an idea. After all, it was about time I decided what I want to be. Edie had said so just a few months before.

A news photographer.

A photojournalist! Sure, I'd have to work on the writing part, but how hard could it be?

THE NEXT MORNING, my photograph was printed on the front page, while Edie's article continued on for several pages, our names boldly printed at the bottom. Dad read the article aloud to all of us gathered around the kitchen table. Edie had done a flawless job at capturing the story.

It was as though you were there. You saw the Nazis throwing Chaim and Judith out of their home. You saw my cousins' neighbor, a defenseless dentist who wouldn't harm a fly, being beaten to death by a mob on Kristallnacht.[6] You saw my cousins forced to hide in a tiny grotto, denied education and decent work. You saw the thousands of books burning in the quad of the university.

Then you saw the men in striped uniforms, with their vacant stares and hollow cheeks. You saw it all. You forgot the words, forgot it was an article. It was real. Horrifically real.

The sort of words that can change the world.

Edie concluded her article with, "This is why we fight. Not only to protect our precious soil. No! We fight to set the captives free, to deliver the oppressed and the needy. The blood of the innocent cries out to us from Germany. We will not rest until they are vindicated."

My father's voice cracked, and he set the paper down, visibly moved. Everyone was still.

"You did a great job Edie," Horatio said finally. "I've never been so proud of you."

"Thank you, dear," Edie responded after a moment. "It was a wonderful feeling to have something to write again. Something real. Something that matters."

"It's true," Katrine said, her voice betraying a storm of emotions. "You wrote it exactly the way it really happened. *Is* happening."

I felt my mother's hand rest on my back. "Thank you for taking that photograph, Agatha. For Chaim and for Judith. For all those men."

She gave me a sad smile as tears welled up in her eyes. I didn't know how to reply. Mindlessly, my fingers traced the grain in the knotted pine of the table, worn in places by decades of use long ago.

Horatio carefully gathered the paper. "I'm getting this framed."

Edie stretched. "And I'm going to bed. I'm thoroughly exhausted, if you know what I mean."

"Shall I draw you a bath, ma'am?" Ferguson asked.

"No, I'd fall asleep in the tub."

"I'm going for a walk," Katrine said abruptly, quickly standing and moving towards the back door. Lorelei and Grace were on her heels.

"Bring your sweaters, girls. It's cold!" my mother warned. "And it looks like rain."

"No need, Aunt Rose," Katrine answered, her voice bitter and angry. "I've so much heat inside. I need to cool off."

"You want me to go with you three?" Frank asked hopefully.

"No. We need to be alone," Lorelei answered.

With that, the sisters were out the door. Peter put his hand on Frank's shoulder. "Harsh."

But Frank was actually smiling. "She spoke to me! I think I'm making some headway."

From the kitchen window, we could see the girls walk high up on one of the moors. Katrine's red dress popped out of the mist and heather like the poppies back home in California. They were so high that they could almost be flying.

"They look like three little sparrows," my mother said. "Flitting about, not knowing which way to fly."

"No," Edie replied, staring at them. "They are too strong and too angry to be sparrows." Edie paused before turning back. "Hawks, Rose. They are seahawks."

"Seahawks?" My mother looked confused.

"Well, for one thing, they all have big eyes. But it's more than that. Seahawks, like the Jews, are found on all continents, except Antarctica. They are special because they can tolerate a wide range of habitats, nesting in any location where there is water or food." She looked back toward the girls. "They don't know where to nest yet, but once they decide where to settle, they will thrive." She nodded her head. "Seahawks. Definitely seahawks. I ought to paint them someday."

Then to me she said, "Piper, do you have your camera handy?"

I did actually. It was at the end of the table where'd I'd left it earlier.

"Then take the picture! I want to remember them on that mountain always."

# CHAPTER 36

## WAITING

"The Brophy twins were drafted today," Horatio said that night at dinner. All of our faces were aglow in the candlelight as we finished up the remains of a lamb roast. "Cookie's volunteered. And Sebastian took a position on a freighter that supplies to the army." He frowned. "I am, to put it bluntly, without a crew."

"What of your lobster fleet?" Peter asked, mouth askew.

"All able-bodied seamen were drafted. The British ones, that is."

"And the fleet?"

"I've chosen to dry dock the fishing boats."

"What does that mean?" Edie asked, wiping Anna's mouth with a napkin.

"It means the lobster business is on hold until the war is over." He put his elbows on the table. "We've got enough in savings to hold out for years, but still…"

Ferguson came into the room and waited patiently for Horatio to finish.

"Sir, a telegram has arrived. From Germany." He looked at my cousins, his mouth turned down slightly at the corners. "I do hope it is good news," he added softly as he gave Katrine the thin envelope.

Dinner was instantly forgotten, and we huddled around Katrine, who held the message with shaking hands. "It's from Betty, the night maid at the jazz club."

"How did she know where to send the message?" Peter asked.

"I gave Rolf our address," Horatio answered. "Perhaps he gave it to her?"

By now, Katrine had read the message. She sunk into her seat, stunned. My mother took the note and read it. She put it back down on the table and looked for the right words. "The Gestapo took Rolf in. They questioned him severely. When he was returned to his apartment, he was beaten quite terribly. He... Oh, Lorelei."

Lorelei knew. "He's dead, isn't he."

My mother nodded. But there was more. Her eyes continued down the page. Before Rolf had been taken in, he had informed Betty that Chaim and Judith's names had been discovered on a list of those sent to a camp called Birkenau. Apparently, they had caught some sort of influenza. She didn't know if Chaim and Judith had died, but the odds of their survival was slim. Hundreds had. She had tried to find out more, but it was as though they had disappeared. Their trail had gone cold. She had no idea if they were alive or dead or even if they were still in the camp.

"There was no flu," Peter said. We had seen the camps. We knew the truth. If Chaim and Judith had died, it was from forced labor and a lack of food and decent medical care and who knows what else.

My mother began to cry and my father did his best to comfort her. She pulled away from him and gathered my cousins in her arms, like a mother hen. The four of them quietly cried together, oblivious to the rest of us. They were all alone in their suffering, and there was nothing we could do to alleviate it.

Frank wrung his hands and paced back and forth. Peter, by my side, watched silently, his eyes growing wide with the reality of their pain.

Horatio looked at Ferguson and signaled for him to take the

children out of the room. "They can finish their supper upstairs," he whispered. "No need to cause them concern."

I moved towards them and leaned my head on my mother's shoulder. "I'm so sorry, Mother."

"It wasn't supposed to end like this," she said. "I thought that after everything, we would have a happy ending."

"It isn't over yet," my father said. "It isn't over yet," he repeated. "He's already won the war, you know."

"I don't understand," my mother looked up at him angrily. "I don't understand how we have victory in something like this!"

With that, she sunk her head into her hands and sobbed.

GRACE TOLD me that night in bed that she felt trapped indoors, like she couldn't breathe.

All three of them constantly needed to be moving. It was as though they believed that if they kept walking the moors, they would eventually escape the vast sea of sadness that had engulfed them. And over the next two days that's exactly what they did.

I went with them once or twice, but the truth was that they wanted, and needed, to be alone.

My mother, on the other hand, retreated to her room and came out only for meals.

It was on the third morning after we'd received the news that I walked down to the water, longing for comfort in the midst of all the unknown. The waves called my name, and I moved towards them, my pocket Bible tucked under my arm.

The water crashed violently on the rocks, sending sprays in every direction.

*I have seen them riding seaward on the waves*
*Combing the white hair of the waves blown back*
*When the wind blows the water white and black.*
*We have lingered in the chambers of the sea*

*By sea-girls wreathed with seaweed red and brown*
*Till human voices wake us, and we drown.*[7]

Once again, the cadence of T. S. Elliot. I was shivering, but whether from cold, fear, or dread, I did not know. I leaned against the base of the cliff, watching the steady motion of the water.

"Be brave!" shouted a voice out of nowhere. I looked to the left and right and up above. There was no one there.

"Who's there?" I asked out loud.

"It is I. Don't be afraid."

I leaned into the rock. Was the voice in my head?

"Don't be afraid, Piper," the voice urged.

I dropped my Bible in surprise, Prufrock's song of defeat disappearing into the wind. The pages blew open to Matthew 14.

> *"When evening came, He was there alone. The boat was already a long way from land. It was being pounded by the waves because the wind was blowing against it. Early in the morning, Jesus went out to the disciples. He walked on the lake. They saw Him walking on the lake and were terrified. 'It's a ghost!' they said. And they cried out in fear... Right away Jesus called out to them, 'Be brave! It is I. Don't be afraid.'"*

"Piper! Is that you?"

I looked up towards the crest of the cliff. It was my mother. She slowly wound her way down to the water, wrapped her arms around me, and did not try to hold back her tears.

"Are you all right?" I asked after a moment.

She shook her head. "I don't know."

"Do you ever think anything will be the same again?" I asked.

"No." She looked out at the sea, pushing the tears away. "Nothing will ever be the same. Our world is very different now. I've been thinking about what your father said."

"About what?"

"About Christ having already won the war, how the victory is ours. It was so easy to believe that when I walked out of the sanitarium." She inhaled heavily and continued, "But I didn't believe it that night when the message came about Rolf and Judith and Chaim. I couldn't see the victory. I could only see loss. The most painful loss I've ever experienced."

My voice trembled as I said, "I don't see how any good can come of this."

"Neither do I, Agatha. Not with my natural eye." She faced the waves stoically. "But I know he wants us to be brave. And he wants us to believe that he really will work all things out for our good. He's faced bigger storms than this." The wind kicked up, blowing our skirts and hair wildly round us. "And he walked on the waves."

"He even stilled the storm," I whispered to the wind.

"We might just have to wait a while." She squeezed my hand. "He stills storms on his clock. Not ours."

I sighed and nodded. "How about we head back to the house? I'll make us some proper Scottish tea and maybe even try to make some scones. Do you think they are very difficult to make?"

She managed a smile and said, "What do you say we find out together? We'll be proper ladies by the time we get back to California."

"YOU KNOW WHAT PATIENCE IS, don't you?" Peter chucked his apple core over the edge of the cliff where we sat. It was a clear day, not a cloud in the sky. It was now two weeks to the day from when the tragic news of Rolf and my aunt and uncle arrived on our doorstep.

"Sure, it means waiting." It was all we'd been doing, day in and day out. There was nothing to do, nowhere to go.

"Nope, it means having the right attitude *while* waiting."

I could feel him smirking, and I playfully smacked him. "I know you're always right, but do you have to be so smug about it?"

"It's like when we develop those pictures. We're in the middle of the process right now. The future is still blurry. But at just the right moment, it will all become clear."

Why did he always have to be so calm, so composed? It was deeply annoying.

"Don't tell me you're not just a little impatient," I needled.

"Not at all. I've never felt so patient in my life," he said sarcastically. He picked at blades of grass methodically. "I'm preaching to myself as much as you. Honestly, I have no idea what to do with myself anymore. This monotony is driving me crazy. I feel useless."

He gazed out at the ocean. "Maybe I'll build a sailboat."

I snapped a photo of the waves. The light had a peculiar quality to it that I liked. I wanted to remember it.

A strange rhythm had been evolving in our little crew each passing day. Edie had dived headfirst into motherhood, under the tutelage of my mother. She took a few hours every morning to teach the children English, while enlisting my mother to help her learn German. Each afternoon, she worked on a portrait of her new "family," with Peter and me sitting in for her and Horatio. It was difficult to get the children to stay still, but with bribes of Horatio taking them out on the little fishing boat, we could normally get in at least a half-hour of sitting.

Anna was Edie's little girl, no doubt about it, but the boys were all Horatio's. They followed him everywhere, copying his mannerisms, picking up his lilting Scottish brogue with their limited English vocabulary.

The castle's garden had been neglected for years and years, but Edie had great plans of rehabilitating it in the spring. She was beginning to love the castle, and there she planned to stay. Well, for the time being anyways.

But as for the rest of us, the future was remarkably uncertain. My father tried to get us passage back to the States on an ocean liner, but fares were booked out for over a month. Commercial flights had only been flying over the Atlantic for a few months, and tickets were exorbitantly expensive. Horatio offered to buy them, but my mother declined. "Over the entire ocean? Absolutely not! I flew once to Santa Barbara. It was only an hour long flight, but it was an hour too long! When we go home, it will be on a boat. The way people have been traveling for centuries."

But sailing was dangerous as well. There was the chance that the ship could cross paths with a German U-boat and be blown out of the water. It had already happened to two passenger ships in the last week.

No one quite knew what to do, and so we remained undecided. Should we stay? Should we go? We spent our days vacillating back and forth, doing odd jobs about the house, or huddling around the radio listening to the BBC's latest news bulletins.

There was nothing to do but, as Peter said, wait.

I gazed at the waves. They were certain of their path.

Peter took the camera out of my hands and looked through the lens at nothing in particular.

Sighing heavily, I continued, "I am counting down the minutes till things are dependable again. I remember the days when I would wake up and know what the day was going to hold. Things like my mother's breakfast and school. Band practice. Homework. Football games. Hamburgers with the gang. These days, all I can depend on is breakfast."

Peter looked at me. "Yeah. I guess oatmeal's dependable enough."

There was so much I didn't understand. So many knots my brain sought to unravel.

How could God heal my mother and then allow Judith and Chaim to die? Well, possibly die, that is. But Rolf *was* dead. He was such a good man. And so young. If Peter had been in his place, I don't know how I could have gone on.

I looked back and forth from the sea to Peter and back again. It was all so confusing.

"I bet the boys would enjoy building a sailboat," Peter said changing the subject.

"Don't you think they are a little young? Besides, do you know how to build a boat?"

He looked back at me. "No, but I can learn."

"And I can teach you!" Frank said as he heavily flopped down beside us. "I used to work in the shipyards." He was breathing heavily from the climb up the hill.

"What have you been doing?" Peter asked.

"You know me," Frank answered. "Nothing. There's nothing to do, except babysit those kiddos. Which is fine, but I'm not a babysitter. I'm going crazy."

"You and me both," I grimaced. "Lorelei still giving you the cold shoulder?" I hugged my sweater closer. With each day, winter seemed nearer. It loomed on the horizon, as uncertain and ominous as the impending days.

"More like the frozen shoulder. That girl is as cold as ice. But you give ol' Frank some time. She'll start to melt like an iceberg in the sun. Believe you me, the great thaw is coming."

I LAY AWAKE IN BED, listening again to the stifled sobs of Grace in the bed beside mine. Finally, her breathing evened out.

She'd fallen asleep, but I couldn't.

I tiptoed out of the room and made my way down to the kitchen.

My aunt had beat me to it.

It sort of felt like the old days, back in the lighthouse. Funny, I thought. The old days were only a couple of months ago.

Edie glanced at me with a "so, the late-night munchies got to you too?" look. She was in front of the icebox, pulling out the milk jug. She poured two tall glasses and pushed one towards me. We sat at the table, silent and still.

Finally, Edie reached across the table and took my hand in hers.

As though reading my thoughts, she whispered, "Don't try to make sense of it all, Piper."

I looked at her questioningly, her eyes were tired but still peaceful, holding the peace I longed for at that moment.

"We live in a fallen world. Good will win in the end, but we are not yet at the end, are we?" She squeezed my fingers gently.

"I guess we're not at the end yet. But I'm sure looking forward to it."

I took a sip of milk and wiped the mustache off my upper lip with the back of my pajama sleeve. I was wearing new pajamas from the Bijenkorf. They were pink flannel with long sleeves and tiny ruffles around the hem. It felt appropriate for the castle. "I was never much of a milk person back home, but Scotland is converting me."

"I know. I could live off of oatmeal with that cream on top. Can you believe it? Me eating breakfast?" She lovingly looked about the dimly lit kitchen. "Oh Piper, I absolutely love it here. I've never loved anywhere so much, and I've never been so happy."

"You've really settled in here, haven't you, Edie?" It was funny. This journey had brought her home, but had only raised a million questions of uncertainty for the rest of us. Where we felt uprooted, she felt grounded.

She looked at me pensively. "I suppose I have. Never thought I could feel at home anyplace but Maine. But here I am. I think," she chuckled, "I was always made to live in a castle."

"With children?"

She nodded. Motherhood became her.

"Sometimes I can't believe how much I love it. I was a fool to wait so long. But I suppose God had his purposes. His timing. Look where it brought us." She paused, scrutinizing me. "You know, I think you've grown."

"You think so?"

"Yes. You have. Stand up."

I stood up, her sharp eyes taking me in. "At least an inch. I'll have to re-cut yours."

"My what?"

"Oh," she waved slightly, "I bought Horatio's family clan's tartan. Several bolts. I'm sewing matching sashes for the girls and new kilts for the men." She hugged me tightly."Okay, back to bed. Who knows what tomorrow holds?"

Indeed. Who knew?

## CHAPTER 37

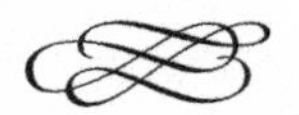

## WHAT TOMORROW HELD

"But you don't really think the bombs are going to drop here?" I asked. "We're in the middle of nowhere. A mile from Kingsbarns? A half-hour drive to St. Andrews! Two hours to Edinburgh!"

All over the village, families were out in their gardens expanding cellars for when the bombs might begin to drop. And it was all done under the watchful eye of Mrs. Sybil Butterfield. The government issued pamphlets explaining exactly how to create the air-raid shelters. I put the pamphlet down. "Seriously! What could the Germans possibly want with the village?"

"Obviously," Peter chuckled, "to destroy this year's cabbage plot and take out the armies of sheep."

Our own shelter was in desperate need of a good cleaning. The mansion's basement was filled with old junk and dust, and Edie was concerned that it might harm the children's health. So we rolled up our sleeves and scrubbed and dusted and chucked out the bizarre collection of old lamps, boxes of screws and rusty nails, and the trunks of moth-eaten clothing.

Katrine threw herself into the work as though she were scrubbing for her life.

Ever since the tragic news of Rolf and her parents' disappearance, she hadn't stopped working. Cleaning, cooking, reorganizing the endless closets in the mansion. If she couldn't find something to do, she would invent an activity. Then, she would walk for hours and hours on the hills. She said that if she didn't exhaust her legs, she couldn't sleep. My mother tried several times to make her rest, but she wouldn't, for if she stopped, she feared she may not be able to start again. Grace was always by her sister's side, silently helping with whatever task Katrine gave her. Her smile was very rare, her giant blue eyes no longer bright.

For Lorelei, the blow of Rolf's death went very deep. She would lock herself away in the music room, playing sad melodies on the keys, refusing to answer when we called her. She joined us only at dinner, sitting silently in her chair and staring at her plate.

Frank and Peter lugged down to the shelter a few old armchairs, a couch, and what was left of the tinned beans and tuna.

Edie carefully descended the rickety stairs. She carried a box of candles in case of a power outage and was wearing one of her "going out hats." Looking approvingly at the set-up, she said, "Well, this certainly looks a lot more cheerful. Excellent work, young people." Edie set the box down. "I do love seeing industrious young people."

"Where are you going?" Katrine asked, looking up, dust and grime stuck to her face, her hair tied up in a kerchief.

Edie turned back around and replied, "I've got to run into town and pick up the curtains."

"Curtains?" I couldn't imagine why Edie would want to replace the curtains at a time like this. Sure, they were a little faded, but really?

"Blackout curtains, Piper. Government issue."[8]

Frank followed her up the stairs. "Need some help, Edie? I've had enough of this mamsy-pamsy decorating business. I need some man's work. Like buying some curtains."

"Of course, Frank. I can always use a good strong sailor to carry my packages and things."

~

"YES! YES, JUST SO." Ferguson directed. "A little more to the left. And... perfect!"

Every window in the mansion, all 483 of them (I know the exact number because it took Grace, Peter, and I an entire afternoon to count them) needed to be covered with the thick black curtains that, at night, would keep out any shred of light that might guide the German Air Force to our home and bomb the living daylights out of it.

"Now," Ferguson puffed out his chest slightly, "as the designated Air Raid Warden[9] for Kingsbarns, I am determined that our home will set an example to all the village. Not one cottage is going to be blown to smithereens while I'm on the job, do you hear me!"

"Aye, aye, sir!" Horatio saluted his butler.

It took us a long time, even with all of us working our way through the old place, to cover each window. As my father and mother hung a curtain over the dining-room window, I heard him murmur, "Feels good to be busy."

So it was getting to him too. All this unknowing. All this monotonous not-really-doing-anything-ness.

With every window now covered, we gathered after dinner in the parlor. It was raining very hard. The Scottish Sheets, I'd dubbed it. It wasn't normal rain. It was more like a waterfall had broken free from the heavens. I broke regulation and peeked out the window. Where normally I might be able to see the glow of the village's lights, tonight all was black. It was stifling and sent chills up my spine.

"Piper!" Ferguson ran over and shut the curtain. "None of that, now. You know better than that." He looked at me like a disappointed parent and checked his watch. "Ah, it's time for my rounds."

He slipped on his government issued uniform jacket and the special helmet with a big 'W' on it (identifying him as the warden).

"What exactly are you going to do on these rounds?" Peter asked.

He snapped the clasp of the helmet under his chin.

"Why, Ferguson!" Edie exclaimed. "You look very official in that uniform. But you can't go out without some sort of parka or something. You'll freeze!"

Ferguson grinned. "Not to worry, ma'am. I've a poncho that's just the thing. I'll retrieve it before setting out." Then, turning back to Peter, he said, "The very short training seminar at the police house this afternoon taught us how to sound the sirens in case of a raid, how to check gas masks—"

"We don't have any gas masks," my father interrupted.

Ferguson nodded. "A shipment is coming soon, I am assured." He scratched his chin. "Well, I'm off then! If you hear the siren, run to the cellar. Don't come out until I sound the all-clear. And Piper, keep that curtain closed! The German pilots can see the glow of a cigarette. Imagine the bright light of the parlor!" His face registered horror.

"I hope we don't hear anything at all." Edie said. "You have a nice time now, Ferguson. And try to stay dry, won't you?"

He bowed slightly, "Goodnight then! I'm really off now!"

I wondered if he was nervous. I'd never heard Ferguson talk so much at one time. He was taking this air raid business quite seriously. We watched him march out of the room, a true soldier going to battle.

A clap of thunder shook the house.

"I doubt there will be a raid tonight. Any pilot would be an idiot to go out in this weather." Horatio said drolly.

"What we need is some music," Edie said, "Lorelei? Perhaps we could all go into the music room, and you could play us something?"

Lorelei was staunchly opposed to this idea. She couldn't! Not in front of everyone. Besides, she was too sad to do anything like putting on a concert. She didn't say that, but it was exactly what she communicated.

Edie looked around, tapping her long fingernails on the arm of her chair. "Enough with all this doom and gloom. We need some fun around here. I haven't laughed in days, and that's just not healthy." And she was determined to do something about it! She stood up and marched to the record player. Putting an Andrews Sisters record on, she carefully adjusted the needle and looked at my cousins. "Lorelei, Grace, Katrine? Up off your bottoms. I need your help."

"I don't understand," Katrine protested as the frenetic singing to the hit song *Cuanto la Gusta* started up.[10]

She was starting to sway. "You and your sisters were singers in a hip underground jazz club. You must have picked up some of the new moves. Why don't you teach us how to swing a little? Horatio, come here! Peter, you take Piper. Lorelei, you can demonstrate with Frank."

"He can't dance!" she snapped.

"I can too!" he retorted, taking her in his arms. "Well… I can try."

She rolled her eyes, but didn't pull away. Frank looked triumphant.

Edie had Horatio in her arms now and was attempting a two-step. "You girls have got to help me. I really don't know what I'm doing! But I've always wanted to swing with the best of them."

Looking over at my parents, she said, "Nathan, Rosie, you two don't get off so easy. Up and at 'em you two. Move the feet."

Edie laughed at the lyrics, "I think this is our family song! They don't know where they are going, we don't know where we are going…"

The trio crooned on and on about handsome caballeros and surprises and going *somewhere,* and we all began to try to dance.

Edie had a way about her where you simply could not argue with what she wanted.

Grace took over, showing us a modified Balboa. We all tried to follow my cousin's instructions. It was a little complex, but I started to get it.

Anna, Willem, and Raffi moved right along with us. The joy of movement and my Aunt's crazy antics showed radiant on their little faces. Frank swung Lorelei around like a sack of flour, which remarkably succeeded in producing a tiny smile on Lorelei's rosebud lips.

He looked knowingly at Peter and me. "Told ya! The ice age is ending!"

Edie turned the record over, and we moved on to faster stuff. Peter and I did our best with the West Coast Shag, but Peter was distracted. Sure, he hung in there, but he kept stepping on my feet and forgetting the timing, apologizing that he just wasn't a good dancer.

It wasn't that though. I knew him too well. He was thinking about something. In the end, he excused himself before the song ended.

As I was about to follow Peter, my father caught my hand and pulled me in. "Come on, Agatha, Conga Line!" The children laughed gleefully, keeping time with the music and nearly screaming with delight.

We danced and danced, all of us whirling around that room till the needle fell off the record, and we collapsed on the floor, quite breathless. Before Edie could start another record, I made a quick exit to find Peter.

There he was, sitting alone on the stairs in the dark front hall.

Surprised by my presence, he looked up.

"Peter? What in the world is on your mind?" What was the point of beating around the bush. Ask straight questions, get straight answers.

In a bit of an angry tone, he spouted, "Piper, I can't sit around this house anymore doing nothing. I'm not in school. I've no real work now that the fleet and crew are all with the British Navy. I feel useless."

And restless, I thought. Like me. And Frank. Like Grace and Katrine and Lorelei. Like my parents.

"It's late." He stood up and gave me a searching look before heading up the stairs.

"Do you want to talk about it?" I called up after him.

"There's nothing to say."

I watched him march up the stairs, feeling sorry for him. Feeling sorry for myself.

The words of that song stuck with me all night through my dreams. I was whirling through Europe, dancing while my cousins sang *Cuanto le Gusta*. But in my dream, the caballeros were actually German Gestapo. And then the song faded, and we were lost in the ocean with nowhere to land. No home to go to, just adrift at sea.

# CHAPTER 38

## DECISIONS

"Oh my. Frank? Peter?" Edie's hand slowly rose to her mouth. "What have you boys done?"

I turned around from the pot of oats I was stirring for breakfast. My hand stopped dead still. They were both in uniform.

"We couldn't take it anymore," Frank began. "We volunteered for His Royal Majesty's Navy," Peter finished.

"But you're Americans!" I gasped. "We're neutral. We're not in the war!"

"Piper," Peter started, "I couldn't let one more day go by with all the rest of the guys joining up. Not after what we've seen. It wouldn't be right."

Frank butted in, "And I wasn't about to let him go off and have all the fun." He looked at Anna, Willem, and Raffi. "No offense, kiddos. It's not like it wasn't fun playing blocks and all."

"They need men like us," Peter said slowly.

Edie, still in her robe, put her coffee down and seemed to choose her words carefully. "Well, I'm right proud of you both."

I turned back to the oats, stirring without thinking and trying to hold back my fear, my anger, my tears. How could Peter go off and leave me like this? Go off and be a hero! Go off and maybe die? With every breath, I could feel my heart sinking further.

"Don't be angry at me, Piper." Peter stood behind me. "I can't stand it when you're angry."

"I'm not angry," I lied. "I'm not. I'm just trying to get breakfast on the table."

"Is that all you're going to say?"

Before I could answer, Horatio came in and saw the uniforms. In a split second, he perceived it all.

He gathered both boys into an enormous bear hug. "If I was younger, I'd be right in there with you."

"You know, sir," Frank said, "you're not too old."

Edie's face turned white.

Horatio stroked his beard. "True, true. Actually, I did get a call from the admiralty earlier this morning."

"You didn't." Edie's eyes widened.

"Now don't go worrying your pretty head, Edie. I'm just a bit too old for combat, but not too old to give advice. I've been given the rank of Commodore, but in reality, I'll just be training new captains. Specifically, the ones stationed at the new base in Edinburgh."

"When?" Edie asked, relaxing only slightly.

"Every other week to start," Horatio sighed. "When His Majesty calls, there is no saying no." He turned his focus back to Frank and Peter, rubbing his hands together briskly. "So, when do you boys ship out?"

"Tomorrow morning," Frank answered, easing into a chair at the table. "Piper, a bowl of that oatmeal, please. And some thick Scottish cream!"

"Make it two, Piper darling," Horatio said.

"Do you want some, Edie?" I asked.

"I can't stomach food on a morning like this! Too much excitement!" Flushed, eyes wide, she flitted about the kitchen, not knowing what to do with herself.

I pushed Peter aside, ignoring him and the tear that escaped down my cheek. My best friend was leaving, and I might never see him again.

Just then, my cousins marched into the kitchen. All three were still in their pajamas, their hair all over the place.

Frank chuckled, "Looks like you girls were up all night."

Katrine, not noticing the uniforms, commanded our attention.

"I've decided, or rather, *we've* decided to go to Palestine."

"You've what!" Frank's spoon clanged against his bowl as collective shock stunned the rest of us.

"Harry was right. I was wrong."

My mother rushed over to Katrine and put her arms on her shoulders. "Whatever are you talking about? Harry was right about what?"

Katrine shook her head. "He… I…" Gathering her thoughts, she said, "Look, it doesn't really matter. He said he needed help. I want to help."

"*We* want to help," Grace threw in.

"Lorelei?" Horatio said seriously. "You too?"

"There is nothing for us here," she answered sadly. "Nothing in Germany. No one… It's what we must do."

"You have us," my mother said, grabbing her hands, "You know that."

Frank nodded. "Yeah! You've got us!"

"Oh shut up," I spat. "You won't even be here."

"And you have been wonderful." Katrine gazed into my mother's eyes. "You are family. But this is something we must do."

Katrine looked at Edie and Horatio. "And you've been the best adoptive parents a girl could want. We will never forget how kind you've been. You saved our lives." She stopped and inhaled. "But one must go where one is needed."

Horatio's face was grim. "And Harry and his Jewish National Fund needs you, eh? I sure hope you girls know what you are signing up for."

"Our minds are made up," Grace replied firmly.

"But you are *quite* sure you are want to go all the way to Palestine?" my father asked, turning towards his nieces. He looked at them tenderly, searching for the right words. "Katrine, I feel responsible now that..."

"Now that our parents are gone?"

Grace answered, "That's exactly why we must go. Because they are gone. It's no use pretending otherwise."

All three were stoic and brave.

"Maybe there is something for us there. There is nothing left for us anywhere else." Grace looked from one sister to the next.

The kitchen was silent. No one moved.

Suddenly with a burst of energy, Edie sprang up. "You girls must be famished after so many decisions. Sit!" she commanded. "As long as you're in this house, you're still my daughters. And as your mother, I say it's time to get some breakfast into those skinny frames of yours. I want you strong and healthy for your trip. Who knows what sort of food Harry's got lined up for you."

The girls sat down, and soon the table was filled with chatter. So many plans to be made. What to pack. What they might need in Palestine. The boys debated what their basic training would entail. Horatio and my father dove into a discussion on naval history and new maritime technology.

It looked like everyone's mind was made up... made up to abandon me here in Scotland in the middle of nowhere. I pushed my oats away. I'd completely lost my appetite.

~

"ENJOY THE CAKE," my mother said, putting the frosted layers of yellow chiffon and white marshmallow creme in the center of the table. "It's the last real one we are going to get for a while."

"And as long as we're at it," Edie set out a few bars of chocolate from the Bijenkorf, "why not push the limits of sugar consumption. It's our last chance to really go hog wild on the sweets."

Beginning next week, the whole country would officially be rationing food. Bacon, butter, and sugar were to be the first casualties of the war, followed by meat, jam, tea, and eggs. Not to mention cheese, breakfast cereal, milk, and canned fruit. I wondered what was left to eat? Potatoes and dandelion greens probably.

We were "celebrating" Peter and Frank's departure, along with that of my cousins'. Some bug must have gotten loose in the house the night before, biting everyone with the "must get out of here!" virus. Only, it had forgotten about me. I was stuck here, and everyone else was leaving. Even Horatio was leaving, even if it was only part-time. And Ferguson was gone every night on his rounds as the warden. Everyone was getting to help with the war effort. Everyone was getting to do something new and exciting. Everyone but me. I took a bite of cake. Personally, I was celebrating a full-on pity party.

"We'll catch the train tomorrow morning to Chelsea," Katrine said, "if you don't mind loaning us Ferguson to take us to the station."

"I'll do better than that," Horatio smiled. "I'll take you myself."

"Yes," Edie agreed. "Horatio, you take them. Ferguson is so sleepy in the mornings now that he's up half the night telling people to close their curtains. I don't feel comfortable with him driving long distances."

"Really! Ma'am," Ferguson felt quite slighted, "I must say that I think-"

"Don't even try, Ferguson." She silenced him with a look. "There is one thing and one thing only I want you doing until 10:00 every morning, and that is sleeping."

I took a large bite of cake. It was the only sweet thing about this party. Everything else was sour. Bitter even.

Peter kept catching my eyes with a mournful expression that

sent a horrible longing ache into my stomach. He tried to stop me at the bottom of the stairs before I went up to bed.

"Please don't be mad at me, Piper. I had to. I'm sorry."

I ran up the stairs before he could see me cry. "I'm not mad, Peter."

"Yes, you are!"

"Goodnight."

I shut the door to my room before he could answer. Grace was there already, brushing her hair and putting night cream under her eyes.

"You sure were quiet this evening," Grace said as she crawled into her bed.

"You'd be quiet too, if you were me." I kicked my shoes off and sat on the edge of my mattress. "At least you know where you're going. I'm stuck in limbo land."

"And Peter is leaving."

"Yeah," I said quietly. "And Peter is leaving."

I took a stack of my photographs from the nightstand and picked through them one by one, until I found the picture of Peter playing with the collie on the shores of the Black Sea in the Netherlands. It was of his back, but it sort of captured him. All alone. A man and the sea.

In bed now, I lay awake staring at the ceiling. Praying that God would make a way for me. That He would make a way for me and Peter. For me and my parents. For my cousins. For all of us.

THERE WASN'T room in the Bentley for us all to go to the station. Just Peter and Frank, the girls, and Horatio. He would drop the girls off at the train and then head down to Leith Harbor with the boys.

My cousins kissed my mother and Edie. Then they lovingly embraced Willem, Raffi, and Anna, whispering to them in German that maybe one day they would meet again.

It was all ending so suddenly. I wasn't ready when the three of them hugged me close and promised they'd always stay in touch, if they could. Before I knew it, they had disappeared into the car. I wondered if we would ever reunite.

Next came Frank. He shook hands with everyone like a gentleman. As he shook mine, he asked if he could write me, as a guy in the Navy had to have a girl to write to, or all the other guys would beat up on him and who knew where Lorelei would be in the world? That was fine, and I agreed that Lorelei most likely wouldn't get jealous or anything. Frank wished she would get a little jealous, and I told him to give it some more time.

Rolf wasn't the sort of person you got over in a week. Or a month. Or a year...

"Yeah. You're right, Piper," he said. "I uh... I guess I better get in the car now. You be watching for those letters, okay?"

"Okay." I reached out and hugged him quickly, taking him by surprise.

That left just Peter.

"Samuel," my aunt said.

"You called me by my real name!" he said, shocked. I'd almost forgotten his real name was Samuel.

"I save it for use on only the most important of occasions." She opened her arms wide and held him close. "Now, you be careful. Remember your manners. And remember you have a family who adores you."

He shook hands with my father, kissed my mother's cheek, and then stood in front of me.

"Can I write you too, Piper?"

I shrugged as nonchalantly as I could. Before I could stop it, one tear fell from my eye and made its way down my cheek.

He pulled an envelope out of his pocket. "I went ahead and started." Handing it to me, he whispered, "Read it once I leave, okay?"

"Okay." I looked down. I didn't want him to see me crying.

Holding the envelope in my hands, we who remained watched

the car drive out of the courtyard and disappear over the hill. I felt life drain out of my veins. Had I stopped breathing?

My mother's arms wrap around my back. She whispered that it would be all right, that God had a plan. I tried desperately to believe her. I felt her clasp my birthday locket back around my neck.

"There," she said turning me around. "That looks good on you, right now. Hope suits you."

I managed a small smile as our eyes met.

"Well, everyone back inside." She clapped her hands together. "It's cold out here."

Edie held her stomach a moment. "Are you feeling alright?" my mother asked, taking the children by the hand.

Edie looked at my mother, surprised. "Yeah. I just feel a little sick to my stomach."

"You look like you need to lie down."

"Yes. A nap. There's been so much activity."

Growing concern in her voice, my mother asked again, "You're sure you're okay?"

Edie nodded and walked slowly inside. "Just a little dizzy."

"I hope it's not the flu," my mother murmured, following her inside.

Alone at last, I tore open the letter. Out popped something small and round. It rolled to the ground, and I picked it up, my curiosity rising. Upon closer examination, I started to shake.

It was the ring from Casablanca. From that little shop. I'd know it anywhere! Somehow, Peter had bought it. And he'd bought it for *me*. My heart was beating now, very hard. I had a feeling I knew what the letter was going to say. Hands shaking, I read Peter's words.

It said what I'd hoped he would say for a long time, but never really thought he would.

Looking up towards heaven, I winked. I'm sure God was winking back. Something good was coming from all of this after all!

~

"I've got big news!" Horatio bellowed coming through the front door. "Everyone downstairs!"

I was in my room, in front of the open window, examining the ring on my finger. It fit perfectly. He wanted to marry me. Peter wanted to marry me! Just as soon as I turned 18.

What were two years? Nothing at all! I read the letter over and over.

I had it all planned out. We would hold the wedding in the courtyard of the castle. Anna would be my flower girl. I'd seen a dress at the Bijenkorf that would be perfect. My mother was a passable seamstress, and I was sure we could work out something similar.

I'd never felt more joyous.

And I'd never felt more desolate. Here I was, engaged. And my fiancé was on his way to fight the Nazis. We'd never even kissed. We'd never even said "I love you." It was pitiful.

*And* I still had two years to wait. But I knew I could wait decades if it meant that Peter would be my husband.

Of course, there were the little details to sort out. Like the need to finish high school. Correspondence courses were just the thing, I decided excitedly. Maybe I could even do an accelerated course and graduate early. Now that was a thought!

Then it hit me that I might not be in Scotland when he returned for leave.

My parents might decide to go back to the States. Oh, goodness! My father was going into town that very afternoon to check on the fare for another ocean liner. What would I do then?

My heart raced. This could get complicated. No, it was *already* complicated.

Calm down, I coached myself. You've got two years to go, girlie. Hold your horses.

Peter and I would make our relationship work, no matter the distance, time, or space.

It was all so terribly romantic. The ring glistened in the light. I loved it.

"Downstairs!" Horatio bellowed again, breaking my reverie. "Everyone! Stop dawdling!"

~

I RAN DOWN THE STAIRS, floating on a cloud.

Edie was there, holding Anna's hand, and my mother and father. Ferguson walked in, trailed by Willem and Raffi, all three of them covered in flour. "We are attempting to bake bread, sir," he said in explanation for his appearance, rubbing his hands on the apron. "Bread! Bread! Bread!" the boys sang.

"Their English is improving," Edie said cheerily. "Excellent work, Ferguson."

"Thank you, ma'am." He grinned down at his wards.

Horatio looked at the little boys and then back at Edie and Anna.

"So..." Edie urged him to continue, slightly impatient. "What is it? We all are here. What's the big news?"

Inhaling, Horatio looked straight at Edie. "How'd you like some more kids?"

Edie turned white. She sunk down to the steps. "How ever did you know?"

Horatio looked completely confused. "How'd I know what?"

"That I'm going to be a mother?"

"How'd I know? How'd you know?" he stuttered. "I only just now volunteered us. They are evacuating all the school children out of London. We've got enough room for at least 40. So I said, why not? We've got the time, and we've got the money! The boys have been so much fun," he chuckled, looking at Willem and Raffi, "I thought, the more the merrier."

"The more the merrier?" Edie swallowed. "How about 41 more the merrier?"

"I told the organizers we only had room for 40."

"It will be a very tiny extra one." Her voice rose very high.

It hit him like a load of bricks. "You mean, I'm going to be a father? A real father?"

She nodded, and he picked her up off the steps and kissed her face. "Imagine that! A real father. At my age!"

Ferguson blushed and offered his heartiest congratulations. My mother hovered around Edie and began pestering her with a million questions. Horatio nearly ran to the phone to call for a doctor, but we pulled him back, assuring him it wasn't necessary quite yet.

It was as good a time as any to break the news. I coughed loudly for attention, announcing, "I've got some big news of my own." Then, holding up my finger, proudly wearing Peter's ring, I said, "Peter and I are getting married."

"You're what!" my father exclaimed.

"Don't worry, Dad. Not for another two years." He looked only barely relieved.

Edie was beaming. "What'd I tell you, Piper. He'd come around in the end."

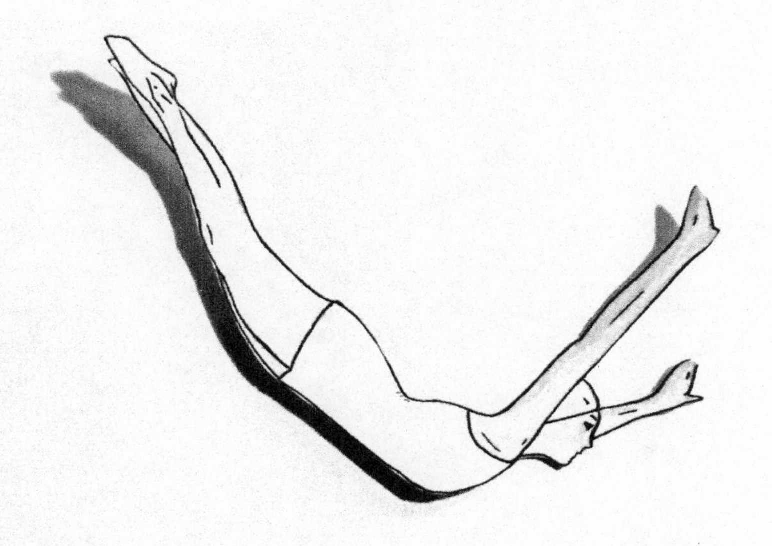

# ENDNOTES

**Part One**

1. Eliot, T.S., *The Poems of T. S. Eliot Volume I: Collected and Uncollected Poems* (Faber & Faber, 2015), 1250.

2. Eliot, T.S., *The Waste Land, Prufrock and Other Poems* (Dover Publications, Inc.1998), 39.

3. Eliot, *The Waste Land, Prufrock and Other Poems,* 4.

4. In 1936, King Edward VIII of England abdicated the throne in order to marry Wallis Simpson, a twice divorced American woman. The love affair was closely followed by the press.

5. Eliot, *The Poems of T. S. Eliot Volume I: Collected and Uncollected Poems,* 1250.

6. *Holy Bible,* Lamentations 3:22-23 (New International Version).

7. Prior to WWII, people of German ancestry all over the world formed citizen groups to promote German values and lobby on behalf of the Nazis. This included youth summer camps and large demonstrations, such as the 'Americanization' rally held in Madison Square Garden in 1939. Taylor, A. (2017, June 05). American Nazis in the 1930s-The German American Bund. Retrieved March 26,

2019, from https://www.theatlantic.com/photo/2017/06/american-nazis-in-the-1930sthe-german-american-bund/529185/.

8. On March 11,1938, under growing pressure from the Nazis, Austrian Chancellor Kurt von Schuschnigg resigned from his position and plead with Austrian forces not to fight against the advancing German army. The next day, German troops officially incorporated Austria into the German Reich, an event known as *Anschluss*. No nation was brave enough to respond with more than moderate verbal protests against the action, which went against both the Versailles Treaty and the St. Germain Treaty.

9. Greta Garbo was a well known Swedish-American film star and style icon.

10. Elliot, T.S., *Four Quartets,* (Harcourt, Inc., 1943), 58.

11. The Nuremberg Laws, or German racial laws, forbade marriages between Jews (non-Aryans) and Germans and declared that only those with 'pure' German blood could be citizens of the Reich. Non-Aryans were excluded was from various professions and subject to harassment and imprisonment. Due to the fact that a heavy tax was placed on Jews trying to immigrate, few made it out of the country. As a result, millions died in the Nazi death camps.

**Part 2**

1. Fred Astaire and Ginger Rogers were popular dance partners who starred in 10 films together from 1933 to 1949.

2. "Jim Crow Laws" refer to state and local laws in the Southern United States enforcing racial segregation. These laws extended to public transport and education, institutionalizing social disadvantage for Americans of African descent.

3. The "Kriegsmarine" was the Nazi navy from 1935-1945.

4. The International Ladies' Garment Workers' Union was one of the largest female labor unions in the United States. The awful conditions of the 'sweatshops' or factories the women worked in inspired them to unionize to improve conditions. The union was

closely linked to socialism and communism as many members leaned towards the political left.

5. After France fell to the Nazis in 1940, Casablanca became a jumping-off point for escaping refugees, many of whom were Jewish. Getting to Casablanca was easy enough, but leaving was another story. Exit and transit visas all issued by various governments were difficult to obtain and often expired within a matter of days. Some refugees wound up stuck for months or even years.

6. After their defeat in WWI, Germans were required to make payments (called reparations) in cash to the Allies. The 112 billion marks were scheduled to be paid in full by 1988. However, in 1931, Germany's economy completely collapsed. By 1932, all reparation payments were cancelled. German citizens viewed reparations as a national humiliation. Part of Hitler's appeal came from his determination to restore Germany's power and dignity.

7. The Chateau d'If is a fortress that was later converted into a prison offshore in the Bay of Marseille. The prison is known as one of the primary settings in *The Count of Monte Cristo*, a novel by Alexandre Dumas.

8. The Palais Longchamp was built to bring water from the Durance River to Marseille by the Duke of Orleans from 1839-1869.

9. The Maginot Line was a line of concrete obstacles and weapons built by France to deter against an invasion by Germany in the 1930s. The Germans bypassed the line altogether, invading through the low countries and taking the French by surprise.

10. In the late 1800s, Italian composer Giuseppe Verdi built a mansion with the intention of providing sanctuary for struggling professional musicians. For over 100 years, the mansion has housed hundreds of elderly players and continues to do so today.

11. Verdi's opera Falstaff is a comic opera based off of Shakespeare's character Falstaff, who appears in the Merry Wives of Windsor and Henry IV.

12. Hitler's dream to become a professional artist was cut short

when he failed the entrance exam at the Academy of Fine Arts in Vienna--twice. He pursued politics as an alternative.

13. La Scala is a famous opera house in Milan, Italy open since 1778. The world's greatest operatic talents have performed there, and La Scala's ballet theatre is one of the most highly regarded in the art world.

14. *A Midsummer Night's Dream* is a comedy by William Shakespeare. The story centers on four young Athenian lovers beset by problems. It is one of Shakespeare's most performed plays around the world. Quote from Act III.

15. *A Midsummer Night's Dream* Act V.

16. The Kindertransport (or 'children's transport') was an effort to rescue Jewish children from Germany, Austria, Czechoslovakia, Poland, and the city of Danzig in the months leading up to the Second World War. Over 10,000 children, mostly Jewish, were saved.

17. Geertruida Wijsmuller-Meijer was a Dutch resistance fighter who saved 10,000 Jewish during the through her work with the Kindertransport.

**Part 3**

1. Stuttgart dates back to the 10th century stud-farm for Herzog Luidolf's horses. During the first half of the 19th century, the city became an industrial hub for Bosch. *Stuttgart Information*, www.s-tuttgart.biz - Stuttgart's History. (1995-2014). Retrieved March 26, 2019, from http://www.stgt.com/stuttgart/historye.htm.

2. Nazi Germany and its allies established more than 42,000 camps for German communists, Jews, Roma, Jehovah's Witnesses, Socialists, Social Democrats, and persons accused of anti-social behavior. These camps served as forced labor camps, ghettos, and extermination centers. At the Auschwitz camp complex, 6,000 Jews were gassed (murdered) each day. By the end of the war, nearly 6 million European Jews had died.

3. The Leipzig Synagogue, built in 1855 by German Jewish

architect Otto Simonson was one of the most beautiful in the city. It was destroyed on Kristallnacht by the Nazis.

4. Eliot, *The Waste Land, Prufrock and Other Poems*, 1.

5. Hitler was known for his love of Wagner, a composer whose anti-Semitic and extremely nationalistic writings possibly had a strong effect on Hitler's theories of racial purity. Hitler and Wagner. (2011, July 25). Retrieved from https://www.telegraph.co.uk/culture/music/classicalmusic/8659814/Hitler-and-Wagner.html.

6. Wagner was vocal in his hatred towards the Jewish composer Mendelssohn, who was, ironically, in his faith, a strong Christian. Threatened by Mendelssohn's genius, Wagner's vitriol came out in essays, letters, and diatribes against the Jewish genius. Service, T. (2009, May 04). Tom Service on why Richard Wagner set out to destroy Felix Mendelssohn's reputation. Retrieved March 26, 2019, from https://www.theguardian.com/music/2009/may/05/felix-mendelssohn-richard-wagner-classical-music.

7. The statue, erected in 1892 was destroyed in 1936 by a hostile Nazi band as an, "An act of 'homage to the spirit of Aryanism,' or pure German values. ArchiveAuthor. (1936, November 16). Mendelssohn's Statue Destroyed by Nazis. Retrieved March 26, 2019, from https://www.jta.org/1936/11/16/archive/mendelssohns-statue-destroyed-by-nazis.

8. The original Hotel Adlon was a luxury hotel in Berlin built in 1907 and destroyed in 1945 at the close of WWII by allied bombs. It was a watering hole for the wealthy and German nobility.

9. "Grand Hotel Quotes." https://www.rottentomatoes.com/m/grand_hotel/quotes/.

10. Eliot, *The Waste Land, Prufrock and Other Poems*, 1.

11. Eliot, *The Waste Land, Prufrock and Other Poems*, 1.

12. The 'swastika' is a geometric figure that became the co-national flag of Nazi Germany.

13. During the 1920s, jazz swept through Germany much to the horror of nationalist conservatives and the right wing. Once Hitler took power in 1933, the government began to clamp down on jazz

music. By 1938, jazz, swing, and swing dancing was prohibited as degenerate.

14. The exclusion of Jews and those of African descent from performing publicly in Germany reflected Aryan racial values. Both were thought to jeopardize German culture.

15. The Andrews Sisters, *Hold Tight (Want Some Seafood Mama?)* (Decca 1938), https://genius.com/The-andrews-sisters-hold-tight-sea-food-lyrics.

16. The Gestapo refers to the German Secret Police under the Nazi regime.

**Part 4**

1. It was not uncommon for Jews to hide in attics, basements, or elsewhere for months at a time to escape discovery by the Nazis. Home. (2019, March 19). Retrieved March 26, 2019, from https://www.annefrank.org/en/.

2. Originally, Zionism referred to a movement that called for the re-establishment and development of a Jewish homeland in what is now Israel.

3. It was not unusual for Jewish children who escaped on the Kindertransport to stay in holiday camps converted to become youth hostels. Madchen des Kindertransport ~ Girl Museum. Retrieved March 26, 2019, from https://www.girlmuseum.org/project/madchen-des-kindertransport/.

4. The Women's Institute, or WI, was formed during WWI to encourage food production among British rural communities. During WWII, the WI ran Government Sponsored Preservation Centers that oversaw excess produce, which they canned or made into jam sent to the front in addition to regular rations. About the WI. Retrieved March 26, 2019, from https://www.thewi.org.uk/about-the-wi.

5. Eliot, *The Waste Land, Prufrock and Other Poems*, 2.

6. Kristallnacht, or the Night of Broken Glass, refers to the series

of pogroms in November 1938, when German Nazis viciously attacked Jewish property and persons.

7. Eliot, *The Waste Land, Prufrock and Other Poems*, 5.

8. Blackout regulations during WWII required all windows and doors be heavily curtained, covered with cardboard, or painted to prevent any glimmer of light to escape and give the enemy an advantage.

9. Air Raid Wardens main duty during WWII was to patrol the streets at night, ensuring no light escaped windows or doors. They were also to report and assess bomb damage for rescue service workers, organize public air raid shelters, and distribute gas masks.

10. The Andrew Sisters, *Cuanto Le Gusta* (Decca 1948), https://genius.com/The-andrews-sisters-cuanto-le-gusta-lyrics.

# BIBLIOGRAPHY

*Anne Frank.* Anne Frank House, https://www.annefrank.org/en/. Accessed March 26, 2019.

Elliot, T.S., *Four Quartets,* Harcourt, Inc., 1943.

Elliot, T.S. *Poems of T.S. Eliot Volume I: Collected and Uncollected Poems*. Faber and Faber, 2018.

*Madchen des Kindertransport ~ Girl Museum.* Girl Museum, https://www.girlmuseum.org/project/madchen-des-kindertransport/. Accessed March 26, 2019.

Service, T. (2009, May 04). "Tom Service on why Richard Wagner set out to destroy

Felix Mendelssohn's reputation." *The Guardian,* May 4, 2009, https://www.theguardian.com/music/2009/may/05/felix-mendelssohn-richard-wagner-classical-music. Accessed March 26, 2019.

Shakespeare, William. "A Midsumer's Night's Dream." *Stuttgart Information, www.stuttgart.biz - Stuttgart's History*, 1995-2014, http://www.stgt.com/stuttgart/historye.htm. Accessed March 26, 2019.

Taylor. "American Nazis in the 1930s-The German American Bund." *The Atlantic*, June 5, 2017, https://www.theatlantic.com/photo/2017/06/american-nazis-in-the-1930sthe-german-american-bund/529185/. Accessed March 26, 2019.

The Andrew Sisters, "Cuanto Le Gusta." Decca 1948. Genius, https://genius.com/The-andrews-sisters-cuanto-le-gusta-lyrics. Accessed March 26, 2019.

The Andrews Sisters. "Hold Tight (Want Some Seafood Mama)?" Decca 1938. Genius, https://genius.com/The-andrews-sisters-hold-tight-sea-food-lyrics. Accessed May 25, 2019.

"About the WI." The Women's Institute, https://www.thewi.org.uk/about-the-wi. Accessed March 26, 2019.

"Grand Hotel Quotes." https://www.rottentomatoes.com/m/grand_hotel/quotes/. Accessed May 25, 2019.

"Hitler and Wagner." *The Telegraph*, July 25, 2011, https://www.telegraph.co.uk/culture/music/classicalmusic/8659814/Hitler-and-Wagner.html. Accessed May 25, 2019.

"Mendelssohn's Statue Destroyed by Nazis." *Jewish Telegraphic Agency*, November 16, 1936, https://www.jta.org/1936/11/16/archive/mendelssohns-statue-destroyed-by-nazis. Accessed March 26, 2019.

OTHER BOOKS BY

# JESSICA GLASNER

To Order
Visit Amazon.com and
hopehousepress.co

Faith-based historical fiction for the tween, teen, and fun-loving adult!

*The Seabirds*
TRILOGY

MEET THE GREY GOOSE GANG AND SET OUT ON THE WWII ADVENTURE OF A LIFETIME THAT WILL CHALLENGE, INSPIRE, AND ENCOURAGE READERS!

CURIOUS ABOUT PIPER'S FIRST JOB AS THE GIRL REPORTER? NOW'S YOUR CHANCE TO FIND OUT WITH THESE BELOVED NANCY DREW STYLE MYSTERIES SET BETWEEN VOYAGE OF THE SANDPIPER AND FLIGHT OF THE SEAHAWKS!

GIRL
REPORTER

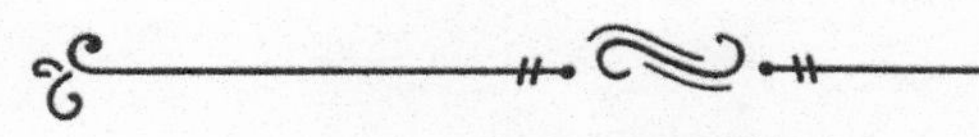

PICKING UP WHERE THE SEABIRDS TRILOGY LEFT OFF, THE COLUMBA DIARIES FOLLOWS THE GREY GOOSE GANG ON NEW ADVENTURES SORTING THROUGH THE AFTERMATH OF THE HOLOCAUST AS THE WORLD SPINS TOWARDS THE COLD WAR.

# ABOUT THE AUTHOR

Jessica Glasner is an author and screenwriter. Young and old alike agree that her lively characters, colorful settings, and laugh-out-loud vignettes display the goodness of God in the darkest moments of the past. Known for instilling hope, faith, and godly values through page-turning stories inspiring tears and laughter, her books are those that are read over and over.

For more adventures with Piper and the gang, check out Jessica Glasner's other stories on Amazon and Barnes and Noble.com.

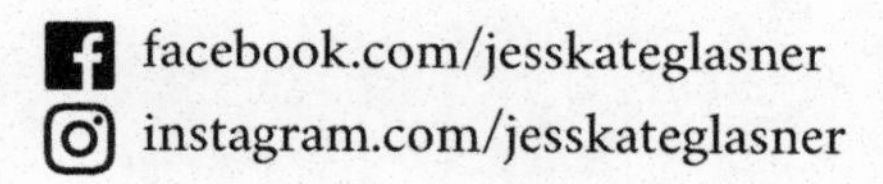

facebook.com/jesskateglasner
instagram.com/jesskateglasner